A LION ROARETH

AN ALTERNATE HISTORY ADVENTURE

Book Two from the *Annals* of *Zebulon*

WILLIAM WHITTENBURY

 ZENNA
BOOKS

ZENNA BOOKS

A Lion Roareth: An Alternate History Adventure

Paperback Edition ISBN: 978-1-7349976-2-0
Library of Congress Control Number: 2021911594

Published by Zenna Books
Rancho Palos Verdes, California
WilliamWhittenburyAuthor.com

This book is dedicated to anyone who fights against the odds for something they believe in. No righteous cause is ever truly lost.

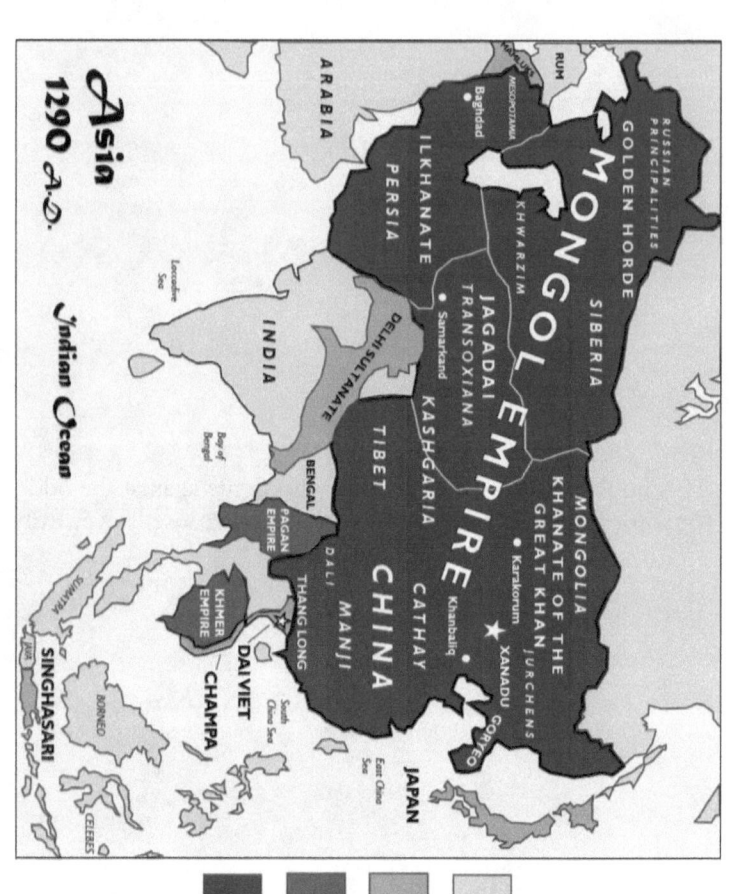

Asia
1290 A.D.

Indian Ocean

GOLDEN HORDE

RUSSIAN PRINCIPALITIES

RUM

ARABIA

MESOPOTAMIA

Baghdad

ILKHANATE
PERSIA

KHWARZIM

MONGOL EMPIRE

MONGOLIA

JAGADAI
TRANSOXIANA
Samarkand

KHANATE OF THE
GREAT KHAN

Karakorum

JURCHENS

Caucasus Sea

DELHI SULTANATE

INDIA

KASHGARIA

TIBET

Khanbalig

XANADU
GOYEO

Bay of
Bengal

BENGAL

DALI

CATHAY

CHINA

Karakorum

JAPAN

PAGAN EMPIRE

THANG LONG

MANJI

South
China
Sea

East
China
Sea

SUMATRA

KHMER
EMPIRE

DAI VIET

CHAMPA

BORNEO

SINGHASARI

JAVA

CELEBES

Mongol
Empire

Mongol
tributaries

Nations resisting
the Mongols

Non-aligned
nations

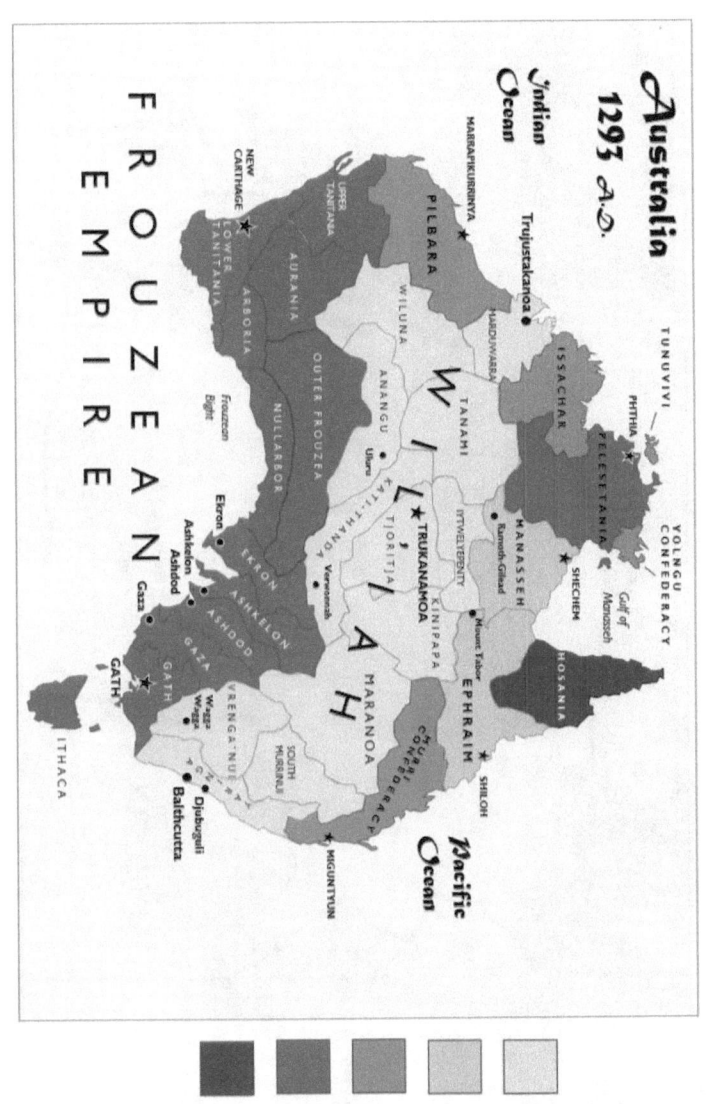

Australia
1293 A.D.

Indian
Ocean

FROUZEAN EMPIRE

Pacific
Ocean

Hosania

Frouzean
Empire

Wii'rahn allies

Ephraim-
Manasseh

Wii'ah

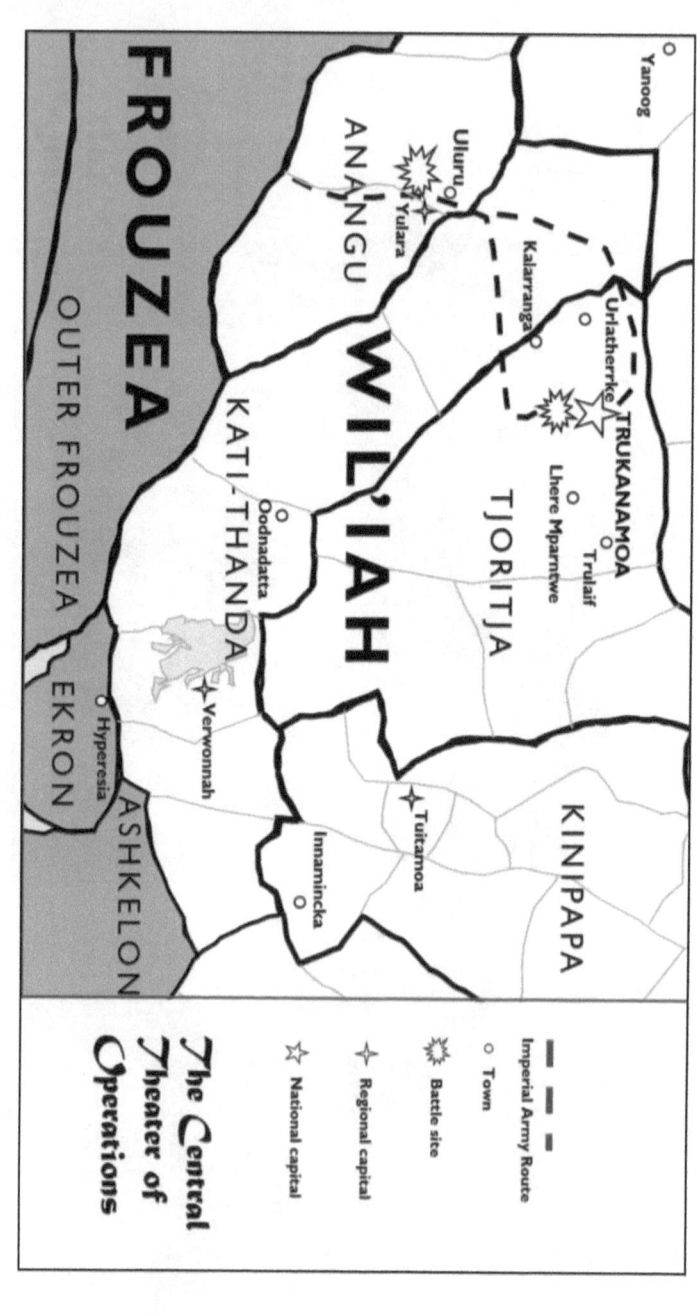

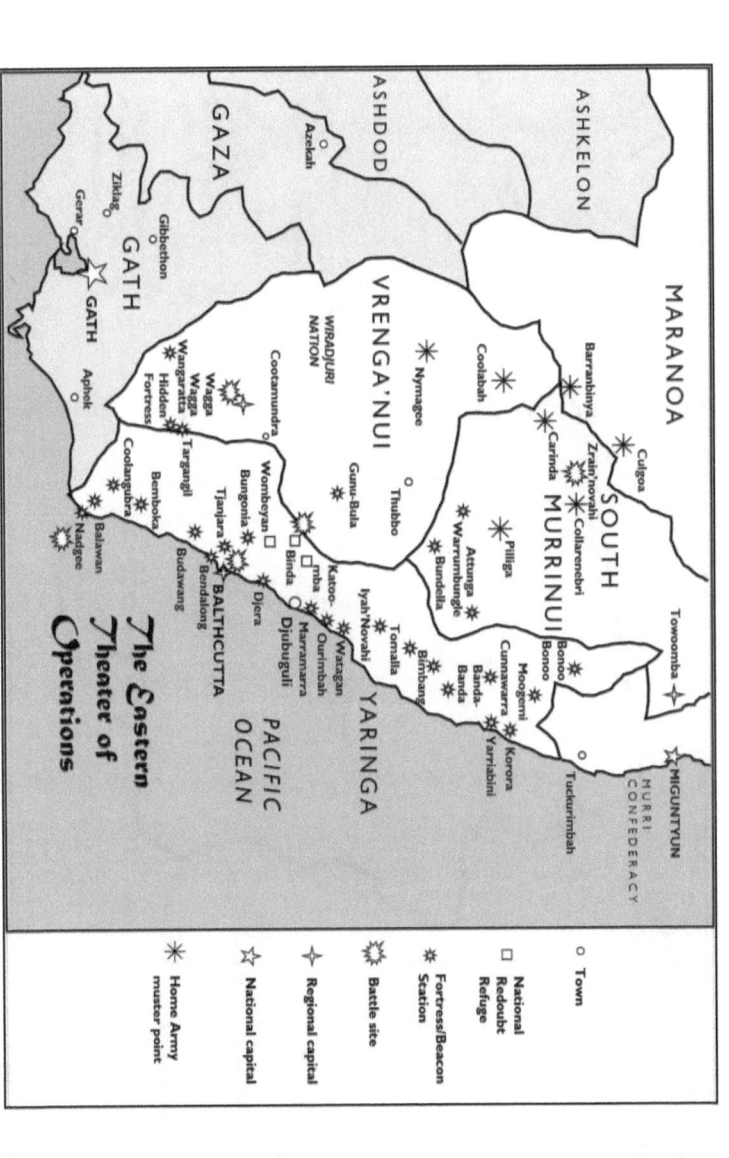

The Eastern Theater of Operations

Legend:
- ○ Town
- □ National Redoubt / Refuge
- ✳ Fortress/Beacon Station
- ✴ Battle site
- ✧ Regional capital
- ✩ National capital
- ✳ Home Army muster point

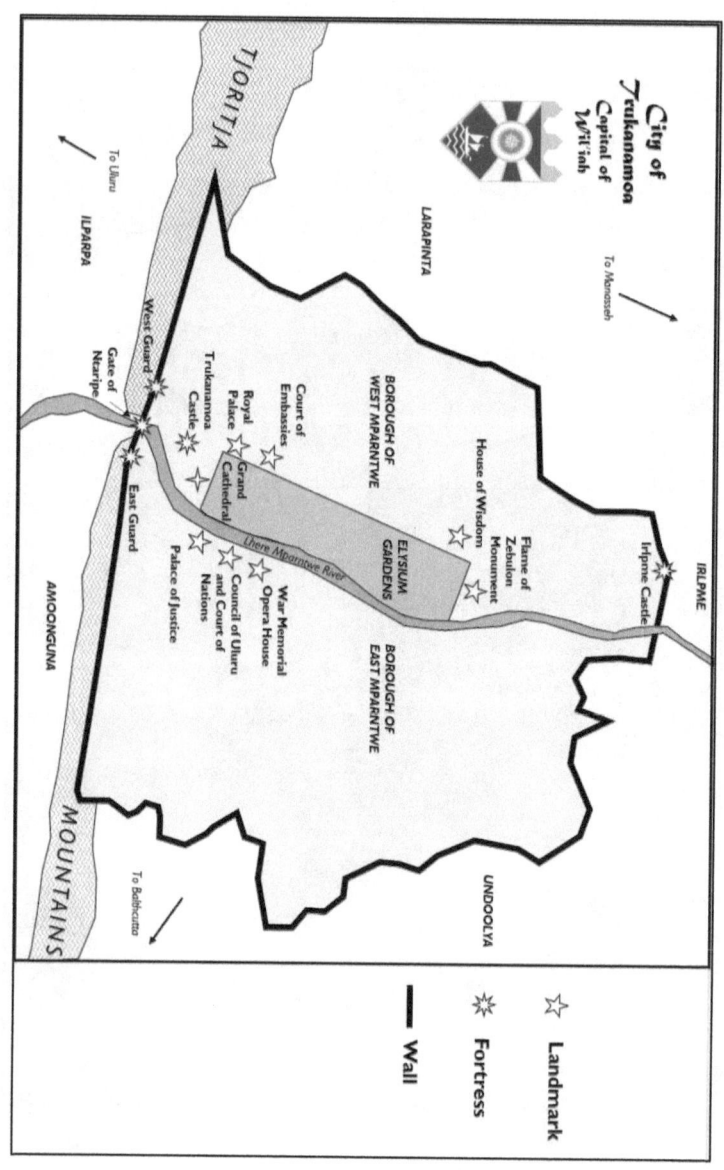

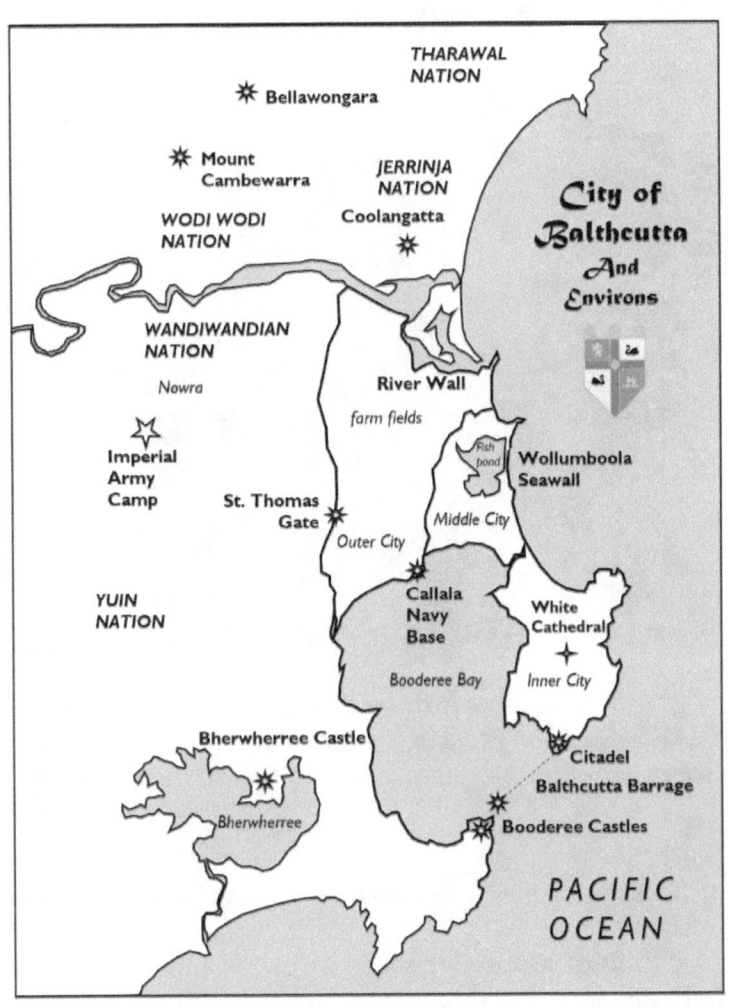

GUIDE TO PEOPLE, PLACES, AND PRONUNCIATIONS

Left to right: Top row: Briseis, Delilah, Avora'tru'ivi, Tamino, Middle Row: Salome, Ajax the Lesser, Kublai Khan, Adirah, Jeremiah. Bottom row: Jason, Achilles, Heracles, Lady Deborah, Jessica

Abigail: Artillery Commander in the Royal Wil'iahn Army

Adirah of Mangala: queen and co-founder of Wil'iah and mother of Tamino, Jessica, and Jeremiah; born 1226

Ajax the Lesser of Gath: Prince of Gath and commander of the Imperial Army Group East

Alinta: Commander of Balthcutta's sea defenses

Allira: Prime Minister of the Council of Uluru, Wil'iah's representative legislature.

Arigh Khaiya: Mongol general. Real historical figure.

Atrides: Frouzean army commander.

Avora'tru'ivi: A-VORE-uh troo EEvee: Princess of Ephraim and Manasseh and queen of Wil'iah; Born 1259

Balthcutta: Large city on the east coast of Wil'iah and Wil'iah's primary pacific port. Located at real-life Jervis Bay, in the Australian Capital Territories.

Bao: Kublai Khan's minister

Bayan of the Baarin: Mongol general and mentor to Temur Khan. Real historical figure who led the conquest of China.

Briseis: Handmaiden to Frouzee Delilah

Chabi: Kublai Khan's late wife. Real historical figure.

Champa: Sovereign state in present-day southern Vietnam

Dai Viet: Sovereign state in present-day northern Vietnam ruled by the Tran Dynasty; also sometimes known as Annam.

Deborah of Dhirari: Captain of Zebulon, commander of Wil'iah's armed forces.

Delilah: Frouzee of the Frouzean Empire

Diomedes: Prince of Ashdod

Gamaliel IV: King of Manasseh and father of Avora'tru'ivi and Gideon

Gath: Capital city of Frouzea, located where real-life Melbourne is. Named for the hometown of the Biblical villain Goliath.

Gideon: Prince, later King, of Ephraim and Manasseh

Goliath: Delilah'

Harijit: Crown Prince of Champa. Real historical figure

Heracles: Manservant and Champion of Frouzee Delilah

Hezekiah: founder and king of Wil'iah from 1256-1291. Born 1223.

Hoglah: Member of the Judith Corps, the queen of Wil'iah's elite guard

Hung Dao: General in command of the armies of Dai Viet; real historical figure

Italereme: King of the Arrernte Nation, an Aboriginal people that live in central Australia.

Jason: Prince of Pelesetania

Jaya Indravarman V: King of Champa. Real historical figure

Jeremiah: Prince and Sovereign Protector of Wil'iah; Born 1262

Jessica: Princess of Wil'iah and commander of the Royal Wil'iahn Navy's Eastern Fleet; Born 1260

Karakorum: Former official capital of the Mongol Empire, located in present-day Mongolia

Kertanegara: King of Singhasari (modern-day Indonesia); real historical figure

Khanbaliq: Part-time capital of the Yuan Dynasty in China, present-day Beijing

Kublai Khan: Emperor of the Yuan Dynasty and Great Khan of the Mongol Empire; real historical figure

Kurultai: The traditional Mongolian tribal process for choosing a new leader. Kublai Khan's kurultai was held in China, leading some of his rivals to question its legitimacy.

Luana: Woman who takes command of the defense of Trukanamoa

Lu Xiufu: Prime Minister of the Southern Song Dynasty and one of the "Three Loyal Princes of the Song." Real historical figure. In real life, he committed suicide with Emperor Zhao Bing at the conclusion of the Battle of Yamen, where this story begins.

Medea: escaped Frouzean slave

Menelaus of Gath: commander of the Frouzean Center Force.

Milcah: MILL-kuh Maid and governess in the Court of Wil'iah

Minh: Associate of the Order of the Flame of Zebulon in Champa

Minos of Ashkelon: Prince of Ashkelon and commander of the Imperial Army's Balthcutta attack force

Nasir-al-din: Mongol general of Persian descent. Real historical figure.

Raden Wijaya: general of the Kingdom of Singhasari, and later founder of the Majahapit Empire. Real historical figure.

Salome: Handmaid to Frouzee Delilah and former harem girl of Achilles of Gath

Shechem: Capital city of the United Kingdom of Ephraim and Manasseh, located on the real-life Gulf of Carpentaria in northern Australia.

Sheerah: War Queen of Ephraim and mother of Avora'tru'ivi and Gideon

Singhasari: Kingdom located on present-day Java, a forerunner to Indonesia.

Tamino: Tuh-MEE-no; Born 1258, Prince, later King, of Wil'iah from 1291-1327.

Temur Khan: Grandson of Kublai Khan and second ruler of the Yuan (Mongol) Dynasty of China. Real historical figure

Thang Long: Capital of Dai Viet

Toghon: Son of Kublai Khan, who led the disastrous invasion of Dai Viet in 1285 and later leads Mongol forces against Wil'iah. Real historical figure, who was exiled to Yangzhou and disowned by his father after failing to conquer Dai Viet.

Tran Anh Tong: Crown prince, later emperor, of Dai Viet; ruled from 1293-1314. Real Historical Figure.

Tran Nanh Tong: Emperor of Dai Viet; ruled from 1278-1293. Real historical figure.

Tran Tranh Tong: Retired emperor of Dai Viet; ruled from 1258-1278. Real historical figure.

Tribhuwaneswari: Princess of Singhasari. Real historical figure

Trujustakanoa: TRUE-just-uh-kuh-nowa: large city on Wil'iah's west coast and former capital of the ancient Kingdom of Zebulon, located at real-life Derby, Western Australia, on King Sound. Wil'iah's primary port for trade with Asia and the Indian Ocean.

Trukanamoa: TRUE-kahna-mowa: capital of Wil'iah, located where real-life Alice Springs stands at the center of Australia.

Uluru: Also known as Ayers' Rock, a sacred site for Aboriginal Australians and, in this story, the site of the founding of Wil'iah.

Wil'iah: Will-Lee-Uh: country in Australia, formed from an alliance of Zebulite tribesmen descended from one of the Tribes of Israel and indigenous Aboriginal nations.

Xanadu (Shangdu): the legendary summer palace of Kublai Khan; real historical location described by Marco Polo.

Zhang Shijie: Admiral of the Southern Song, and later Royal Wil'iahn, navies. One of the "Three Loyal Princes of the Song." Real historical figure.

Zhao Bing: Last emperor of the Song Dynasty, also known as the Xianxing Emperor. Real historical figure. In real life, he perished, at the age of seven, at the Battle of Yamen when Prime Minister Lu Xiufu and he jumped off of a warship to their deaths.

AUTHOR'S NOTE

Wil'iah is not a real country. Nobody really knows what happened to the Tribe of Zebulon and the other lost tribes of Israel. There are many theories, but none of them posit that they fled to Australia. Thus, this is a work of pure imagination and does not pretend to endorse any actual anthropological or historical theory. However, the events leading to the plot of this book are grounded in real history, even if the war between the Kingdom of Wil'iah and the alliance composed of the Frouzean Empire and the Mongol Empire is entirely fictional. Many of the characters in this book are real historical figures, and though the author has taken some artistic license regarding their response to the fictional events of this story, he has tried to ground their characters in reality.

SUMMARY OF *THE SEVEN THUNDERS*

*I*n the year 1279 AD, the brave Song Dynasty's decades-long resistance to the Mongol hordes of Kublai Khan came to a disastrous end at the Battle of Yamen. Free China's last stand against the inexorable enemy ended with the destruction of the remnants of her navy and total occupation of the country – but defeat was not complete, for the last emperor of Song China, the young boy Zhao Bing, was snatched from the teeth of the Mongol fleet by the intrepid forces of Hezekiah, King of Wil'iah, a mysterious nation in an unknown land far to the south.

Now, however, the baleful eye of the Great Khan turned its gaze to this faithful kingdom and gathered the Mongol forces, waiting for the day when he could reach out his hand and destroy Wil'iah.

Four years later, Khan's strength had grown sufficiently that the day had come. His armies moved to threaten the kingdoms of Champa and Dai Viet, two of the last free countries in Asia. King Hezekiah realized that if these nations fell, Wil'iah would be next, and not even the wide reaches of the ocean would be able to protect his country from its implacable foe. He called an emergency meeting with his ancient ally, the United Kingdom of Ephraim and Manasseh, whose Princess Avora'tru'ivi suggested creating an alliance of all of the free nations remaining in Asia and the Pacific. If they worked together, they might just have a chance of containing the ambitions of the Great Khan. Together, she and Wil'iah's brave Prince Tamino embarked on a mission to rally these nations together, daring to infiltrate enemy-occupied territory and the decadent courts of would-be allies. Before they left, she gave him a red waratah flower as a sign of her friendship – and the growing, unspoken love between them.

However, unbeknownst to them, Wil'iah's own ancient nemesis was stirring at their back door. The wicked Frouzean Empire, defeated by Wil'iah decades before and left in shambles, became acutely aware of the Mongol menace when Temur Khan, grandson of the Great Khan, arrived with a dire threat – in seven years, if Frouzea didn't offer up an enormous tribute, the Mongol fleet would arrive to crush the country. The Circle, a wicked cult dedicated to the restoration of the empire, prayed to their mother goddess Astarte to descend back to earth and take the form of an empress to lead her people to triumphant conquest, but no answer came. The slave girl Iphigenia, in service to the Circle as a potion-maker, became increasingly distressed as her eligibility period to become the host for the earthly manifestation of Astarte – and thus her life -- drew to its close. In a moment of desperation, she resolved to impersonate Astarte, in the guise of the Frouzee Delilah, Empress of Frouzea, and seize the throne of the empire itself. She succeeded in duping the Circle and set about to reunite Frouzea's five warring principalities – by any means necessary. She beguiled Achilles, Prince of Gath, and became his consort, helping him to seize the throne by killing his own father. With the powerful armies of Gath at her command, Delilah launched on a wave of conquest that would shake the world.

Tamino and Avora'tru'ivi succeeded in recruiting the kingdoms of Dai Viet, Champa, Singhasari, and the Yolngu Confederacy to join the alliance, but Tamino's intervention in the Mongol's attempted control of Dai Viet set the alliance on an unavoidable path to war. For her part, Avora'tru'ivi rejected the disgusting advances of Jason, Prince of Pelesetania, her nation's mortal enemy, though it placed her country in grave danger. The allied fleet managed to defeat the Mongols in a furious sea battle off the coast of Dai Viet, but a misunderstanding led Tamino to believe that Avora'tru'ivi had decided to join a convent.

Meanwhile, Delilah successfully conquered all five principalities through a combination of murder and intimidation. Her confidante, Briseis, a fellow former slave to the Circle, became increasingly uneasy with her situation, while the sycophantic Salome exploited her position as Delilah's other handmaiden for personal gain. Delilah next set her sights on the Tanitanian Empire, a rich country formerly part of the Frouzean Empire. She persuaded her consort, Achilles, to challenge Hasdrubal, King of Tanitania, to a duel, with Delilah and the combined empire as the prize. However, knowing that the Tanitanian populace would not accept Achilles as the victor, she drugged him so he became paralyzed during the fight, causing his death. Delilah then married Hasdrubal, but murdered him on her wedding night, making it appear accidental. With the entire empire now united with Delilah in sole control, she fixed her gaze on her next victim – Wil'iah.

Tamino and Avora'tru'ivi resolved their misunderstanding, confessed their feelings, and married. Shortly after, Tamino led a military expedition to help stave off another Mongol attack on Dai Viet, achieving victory at the Battle of Bach Dang and arriving home in time to help with the birth of his daughter, Princess Judith. Subsequently, King Hezekiah of Wil'iah decided to retire, and Tamino was elected as his successor by the Council of Uluru, Wil'iah's representative legislature.

To "congratulate" him on his accession to the throne, Delilah sent Briseis to Wil'iah to bear a message of goodwill – and gather tactical information. Briseis found that Wil'iahns did not conform to the savage stereotypes she had been raised to believe. Nevertheless, Delilah came to Wil'iah's capital of Trukanamoa for a state visit, with an ulterior motive. She attempted to seduce Tamino, offering him a military alliance against the Mongols in exchange for his attentions. However, Tamino threw her out, willing to fight both empires rather than sacrifice his principles. Thus scorned, and with time running out before the Mongols were due to attack Frouzea, Delilah turned her gaze to the last option remaining to her – Kublai Khan himself.

Delilah arrived at Khan's palace of Xanadu in splendid array and charmed him with her wit – and with the secret that Zhao Bing, the last Emperor of China, was in hiding in Wil'iah. Offering herself up as a worthy successor to

Khan's late wife Chabi (with the aid of some drugs), she bewitched Khan into offering his hand in marriage. Thus, Delilah formally became empress of China, and all the lands of the Mongol Empire, stretching as far as Europe. Her conquest of the world was almost complete – all that remained was Wil'iah, and the faithful kingdom's few allies. Delilah began to secretly gather her forces for an all-out assault.

In the meantime, Tamino's father, Hezekiah, fell ill and appeared to be dying. Nevertheless, Hezekiah insisted that Tamino and Avora'tru'ivi fulfill their royal duties and dedicate the recently-completed White Cathedral of Balthcutta, far from the capital, leaving Tamino's brother Jeremiah in command of Trukanamoa's defenses. While Tamino was in Balthcutta, Hezekiah passed, and Delilah seized the moment to strike, launching a massive invasion of Wil'iah on three fronts. The news of Hezekiah's death and Delilah's treacherous attack simultaneously reached Tamino in Balthcutta, devastating him.

Now Wil'iah girds for a battle she has little hope of winning. Only an ancient power, the hidden source of Wil'iah's strength, can save her now…

CHAPTER ONE

ALL HAIL FROUZEE

Nadgee, Bidawal Nation, Southeastern Wil'iah, 1293 AD

*T*he stirring blare of five hundred trumpets reverberated over the wide coastal plain as an angry red, white, and black flag unfurled in the gathering breeze, held aloft by a hulking warrior. Heracles, first servant of Frouzee Delilah, ascended a dais, flanked on either side by gleaming detachments of the fabled Homeric Guard, their spotless, burnished armor reflecting the blinding sunlight. Behind them, an enormous, horned altar loomed ominously.

"Here stands the Eastern Division of Her Worship's Imperial Army!" Heracles triumphantly bellowed, bringing a hearty cheer from the assembled hordes that blanketed the beach before him. "As the armies of Ashdod, Gaza, and Gath attack Wil'iah in the west, in the center, and the backcountry, we will strike the lethal blow at their greatest city, Balthcutta!"

"Now we shall pay our homage to our goddess and call her to descend to Earth and lead us to victory!" Heracles dramatically unrolled a scroll and began to call the roll of the army. "Ekron!"

The heralds flanking Heracles let out a triumphant fanfare as a great chariot pulled by four white horses swept in front of the altar, flanked by two riders, one carrying the red, white, and black battle-standard of the empire, the other flying the purple flag of Ekron, emblazoned with a golden horsefly. Standing ramrod-straight in the chariot was Diomedes, Prince of Ekron, his golden armor gleaming in the sun and his purple cape whipping in the wind. His stony, bearded face masked the storm of emotions within – and the hatred that flared in his heart at the sight of the altar.

He fought to shake the imagined image from his mind of his brother, Theseus, dropping into the writhing pit of spiders in Delilah's debauched palace. Theseus' murder had installed Diomedes in his current role as prince, but the title lacked any real power. He was just another pawn in Delilah's game, and he knew it. He clenched his jaw as his thoughts strayed to his other, more important relative – his infant son, Perseus, just recently born. Diomedes then had to fight to clear the mist from his eyes as he thought of his noble wife, Ismene, who had died in childbirth. Diomedes had been ripped from both by this invasion.

I'll return to raise you, I vow it, Diomedes thought as the chariot ground to a halt in front of the altar. Then, Diomedes dutifully stepped down from it and lay prostrate on the ground before the altar, kissing the dirt – and hating every second of it.

Heracles triumphantly smiled, and called the next name on the scroll. "Ashkelon!"

Another chariot swept into view. This time, the escorting standard-bearer held aloft a flag of red, white, and gold stripes, with roses at its four corners and a strange symbol emblazoned on its center- a circle surmounting a cross. Minos, Prince of Ashkelon, wearing a crown of dove feathers, stepped down and rendered similar obeisance to the altar. The deafening cheers of the assembled army did nothing to drown out his thoughts.

When this farce is over, my time will come.

"Now," Heracles bellowed, "Let us all unite to call forth our goddess!"

A tidal wave of humanity surged toward the altar as fanatical soldiers fought each other for prime worship positions.

✳ ✳ ✳

Inside a chamber of the altar, two women huddled over an iron pot. The taller of the two, dressed from head to toe in a malevolently red costume designed to resemble a cobra, spoke in a low hiss.

"Not that much Powder of Persepolis, Briseis! The mixture must be perfect if we are to get the right effect! It must be convincing!"

Briseis, the shorter of the two, poured a vial of red powder into the pot with shaking hands. Her eyes, filled with concern, flicked over to her companion. "Iph—I mean Delilah," she quickly corrected as the other woman flashed her a murderous glare, "Don't you think you're pushing your good fortune with this invasion? You and I both know how this started out – we just wanted to save our own skins. Now, you are the empress of China. Isn't that enough? Aren't you satisfied?"

The look Delilah gave her nearly stopped her heart. Delilah leaned in closely and grabbed Briseis' jaw with her long-nailed finger. "Briseis, darling, there is no way to go but forward. I must fulfill the earthly mission of the goddess Astarte and destroy Wil'iah once and for all! Then my power will be complete."

"But you're not the goddess—"

Briseis gasped as one of Delilah's nails pierced her cheek and drew blood.

"We've talked about this before. No one – *no one* – can ever know that, if you value either of our lives – but especially yours. You have been my most trusted confidant, but that can always change. Nobody is essential – except me, of course."

Briseis shuddered as the visages of Delilah's murdered, disposable husbands flashed before her eyes. She weakly nodded.

Delilah turned around in the cramped chamber and lifted a headdress from a shelf. Shaped like a rearing cobra's head, it was crowned with two polished horns and a burnished pentagram, the symbol of the empire. As she triumphantly lowered it onto her head, Delilah spoke once more.

"Besides, how do we know that the inspiration to set this scheme in motion w*asn't* Astarte choosing me as her vessel? Goddesses have many methods."

Neither of them noticed the small crack in the wall of the chamber beside Delilah, or the two serpentine eyes that triumphantly narrowed behind it.

※ ※ ※

"Now, how do we show our gratitude and homage to our glorious goddess?" Heracles thundered.

Maniacal soldiers hefted platters piled high with the bounty of the sea – dead-eyed fish, squids, clams, eels, and all manner of benthic denizens. They robotically began dumping the offerings into the wooden channel that surrounded the altar, all the while chanting, "All hail Astarte! All hail the Frouzee! All hail Delilah!"

As Heracles egged them on, the displays of ardor and worship grew more and more frenzied. Soldiers wheeled about in frantic dance, foaming at the mouth as their wild eyes opened wider than seemed possible.

Suddenly, the scene of bacchanalia froze as an enormous, angry plume of red smoke shot into the sky. Mouths trembled in reverence at the sight, and Heracles' chest swelled in an entirely genuine show of pride and zeal. When the smoke cleared, Delilah stood on a platform high on the altar, resplendent in her full "formal invasion wear." She was greeted by a deafening cheer.

"Yes, yes!!!" she yelled, reveling in the ardor of her armies. "Today, the hosts of our glorious empire have assembled once again to trample the world! Once, our enemies thought they had defeated us, humiliated us, left us destitute and broken. But had they?"

"NO!!!" the assembled army bellowed. Nobody could see Minos of Ashkelon roll his eyes.

Delilah, Frouzee of the Frouzean Empire

"For years the mudfaces of Wil'iah have sat in the luxury of the land they stole from us while we suffered in squalor. But no more! Today we embark on the great quest to restore our empire to greatness! Today we take back what is rightfully ours! And today we restore the subhuman creatures that call themselves Wil'iahns to their rightful status!!" She cupped a hand over her ear, as if expecting an answer.

"SLAVES!!!" came the jubilant response from the assembled armies.

"That's right! Soon the whole world will quake at the sound of our boots, just like they did before! Once again we will be acknowledged as the rightful masters of this Earth, alongside, of course, our esteemed allies," Delilah hastily added, stretching her arm out to regard the massive Mongol army that stood alongside the Frouzeans, watching the proceedings with a mixture of curiosity and horror.

"Together, my husband, Kublai Khan, and I will expand our empires beyond our wildest dreams! We are more powerful together than we ever were apart. And, through our alliance, Frouzea has reached a splendor beyond the wildest imaginations of our ancestors!"

She now swept her arm to regard the land that stretched out before them – a coastal plain leading to sparkling blue waters to the east, and forbidding mountains to the west.

"Today we strike when our enemies are at their most unprepared, for I have received news that Hezekiah, the wretched warrior whom the mudfaces claim as their national hero, is dead! Now, nobody is there to save them! His son, Tamino, is an effeminate weakling, and their armies are no match for our forces! We will sweep over them like a tidal wave, and crush them like ants!"

At the news of their legendary enemy's death, a lusty cheer rang out from the army.

"*Now,* where shall we go?" Delilah asked, with a devilish gleam in her painted eye as she dramatically raised her arms over her head, letting her voluminous red sleeves whip in the wind.

"FORWARD!"

"What shall we do?"

"KILL!"

"Who do we love?"

"YOU!!!!!"

With that, the army began to rumble forward, led by a surging tide of Mongol cavalry. Hundreds of banners of the Frouzean and Mongol Empires snapped in the breeze as the very earth shook with the mass of humanity, beasts, and machines that passed over it. As the first legions of the army crossed the border, they gave a jubilant shout.

"See, our enemies are so cowardly that they don't even dare oppose us at their own border!" Delilah laughed maniacally.

Her laugh died on the wind as a flicker of light caught the corner of her eye.

On the peak of the mountain that overlooked the plain, an angry red flame flared into life. Shortly afterward, another flame ignited on a distant mountain in answer.

Diomedes watched the flames with a sinking feeling.

They knew we were coming.

CHAPTER TWO

THE SAMSON PLAN

Balthcutta, Yaringa, Southeastern Wil'iah,

*T*he line of fire marched along the mountains to a sparkling turquoise bay, guarded on its northern and southern ends by great headlands jutting defiantly into the sea. On one of them, a white citadel towered over its surroundings, commanding the approaches to the city. Inside one of the fortress' corridors, King Tamino of Wil'iah fought to regain his composure. The simultaneous news of his father's untimely death and the invasion of his country had struck him with the force of a sledgehammer. He fought back tears as he hurried towards the War Room, silently berating himself for his absence from the capital at his father's moment of need.

You should have been there.

Even worse than the grief was a sinking feeling that, at this moment of crisis, he was alone – and not up to the task.

My father was a larger-than-life legend who freed his people against impossible odds. Next to him, I'm nothing.

Tamino forced himself to remember what his father had always told him – that the nation had an ultimate defense that was just as present now as it had been when his father had overthrown Frouzean rule of the country thirty-five years prior. Tamino wasn't really alone – he just needed to understand that. Of course, that was much easier said than done, especially with enemy troops roaring over the border.

Reaching the end of the corridor, Tamino found himself standing in front of two rough-hewn wooden doors deep within the bowels of the castle, surrounded on all sides by twenty-foot thick walls with no windows or arrow-loops.

You can do this, he reassured himself as he took a deep breath. Then, not allowing his self-doubt to paralyze him any further, he stepped forward and pulled the doors open.

They revealed a Spartan room lit by a dozen blazing torches, its far wall festooned with maps of the entire continent as well as of the immediate region, the judgates of Yaringa and Vrenga'nui. With a sigh of relief, he realized that all of the faces were friendly. Seated on the right of the table was General Teva'ivani, the woman in command of the Army of Yaringa, which was tasked with the defense of Balthcutta and its environs. In the flaring torchlight, her slight figure cast an outsized shadow, and her gaunt, grandmotherly features took on an unexpected keenness. Set in her deeply lined face were two fierce specks of light that stared down Tamino with an intensity that reminded him of his mother. Tamino wasn't sure exactly how old she was, but a scar over her right eyebrow bore witness to her service in the War of the Vow forty years prior.

Next to her was Lady Deborah of Dhirari, Captain of Zebulon, the enormous woman tasked with organizing the defense of the kingdom. Piled atop her humorless, intimidating face was a three-tiered, severe bun, from the center of which rose a wickedly sharp, burnished spike. She gave Tamino a curt nod as he appeared at the door.

Flanking her was Zhang Shijie, the refugee Chinese admiral who now commanded Wil'iah's navy, his face lined with concern as he realized that he would once again face his nemesis.

Next at the table was Tamino's sister, Princess Jessica, who was serving in the Navy's Eastern Fleet. Her fierce features might have scared another man, but they reassured Tamino.

And, of, course, next to her sat the queen. Even in this serious moment, Tamino felt a warmth kindle in his heart as the torchlight reflected off her shining armor and the gleaming war crown that framed her serious face.

There was an empty seat at the head of the table. Tamino swallowed hard as he realized it was for him.

"Thank you for coming on such short notice," he said as he gingerly took the seat.

"I just can't believe he's gone." Deborah responded.

"I know exactly how you feel, but there will be time for that later. Now, we must defend his dream." Tamino stared the generals directly in the eyes, attempting to muster an authority that he didn't really believe he had. "Alright, what are we up against?"

"The first reports from the border fortifications are astonishing. Enemy forces are streaming into the country flying both the Frouzean and Mongol flags." Lady Deborah stated matter-of-factly.

Queen Avora'tru'ivi started. "Mongols? Here?"

Zhang nodded, his face an unemotional mask. "That's what the intelligence reports stated. I don't know how they got here though – there have been no naval reports of massed Mongol troop shipments. We would have done something about that."

A sudden cloud crossed Princess Jessica's face. "Those 'trade missions'…"

Deborah pursed her lips. "The possibility has crossed our minds."

Tamino cleared his throat. "Regardless of how they got here, we have a Mongol army to deal with in addition to the Imperial Army. Do we have any sense for how many they have?"

"We have no idea how many Mongols there are, but according to an Order communique I received from the fortress of Balawan, the Imperial Army gathered something like one hundred thousand soldiers from each of the five Principalities. We don't know how many will be deployed in this theater," Deborah responded.

Tamino turned to Teva'ivani. "General, it's my understanding that the standing forces in the Army of Yaringa are just under twenty thousand. Is that still correct?"

The severe woman nodded. "The Army of Yaringa has twenty thousand standing forces, and the Army of Vrenga'nui can muster eighteen thousand immediately. When we mobilize the reserves, that number will increase tenfold."

Tamino nodded. "That at least gives us a chance, but mobilization will take time. And we won't just need the reserves," he said, turning to Deborah, "We will need the Home Army as well."

The general nodded enthusiastically. "We're ready. We've been ready for this for thirty-five years."

Avora'tru'ivi added, "We can also count on the support of our allies in the League of Trujustakanoa. We will send ships immediately to invoke the Articles and call on their assistance. You can all at least trust that help from Manasseh will not be tardy in its response to our call."

"That's if Gideon doesn't roll over immediately to that detestable Prince Jason," Deborah said ruefully.

A dark look crossed the queen's features.

Tamino regarded Zhang, trying to make sense of the conflicting emotions on the Admiral's face. "Admiral, ever since your arrival in the Kingdom, the care of Emperor Zhao has been entrusted to you. However, at this crucial juncture in history, it is vital he be given the utmost protection. He will come here, to Balthcutta, where he will assume the identity of my "squire." I can assure you, he will not see combat."

Zhang gravely nodded. "He is already in the city, as I have foreseen this. I agree that he must be kept off the front lines, but you must understand that he is a young man of twenty-one who is anxious to help defend the country that saved his life. He will not take kindly to being kept off the battlefield."

Tamino nodded. "Surely he must understand how valuable he is. He is the key to a free China. In the meantime, Zhang, maintaining sea control is essential. We are likely to face a siege situation in Balthcutta and need to keep sea supply routes open."

Jessica interjected, "The Eastern Fleet has two hundred fifty ships in Balthcutta, with additional forces positioned further north at Djubuguli. My recommendation is to take two hundred ships and position them off Cape Nadgee to head off any enemy sea assault and to interdict their sea supply lines. We'll leave the other fifty here as a defensive reserve."

Tamino responded, "Alright, Jessica, that plan is sound. You and Admiral Zhang will lead the fleet from the *Ava'ivi* and the *Reliance*. Please be careful."

Zhang gravely nodded.

Tamino passed his eyes to each of the generals in turn. "I don't think I need to emphasize the seriousness of this situation. Until the reserves are mobilized, we might be outnumbered twenty to one, or worse, depending on how many Mongol troops are in the area. We also cannot hope to defeat the Mongol cavalry in open battle- many have tried and failed. Fortunately, my father left behind a plan. I think you all know it."

A dark look crossed Lady Deborah's eyes. "The Samson Plan is incredibly costly."

"Do you see a better option?"

"We've run many analyses and simulations. None of them go well. I hate to say it, but Samson is our best hope," Lady Deborah sighed.

"Are the muster points and the Redoubt prepared?" Tamino responded.

"What do you take me for?" the general chided, an unexpected twinkle reaching her eye. Tamino hadn't thought that the woman was capable of smiling at all. "The principal mountain fortresses are all garrisoned – Kumana Namagdi, Balawan, Budawang, Bendalong, Tjanjara, Jerrawangala, Barrengarry, Cambewarra, Bellawongara, Wombeyan, Binda, Katoomba, Mugli, Wollemi, and Gunu-bula," she rattled off the names of castles with admirable recall. "If you go with this plan, I will depart for Gunu-bula immediately to begin executing it."

"Alright, Samson it is," Tamino responded. "We may not know the situation in the rest of the country if the signal system fails and communication cannot get through. We'll have to place our trust in the local commanders."

"Eleazar is capable," Deborah referred to the general in command of the Army of Tjoritja, the main force tasked with the defense of the capital.

"So is Jeremiah. He wanted his chance to fight the Frouzeans, now he'll get it," Avora'tru'ivi added, referring to Tamino's hot-headed younger brother.

"I hope he can control himself," Tamino said, before turning to address the rest of the group.

"I don't have to remind you that we are facing two enemies known for their singular brutality. Both are likely bent on our total annihilation. But to defend our dream, we must live up to its ideals. We cannot allow ourselves to sacrifice our principles and descend into the same levels of savagery. In every action and encounter in this war, the Code of Wil'iah will be followed to the letter. No non-military targets, no killing or torture of prisoners, and no unnecessary violence wherever possible. You can call me an unrealistic optimist, but I am determined that this war will be an affirmation of everything Wil'iah stands for, rather than the moment we descend into darkness. We all know that there is a higher way. We must walk in it. And we must remember that no enemy is beyond redemption. At this critical juncture we are forced to take up arms, but ultimately divine love is the true defense of Wil'iah. And it is by loving them that we will disarm our enemies. Never forget this. We are going to win this war, but we are going to win it the right way."

"That's why we love you," said Avora'tru'ivi, her eyes crinkling with a smile as she noticed the waratah flower fastened to her husband's armor.

"Alright, we have our marching orders." Tamino addressed the gathered generals, who all stood, rendered the military salute, and yelled in response,
"Ivrae'ia Va'a'kau'lua!"

King Tamino I of Wil'iah, 1293 A.D.

CHAPTER THREE

WATCHFIRES OF HOPE

*A*fter leaving the War Room, Tamino and Avora'tru'ivi ascended a spiral staircase to the tallest keep of the castle, which towered over the rest of the complex. From its ramparts much of the surrounding environs were visible. A stern-faced guard looked resolutely to the south, the direction from which enemy forces were expected. However, hearing the clinking of armor, he spun on his heel to face the new visitors, and, with a start, hastily rendered the military salute.

"At ease." Tamino said, then motioned to the red flame on the mountain, which was beginning to die down, its mission accomplished.

"It's time we gave our answer."

The guard grimly nodded, then walked over to a cabinet and unlocked it with a ring of keys he carried on his belt. Inside were a group of more than a dozen barrels, each containing a fine powder.

"What color?" asked the guard.

"Blue."

"We're going with the Samson Plan?"

"You heard me."

The Guard didn't know what the Samson Plan entailed, but he knew that a blue beacon atop the Castle of Balthcutta would set whatever it was in motion. He and Tamino removed the barrel from the cabinet and began shoveling its contents onto a gigantic wood pile in the center of the keep. The task accomplished, he withdrew a ceramic pot from the cabinet and poured its oily contents over the pile. Reaching inside his hip-bag, he retrieved a piece of flint and struck it against his dagger. Almost instantly, a towering blue flame roared to life, crackling with intensity.

"It's done," the guard said.

In answer, beside the dying embers of the red alarm fire, a blue light leapt into existence on distant Mount Cambewarra, its bold color blazing defiantly against the atmosphere of terror that seemed to grip the surrounding countryside. Tamino felt his heart leap inside him as he beheld the distant flame, even as apprehension about the plan gnawed at his stomach.

"It's beautiful," Avora'tru'ivi said as the distant fire danced in her eyes.

"Hope is always beautiful," Tamino replied, squinting even further into the distance. With a sigh of relief, he saw the next two beacons, Jerrawangala and Bellawongara, flare into light.

"The Lights of our defiance will soon blaze all over Wil'iah. I'm just glad the Order trained for this. The National Smoke Signal System will relay the information to Trukanamoa, since there are no permanent beacon stations on that route."

The guard awkwardly cleared his throat. "If you don't mind me asking, what exactly is the Samson Plan? How many people know about it?"

"Only a dozen people in the whole kingdom know the plan in its entirety. We have reason to believe that the Frouzee may have spies in our courts. But all over Wil'iah, in every village and enclave, those who have a role to carry out in the plan know what they need to do," Tamino responded. He gave the guard his best approximation of an easy smile. "You have done your duty."

"Many thanks, Your Faithfulness," the guard responded.

Tamino looked into the distance, his face tinted blue by the leaping fire beside him.

"And now we wait."

CHAPTER FOUR

THE DESERTER

Great Coastal Road, Southeastern Wil'iah

O *star of the morning!*
O star of the evening!
O goddess of love!
O empress of war!
O queen of all the heavens!
Beautiful, inexorable, exalted!

The reverent, fanatical tones of the chorus filled Delilah's sumptuous pavilion as troupes of dancers manically cavorted before the throne. Perched on a small dais beside it, Delilah's handmaid Salome gleefully led the signing, casting insincerely adoring looks at the woman who reclined on the throne, fanned by members of the Bull Pen, her personal harem, who wielded large plumes of cockatoo feathers. Heracles, the bodyguard, beamed down on Delilah, occasionally scowling at the Mongol general Toghon, son of Kublai Khan, who watched the scene of debauchery play out with a mixture of disgust and bemusement.

Briseis, Delilah's confidante, also watched the worshipful dance with conflicting emotions. Barely ten years before, she hadn't been much better than one of the enslaved dancers. She suppressed a shiver as she thought of her time in service to the Circle. Images of dusty, dimly lit temples and macabre rituals danced through her mind in time with the dancers before the throne. Only Delilah's resourcefulness and cunning had saved them both from the Circle's sacrificial knives, and set them on their careening journey to world power. However, as Briseis regarded the fanatical, groveling faces of the "eternal empress'" courtiers, her stomach churned with fear that they would be discovered – that it was all a lie. Delilah's scheme to pose as a goddess to save her own skin had gradually spiraled out of control as her efforts to maintain the charade had required ever more-grandiose displays of power. It had begun with conniving murders of certain key political figures in Frouzea, and had staggered on to the present alliance with Kublai Khan and invasion of Wil'iah.

When will it be too far? Briseis thought as she watched the deranged gleam in Delilah's eye.

The bacchanalia was suddenly interrupted as two members of the Homeric Guard, Delilah's elite cadre of hand-picked warriors, dragged a soldier into the pavilion. The dancers scattered to the edges of the tent; Briseis noticed that their eyes' feigned reverence actually masked all-consuming fear.

"*Well,* what do we have here?" Delilah huskily intoned as she sat up in the throne with renewed interest.

"Your Worship!" one of the guards snapped into an adoring salute. "This scum was caught attempting to desert!" The soldier was shoved roughly to the ground before the throne, where he groveled in terrified subjection.

"*Desertion!?* You would desert your beloved, your eternal empress, your goddess? The one who restored your nation to the pride and greatness that is her birthright? Unthinkable! What do you have to say for yourself?"

The trembling soldier managed to force out a few words. "I-I-I'm scared. I've heard the stories. It's a m-mistake to invade W-Wil'iah. They have mysterious powers that we don't understand."

"Mysterious powers?! Nonsense! Surely you know that *I* am all-powerful!?"

Whether her acting was convincing, or she truly believed her words, Briseis couldn't tell.

"I will give you one chance to show your loyalty, your love for me." Delilah turned to Briseis and smacked her lips.

Briseis' blood ran cold.

"Run along, dear," Delilah said blithely. "You know what to do."

Briseis forced herself to walk over to an ornately inlaid cabinet that stood behind the throne. Fumbling through a drawer, she retrieved a palette of lipstick and an applicator. Returning to Delilah, she proffered the cosmetic without meeting the empress' eyes.

After applying the lipstick, Delilah rose from the throne and held out her arms to the soldier, indicating an embrace. "Now, come and show me how much you love me."

With wide-eyed terror, the solider seemed to look for an avenue of escape, but the Homeric guards roughly shoved him forward. "It is a great privilege to kiss our goddess," one of them said fanatically.

The soldier, with shaking steps, ascended the steps to the throne. Delilah wrapped him into an embrace and theatrically kissed him. The solider struggled and thrashed for a few moments, then fell still, his wide eyes turning glassy. Delilah released her grip and let her limp victim collapse to the floor. Briseis winced.

Indicating an albino crocodile that lay chained in a pool of fragrant water to the right of the throne, Delilah issued orders to the guards.

"Goliath hasn't had his dinner yet."

As the crocodile's next meal was dragged away and the dancers cautiously resumed their routine, Toghon approached the throne.

"Delilah—"

The empress cut him off with a single hand motion. "That's 'Your Worship' to you, or, if you're feeling familial, 'Mother.'"

Toghon visibly had to force himself not to roll his eyes. "Very well, *Mother,* as disloyal as that soldier was, he has a point. We expected the Wil'iahns to offer battle as soon as we crossed the border. Their armies have not appeared. However, as we've seen from the beacon signals, there are fortresses in the mountains from which they could easily attack our supply lines. We must stop to besiege these fortresses before we proceed any further."

"Halt our advance now, at the height of success? Nonsense! The only way is forward. We must chase the

Wil'iahns until the cowards finally turn and fight, and then we shall destroy them."

"With all due respect, you have proved adept at politics, but you are not a military commander."

"Remember your place, Toghon. You are only here because of my mercy. Before I became your mother, Kubi had abandoned you owing to your miserable performance in Dai Viet. I would expect you to show more gratitude."

Toghon grimaced and looked like he was about to say something, but a glance at Heracles, who protectively loomed over the empress, seemed to put a stop to the notion.

Kubi? Briseis had never heard Delilah refer to the Great Khan of the Mongols so flippantly. As she returned the lethal lipstick to the cosmetics cabinet, she couldn't help but think that the deserter might have been right.

Is this the fatal error? Have we gone too far?

CHAPTER FIVE

PRINCESS JUDITH

Balthcutta

Tamino and Avora'tru'ivi strode down the long hallway towards their quarters in the castle. As unpleasant as the invasion preparations were, Tamino was looking forward to this part the least.

"How much are we going to tell her?" He asked.

"We're going to tell it to her straight. There's no use coddling her at this point. She's smart. She'll figure it out," Avora'tru'ivi responded.

"You're probably right."

"I might leave out the actual troop numbers involved, though. There's a difference between making sure she knows what's going on and scaring her out of her wits."

"I'm glad she's with us, but a big part of me wishes that she were somewhere else, away from the war zone. We should have sent her to Manasseh."

"Galbi, this is probably the safest place she can be. Balthcutta is the best-defended city in Wil'iah. I don't think Manasseh will be any safer. We don't know if the shadow of evil has fallen there as well. The Frouzee certainly knows that they would come to our aid. I would be surprised if she left my old country out of her plans."

The two monarchs arrived at a wooden door. Tamino gently knocked.

The door opened to reveal the gaunt face of Milcah, the governess and maid.

"Oh good, you're here," she said. "She's been asking for you. I've been trying to explain to her what is happening, but I don't completely know myself. Based on the beacon, I suspect…"

"Your suspicions are correct." Avora'tru'ivi said.

"Do we have a plan for the defense of the city? For that matter, do we have a plan for the defense of the whole country? This is disastrous. What are we going to do?" The normally taciturn maid pleaded.

"I'm afraid I can't reveal the details, but we do have a plan," replied Tamino. "I wish I could tell you, but we have to be very careful. The Frouzee could have spies everywhere. You never know who might overhear."

"Indeed," said Milcah as she deferentially bowed her head and led them into a small, brightly painted room filled with toys, dolls, and stuffed animals.

"Momma! Daddy!" Princess Judith's greeting was a mixture of relief and alarm.

"Hi, sweetie!" Avora'tru'ivi tried to manage the brightest tone she could.

"What is happening?" Judith said as she hugged Alinta, her stuffed koala, with surprising force.

"Well, sweetie, some bad guys have decided to come to Wil'iah." Avora'tru'ivi said matter-of-factly.

"It's that mean lady, isn't it?" Judith responded, her diminutive eyebrows furrowing in concern.

Tamino gently laughed. "Yes, it's that mean lady. But don't worry, sweetheart, we are going to take care of it."

Judith gave Tamino an unexpectedly intense stare. "How many troops does she have, Daddy?"

"We don't know yet, sweetheart. But we're going to find out, and when they get here, we will be ready."

"I like your armor, Momma," Judith said as she turned to her mother.

"Thank you, sweetie."

"What's going to happen?" the princess asked.

"Well, sweetie, we're going to have to fight off the bad guys. Momma and Daddy are going to be pretty busy, so Milcah is going to take care of you."

Judith screwed up her face as though she found the idea distasteful, but simply responded,

"Oh."

"Come, child," Milcah said, stretching her bony arms out to embrace the princess. Judith reluctantly hauled herself out of bed and trundled over to the governess.

"We love you, and we are going to keep you safe," Tamino said to his daughter.

Milcah opened her birdlike mouth to respond.

"Don't worry, Your Faithfulnesses, the princess will be well taken care of."

CHAPTER SIX

CU QUOC NGHÊNH DICH

Thang Long, Dai Viet, northern Vietnam

The serenity of the Tran Court at Thang Long shattered in an instant when an exhausted messenger staggered into the throne room.

"Your Highness!" he breathlessly gasped, "Our intelligence forces in China indicate that the Mongols have launched a major military operation!"

Tran Anh Tong, the new emperor of Dai Viet, leaned forward on his throne with concern. Hung Dao, the commander of Dai Viet's forces, stepped forward and addressed the herald.

"Where are the forces headed?"

"All indications are of a major amphibious invasion."

"Japan? Again?"

"We don't think the target is Japan. Based on a semi-reliable informant in Khan's palace of Xanadu, we believe the target is Wil'iah. This is consistent with his recent marriage to Frouzee Delilah."

Hung Dao gravely nodded.

The emperor regarded the general. "As members of the League, we are obligated to respond."

"Indeed, after all of the assistance Wil'iah has rendered to us against the Mongols, we must return the favor."

"What forces do we have available?"

"We can call up 200,000 troops on short notice, but we cannot afford to send a large army all the way to Wil'iah without exposing ourselves to invasion. We barely survived the last one."

The emperor pondered the situation for a moment, then responded. "We will send 50,000 troops. We cannot allow Wil'iah to fall." Turning to the messenger, he continued, "Send a message to the naval base at Van Don. Tell the Binh Hai Quan fleet to begin to mobilize and to receive a large army. On their way to Wil'iah, they are to stop at Singhasari and gather their fleet before proceeding south. We will also send ships and soldiers to Manasseh, which we expect may also be under attack."

The messenger nodded, then turned and raced back out of the throne room.

The emperor turned to Hung Dao. "I trust you to lead our forces to victory. Last time, when the Mongols invaded, our slogan was '*Cử quốc nghênh địch,*' 'the whole country face to face with the enemy.'"

Hung Dao nodded. "And now we will stand with our allies. Now our slogan will be 'the whole *world* face to face with the enemy.'

CHAPTER SEVEN

THE EVACUATION

Balthcutta

Leaving the peaceful sanctuary of their daughter's room, Tamino made his way through the halls of the castle to the main gate, then proceeded into the city, eventually coming to the St. Thomas Gate of Balthcutta. The gatehouse was a massive, double-layer structure flanked on either side by D-shaped towers; glistening black cannons ominously yawned from between the crenelated battlements. The gatehouse included several layers of internal defenses, including machicolations, which would allow defenders to hurl missiles down on any forces that managed to pierce the main gate. But today, the main gate was flung open, the portcullises were up, and the sturdy drawbridge was lowered over the moat.

Stretching into the distance was a paved road which led to the upcountry of the Blue Mountains and the patchwork of farming communities that lay between it and the city. The road was always busy, but today it was a teeming morass of humanity and livestock as wagon after wagon trundled through the gates and people from all over south Yaringa streamed into the city with their livestock, each village group accompanied by its assigned Marshal of the Order of the Flame of Zebulon who had sprung into action as soon as the blue fires were set alight on the mountains. Knowing full well that the countryside could not be held against the unstoppable Mongol cavalry, Lady Deborah had made the decision that all civilians in Balthcutta's environs would be evacuated to safety within its staunch walls, and those of its sister city of Djubuguli, one hundred and twenty miles to the north, taking with them all the food they could gather in a hurry. These two great fortresses would have to contain all the civilians of the Judgate of Yaringa. Ominously, great billowing plumes of ugly black smoke filled the sky in all directions as the countryside and its food resources, which might otherwise sustain the Mongol cavalry, burned.

Tamino squeezed his way through the mass of civilians, eventually reaching the other side of the drawbridge. There were perhaps more important matters to attend to at the moment, but he felt his place was here. A battered-looking wagon drawn by two mules clattered up to the drawbridge, piled high with hastily-gathered belongings and crowned with five young children and two elderly people. Next to it walked an exhausted-looking woman, obviously the mother of the children, and her husband, who gently led the mules. As they neared Tamino, he rendered the civilian salute, ending with the open palm extended toward them in welcome. The woman noticed the gesture and began to return it, but suddenly stopped cold when she recognized the Signet of Hezekiah emblazoned on Tamino's armor. She grabbed her husband's arm.

"Va'a'heva, It's....It's..."

"Welcome to Balthcutta. You and your family will be safe here," Tamino said, bowing his head in respect. He then stepped forward and wrapped both parents in a hug.

Above all the streaming mass of refugees flapped the brave battle-flag of Wil'iah.

CHAPTER EIGHT

BALTHCUTTA GIRDS FOR BATTLE

Balthcutta

*F*or her part, Avora'tru'ivi returned to the depths of the castle, finally reaching an office deep within its basement, not far from the war room. A woman sat at a desk carefully reviewing scrolls, muttering to herself as her tightly-wound hair bun bounced up and down with each movement of her head.

"Can I help you?" the clerk said as she looked up from the scroll, then hastily snapped into a salute as she realized who had entered.

"At ease. Are the storehouses ready?" Avora'tru'ivi asked in a businesslike tone.

"Yes, your faithfulness. I was just checking over the inventory records."

The woman grabbed an enormous ring of keys that were hanging from a peg on the wall, then motioned for Avora'tru'ivi to follow her. They eventually came to two ponderous steel doors, each guarded by a dour-looking soldier in full armor.

"Her Faithfulness informs me it is time to open the storehouses," the clerk said.

The soldiers stoically nodded, then set about unlocking the doors, which swung open with a groan, and the clerk lit two oil lamps.

Their dim but insistent light illuminated a vast hall stretching into indiscernible darkness, in which thousands of barrels were stacked in neatly-organized rows.

"This is Rice Storage Facility Fifteen," the clerk said with a note of pride. "There are twenty like it in the city, with similar storage facilities for grain, dried fruits, roots, and other non-perishables. There's enough for at least six months, possibly eight if we stretch it."

"Very good. Instruct your staff to deploy the ration stations immediately. It's very possible our sea resupply could get cut off."

"Of course, Your Faithfulness."

With a mixture of apprehension and wonder, Avora'tru'ivi looked at the seemingly endless food supplies.

I'd better get used to eating rice.

CHAPTER NINE

COOTAMUNDRA

Cootamundra, Vrenga'nui, eastern Wil'iah

On the other side of the mountains, in the Judgate of Vrenga'nui, the knight Jiemba stood atop the keep of the castle of the town of Cootamundra, carefully watching the distant Mount Burrinjuck for the next signal. The angry red fire that had announced the invaders had set the town into motion; families had begun to gather in the town square to await further instructions. As the local marshal, Jiemba had special responsibilities. Next to him atop the keep flapped three flags; the battle-flag of the Kingdom of Wil'iah, the flag of the Judgate of Vrenga'nui, and the standard of the

Wiradjuri Nation, which held sovereignty over the area. Next to him stood another knight, Brindabella.

"What do you think it's going to be? Mizpah, Elah, Geba, Samson, or one of the others?" Jiemba asked.

"My money's on Mizpah," Brindabella responded.

Suddenly, both knights' eyes narrowed as a blue flame roared to life atop the mountain. Jiemba sharply took in his breath.

"Samson."

"Well, we'd better get to work," Brindabella responded, hefting her spear.

"The situation must be really serious if they picked that plan," Jiemba responded.

"Look, all we know is what we're supposed to do."

Jiemba and Brindabella made their way from the castle, a minimal structure consisting of a circular wall surrounding a single tall keep, to the town square, where the town's population of about a thousand nervously waited.

Jiemba cleared his throat.

"Alright, the lights are blue. This means that we must institute the Samson Plan."

A murmur ran through the crowd as people conferred. Nobody knew what that plan was.

"This appears to be a major invasion," Jiemba continued. "Our tasks must be carried out immediately. All civilians are to follow Brindabella. She knows where to go. Any Home Army members designated to Home Army Upcountry Command are to proceed with her as well. However, all individuals in the Army of Vrenga'nui Reserves or the Home Army Backcountry Command are to follow me. I hate to say this," Jiemba apologetically looked at the assembled villagers, "but the entire village and all the farmland must be put to the torch to deny these resources to the enemy. We are instructed to remove any valuables with us when we evacuate. When possible, space priority should be given to food. We also should bring as much livestock as possible with us. We need to move quickly. The enemy is highly mobile."

A gasp ran through the crowd as the full gravity of the situation hit them. Some family members grimly embraced each other as they realized they would be split up, with some members heading with Brindabella and some with Jiemba.

"And just where are we going?" asked one villager angrily.

"Neither of us knows the end destinations," Brindabella responded. "We will be following songlines specially prepared for this operation. You can trust us."

The villager nodded in response, his eyes still filled with some skepticism.

Jiemba addressed the gathered audience.

"Alright, you have your orders. We will reassemble at the entrance to town in two hours."

※　※　※

Two hours later, a hastily-assembled caravan stood in some semblance of order at the entrance to the village, as the evening darkness gathered. Carts loaded high with food and livestock stood at the ready in Brindabella's column, while a line of horses and riders formed up behind Jiemba, the green pendant of the Home Army flapping from the knights lance. A middle-aged woman in Brindabella's group hugged her daughter tightly, tears streaming down both of their faces, before they parted, and the daughter, her face set in a resolute mask, marched over to join

Jiemba. Behind them, the village and its associated farm fields consumed themselves in an angry orange conflagration. Jiemba couldn't help but see hopelessness plainly written on many of the villagers' faces as all that they had ever known went up in flames.

With nothing left to do but go forward, both Brindabella and Jiemba began to quietly sing to themselves, recalling the words to the Samson Song that they had drilled into their minds. The song would lead them from landmark to landmark until they finally reached their end destinations, wherever they may be. Each of them picking out their first mark, Brindabella and Jiemba advanced forward, haltingly followed by the columns of villagers.

Jiemba allowed himself a brief glance skyward, his eyes instantly alighting on the Southern Cross that blazed defiantly against the black firmament.

This had better work, he thought.

CHAPTER TEN

THE HIDDEN FORTRESS

Kumana Namadgi, Vrenga'nui, southeastern Wil'iah

$\mathcal{T}$he mountain of Kumana Namadgi, Australia's highest peak, stood tall and proud amongst the other high mountains near the Frouzean border, a gentle blanket of snow covering its highest reaches. At the summit, a small, unassuming tower, virtually invisible to someone at the base of the mountain, kept watch over the valley below. A sentinel paced back and forth, his eyes squinting at another mountain in the distance, Targangil. Beside him was a brazier filled with oil and sticks. Now, he awaited the response from Tamino.

Suddenly, the sentinel's eyes widened in recognition as a blue light ignited atop Targangil.

"*Samson,*" he whispered to himself, then immediately fumbled for a pouch of powder which was kept ready at all times atop the mountain. He spread the powder over the sticks, then ignited a spark with his flint. A blue flame roared into life in the brazier. Waiting for a moment to make sure that the fire didn't sputter out immediately, the sentinel then raced down a set of spiral stairs that plunged him into darkness.

The small watchtower atop the mountain was the only visible sign of the massive fortress that filled a warren of passageways painstakingly carved into the mountain itself. The Hidden Fortress had first been built long ago, during the days of the Wil'iahn Revolt against Frouzea, when secrecy was essential. Now, it stood as the clandestine forward base of Wil'iah's armed forces, a subtle spearpoint aimed directly at the Frouzean border just a few miles away. It formed a crucial part of the Samson Plan.

The sentinel raced through a maze of passages that he knew by heart, lit sparingly by sputtering torches. After several minutes of navigation, he arrived at the command center of the fortress, where a stern-looking knight hunched over a map of the border region.

"It's blue, sir. Samson."

The knight stood up straight, a dark look crossing his face as his eyes scanned the map one more time.

"Very well. Muster the mobile strike force. We will depart immediately. Signal to Balawan, Wangaratta, and Wagga Wagga to do the same. "

Inscribed on the map was a series of dotted lines indicating likely supply lines for the Frouzean armies as they penetrated into Wil'iahn territory. With practiced precision, the knight hurled his knife, the point burying itself perfectly in one of the lines.

"They won't know what hit them."

CHAPTER ELEVEN

THE EAST GUARD

Trukanamoa, Tjoritja, central Wil'iah

Jeremiah, Tamino's younger brother and the sovereign protector of Wil'iah, paced along the battlements of the Castle of Trukanamoa, trying to regain his composure. Regarding the splendid capital of the nation spread out before him, he reflected on all that his father had built, against impossible odds. Now, he was gone. Jeremiah's heart felt like a leaden weight as sorrow pulled him into the depths, but he knew he needed to be strong for his people at this crucial hour.

Especially since Tamino isn't here.

However, he was pulled from his reverie by an abrupt, anguished shout.

"The Beacon of the East Guard!"

Sudden panic gripping him, Jeremiah whirled around to see a red fire flare from the top of the fortress that guarded the east end of the Gap of Mparntwe, the notable chink in Trukanamoa's defenses.

"*What?*" he hissed under his breath as the castle around him erupted into a flurry of activity. Of course, the beacon could only mean one thing. Hazarding a glance back at the old palace, which looked pitifully small to him from this height, he knew what he needed to do. He raced down the spiral staircase in the nearest tower and made his way through the gates toward the palace.

At length, Jeremiah arrived at a door in southwest corner of the palace's upper level and paused for a moment, holding his breath. Then, with resolution of purpose, he raised a fist to knock on the door.

Hearing no response, he tried the knob, which willingly twisted in his hand. The door slowly creaked open, to reveal a darkened room lit only by the much-attenuated glow that diffused through gossamer curtains drawn across a window, a glow which betrayed the black silhouette of a lone figure.

"Mother," Jeremiah softly entreated.

"What is it, Jeremiah?" Adirah of Mangala, co-founder of Wil'iah, asked, her voice a flat, emotionless monotone.

"There's some bad news."

"Could any news be worse than the blow we have already been dealt?"

"I'm afraid so. The beacon of the East Guard glows red."

The figure against the window briefly straightened, then slumped again as it turned toward him. His eyes adjusting to the dimness of the room, Jeremiah could make out the blank look plastered across his mother's face.

"The beacon…"

"Yes, the beacon. This time is difficult for all of us, but Wil'iah has need of you at this hour."

"What does Wil'iah need an old woman for? I am nothing but a wispy wraith of what once was. We all are. My time passed with my husband. It is your time now. Go to them, Jeremiah. Be the hero that Wil'iah needs."

"What is this? You know better than this, Mother. Your greatness was never dependent on him."

"Dependent or not, its fire has been passed down now. Leave me to my peace, Jeremiah. It's all that I have left." Adirah turned and resumed her vacant vigil at the window.

A sinking feeling dragging on his gut, Jeremiah exited the room and took a deep breath.

What is wrong with her?

Jeremiah Tru'maua, Sovereign Protector of Wil'iah

CHAPTER TWELVE

THE DEFENSE OF TJORITJA

Trukanamoa

That evening, Jeremiah sat with his generals in the command center of Trukanamoa Castle, trying to make sense of the situation.

"The border fortifications report seeing four tumens of Mongol cavalry and approximately forty thousand Frouzean troops cross the defensive perimeter near the border between Anangu and Kati-Thanda. As far as we could tell, they're headed straight for Uluru." Jeremiah said.

"We don't know how many forces the enemy has in this region, or even if they plan to attack here at all. The initial alert came from the east," said Eleazar Va'i'tavi, a Knight Commander of the Order of the Flame of Zebulon who served as General of the Army of Tjoritja, Wil'iah's main force in the center. Towering even over Jeremiah, his powerful frame, close-cropped hair, and intense, angular face punctuated by piercing eyes lent a muscular presence to the occasion.

"It would be strange for the enemy to attack only in the east and ignore the capital. They'll be here," Jeremiah responded.

"But in what numbers?" asked Allira, Prime Minister of the Council of Uluru and head of Wil'iah's civilian government.

Eleazar swept his hand over a map of central Wil'iah, emphasizing the alarmingly long, perilously porous border of the judgates of Anangu and Kati-Thanda that tenuously guarded Wil'iah's southern marches against the lawless wilds of Outer Frouzea. "We have yet to hear anything from our border fortifications, but the enemy likely knows where they are and have circumvented them. We cannot possibly watch every segment of a border over a thousand miles long. We have no idea from what direction the Frouzee's forces will strike, but we know that there is one target she couldn't possibly resist."

"Uluru," ruefully grunted Allira.

Eleazar continued. "We don't know the full extent of the Frouzee's forces. But we do know what we have at our disposal. Our standing forces in Anangu number seven thousand, with another seven thousand in Kati-Thanda. If we call the reserves, we can add another twenty-two thousand to those numbers. The border provinces are the first line of our defense."

"And how many do we have here in Tjoritja?" the Prime Minister asked.

"Twelve thousand, with much more significant reserves. Last I checked, if we really mobilized everyone, there are over one hundred thousand trained troops in Tjoritja."

"We only mobilize reserves to that extent if we face a truly existential threat."

"That's exactly what we're looking at," Jeremiah said. He turned to Eleazar. "I suggest that we deploy the Armies of Anangu and Kati-Thanda to their border defense positions and call up all available reserves immediately. I think our best chance, assuming we will receive no further instructions, is to meet the enemy head-on."

Allira nodded in assent. "We cannot allow the enemy to capture Uluru."

"Such a humiliating defeat would be disastrous. It would be unwise for us to leave the capital completely undefended, but if we mobilize the full reserves, we can bring fifty thousand with us to reinforce the defenses at Uluru. Before the Great Rock, our enemy will be shattered!" Jeremiah roared, pounding his heavy fist on the table.

Eleazar placed a staying hand on Jeremiah's outstretched arm. "Let's not be hasty. Tjoritja's strength is the desert and the deleterious effect it has on enemy forces. We would be wise to let the country itself sap them before we strike."

"Besides," interrupted Italereme, "Don't we have a national defense strategy? I would think this had all been planned out already."

Jeremiah scoffed. "My brother is too busy dedicating churches to make these kinds of decisions. We're going to have to make do without him or his leadership."

Just then, a guard burst through the door and breathlessly yelled,

"Another beacon! This one is blue!"

A dark look covered Jeremiah's face.

"The Samson Plan," he said, giving Eleazar a significant look.

"And you thought he couldn't make any decisions," Allira said, her brows furrowing in concern as the full import of the order hit home. "The council's not going to like this, but they must defer to the Crown on military matters."

"All the same, the plan leaves us some flexibility," Jeremiah interjected. "It's safe to assume that the vast majority of the enemy's forces will be concentrated in the east, where both they and we have the most population. The only parts of Frouzea directly to the south of us are nearly depopulated. I think we still have a chance to smash them at Uluru. We'll retreat to the prepared defenses if necessary."

"Jeremiah, that is a dangerously large troop commitment to this plan," Eleazar said.

"Who is in command here? Am I not the Sovereign Protector with responsibility for the defense of Wil'iah's capital?" Jeremiah retorted.

"That's exactly right. The defense of the *capital*," Eleazar said darkly.

Not taking the bait, Jeremiah turned to the guard who had announced the beacon.

"Go to the courier's office and tell him to send riders to Uluru and Verwonnah immediately. Tell them that the Armies of Anangu and Kati-Thanda are to mobilize and report to their stations along the border, but that the majority of Anangu's forces, and all of their reserves, should concentrate at Uluru for now. We aren't positive that that's where the enemy will strike, but it's a high-value target."

The guard snapped into a military salute, then ran out the door.

CHAPTER THIRTEEN

SALOME'S SCHEME

Imperial Army camp, Great Coastal Road, southeastern Wil'iah

"*N*o-one *can ever know.*" Delilah's words reverberated through Salome's mind as she slunk between rows of tents in the Imperial Army's camp on the coast. At first, confirmation that Delilah wasn't actually a goddess had shocked her to her core. Doubt had always gnawed at her, of course – Delilah's appearance in a puff of smoke in the hour of Frouzea's greatest need had been exceedingly convenient – but she never expected to have to confront these doubts so dramatically.

But almost as soon as she had done so, a plan had started to grow in her mind's garden, like an uncontrollable weed. She was exceedingly grateful to Delilah, of course, for rescuing her from slavery at the hands of the handsome but depraved Achilles of Gath, but, from the very beginning, Salome had recognized an opportunity to increase her own prestige by growing ever-closer to Delilah. Now though, that she knew that Delilah had essentially acted and fooled her way into the thrones of not one, but two empires…

Salome suddenly found herself in front of a large purple pavilion with embroidered golden horseflies.

A perfect opportunity had presented itself.

A few short minutes later, Salome returned to the pavilion with a platter piled high with delicacies filched from Delilah's private stores.

She's so overflowing with riches that she'll never know, Salome thought, reveling in the access that "Preferred Handmaiden" status gave her to her mistress' resources. Arriving at the entrance to the pavilion, she coquettishly smiled at the two stern-faced guards that flanked it.

"I bring some *gifts* for your master, courtesy of Her Worship."

"His Excellency Prince Diomedes does not want to be disturbed," one of the guards growled.

"Goddesses can disturb anyone whenever they want," Salome countered. The guard winced, but let her through, chastened by the veiled threat behind the handmaid's words. As Salome passed through the tent flaps, she turned back over her shoulder and blew the guard a kiss. He turned beet-red.

Inside, the tent was the picture of imperial splendor, with luxurious cushions and deep-pile carpets strewn about, lit by ornate paper lanterns that cast their golden glow over intricately-embroidered walls. Diomedes reclined on a lounge trimmed with sumptuous furs, gazing longingly at a marble bust of a woman on a plinth next to the lounge.

Suddenly, his beady, dark eyes focused on Salome, and he grunted in surprise.

"What do *you* want?" he asked gruffly.

"I bring the felicitations of Her Worship. She recognizes that you have suffered an agonizing loss recently and wants to help. After all, she knows the heartbreak that comes when losing a spouse."

Diomedes looked like he was about to scoff at the comment, but clearly remembered who he was talking to (or, rather, who she worked for) and recovered, instead nodding gravely.

"Is that her?" Salome said soothingly, motioning to the bust.

"Yes," Diomedes responded shortly, his voice wracked with pain.

"She was beautiful," Salome responded in a low voice.

"Yes, she was."

"What a shame to lose her so young. At least she bore you a son. I trust he is being well-taken care of?"

Diomedes winced, but then recovered again, as though he thought he was being tested.

"Perseus is in the care of my mother, Andromeda, and my brother, Adrastus."

"He must be a darling child, handsome and strong – like his father."

Diomedes's beady eyes flashed to meet Salome's for a moment in surprise. However, he suddenly gave a wry smile and began to laugh. "You learn quickly, don't you?"

Salome feigned insult. "I don't know what you mean."

"I'm sure you don't." Diomedes eyed the platter that Salome balanced on one hand. "What have you brought?"

"My mistress wishes to bring you *comfort* in the hour of your loss. You moving act of patriotism, abandoning your family and infant son to lead her armies to victory, has not gone unnoticed."

Another dark look filled Diomedes' eyes, and he beheld the tray with suspicion. "How easy. How convenient. No, I am not a simpleton like my brother was. I eat only from my own supplies. You can tell your mistress that her 'gifts' are appreciated, but I'm doing just fine on my own."

"I understand," Salome said. "And I know how it must feel to lose your brother. What a terrible way to die. It almost makes one feel that whoever did it deserves the same, or worse."

"But Her Worship was responsible...I will not question the Goddess," Diomedes forced himself to say, "and, after all, it did give me the throne." To his surprise, however, Salome winked, then sidled over and whispered in his ear.

"It is well known that Ekron was one of the most independent-minded principalities in the old empire. I have recently come into knowledge of a secret that could greatly benefit us both. If you are interested, meet me at the northeastern edge of the camp at midnight. You won't be disappointed."

Diomedes' eyes widened in shock. Salome, however, simply got up and slunk toward the tent flap, leaving the tray behind. When she reached the opening, she looked back over her shoulder at Diomedes.

"Your wife was beautiful, but it would be a shame for you to be all alone now. There are other options. They are ready and waiting."

With that, she disappeared.

CHAPTER FOURTEEN

TRANQUILITY BEFORE THE TEMPEST

Balthcutta

*T*amino and General Teva'ivani strode along the ramparts of the inner wall of Balthcutta, surveying the row of black Chinese guns that stared out between the crenellations. Behind them were a row of finely-oiled trebuchets, with piles of boulders standing at the ready, and with furnaces for heating projectiles spaced between the engines. Tamino approached a heavyset woman who stood next to one of the catapults, excitedly speaking with a soldier who was coiling a thick rope.

"I trust all is ready, Abigail?" Tamino asked. The siege engineer broke off her conversation and snapped into a military salute.

"Yes, your Faithfulness, we're ready."

Tamino looked out on the fuming ruins of the countryside all around Balthcutta, wisps of black smoke rising all around the city. Suddenly, his eyebrows narrowed as he espied a single rider thundering across the smoldering plains at breakneck speed.

"Thank you for your diligence, Abigail," he said before turning and descending to the level of the main gate, which laboriously creaked open to admit the rider.

The wild-eyed horse, foaming at the mouth, staggered across the drawbridge, and the exhausted rider jumped down to come face-to-face with the king. Tamino immediately noticed a white six-pointed star emblazoned the rider's armor.

"You come from the Hidden Fortress," Tamino said.

The rider nodded, taking a moment to catch his breath. "The Imperial Army has penetrated the border. They appear to have split into three main groups- one is advancing into the Backcountry, one has turned west toward Wagga Wagga, and the third appears to be headed straight for Balthcutta."

Tamino clenched his fist as his stomach churned at the news.

"How many?"

"It's difficult to estimate the numbers. Based on the different legionary standards we were able to identify in the Balthcutta force, there appear to be at least fifty thousand Frouzeans, and an equal number of Mongols. They appear to have brought advanced siege equipment with them."

Tamino grimly nodded. "I suppose that's to be expected. How long do you think we have?"

"My guess is two days, three at most."

"Are the Order's forces in position?"

"Yes, your Faithfulness. When the time comes, we'll be ready."

CHAPTER FIFTEEN

THE SECRET PLACE OF THE MOST HIGH

Vrenga'nui, southeastern Wil'iah

*T*he smoke of a thousand dying fires obscured the bravely defiant light of the stars as Brindabella picked her way through the darkness, the carts and wheelbarrows of her column creaking behind her, masking the constant swishing noise as the rear guard swept over their tracks with brooms. Constantly, the knight softly sang, her alto voice audible only to the very vanguard of her group. As she felt the rhythm of the song wash over her, her sharp eyes constantly darted from side to side, picking out the various landmarks that the song called out, and always noticing the mountains that loomed before the small party of older people, new mothers, and children. Brindabella also kept her ears open, listening constantly for any sign that the Imperial Army was in the vicinity, although she supposed they had not gotten this far north yet. All the same, she gripped her woomera tightly, ready to hurl the spear at a moment's notice. She had never been in this part of the country in her life, but the song did not fail her as she recognized waypoint after waypoint. Although she was unfamiliar with the territory, she began to suspect that she knew where they were going- a place spoken of in the legends of her people.

At length, the song led her directly to the foothills of the mountains. Squinting in the darkness, she was able to make out a speck of light high on the peak. Her eyes straining for details, she could barely see the blocky outline of a fortress tower. According to her Order training, the mountains were crowned with hundreds of small castles. This must be one of them.

"I think we're almost there," she hissed back to her group.

"Almost where?" a twelve-year old boy next to her said.

"We'll find out," Brindabella responded grimly.

The group began to wind its way up a barely-discernable track along the crest of the foothills, ascending higher and higher, despite the protests of the mules. Soon, the foothills gave way to full-fledged mountains.

"Are we going to go over the whole mountain range?" a grandmotherly woman complained as she rubbed her ankles.

"I don't know," Brindabella responded. "If my suspicions are correct, I don't think so."

A sudden shriek sounded from the back of the column as a woman lost hold of a wheelbarrow laden with grain, which plummeted down the side of the mountain, tumbling with a terrible clatter.

"Leave it!" Brindabella hissed. She turned to the rest of the group, which panted with exertion.

"My directions are clear and have yet to fail us. I ask that you just trust me a little while longer. I believe our salvation is nigh."

"Ummm, Brindabella, what's that?" a ten-year-old girl squeaked from the rear of the column.

Brindabella whirled around, and her stomach dropped to the ground as she beheld a mass of torches in the distant plains, far below. The Imperial Army.

"We must make haste," she said to the crowd. "Don't be afraid. There's no way they can see us. I think I know where we're going. We will be safe there."

"It's time you leveled with us," an old Tharawal man grumbled. "Just where do you think we are going?"

"If you must know, I think you would call it Binda."

The old man's eyes grew wide.

"Well, that changes things. Let's get moving."

Now the party moved with increased urgency, throwing a nervous glance over their shoulders every so often to espy the advancing invasion force below. After what seemed like an eternity, they began to descend slightly into a valley. Soon, the exhausted group came face to face with a yawning gash in a rock face, only haltingly illuminated by the weak light of the waning crescent moon above.

Suddenly, the rock face itself seemed to come alive in a flash of movement as two expertly-camouflaged knights emerged from their hiding places and leveled spears at the party.

"Who goes there?" one of them asked.

"Brindabella of Cootamundra, Knight Commander, with my allotted party." Brindabella reached into her pack and pulled out a badge in the shape of a six-pointed star.

One of the knights looked over the bedraggled group of civilians and tersely responded,

"Password?"

Brindabella froze for a moment, as the realization hit her that she had not ever been told a password.

"Umm…"

The knight moved up his spear ever so slightly, so it now pointed directly at Brindabella's throat.

Just then, she remembered that there was one last piece of the song to be sung, a verse familiar to many Wil'iahns.

"He that dwelleth in the secret place of the Most High…"

The knight visibly relaxed and withdrew the spear. With an easy smile, he rendered the civilian salute to the exhausted refugees.

"You can never be too careful. Welcome to the Refuge of Binda." He spun on his heel and walked into the entrance, motioning for the rest of the group to follow.

A narrow passageway, nearly completely dark, stretched before them. The group picked their way through the gloom, doing their best to navigate the carts and barrows between sharp stalagmites that thrust their way up from the uneven floor.

Gradually, a diffused yellow glow began to permeate the darkness, growing steadily stronger, until Brindabella could easily see the faces of her charges, as well as the path forward. Finally, they came to the end of the tunnel, and gasped at the sight before them.

A huge cavern, lit by the reassuring light of a thousand golden torches, stood before them, punctuated throughout by astonishing, swirling columns and stalactites that looked like some sort of alien landscape. At the floor of the enormous space was a pool of crystal-clear water that gently whispered as it flowed through the cavern. Surrounding it were hundreds of people, huddled around campfires that added to the brilliance of the cave's lighting.

Brindabella turned to the group behind her as they stared in wide-eyed wonder.

"This is it. The secret place of the Most High."

CHAPTER SIXTEEN

MIDNIGHT ASSIGNATIONS

Imperial Army Camp

$\mathcal{S}$alome crept into position on the northeastern corner of the camp. The sound of surf crashing on the nearby beach filled the warm evening air, as the dark Pacific stretched like a blanket beyond. Still, Salome's ears strained to hear any noises that might indicate a marauding patrol. Her heart hammered in her chest. Her plan had a chance at success, but it was slim.

Suddenly, a hand shot out from the darkness and clamped over her mouth, stifling the scream that Salome gave off in response. Brusque arms picked her up and hauled her off to a certain destination as a blindfold was roughly tied over her eyes. At first, she tried kicking herself free, but it was to no avail. Her hand reached for the stiletto she kept concealed in her waistband, but it was quickly grabbed and restrained.

After what seemed like hours but was only a couple of minutes, Salome was unceremoniously dumped on the ground, and the blindfold was removed. She found herself in a secluded copse of trees. Diomedes towered over her, his powerful arms folded and a scowl on his bearded face. One of his guards loomed over her from behind – he must have been the one that kidnapped her.

"Alright, sweetheart, we can talk now, away from whatever trap you laid," Diomedes growled.

Salome batted her eyelashes in feigned insult. "Surely you don't think I could have laid a trap—"

"Save it for your mistress," Diomedes cut her off. "What were you planning to tell me?"

"What do you offer in return?"

"Do you want this war, Diomedes?"

"I have no love for the Wil'iahns."

"Nobody does. But do you want to fight this war *for Delilah?* Or would you rather fight it for yourself?"

"What are you playing at?"

"Like I said, Ekron is a proud and independent principality. Half of the troops in the Frouzean part of this army belong to you. The glory of this conquest should go to you. This glory is what I offer."

"What does any of this have to do with the secret you purport to know?"

"Delilah isn't actually a goddess."

Diomedes stood in stunned silence for a moment, then allowed himself a fit of stifled, quiet laughter. As it died down, he asked incredulously, "You actually believed she was!?"

Salome gave him a terse frown. "Whatever I thought about it, most of your troops believe it. But we know the truth."

Diomedes glared down at her, a mistrustful gleam in his eye. "Exactly. I don't understand what you are suggesting, but it is dangerous for either of us to go against the will of the 'goddess.' I wouldn't be surprised if this charade of yours was some sort of elaborate loyalty test."

"That's the thing with goddesses," Salome said with a sly grin. "The beauty of polytheism is that you can have more than one of them."

※ ※ ※

Briseis tossed and turned in her cot inside Delilah's luxurious pavilion, wracked with worry. Delilah's collected demeanor notwithstanding, Briseis was very concerned that the Wil'iahns had yet to show themselves. Despite the frequent insults hurled at them from Frouzean mouths, the Wil'iahns were known to not be cowards.

They must be planning something, and I don't think we're going to like it.

Finally, sleep evading her, Briseis decided to go for a walk to clear her mind. As she slipped out of the pavilion and began to make a circuit of the camp, she took the opportunity to examine her surroundings. This was not the first time she had walked on Wil'iahn soil — Delilah had sent her as an envoy to Trukanamoa two years before, to attempt to gauge Wil'iah's willingness to negotiate. She had found an unexpectedly warm reception there. She couldn't shake the feeling that these people weren't as contemptible as she had been led to believe.

Nonetheless, Delilah's right. We've gone too far to stop now. The only way is forward.

Suddenly, movement caught her eye to the left. Briseis turned to see a copse of trees, and a lone figure stalking away from it.

"*What?*" she muttered under her breath. Thinking the shadowy menace must be a Wil'iahn spy, Briseis crept forward, trying to get a closer look. She took in a sharp intake of breath as she recognized the unmistakable silhouette of one of her least-favorite people.

Just what are you up to, Salome? She thought.

She prepared to follow her fellow handmaiden when another noise sounded from the copse. A man exited the stand of trees in the opposite direction.

Got a boyfriend, do you?

Gripped with curiosity, Briseis got as close as she dared and dropped down into the grass. As the man confidently strode away from the trees, he looked toward the coast for a moment, and his face was bathed in moonlight.

Diomedes?

That settled it. Briseis had to watch Salome carefully. Her life might depend on it.

CHAPTER SEVENTEEN

THE FLOWER OF CHIVALRY

Trukanamoa

*T*he staunch walls of Trukanamoa loomed over the flat plain that fronted the Tjoritja Mountains. While the resolute ridge formed the primary bastion of the capital's defense, right before it lay the crucial Gap of Mpartnwe, where the mountain range split. Where nature had failed, humanity had improvised, and three great ramparts rose in succession, blocking off the otherwise vulnerable gap. At its center was a great fortified gatehouse, with two gates flanking a grate that admitted the ephemeral waters of the Trukanamoa River, which only flowed in times of heavy rain. Here in the desert, the tears of heaven were too precious to be wasted on water defenses, so Trukanamoa made do with a huge ditch that wended its way across the gap. Within the walls, only the faithful bubbling spring that had lent the city life in the first place saved it from exhaustion. The impressive fortifications were always a triumphant sight, but, today, they took on a somber demeanor. Beside the gates limply hung two great black banners. With an ominous groan, the gatehouse's two great mouths opened to permit the exit of two shining columns of soldiers, dressed in a glittering array of Wil'iah's finest armor. Above them fluttered the flags of the dozens of military units that formed the assemblage; the Army of Tjoritja, with its mostly conventionally-armed Zebulite forces; the Armies of Arrernte, Andegerebendha, Wankanguru, Anmatyerre, and Alyawarre, armed with the iconic woomeras, long spears, polished boomerangs, and fluted shields; and countless smaller formations of the Home Army.

In a seemingly endless array they streamed out of the gate, led first by the brave mounted Knights of the Order of the Flame of Zebulon. Excited children in the crowd made out many of the heraldic devices of heroes whose names counted in the roll of living legends. Elhanan of Arltunga, Ishbaal of Urlatherrke, Azmaveth of Kalarranga, Karinda of Antakarinja, Alkawari of Anangu, Anatjari of Pintupi, and countless others. Proudly astride their war-chargers at the front of the columns rode Jeremiah, bedecked in the finest armor of the Sovereign Protector, and Eleazar, his black horse a complement to Jeremiah's milk-white steed.

As the flower of Wil'iahn chivalry passed through the gates, the civilians that lined the streets feted them with flowers of their own, tossing wreaths and leis with a mixture of patriotic exuberance and worried solemnity as the full gravity of the situation struck them. More than a few wept with increasing intensity as first the mounted knights and cavalry, then the infantry pikemen, and lastly the bowmen and boomerang throwers passed through the gate. At the close of the seemingly endless parade, the crowd looked on at the increasingly-distant soldiers as the gates groaned shut once again, slamming shut with a sound like thunder that rolled over the advancing army and reverberated across the desert. In an instant, the army was gone, and the civilians' longing gaze was met only by a wall of cold, unyielding steel.

CHAPTER EIGHTEEN

ANY OTHER COUNTRY

Balthcutta

Tamino and Avora'tru'ivi's eyes snapped to attention as the doors to the throne room were flung open, and two members of the Judith Corps, the queen's guard, dragged a Mongol soldier through the door and hurled him to the ground at Tamino's feet. The man curled on the floor, sputtering.

"A Mongol scout. The Order caught him skulking outside the walls last night."

Tamino regarded the pitiful sight on the tiles before him. Bending down, his eyes widened in surprise as he saw that this soldier was no battle-hardened Mongol ruffian, but a boy, probably no older than eighteen. And he was no Mongol.

"*Ni shi Zhongguo ren,*" Tamino whispered.

The spy's eyes widened in surprise as they darted up to the unexpectedly kind features of the king.

"*Dui,*" he said softly.

As if on cue, Admiral Zhang stepped out of the shadows by the map table and dragged the soldier to his feet. Behind him stood a young Chinese man with intense features.

The soldier's jaw dropped as he seemed to recognize the legendary figure.

"*Ni shi…ni shi…*"

"*Dui a, wo jiao Zhang Shijie.*" The admiral responded. "*Na ge ren shi ni de pengyou,*" he said, motioning to Tamino and Avora'tru'ivi. He then gestured to the man behind him.

"*Ta jiao Zhao Bing.*"

The soldier's eyes grew wide as saucers.

"*Zhao Bing? Ta huozhe?*"

Emperor Zhao Bing stepped forward, a regal look on his face.

"*Dui, wo Shenghuo le. Wo shi zhenzheng de Huangdi.*"

The soldier looked like he had seen a ghost.

Tamino hastily motioned to the Judith guards.

"Get this man some water and a square meal. Preferably something he would be familiar with, *jiaozi* or something."

"But, your faithfulness, this is an enemy spy!" one of the guards responded through gritted teeth. "If this were any other country he would be tortured for information or killed on the spot."

"This isn't any other country. Get the dumplings."

Her face still somewhat incredulous, the guard rendered a military salute and raced off to the kitchens.

Half an hour later, Tamino sat across a nicely-prepared table from the hesitant soldier, who looked incredulously at the priceless porcelain that had been saved from Song China. The two spoke in Mandarin.

"I don't think I ever got your name," Tamino offered.

"My surname is Yeh."

"Alright, Mr. Yeh, I need to know how many troops are coming here. I'm sure you can understand." Tamino said gently.

Yeh poked at a juicy dumpling with a chopstick, his eyes filled with a mixture of hunger and suspicion. In answer, Tamino picked up the dumpling with his chopsticks and bit off half of it, conspicuously swallowing before placing it back on the plate.

"There, now. I'm not dead," he said.

Yeh immediately plowed into the dumplings, the juices running down his chin. A single tear ran down his face.

"Remind you of home?" Tamino asked.

Yeh nodded.

"You know, we're fighting for China, too," Tamino said softly, motioning to a blue banner with a black character inscribed on a white oval hanging on the wall behind him -- the flag of the Song Dynasty.

Suddenly overcome with emotion, Yeh began to quietly cry.

"Do you want to be here?" Tamino asked gently.

Yeh shook his head, gathered himself, and began to speak. "My people are third-class citizens in our own country. We have few rights, and most of us are desperately poor thanks to the mismanagement of Khan's villainous ministers. Now, we are being conscripted for this invasion, to fight a war we want no part of. But we were threatened into coming. Now there's no turning back."

"Maybe you don't have to go back," Tamino said softly.

"What do you mean?"

"We have no desire to fight you either. The Chinese are our friends. We were proud to stand with them against the Khan, and even now your wisdom gives us the strength we need to continue to resist. When this war is over, you are welcome to stay here. We will grant you full asylum."

Yeh almost dropped his utensils. "What? Why?"

"Why kill an enemy when you can make him into a friend?"

"Would you do that for all of the Chinese soldiers in Khan's army?"

"Depends. How many of them are there?" Tamino asked with a wry smile.

Yeh suddenly laughed.

"You almost got me."

Tamino merely looked at him expectantly. The suspicious mirth in the soldier's eyes suddenly turned once again to incredulity.

"You're serious."

"I will think about it. We're a big country with a lot of open space, and few people to fill it."

Yeh quietly sat for a few moments, then began to speak.

"The expeditionary force in the East has two hundred thousand men. The force in the center has another three hundred thousand. Out of the total, about four hundred thousand are Han Chinese. There aren't so many Mongols as they want everyone to believe."

Tamino let out a whistle. "That's still quite a bit. And I imagine that the Frouzean forces are similar in number?"

"I'm less familiar with their troop arrangements, but it's my understanding that each Frouzean Principality sent one hundred thousand men. I don't know how many Tanitania sends against the west."

Tamino took a deep breath.

Over one million enemy troops. Wil'iah's entire population was four million.

"Are all five hundred thousand troops in the East coming here?"

Yeh shook his head.

"No. Two hundred thousand are headed for the city, led by Minos of Ashkelon and Diomedes of Ekron. Two hundred thousand more are to push into the country under Ajax the Lesser of Gath, with the goal of severing Wil'iah's east coast from the rest of the country. One hundred thousand will follow behind to mop up local resistance and eliminate any strongholds that threaten the rear."

"Interesting," Tamino responded.

Yeh suddenly looked the king directly in the eyes, his own betraying a distinct sadness.

"I believe you that you would take us in, Your Highness," he said. "But I don't think there will be a Wil'iah left to do so when this is all over. I'm sorry."

Tamino patted the soldier on the shoulder. "That's for me to worry about, not you. And though our forces be few in number, we are not so weak as you have been led to believe. We've got something at our backs that Khan, and certainly Frouzee Delilah, will never have."

"What's that?"

Tamino winked.

"You'll see."

CHAPTER NINETEEN

THE SIEGE OF BALTHCUTTA

Balthcutta

*T*he staunch defenses of Balthcutta were without equal in the known world. Three successive walls, each one higher and thicker than the last, rose like artificial mountain ranges before the massed hordes of the enemy. Melding the best of Chinese and Wil'iahn design practices, the formidable ramparts were tapered from their formidable bases to their crenellated summits, their angled sides expertly designed to deflect projectiles. The first wall, the shortest and thinnest, was still forty feet thick and twenty-five feet high, punctuated at regular intervals by protruding curtain wall towers bristling with ballistae and Chinese oxbows. The second wall, sixty feet thick and fifty feet high, was crowned with menacing rows of glistening black cannon. Last and most formidable, the inner wall was eighty feet thick and eighty feet high, punctuated by proud towers one hundred twenty feet high, on which stood enormous counterweight trebuchets. All three's tops were lined with machicolations, their malevolent maws yawning over the flat wards below. While these walls were punctuated by seven gates, six had been walled up, and only the largest and proudest, the great Gate of St. Thomas, stood now in open defiance of the enemy. Its appearance was deceptive, for in each of the places where the walls were pierced by the gate, a succession of barriers lined the interiors-in the outer wall, four gates and three portcullises; in the middle wall, six gates and five portcullises; and in the last and greatest, seven gates and six portcullises. Surrounding the whole magnificent assemblage was a moat some one hundred feet wide and forty feet deep, filled with salt water that freely flowed in from the sea.

Against these impressive fortifications thundered a group of white horses that stopped at speaking distance with the Wil'iahn command post atop the Gate of St. Thomas. Five heralds blasted out a gloating fanfare on trumpets, while the man astride the central horse boldly rode forward, accompanied by two standard-bearers holding aloft the flags of the Frouzean Empire and the Yuan Dynasty. As he grew nearer, Tamino recognized him as Delilah's manservant, Heracles, who puffed out his chest and issued a challenge.

"Her Worship Delilah, Second Incarnation to Earth of the Goddess Astarte and Eternal Empress of the Frouzean

Empire, Everlasting Object of Adoration of the citizens and Denizens of the Principalities and Provinces of said Empire, Ruler of the Principalities of Gath, Gaza, Ekron, Ashkelon, Ashdod, and Ekron, Dominator of the Provinces of Outer Frouzea, Nullarbor, Ithaca, Arboria, and Aurania, Image of the Goddess Tanit and beloved leader of the Imperial Provinces of Upper and Lower Tanitania, Sovereign by Historical Right of Canaan, Egypt, Sinai, Iberia, Utica, Cartagena, Mauritania, Tunisia, Carthage, Africa Proconsolaris—"

Heracles was rudely interrupted by a shout from the walls.

"Whatever!"

Heracles harrumphed, narrowed his eyes, cleared his throat, and continued.

"Attica, Illyria, Argolis, Achaea, Thrace, Epirus, Crete, Cyprus, the Cyclades, Macedonia, and Asia Minor, Queen of the Antarctic reaches and Atlantis and terror of Australia, the glorious, the inexorable, the beautiful, demands your surrender! She promises to be *merciful* if you will give up your pigheaded notions and submit!

"He certainly is a big fellow, isn't he?" Tamino whispered to Avora'tru'ivi. He wasn't wrong. Heracles looked to be a couple of inches taller than even Tamino's father Hezekiah, whose towering height was legendary – and he was certainly much larger than the average Frouzean.

"Do you think he is part Anakim?" Avora'tru'ivi hissed back, referring to a race of legendary Biblical giants rumored to have taken refuge with the ancient Philistines, the ancestors of the Frouzeans. "I didn't know there were any left."

"There were rumors of large Frouzeans serving as a sort of slave-warrior caste during the War of the Vow, but I thought they might have been exaggerations," Tamino responded. "This is interesting."

The speculation helped both of them mask the cold fear that gripped their hearts.

Now the man next to Heracles, General Toghon, in full barbaric regalia, stepped forward.

"The Great Khan, the *actual* ruler—" he stole a rueful glance at Heracles and Delilah, whose eyes narrowed in response, "—of all the known world, of China, Korea, Sinkiang, Inner and Outer Mongolia, the splendors of Khwarazm, the lands of Syria and Arabia, Mesopotamia, the steppes of Turkestan and the Rus', Siberia, Hungary, and Sarmatia, Anatolia, Persia, Georgia, and Afghanistan, offers you mercy just this once. Remember well the fate of all cities who defy us. All the many-splendored halls of Bukhara, of Merv, of Samarkand, and even of great Baghdad could not withstand us. And now those cities stand as empty ruins, the skulls of their inhabitants, to the last child, stacked as pyramids for all the astounded world to see. It is not well to defy the will of the Great Khan. It is wise to submit. Those who surrender to us are treated well. Surely you have heard that even one of the Great Khan's most trusted ministers is a Nestorian Christian, not unlike yourselves. You will be permitted to retain your way of life and your God if you surrender to us. Defy us, and you will be utterly destroyed. It is the natural way of things. What is your answer?"

As the Mongol general's challenge died on the breeze, an oppressive silence replaced it. All eyes on the walls turned to the burnished figure of Tamino, who stood tall on the battlements atop the Gate of St. Thomas. Tamino wordlessly nodded to the plump woman who stood beside him, who herself gave a hand signal to the crew beside her.

Tamino at the St. Thomas Gate

Instantly, the silence was shattered by a roar of thunder as a plume of white smoke erupted from the battlements beside the king. As the report echoed through the air, it was supplanted by a screaming whine as a shell whistled through the air, finally raising a great fountain of dirt not twenty feet in front of the enemy delegation, followed immediately by an explosive detonation that sent debris flying in all directions- including directly into the Mongol general's face.

A hearty cheer roared up from the three successive layers of ramparts, filling the air with defiance as hundreds of Wil'iahn battle flags flapped in the breeze. But no sooner had this song of resistance arisen than it was drowned out by the whooping and hollering of two hundred thousand hostile voices in return, as the invading army charged. The air became a cyclone of boulders as the assembled hundreds of Mongol siege engines set about their deadly work, whistles filling the air as their red-hot projectiles slammed into the steadfast outer wall. With each thunderous shake the defenders winced and quailed, but the wall held firm, a testament to the Chinese engineers that had designed it to resist just such an attack.

In answer, the middle wall exploded into a hedgerow of flame as the guns roared their defiance, their own missiles screaming over the heads of the defenders of the outer wall as they grimly set the advancing army in their sights. The charred plain in front of the city seemed to erupt into a field of volcanic plumes as ball after ball found its target. The very sun itself seemed to dim as great flocks of thousands of arrows darted out from both sides, their deadly arcs finding all too many marks.

Tamino and Avora'tru'ivi surveyed the scene side-by-side from their command post atop the outermost house of the Gate of St. Thomas. Tamino winced as a Mongol projectile smashed into the tower to their right, but the resolute structure held firm. Avora'tru'ivi's eyes narrowed as she stared into the distance.

"The barrage is covering fire for the real operation."

"Naturally," her husband replied as he looked out over the three barbicans that guarded the zig-zag approach to the outer gate. In the distance, armored platoons of enemy soldiers steadily advanced forward, surrounded by the archers whose formations belched dark clouds of wickedly-barbed arrows. The soldiers dragged long wooden structures across the blackened earth, which looked something like rafts.

"They're going to try to bridge the moat," the queen said. She motioned for General Teva'ivani, also in the command post, to come to her.

"Yes, Your Faithfulness?"

"They're going to try to cross the moat. You know what to do."

The reedy woman nodded, not a hint of humor in her steely eyes.

While many of the siege bridges were picked off by cannon shot, or even plunging fire from the trebuchets mounted high on the inner wall, most of them did manage to reach the moat, despite the arrows that now stuck up like grass from its soggy banks. The makeshift wooden structures gently slid into the water and began to stretch like greedy fingers across its still expanse. Avora'tru'ivi could make out siege ladders stowed on the decks.

The first of the bridges ran into the opposite bank with an audible squelch. Tamino winced. Soldiers began to stream across the bridge, holding their shields above their heads against the rain of arrows and other assorted missiles from above.

"Now!" hissed the queen.

Teva'ivani nodded to the knight beside her, who put a conch shell to his lips and let out three long blasts.

From the machicolations lining the top of the outer wall poured a vile mixture of small fish, entrails, and gristle. The slop slid down the walls and entered the water, whose murkiness began to take on a decidedly red tinge.

A glistening, iron gray fin pierced the surface of the water and began circling near one of the siege rafts.

A Frouzean soldier, his red-plumed hat askew from the chaos of battle, looked down with sudden horror.

Seemingly all at once, the moat erupted into a thrashing morass of foam and teeth as hundreds of bull sharks surfaced, attracted by the chum hurled from the machicolations- and finding more than just fish parts to eat.

Tamino raised an eyebrow and looked at his wife.

"I'm glad you're on our side," he said with a mixture of horror and admiration.

"They started it," she replied, the steel in her voice unmistakable.

As the cries of the attacking soldiers, the hunters who now had become the hunted, carried back to the joint Mongol-Frouzean command post atop a distant siege tower, General Toghon turned to Delilah, a look of abject horror crossing his face.

"You didn't warn us about *this,* woman" he seethed.

Delilah looked on, her face oddly proud.

"I didn't know they had it in them. Well, that certainly was *clever,*" she purred.

"You must call off this attack at once!" the general bellowed. "What a terrible waste! There must be another way!"

"Oh, there is *always* a way," she crooned, stroking the general's beard. "Never worry, I'll take care of their champions of the sea. In the meantime, call a retreat, but keep up the bombardment. By the way, that's the first and only time you will ever call me *woman.* Don't you remember what you're supposed to call me?"

Toghon looked disgustedly at the ground. "Mother."

"That's right. Who was it who married your father and convinced him to pull you out of exile to give you a chance at redemption?"

"You."

Delilah gave him a blank stare.

"Mother."

"That's better."

The Mongol command post relayed its commands by a complex series of flag signals and horns, the terrified soldiers at the banks of the moat stopping and sighing with relief as their commanders ceased relentlessly urging them forward. The enemy armies made their best semblance of an orderly retreat, the Mongols making for a much better approximation than the wild-eyed Frouzeans, who stampeded away from the moat like a herd of panicked cows.

"Well, that held them off for now," Avora'tru'ivi said as the defenders cheered at their retreating foes.

"For now," her husband replied as he stared into the distance.

CHAPTER TWENTY

THE VOW OF WIL'IAH

Balthcutta

That night, a brave moon reflected the distant light of the sun onto the staunch walls of Balthcutta, whose battlements answered with a curtain of blazing torches. Confronting them both was the blanket of lights marking the Frouzean-Mongol camp that spread out as far as the eye could see. His baleful eye locked on the Gate of St. Thomas that stood defiantly bathed in moonlight, Minos of Ashkelon started in surprise as Delilah sidled up to him.

"Do you know what one of the most basic forms of torture is, Minos?"

"I can think of a few."

"Sleep deprivation. Exhausted soldiers won't be able to defend these battlements. It's a good thing our Mongol friends brought fireworks."

"What are you suggesting?"

"I think an incessant show would do wonders for our enemies' sleep patterns!" Delilah said, her visage slashed by a twisted smile.

※ ※ ※

Tamino yawned as he hastily arranged a thin blanket that he had spread on a cot in his chamber immediately beneath the command post at the Gate of St. Thomas. The Spartan accommodation was lit only by an arrow loop that faced directly outside, through which the diffused glow of enemy torches invaded the room. His day had been marked by twenty sleepless hours atop the battlements, and he had wanted to stay longer, but General Teva'ivani had ordered in no uncertain terms that he retire for at least six hours. With a sigh, he settled into the cot.

Suddenly, an explosion rang out. Then another.

Delilah must be launching another frontal assault.

Giving the cot a longing look, Tamino forced himself back up and hastily threw on his scale armor and sword belt, forgoing the more elaborate breastplate. Running back up the spiral staircase to the command post, he was surprised to see a brightly-colored firework fill the sky as another thunderous report reverberated through the night sky.

"What is going on?" he yawned at the knight stationed at the battlements.

"I have no idea," the knight responded.

Tamino shakily grabbed the voice trumpet that lay propped against the wall, then turned to face the enemy army camped just out of range of the defensive artillery batteries.

"Your victory celebration is a bit premature, Delilah!" he yelled fruitlessly, his voice drowned out by another burst above.

The knight shook his head. "Nobody's going to be able to sleep with this going on."

Sudden understanding dawned on Tamino. "I think that's the idea."

The knight's eyes widened. "How…dastardly."

Tamino smiled. "And how shortsighted. We're not the only ones who aren't going to be able to sleep," he said, sweeping his arm to mark out the Frouzean-Mongol tents. "We'll see who lasts longer."

His statement was bolder than he really felt. The last few days had taken a heavy toll. He looked around at the walls, blackened with damage from enemy projectiles, and the bleary eyes of their defenders. Casting a glance over his shoulder, he felt his heart leap simultaneously with a churn of his stomach as he saw his beloved city, standing proud and defiant, behind him, the White Cathedral that crowned the North Point resplendent in the steady moonlight.

Everyone has been so brave, he thought, *But to ask such courage in the face of such monstrosity…*

The White Cathedral, Balthcutta

Realizing that the Frouzee's troops were likely in for the night, and that he was off duty but unable to sleep, Tamino descended the staircase of the gate and made it to the stables, where his horse stood wild-eyed and afraid, flinching at each of the ugly blasts that shook the sky. Tamino did his best to comfort the brave charger, nickering in its ear and brushing its mane, before mounting and riding back into the city. As he cantered through the outer city, with its crops defiantly thrusting their way out of the fertile soil, he felt a note of pride at the ingenuity of the defense designs, mixed with a tinge of sadness, which only grew as he passed into the middle city and beheld the homes of the city's beleaguered residents.

What have I led my people into? Our plan has long odds of success, and failure means complete destruction. This entire city, and all five hundred thousand people within it, face probable extermination because of my actions. I had no right to exact such a price for my own defiance. I have failed them. If I had not been so pigheaded and foolish, and had instead reached an agreement with the Great Khan, or even the Frouzee…

His parade of self-condemnation came to an abrupt end as he inspected the houses surrounding him more closely. From nearly every one hung a Wil'iahn battle flag, its bright rays undimmed by the subdued color palette of the night. In every window burned a candle, a symbolic token of trust in the Flame of Zebulon. And all around, on the walls and on the streets, were painted a myriad of slogans.

RESIST.

NEVER SURRENDER.

NO CONCESSIONS.

NO DEAL.

WE ARE UNCONQUERABLE.

I'VRAE'IA VA'A'KAU'LUA.

They're just as committed to this stand as I am. Tamino's breath caught in his throat as he inspected even more details of the various houses on the street, a narrow byway just like any other in the middle city. The house before him hung two planter boxes from its upstairs windows. They were filled to the bursting with red waratah flowers.

His eyes welling with tears, Tamino continued on his way towards the inner city, passing through the gate set in its mighty wall- built to serve as the very last bastion of Wil'iah in extremity. After making a few more turns through streets carefully designed for defensibility, he came face to face with a stunning vista.

At the end of the peninsula, set slightly above the city's level on the gentle hill that marked the headland, stood the White Cathedral, strong and foursquare. Stretching before it all the way to Tamino's position was the long Cathedral Gardens, modeled after the Elysium in Trukanamoa. A reflecting pool filled with seawater stretched almost its whole length, its perfectly calm surface filled with stars.

Tamino and his horse passed down one of the broad, paved avenues that flanked the pool on either side, finally arriving at the foot of the Cathedral. After tying the horse to a hitching post, Tamino gently pushed open one of the heavy wooden doors and ducked inside.

The pristine, brand-new interior of the church was gently lit by a thousand flickering candles, whose soft brilliance played across the spotless, burnished interior of the dome and sparkled across the crystal star set in its center. Passing through seemingly countless rows of ornately-carved pews, Tamino came to the front of the church and quietly knelt down and began to quietly whisper.

"Lord, through my own decisions, brave or foolish, I have led my people on this path of darkness and dismay. Through no fault and no decision of their own they find themselves facing an unimaginably terrible foe, whose blasts now haunt their dreams. Within these walls are innocent young children, pure in your eyes, who do not deserve such a fate. I am prepared to reap what I have sown, but spare them. Deliver my people from my own shortsightedness."

Suddenly, a voice sounded out behind him, warm and reassuring.

"This I vow, that we shall ever keep the watch, and set alight the beacon-fires of Truth;"

Tamino whirled around to see that a great crowd of people had assembled behind him in the church, their eyes red from sleeplessness but filled with an undying fire. At the fore stood a young mother clutching an infant tightly in her arms.

"If they want noise, we'll give them noise," she said calmly.

She opened her mouth again and continued to sing, her sweet, clear voice reverberating through the cavernous building.

"to become as a citadel on the mountain, a strong place that cannot be taken;"

Gradually, the song swelled as more and more people behind her lent their voices to its strength.

"to keep the flame burning bright on the hillside, and never under a bushel;

That we shall build here in this desert a faithful kingdom, which shall never fall while true hearts draw breath;"

Outside the church, the faint strains of the national anthem of Wil'iah were carried on the breath of the gathering breeze, and, all over the inner city, bleary-eyed citizens' hearts blazed with a new fire at its defiant tones. A great ripple of voices began to spread outward from the church as household after household joined the chorus.

"that when the world forgets thee, we shall remember;

that when we are compassed about by darkness, we shall blaze as a defiant light in the night."

The rising song was now punctuated by the sweet but powerful chimes of the great bells in the White Cathedral's towers, which were almost instantly answered by a thousand others as the hundreds of lesser churches of the city added their own determined voices.

"That we shall defeat every false way in our hearts, that we might be nearer to thee;

that we shall stand guard over the innocent;

that our nation shall be built on virtue, valor, courage, and chastity.

That ever shall we keep our eyes fixed upon the Star;"

The song now spread through the middle city, ten thousand sleepless homes joining the chorus, heedless of the blasts of fume that fruitlessly detonated over their heads. Many of the inhabitants ran out onto the streets and jubilantly began to blast instruments, the sounds of sackbuts, psalteries, dulcimers, tambourines, and didgeridoos girding the song even further.

That we shall preserve the glory, the memory, of the power from above;

that we shall be just and merciful to all men;
and create a kingdom where all might be free from the whip and chain;

Finally, the bold tones washed over the steadfast outer walls, the ears of its defenders instantly perking at the beloved melody. Needing no further bidding, the assembled soldiers joined in, turning from their posts at the walls to hug each other and shake their spears in laughing defiance at the fireworks above.

"that we shall harm no man except in defense of all that is good and true;

ever shall we lean on the wings of the Almighty in times of trouble and triumph."

"What is this?" asked Minos as the cacophony of voices, instruments, and bells assaulted the tents of the besieging army, drowning out the explosions of the fireworks.

Delilah rolled her eyes.

"I hate this song."

Ever shall we be faithful, ever shall we act valiantly!
This we vow, we, the Faithful Kingdom!"'

"Well, hopefully they got that out of their system," Delilah scoffed as she motioned for a redoubling of her colorful auditory bombardment.

But she was wrong. The deafening recital continued with song after song. Battle songs, patriotic anthems, and ancient hymns all roared their defiance, forming an insistent, persistent shield against the devices of the enemy. In increasing frustration, Delilah ordered more and more fireworks to be launched, goading her minions onward with constant flicks of her scepter and screaming obscenities.

Finally, General Toghon appeared at her side, red-faced and flustered.

"You know, my men can't sleep either with all of this racket," he blustered. "This is a stupid plan, and you know it. I'm amazed we haven't run out of fireworks yet. Those things actually serve a purpose, you know. They are vital for sending command signals." Almost as if in answer, the fireworks stopped.

A breathless soldier arrived at Delilah's side and threw himself prostrate on the ground.

"Your Worship, that was the last one!"

"What did I tell you?" the general sneered. "You know, you told us that the Wil'iahns were a subhuman, weak people who would surrender to us within hours if faced with a serious challenge. Not only have they not surrendered, but the food caravans you promised us have not arrived. As I suspected, the Wil'iahns have probably cut the supply lines. I think you need to re-examine your intelligence choices." With that, he stalked back to his tent in a rage.

And still, the steadfast tones reverberated out from the city.

In frustration, Delilah motioned for Briseis.

"Yes, Your Worship?" the servant asked.

"Briseis, Darling, in my chests you will find an aquamarine bottle with a red stopper. It should be quite large. This campfire song session that the Wil'iahns are putting on is leaving them very distracted. I want you to take the vial to the moat and dump its contents in the water."

"But…your Worship, that seems very dangerous!"

"Is it as dangerous as defying the will of your savior and Goddess?"

"Well, no…"

"Good girl. Now, run along!"

Seemingly out of nowhere, Salome appeared at Delilah's elbow.

"Can I go?"

Can I feed her to the sharks? Briseis thought.

CHAPTER TWENTY-ONE

THE MUSTER AT ULURU

Uluru, Sovereign Judgate of Anangu, south-central Wil'iah

The enormous Rock of Uluru stood resolutely against the night, its base lit by the defiant glow of thousands of torches, as the assembled Wil'iahn army spread out like a blanket before it. Jeremiah, his face illuminated with a patriotic fire, addressed the mustered forces, pumping his sword into the air for emphasis.

"Citizens! We are gathered here today, at the foot of the most sacred rock in the nation, to defend its glory from the monstrous evil which now threatens to engulf us all. I don't need to reiterate the severity of this situation. For the first time in recent memory, the moment we have all feared has come to pass. The enemy marches in open array on Wil'iahn soil! But, in so doing, he has made a grave mistake. For, as the saying goes, there are three things that are always true! The sun will come up tomorrow, the waves will keep coming in, and Wil'iah will always resist. Our soil is already red. By the end of the day tomorrow, nobody will be able to tell that the enemy ever dared to tread on our blessed ground!"

At this last assertion, a great cheer rose from the assembled armies.

"Our books tells us of many instances like this, when the Faithful stood, outnumbered, against a terrible foe bent on extinction. But in all of those times, the Almighty rose in his terrible array to smite the enemy with his thunderous glory! Remember the folly of Sisera! Remember the annihilation of the hosts of Pharaoh! Remember the mutual destruction of the enemies that sought to destroy Hezekiah! Remember the strike of blindness that crippled the Syrians at Dothan! This new terror will just be another name to add to the lists of fools who dared to oppose us!"

"Get them!" yelled someone in the crowd.

"Tomorrow, we will show them just what it means to attack Wil'iah! They will pay the dearest price for every square inch of ground!"

Eleazar now raised his voice. "Our strategy is simple. The prince and I will lead a primary cavalry charge, covered by archers, that will smash into the enemy's main center and drive it back. This will distract him from the east and west wings of the army, which will circle around and cut off his means of escape. Should the enemy attempt a retreat, the Armies of Anangu and Kati-Thanda, with their guerilla warfare specialties, will be held in reserve to strike them as they attempt to flee. Now, we must take the muster roll of the major army units." Eleazar held out a hand to his steward, who handed him a carefully-written scroll.

"Army of Tjoritja Prime Division!"

"Aye!"

"Army of Tjoritja Arrernte Reserves!"

"Aye!"

"Army of Tjoritja Anmatyerre Reserves!"

"Aye!"

"Army of Anangu Prime Division!"

Aye!

As Eleazar read out each division's name in turn, a hearty cheer rose from the unit in question. As the roll completed, Eleazar stepped back to yield the stage once again to Jeremiah.

"Our scouts indicate the enemy is expected at dawn. Now, let us pray. Dear Father, deliver our enemies into our hands tomorrow. We have ever stood as your faithful kingdom, prepared always to defend thee from the hordes of the enemy. Deliver us with the breaking of the Dawn. Let your majesty, your earth-shaking thunder, smite the depraved armies of the Frouzee and dash them upon the rocks!"

His theologically-dubious prayer complete, Jeremiah turned to the assembled armies and thrust a fist in the air.

"'Ivrae'ia Va'a'kau'lua!"

CHAPTER TWENTY-TWO

RUN OUT THE GUNS

Balthcutta

On the other side of the country, Tamino rubbed sleep from his eyes, grateful for the small amount he had been able to get after the cessation of the Frouzee's firework bombardment. After buckling his armor on, he stumbled out of the ready chamber onto the gatehouse. He could instantly tell from the defenders' ashen faces that something was wrong.

"How? How did she do this?" a soldier asked, her voice trembling.

Tamino followed her horrified gaze down to the moat. He recoiled as he realized it was blood red. Floating in the sickening waters, belly-up, were hundreds of sharks, motionless and rigid. Flies buzzed about in great clouds as a stench rose from the moat and assaulted Tamino's nostrils.

"I don't know how she did this," he said, "but we have to be ready for whatever comes next. Run out the guns."

CHAPTER TWENTY-THREE

DISASTER AT ULURU

Uluru

*A*s dawn's first tentative rays broke over the horizon, the lone wail of a didgeridoo from atop the rock of Uluru shattered the early morning stillness. Jeremiah's eyes flicked open, and he instantly hauled himself off the ground, already girded in full armor. He hastily strapped on his sword belt and threw open the flaps to his pop-up tent. Eleazar already stood outside, his armor gleaming in what morning light already existed.

"It's time," he said matter-of-factly as the surrounding camp erupted into activity. Jeremiah untied his horse from the post he had buried in the ground the night before and mounted, pausing to grab a spear-tipped battle standard hefted aloft by his squire. As the morning breeze caught the banner and splayed its brave rays across the sky, Jeremiah took a deep breath and closed his eyes.

God save Wil'iah.

Eleazar gave a curt nod to a group of drummers that stood at the ready beside his makeshift command station. They instantly began a slow, steady beat. With painful slowness, the various units of the army began to coalesce into tightly-formed units, while the Armies of Anangu and Kati-Thanda melted into the surrounding desert to take up their distant vigils. Jeremiah fixed his hawk-like eyes on the top of the sacred rock, and saw five flashes.

"The enemy is five miles away. We'd best get going."

Eleazar pulled a ram's horn off his belt and blew three long blasts. A formation of mounted knights, the very best that the kingdom had, formed up behind him, backed by a larger, but less trained, group of mounted men- and women-at-arms ten thousand strong. The soldiers, Jeremiah's battle-standard at the fore and the additional columns that intended to encircle the Frouzeans on either side, began a steady canter out of the camp, flanked on their right by the Rock of Uluru and on their left by the dramatic domes of the Kata Tjuta. Behind the horses marched the pikemen in tight phalanxes, each box-like group protecting a cadre of archers within.

At length, an Anangu scout appeared before the massed Wil'iahn forces and signaled that the enemy army was ahead. The Wil'iahn army began to fan out into their assigned positions. Soon, a dark line on the horizon indicated the approaching enemy. In response, Jeremiah withdrew the ram's horn from his bandolier and let out seven long blasts. His ten thousand riders began to move ever more quickly, graduating from first a trot, then to a canter, and then, finally to a full gallop. The very air reverberated with the thunderous sound of forty thousand hooves as great clouds of long-range arrows filled the sky, loosed by the formations of archers that followed the horses. As they grew nearer and nearer to the enemy, Jeremiah could espy a forest of pikes sprouting out from a series of Frouzean phalanxes. On either side of them were two groups of Mongol Cavalry, who now charged forward, letting loose their own flights of arrows, which furrowed down into the Wil'iahn formations.

However, the tide of the Wil'iahn charge was unstoppable. As the knights thundered upon the Frouzean center, they lowered their great lances, festooned with flags and coats of arms, and issued terrifying war cries. Just as they passed between the two Mongol cavalry formations, the Mongols sprang forward to meet them, only to turn around in shocked horror as the left and right wings of the Wil'iahn cavalry erupted out of the desert to strike them from behind.

Unhindered by the Mongols, Jeremiah's knights smashed into the Frouzean infantry and rolled over them like a tsunami, their lances instantly shattering the carefully-practiced formations and driving the terrified Frouzeans under their hooves. Jeremiah gutturally bellowed war cries as he discarded his shattered lance and drew an enormous broadsword, hacking back and forth with all his might as spittle flew from his growling mouth. On and on the Wil'iahn charge drove in triumph, trampling the Frouzeans underfoot, the great battle-standard of the Army of Tjoritja advancing inexorably forward. On either side, the story was the same- the heavy Wil'iahn cavalry smashed into the lightly-armed Mongols with terrifying, bone-crunching force, and everywhere, the enemy was driven back.

Jeremiah's horse was the first to break through the Frouzean formation, the white charger gloriously thundering over the flat desert plains, its nostrils flaring and its flanks heaving with effort. Eleazar was not far behind, his giant broadsword stained red.

Jeremiah pumped his sword into the air and victoriously shouted.

"Take tha---"

But his cry of success was instantly cut short. Out of the desert before him rose, seemingly out of nowhere, a unit of Mongol horsemen.

Then another.

And another.

Soon, the entire horizon was filled with a massed forest of enemies larger than Jeremiah could have imagined in his worst nightmares. His blood running cold, Jeremiah turned to Eleazar.

"This was a giant trap," the veteran knight said, shocked disbelief clouding his piercing eyes.

Suddenly, a wall of sound slammed into the two men as the Mongol army let out a terrifying, guttural war cry, in unison.

"There's only one thing to do. We must retreat," Eleazar grunted.

Jeremiah could only nod as he fought to keep down his panic.

But retreat wasn't an option. While the Wil'iahns had triumphantly charged through the Frouzean Army, or what they thought was the Frouzean Army, a similar forest of enemies had emerged from the desert behind them. There was no escape route.

Jeremiah worked his mouth in cold fear, trying to force himself to think as the charging Mongols grew ever closer.

But, as suddenly as hope had been crushed by the appearance of the vastly larger-than-expected enemy forces, it flared into life again as the drone of didgeridoos filled the air. The Armies of Anangu and Kati-Thanda, the highly mobile strike forces held in reserve to cut off the enemy escape, now emerged from their own camouflaged hiding places to strike the flanks of the new enemy armies. An escape route seemed possible, but the odds of survival were long, especially with the cavalry charge bearing down on them from behind.

A sudden look of determination filled Eleazar's severe features.

"Wil'iah needs its prince. You must escape. We will hold them off and give you that chance."

"But---"

"Don't argue with me."

With that, Eleazar raised his sword and signaled for a group of cavalry to form up behind him. The highly-trained knights obeyed his order without a moment's hesitation, creating an arrow-shaped formation with Eleazar at its head. Pointing his sword in defiance of the advancing enemy, Eleazar let out one last roaring battle-cry, which would forever be seared in Jeremiah's memory.

"'Ivrae'ia Va'a'kau'lua!"

With that, his formation surged forward, a final glorious, defiant charge against the unstoppable tide of the enemy. Jeremiah watched for a moment as their shining armor and bright battle flags receded into the distance against the long dark line of the enemy, his heart yearning to join them. But, then, he wrenched his eyes away, and, signaling to the remaining knights, charged toward the tiny opening in the enemy lines that the Army of Anangu had managed to open ahead.

Through the breach he hacked and jabbed, verbally dedicating each swing of his sword to one of the noble knights that had charged into oblivion behind him. Finally, he, and far too few knights, managed to get through to the relative safety of the Anangu lines.

But any sort of victory was out of the question at this point. The Army of Anangu counted less than sixteen thousand, as did the Army of Kati-Thanda. The vast enemy forces must have numbered in the hundreds of thousands. His stomach dropping, Jeremiah surveyed the scene and realized that the majority of the Wil'iahn infantry and archers had been crushed by the new Mongol and Frouzean forces that had materialized after the initial cavalry charge. The units that remained were broken masses of huddled, terrified soldiers surrounded by enemies.

Jeremiah turned to the Anangu commander, who waited on baited breath for orders.

"We must do what we can to rescue the remaining infantry. Then, you and the Army of Kati-Thanda must melt into the desert. Our only choice is to make for Trukanamoa and make a stand there. This is hopeless!"

The Anangu commander grimly nodded, and his forces sprang into action, charging back into the fray and opening gaps in the enemy lines for the precious few pockets of infantry soldiers to escape. But, as soon as they did so, they were run down by the enemy cavalry and pounded into the dust. Precious few managed to escape into the desert. Finally, his stomach turning in sorrow, Jeremiah realized that the only way to save any of the Wil'iahn army was to make a run for it. He withdrew his ram's horn and tearfully flew three long blasts. His cavalry heeded the order and reluctantly disengaged from the enemy and fled across the desert in open retreat, relentlessly pursued by the enemy.

Between the Kata Tjuta and Uluru they galloped, vicious arrows picking them off one by one. But, gradually, the enemy forces receded into the distance as the faster Wil'iahn horses increased the range. Finally, after what seemed like an eternity, they were safe, for the moment. Jeremiah stopped his horse and took stock of the ragged forces that remained.

There were less than six thousand, out of an original force of over fifty thousand.

The battle had been a disaster unparalleled in Wil'iahn history.

That night, the hated flag of the Frouzean Empire and the equally terrifying banner of the Yuan Dynasty flapped unchallenged over the sacred rock of Uluru.

CHAPTER TWENTY-FOUR

THE CHAMPION OF GATH

Thubbo, Vrenga'nui, eastern Wil'iah

*T*he triumphant blare of trumpets shattered the smoky air as four white horses thundered over the charred ground, dragging an archaic quadriga. The very picture of imperial pomp, Ajax the Lesser of Gath towered over the driver of the chariot, his red-feathered helmet matching the plumes on the horses heads that livelily bobbed before him and the cape that billowed from his burnished armor. His close-cropped beard framed an iron mouth and beady, cruel eyes that narrowed at the sight that greeted them in the distance – the Wil'iahn city of Thubbo, or at least what was left of it.

Ajax the Lesser of Gath

A lowering plume of black smoke loomed over the vast Frouzean Imperial Army that advanced toward the city, dwarfing its proud banners. Thubbo was the first large city the mighty force had encountered since Wagga Wagga, and Ajax was looking forward to gloating as the city surrendered. He tried not to think too hard about the last time he had approached a Wil'iahn city with such expectation. Wagga Wagga had not submitted weakly to imperial rule. Instead, the capital of Wil'iah's Wiradjuri Nation had stubbornly dug in, threatening to take all of the momentum out of Ajax's invasion. He had been forced to leave behind a large force to maintain the siege while the main army proceeded north, but the very thought of the defiant city, with its enormous battle-flags, made his blood boil. Here was a chance at redemption – for victory came with a prize.

Ajax's nostrils flared as his thoughts strayed to what awaited him if he succeeded. A voice, smooth as silk but intoxicating as wine, echoed through his predatory mind.

"You'll get your turn…every time you burn a Wil'iahn village and put its citizens to the sword, think of the rewards that await you. Think of me."

"Delilah…" the name escaped his lips as a reverent whisper.

Unfortunately, however, there had been no opportunities yet to satisfy his fanatical bloodlust. Every village he had come upon had beaten him to the punch. Time after time, all that remained were charred ruins – and nothing of value. The citizens were nowhere to be found. Surely Thubbo would be different – surely the Wil'iahns could not afford to destroy one of their own cities.

The angry black cloud above said otherwise. Ajax suppressed a snort of annoyance as a horse and rider pulled up beside his chariot, and he recognized his Mongol attaché, the Persian general Nasir-al-Din.

"It looks like more of the same," Din said. "We've encountered these tactics before. Our men can survive for a month or more just on horse blood and mares' milk if need be," he added with a hint of pride, "but eventually we will need to find grazing lands."

Ajax spat over the side of the chariot, drawing a barely-concealed glare from the Mongol general. "Detestable stuff. We are conquerors. We deserve to eat like conquerors."

"And where are the promised supply caravans from Gath bearing your delicacies?" Din asked doubtfully.

"They will be here," Ajax growled.

The procession of standard bearers and generals arrived at the main gates of the city. A group of heralds stepped out in front of Ajax's chariot and let out five long blasts on their trumpets, before issuing a demand for the city to surrender.

They were greeted with silence. A group of soldiers cautiously advanced with a battering ram, wincing as they expected missiles to issue from the walls, but none came. At a single thunderous blow from the battering ram, the gates, evidently unlocked, listlessly swung open. The view they revealed was one of ruin and calamity. Not a single building remained that hadn't been put to the torch. Charred timbers and glowing embers added to the hellish impression of utter destruction.

"I have to admit, I'm impressed. It's rare for a people to completely destroy their own cities rather than surrender," Din said.

"Yes, but where did they all go?" Ajax snarled. "This city had a population of thousands. Our scout parties have scoured the countryside, but there's no sign of them – only more burned farmland."

"We'll just have to keep looking. I have a bad feeling about those mountains," Din replied, motioning to the forbidding-looking ridges in the east. "They will be significantly more difficult to conquer than these flat plains."

"Let them run, let them hide, we'll find them eventually," Ajax rumbled. "And then we'll have our fun." The Prince of Gath's eye caught something unusual- the main castle that defended the city, adjacent to the gate, seemed less damaged.

"This will make a decent command center while we're in this area." He motioned to two of his standard-bearers, who immediately snapped to attention. "Gather a raiding party and secure the castle. I want the flag of Her Worship flying from the keep."

"Yes sir!" the standard-bearers gladly responded.

A few short minutes later, the red, white, and black banner of the Empire proudly unfurled over the tallest tower of the castle.

"Where is your vaunted courage now, Wil'iah!?" Ajax taunted into the air. "It evaporated at the first sight of our fla"---

His last word was drowned out by an ear-splitting explosion as a series of hidden, booby-trapped charges within the castle detonated. The assembled Imperial Army instantly scattered into a chaotic rabble, diving for cover as debris flew in all directions and dust filled the air.

When the smoke cleared, the castle was reduced to a pile of ruinous rubble. The Frouzean flag lay crushed beneath a stack of stones, alight with fire.

CHAPTER TWENTY-FIVE

THE ESSENCE OF CLYTEMNESTRA

Imperial Army Camp, Nowra, outside Balthcutta

Diomedes stormed through the Imperial Army camp, fuming as yet another assault on Balthcutta's walls proved fruitless. Noticing his presence, an aide-de-camp scurried over to meet him, holding a large scroll.

"What!?" Diomedes bellowed.

"Today's casualty reports!" squeaked the aide.

Diomedes held out a hand to accept the proffered scroll, then grimly unrolled it. It had been another bad day. Another disturbing question pressed on his mind.

"Have the resupply shipments from the south arrived yet?" he asked the aide.

A dark look crossed his face. "No," came the response.

"They were supposed to arrive with food and ammunition two days ago. Where are they?"

"There's no sign of them. We've sent back scouts to look for them, twice, but none of them have come back."

Diomedes thought back to the threatening flames fuming from the mountain-tops when they had first crossed into Wil'iah.

"Clearly, the mountains are well-fortified. They must have cut our supply lines. We can't send the whole army back to clear them out, if we are to maintain the siege."

"There's still the possibility of resupply by sea, if the fleet gets through," the aide offered.

"Let's hope they do," Diomedes said grimly, then stalked off to his pavilion. Roughly tearing the tent flaps open, he found himself face-to-face with Salome, splayed across the recliner.

"What are you doing here?" he grunted.

"Darling, don't you think this siege has gone on long enough?" Salome purred. "The Wil'iahns are not capitulating immediately like Delilah said they would. It's becoming clear to the troops that she isn't infallible after all. They are losing their enthusiasm. Now is our chance."

With a hungry fire igniting in his eyes, Diomedes walked toward the recliner. "What did you have in mind?"

"This dart has been dipped in the Essence of Clytemnestra," she said, offering a weapon to him on a silk pillow. "I will arrange to walk with Her Worship past the pavilion of Minos at sundown tonight. You or one of your men will throw this dart from behind it. She will die instantly and bleed profusely, fully proving that she is not a goddess. Then, you will emerge and call for the troops to pray for the *true* incarnation of Astarte to appear, and replace the fraud that we've been dealing with. If anyone gives us trouble, it will appear that Minos was responsible, and he will take the blame."

"And then?"

"And *then,*" Salome crooned as she wrapped Diomedes in an embrace, "We will rule Frouzea together – from Ekron. Your brother will be avenged, and we can raise your son to be the emperor he was born to be."

With that, Diomedes yanked her in for a passionate kiss.

※ ※ ※

Outside the pavilion, Briseis held her ear to the tent-clothes, a shocked expression on her face. As much as she detested Salome, she couldn't believe what she had just heard. Her first thought was to warn Delilah, but a thought nagged at her.

She might not believe me. She might think I'm just trying to sabotage Salome- she knows we don't get along.

She realized the only way to take down Salome was to *prove* that she had malevolent intentions. She had to catch her in the act. There was only one person she trusted to help lay her trap.

A few short minutes later, Briseis arrived at a rather simple tent pitched near to Delilah's outrageous pavilion. Briseis cleared her throat loudly, and a bass voice responded, "Enter."

Heracles was doing his daily exercise routine when Briseis walked in. Somewhat embarrassed, she turned to leave, but Heracles put up a hand, ordering her to stay.

"What is it?" he asked.

"S—Salome is plotting with Diomedes to murder Her Worship," Briseis gasped.

"WHAT!?" came the bellowed reply. Veins bulged on Heracles' tree-like neck.

"She is planning to replace Delilah as the true goddess."

"That's impossible. There's only one true manifestation of Astarte, and that's Delilah," Heracles said, crossing his huge arms over his barrel-like chest. His voice was suffused with devout loyalty.

Realizing that he truly believed Delilah was a goddess, Briseis recognized she needed to tread carefully. "Salome plans for Diomedes to throw a poisoned dart at Delilah."

"That won't do anything. She's immortal. She's invulnerable," Heracles said. "Salome knows that too. She would never even attempt such a stupid plan. Are you trying to smear her name?"

"No, of course not," Briseis backpedaled. "I heard the whole thing myself."

"Do you have any proof, except hearsay?"

"I will, at sundown tonight. Diomedes or one of his cronies will be hiding behind Minos' pavilion. We must go there and hide ourselves. At the moment of this treachery, we'll be there to stop them. Then, you'll have the proof you need."

Heracles gave her a doubtful frown, but reluctantly nodded. "Alright, I'll go with you."

Briseis allowed herself a weak smile.

Got you, Salome.

As Briseis exited the tent, she failed to notice Salome hiding in the shadows, listening to her every word.

CHAPTER TWENTY-SIX

THE TIP OF THE SPEAR

Gunu-Bula, Vrenga'nui, eastern Wil'iah

*L*ady Deborah parted the flaps of her tent and strode outside. The hastily-pitched camp in the shadow of the formidable mountain fortress of Gunu-Bula was ready to be broken down at a moment's notice, but it served as an important forward base for the Army of Vrenga'nui, whose banner flapped bravely overhead alongside the flag of Wil'iah. While other units of the army carried out the Samson Plan, this group would keep watch on the advancing Imperial Army and frustrate its progress with

115

continual hit-and-run attacks. Most of the troops gathered around a campfire in the center of the camp, eating carefully-conserved, small ration portions. Normally, such army units could hope to live off the land.

Not this one, Deborah thought as she grimly surveyed the blackened fields all around them. The plan had been set in motion. Now she had to carry it through.

As she approached the campfire, the soldiers snapped to attention. Deborah scanned their determined, but weary and frightened, faces, streaked with dirt, sweat, and grime.

"At ease," she said. "As you all know, we are the tip of the spear of Wil'iah's resistance to this invasion. Our task is to track the enemy at all times and frustrate his plans however possible while the rest of the Samson Plan is carried out. We cannot carry out this effort effectively if we do not have an inside perspective into the enemy's plans."

A murmur rose from the assembled troops.

"What I'm saying is that we need someone to volunteer to infiltrate the Frouzean Army and report back to us periodically about their movements and plans. Unfortunately, there's an issue: none of us look like Frouzeans, or Mongols for that matter. I don't see how any of us can pass for one of them."

"Not all of us," Deborah heard one soldier mutter.

"Excuse me?" the general replied.

Deborah watched quizzically as the crowd of soldiers gradually parted, until standing alone before her was a single woman – whose light features and blue eyes were definitely not of Wil'iahn origin. The woman nervously smiled at Deborah.

"I don't believe we've met," Deborah entreated.

"My name is Medea. I live in Koorawatha."

"I take it you weren't born there," Deborah responded, noting the woman's Frouzean accent.

"No." A dark look clouded Medea's eyes, but she seemed to shake herself free from whatever had disturbed her and forced her shoulders back. "I wasn't. I am fluent in Frouzean and know the ways of their people. I think I can do this."

"This is a dangerous operation. I cannot force you to go."

"This country saved my life once. Now it's time I returned the favor."

Deborah nodded grimly. "Very well. Follow me."

The two women returned to Deborah's command tent.

"Your mission is to infiltrate the Imperial Army and attempt to get close to Ajax the Lesser, their general. If you can overhear his plans, we can be better prepared to counter them. I hate to say it, but the only way that you would plausibly be there is as some sort of servant or slave."

Medea winced. "I think I could play that role convincingly. Let's just say it wouldn't be acting."

Deborah nodded grimly. "You also have a secondary mission. This invasion force consists of soldiers from two *very* different countries with different aims. It's clear that this is an alliance of convenience and has no lasting basis. No doubt, there will be tensions between the Mongol commanders and their Frouzean counterparts. If there's anything you can do to exacerbate these tensions, do it."

"Knowing Frouzeans like I do, that shouldn't be hard."

Deborah smiled, then proffered a mirror and a scroll to Medea.

"Use this mirror to send us flashing messages when it is safe to do so. In the scroll you will find a code that you can use. Once you have memorized it, and I suggest you do that before you reach the Frouzean camp, destroy it."

"Yes Ma'am."

Deborah now reached forward and pulled Medea in for a grandmotherly hug.

"You are very brave to do this, Medea. Wil'iah will honor your courage."

"I am able to do this today because others once had the courage to rescue me," Medea responded. She gave Deborah a salute, then turned to exit the tent. However, just before she spread open the flaps to leave, she looked back over her shoulder at the general.

"'Ivrae'ia Va'a'kau'lua," she said, then disappeared through the flaps.

"And the same to you," Deborah said, then briefly cast her eyes skyward.

"God protect her."

CHAPTER TWENTY-SEVEN

THE KISS OF SALOME

Imperial Army Camp, Nowra, outside Balthcutta

As the sun entered its terminal descent to the horizon, bathing the sky in pink rays and turning the clouds into glowing lamps, Salome sauntered into Delilah's pavilion. Overhearing Briseis' plot had shook her to the core. Realizing her plan with Diomedes was doomed to failure, she had been forced to adapt, but adapt she had.

"Your Worship?" Salome asked fawningly.

"Yes, darling?"

"The men of Ashkelon have prepared a present for you in front of his pavilion, to show their gratitude for your leadership. Would you like to see it?"

"I am always happy to accept gifts from my adoring men," Delilah smiled.

As Salome led her toward the pavilion, her heart beat a staccato drumroll against her ribcage. Her new plan was exceedingly dangerous, but, if all went well, would rescue her from her own tangled web.

※ ※ ※

Briseis and Heracles huddled inside the tent next to the pavilion, peering out of a slit they had cut in the fabric. At the moment, there was no sign of any activity in the shadow of the pavilion. Heracles gave Briseis a doubtful look.

"Are you sure about this?"

"I know what I heard."

Suddenly, Briseis started and pointed down the road.

"Look! There comes Salome with Her Worship."

Heracles' nostrils flared like a bull at the sight of his beloved empress possibly being led to her death. His hand involuntarily went to the large broadsword strapped across his back. He drew the weapon with an audible hiss of steel. Briseis shot him a death glare.

"Don't give us away! We need to catch them in the act!"

Suddenly, Briseis' eyes caught movement in her peripheral vision. Surely enough, a sinister figure crouched in the shadow of the tent.

"Look!" she hissed. Salome and Delilah drew closer and closer.

Heracles crept towards the entrance of the tent they were hiding, doing his best to mask the noise of his elephantine footsteps, to little avail.

He was too late.

In a single fluid motion, the shadowy figure hurled an object directly at Delilah.

You conniving witch. Your scheme is about to succeed, thought Briseis as she focused on Salome. However, what happened next didn't make any sense at all.

Salome shrieked, "Look out!" and tackled Delilah, pinning her to the ground. The dart sailed harmlessly over her and embedded itself in a nearby tentpole.

"What is the meaning of this?" the "eternal empress" sputtered, enraged.

Salome pointed into the shadow of the pavilion and yelled, "Seize him! Someone has tried to kill our empress!"

Heracles was only too happy to oblige. The would-be-assassin tried to get away, but Heracles barreled out of the tent and tackled him, dragging him out into the open for all to see.

It was Diomedes.

Salome pointed an accusing finger at the Prince of Ekron. "He has been conspiring against you for days! He plotted to kill you and take over the empire!

Diomedes' face was a tableau of shock. Finally, he managed to force out words of defense.

"Yes, I did conspire to commit this act, but I conspired with you!" The gathering troops, drawn to the theatrical scene of the attempted crime, gasped.

Briseis, still unsure of what was happening but seeing an opportunity, stepped forward out of the tent.

"Diomedes isn't lying. I heard him and Salome talking. This entire plan was her idea!"

Delilah's eyes narrowed as she picked herself up off of the ground. "Is this true, Salome?"

Salome gave a triumphant smile. "Yes, this was my plan, but my plan was to flush out a traitor in our midst- to expose Diomedes, whose secret hatred for you threatened to destroy your plans. Now, he can be dealt with appropriately."

Briseis recoiled in horror. Was this really Salome's plan all along?

"After all," Salome continued, "if I had been planning to go along with this plan, would I have warned you? Would I have saved your life?"

"But--" Briseis' protest was cut off by an imperious hand from Delilah.

"My life does not need 'saving,' as I am immortal. Nevertheless, today, you have demonstrated your loyalty, Salome. It will be rewarded."

What!? Briseis boiled with anger, which only doubled when Salome made eye contact and flashed her a perfectly evil smile.

"As for *you*," Delilah said, stalking towards the restrained Diomedes, still held in Heracles' iron grip, "I am very disappointed. I thought you would have more sense than your brother. There is only one thing to be done. Salome, dear," she said, turning to the handmaiden, "Return to my pavilion. Tell my slaves to bring Goliath. It's his dinner time. I'm sure he's hungry. Since Ekron clearly cannot be trusted, Achish of Ashkelon will assume command of Ekron's forces."

A look of horror crossed Diomedes' face as he began to struggle against Heracles' grip. Delilah rubbed her hands together with glee.

"Who would have thought I would get to feed *two* princes of Ekron to my pets?"

As Salome flounced off to collect the crocodile, she turned back and blew Diomedes a kiss.

CHAPTER TWENTY-EIGHT

THE STANDARD OF PRINCESS JESSICA

Balthcutta

The next day, Tamino winced as yet another Mongol missile slammed into the wall to his right. An answering blast from a cannon on the inner wall behind warmed his heart to a degree, but it nearly stopped as the ball's trajectory fell short and it slammed into the back of his own battlements on the outer wall.

Captain Abigail shrieked in frustration.

"The barrel must be worn out!" Windmilling her arms at the batteries above, she screamed, "Decommission Gun number 498!"

She turned to the king, her face reddened with frustration. "My apologies, your Faithfulness, we haven't quite gotten the hang of making these things ye—" her explanation was cut off by an explosion and accompanied shouts of alarm as another cannon atop the middle wall exploded from a misfire.

Tamino placed a staying hand on the flustered captain's shoulder. "You're doing your best and giving better than you're getting. Take heart."

Suddenly, the king realized that the barrage of stones and naphtha bombs from the army below had abruptly halted. Narrowing his eyebrows, Tamino glared out between the merlons that flanked him to his left and right.

Across the blackened plain thundered two white horses bearing the Frouzean general, Prince Minos of Ashkelon, and Heracles, Delilah's manservant, both of them carrying white flags of truce. Behind them lurched the luridly-painted sedan chair of the "eternal empress" herself, borne on the backs of eight sweating slaves whose bare feet squished through the dirt as they ran.

Another footman emerged from behind the sedan chair as it came to a halt before the gate of St. Thomas. He threw himself prostrate with an audible squelch. The curtains parted, and Delilah, sporting as always her snake headdresses, alighted, standing on the back of the slave.

"Well, well, well," she said as she looked up at the king, twenty-five feet above her. "This has been a most impressive display of determination and fortitude. Your ancestors would be proud. You've done your duty. Don't you think it's time we ended all this bloodshed?"

"You can choose to end it at any time by going back to Frouzea!" yelled Tamino.

Delilah smiled. "That's hardly necessary at this juncture. I think I can end it by withdrawing my forces out of range of your Chinese toys and waiting for you to starve. Many of your people are rather…big," she said, holding her arms out as if to imitate obesity, "so that might take a while. Nevertheless, I am prepared to wait."

"You'll be waiting a long time. We can always be resupplied by sea."

Delilah cocked her head quizzically.

"Can you?"

As the words left her mouth, two of her servants stepped out from behind the sedan chair and unfurled a huge pennant behind her.

Tamino's stomach dropped to the floor.

The personal standard of Princess Jessica.

"I've heard she fought bravely off of Cape Nadgee," Delilah purred. "But bravery doesn't count for much in the face of overwhelming force, does it?" She turned back to the sedan chair, but paused before entering, throwing her head back over her shoulder toward Tamino.

"Oh, and your precious Admiral Zhang? That coward got the death he deserved fourteen years ago. You have two hours to make a decision. Surrender now or face the consequences. I have been exemplary in my patience. Goddesses aren't known for it."

Tamino fought back tears as he imagined the fate of his sister and the heroic old admiral, but he forced his voice into a low register and drew the Zrain'de'zhang, shaking the fabled sword over his head as the battle-standard of the Faithful Kingdom snapped behind it.

"I don't need two hours. This city will never surrender!"

"More's the pity," Delilah said before parting the curtains and disappearing into the gossamer embrace of the sedan chair, which instantly whisked her away.

Suddenly, Zhao Bing appeared on the ramparts.

"What are you doing here?" Tamino hissed in frustration.

"I just came from the Citadel," Zhao said breathlessly. "The enemy fleet has arrived and has assumed a blockading position."

Tamino pursed his lips, trying to figure out what to do next.

"Does this mean that Admiral Zhang is dead?" Zhao asked, his voice cracking with a surprising amount of fear. Tamino focused on the young emperor, who he realized was, beneath the impetuous and hotheaded exterior, surprisingly vulnerable.

"Nothing is for certain. Admiral Zhang is a cunning old fox. He has gotten out of worse scrapes than this before. There is no reason for us to give up hope just yet. Now, get back to the citadel. Now."

As Zhao scurried back down the staircase, Tamino wished he felt as brave as he tried to sound.

CHAPTER TWENTY-NINE

SOURCE APHEK

Balthcutta

That night, a Mongol rider burst into Delilah's command pavilion, red-faced with exertion. In his hand he clutched a green bottle.

Delilah suavely looked up at him.

"Yes?"

"I bring news from the fleet! One of our blockade ships was on station when a light flashed from the highest tower of the Citadel- the signal you told us to watch for. When we sent in the dinghy as you ordered, this was flung from the ramparts."

"Very good," Delilah crooned. She grabbed the bottle from the rider's outstretched hand and uncorked it. A rolled-up piece of paper tumbled out; she unrolled it to reveal a map of Balthcutta's defenses.

"Ah yes, Source Aphek comes through, just as I knew it would!"

"Source Aphek?" General Toghon asked bemusedly.

"You didn't really think I would attack Wil'iah's most heavily-fortified city without sources of information from the inside, did you?"

She spread the map out onto the table.

"Ah, just as I suspected!" She clapped with glee. "The northern wall along the river is thinner than the rest. If we are unable to breach their other fortifications, that is our best chance."

"But, the river rushes quickly past there. We would never be able to get our forces across," Achish of Ashkelon, Minos' lieutenant, interjected.

Toghon smiled. "This isn't the first city we've attacked that's protected by a river. It's simple. We must redirect the river."

Delilah delightedly laughed. "That's the spirit! I knew you Mongols were going to make excellent allies."

Toghon pointed at a bend in the river west of the city. "I suggest we build the dam here. That will cause the river to flow in a different direction. Once it has trickled to nothing, the northern river wall will be laid bare to an assault."

"Begin at once," Delilah ordered. She then turned to a large object in the back of the tent, covered by a silk sheet.

"In the meantime," she continued, "I have another idea for breaching the main walls while we wait for the dam." She yanked the sheet off to reveal an enormous wine barrel- or at least it had started its life that way. Painted on its side was a giant red pentagram of the Empire.

"Behold the Goliath Bomb!" She said, her eyes lit by a maniacal fire. "Tell the sappers to get to work. We have a tunnel to dig!"

※ ※ ※

On the other side of the Frouzean-Mongol encampment, four Chinese conscripts huddled around a campfire, roasting the small fish the food patrols had managed to bring back from the sea.

"These Wil'iahns aren't yielding quickly," one of them grunted.

"Neither did we," said another, with a faraway look in his eye. "I heard these people even tried to help us."

"Hush!" replied the first. "We can't talk of old China here. That's dangerous. Don't you know that?"

The third soldier leaned in, a conspiratorial gleam in his eye, and began to whisper excitedly. "You'll never believe what I heard. Emperor Bing survives, and is here in Wil'iah! King Tamino has even apparently offered to grant asylum to Chinese soldiers who switch sides!"

"Where did you hear this?" the first soldier asked urgently.

"One of the scouts apparently was captured, but then released. He says he saw Emperor Bing."

"Don't speak of this again. Toghon has ears everywhere. We cannot afford to speak of treason. Besides, this might be a trick of the Wil'iahns."

As cynical as the words were, a note of hope unmistakably shone through.

CHAPTER THIRTY

THE GOLIATH BOMB

Balthcutta

Gun number 521, atop the walls in between towers 21 and 22 on the middle wall, roared in defiance for the hundredth time that day, its mouth red hot from the effort. As its superheated projectile arced down over the outer wall and slammed into a formation of Mongol archers, its crew cheered, satisfied with their steadily-improving aiming skills.

However, this hit was different. Rather than just throwing up a shower of dirt and debris like all the others, its effect was much more devastating. The very ground caved in, swallowing the whole formation of archers with an ominous rumble.

"What the...?" said the gunnery captain, his eyes filling with a wondered confusion.

His confusion was not unique. General Teva'ivani squinted from the command post on the St. Thomas gate, her beady eyes focusing on the gaping hole in the ground. Suddenly, her stomach turned as she realized what had happened.

"They've tunneled under the moat!" she yelled to Avora'tru'ivi and Tamino, who started in alarm.

In the far distance, atop her siege tower, Delilah smiled.

"David's not going to win this time," she crooned, licking her lips in anticipation.

In the depths of the tunnel, the crew looked around in wild-eyed alarm as the ground shook with the distant explosion. A great cloud of choking dust and dirt rocketed through the tunnel, sending the men into coughing fits. As the dust settled, one of the men, his face covered in mud, exclaimed to the captain, "The tunnel's caved in! We're trapped!"

The captain gestured to the Goliath Bomb, now in position below the wall. The flaring light from the torch that he held reflected off eyes filled with a maniacal fire all their own as he stroked the weapon.

"We were never going to get out. There's only one thing left to do for our eternal empress."

His hand trembling with fervor and his mouth set in a wolfish, fanatical smile, he touched the torch to the bomb's fuse. Then, he sank to his knees and turned toward the direction where, somewhere in the indistinct distance, Delilah stood.

"All hail Ast—"

He never got to finish his last prayer.

The steady light of the moon was suddenly eclipsed by a blinding flash, accompanied by an earth-shattering boom, as a great fountain of flame exploded upward from beneath the outer wall. The densely packed structure, painstakingly built over the course of ten years, instantly broke into a thousand pieces that became flying projectiles aimed in all directions. Much of the rubble fell directly into the moat, creating a new land bridge.

"Now! Now! Now!" yelled Delilah, manically waving her scepter, urging her hordes forward. They streamed like an torrent over the new bridge, most of them fanning out into the inner ward by the thousands as the rest scrambled up the smoking remains of the cross-section of the wall to the battlements above, where a group of rattled defenders waited with pikes, swords, and halberds, shaken but defiant.

Avora'tru'ivi gripped the battlements atop the gate, her terrified eyes filled with the flame.

"No…" she whispered.

However, her despair was instantly shattered by a steely grip on her arm.

"We were prepared for this!" hissed Teva'ivani. She snatched a conch shell from the trembling hands of the blower, who looked on at the breached wall in horror. Pressing the shell to her lips, she let out five ear-splitting blasts. A series of echoes met her ears as her order was relayed down the middle wall behind.

Deep in the middle wall's lower levels, a group of men anxiously waited next to an enormous wooden capstan, haltingly illuminated in the gloom by a handful of sputtering torches that occasionally sizzled as water dripped onto them.

Suddenly, a breathless woman ran headlong down the stairs behind them.

"Open the gates!" she wheezed.

The men instantly snapped to attention and threw their weight against the capstan, groaning with effort.

Atop the middle wall, the gunners frantically moved to lower the elevation of their weapons, hoping to bring them to bear on the swarming horde below, the glint of thousands of suits armor in the moonlight looking like an incoming tidal wave. Gun number 542 managed to fire downwards, its ball smashing into the densely-packed earth below even as siege ladders clattered against the inclined wall and soldiers began their inexorable ascent.

But the report from the cannon was drowned out by what came next. A creaking sound, barely discernable over the din of battle, gave way to a thunderous roar as great stone gates on either side of the ward opened to admit millions of gallons of seawater. A flood of Biblical proportions surged into the ward, whose level sank below the ground outside the wall, instantly sweeping away the massed attackers and the ladders with them. The awestruck gunners above looked on with a mixture of wonder and horror as the spectacle unfolded below.

Atop the St. Thomas Gate, Teva'ivani gave seven blasts on the conch shell. Inside the machicolations, crews of defenders tipped over great vats, their oily contents thickly pouring out onto the inclined walls below, becoming a black waterfall that encompassed the whole of the inner wall. The water suddenly became iridescent as the oil coated its surface.

Teva'ivani blew on the conch nine more times.

A thousand flaming arrows arced from the battlements of the middle wall onto into the water.

And night turned into day.

The surface of the inner moat almost instantly ignited into a roaring conflagration whose incandescent brilliance rivaled the sun. Its angry, defiant light illuminated the shocked faces of defender and attacker alike. The Frouzean soldiers who kicked and pushed each other for the chance to enter the breach next, the chance to strike the next killing blow against the hated enemy, instantly stopped, their jaws dropping in awe at the terrible effulgence before them. Then, wordlessly, they turned and ran.

"WHAT!?!" screamed Delilah as she tore the snake headdress off in frustration and flung it to the ground. General Toghon winced as the "eternal empress" launched into a full-blown tantrum, stomping her feet and tearing at her hair.

Above the fires that now encircled the city of Balthcutta like the chariots at Dothan flapped the standards of Wil'iah, their red, white, and blue rays tinged gold by the leaping flames below. And higher yet, crowning the firmament above, the Southern Cross blazed against the darkness.

CHAPTER THIRTY-ONE

IN THE DEN OF THE ENEMY

Imperial Army Camp, Vrenga'nui, eastern Wil'iah

Medea silently suppressed a curse, tripping over a blackened branch as she picked her way across the burned backcountry. Ahead, she could just make out the lights of the Imperial Army's encampment. She shook her head as she viewed the destruction all around her.

I never thought I'd see the day when Wil'iah went down in flames.

Steeling her resolve, she exhorted herself forward.

I can still do my part to save it.

Figuring that the Frouzean section of the camp would be more laxly-defended than the Mongol section, she headed for an area flying large banners of Gath. The very sight of the flags turned her stomach, but she knew what she had to do. Reaching the camp perimeter, she discarded her cloak, revealing the costume of a Frouzean slave. She produced from her pouch a pitiful handful of seeds and berries.

"Where do you think you're going?" a half-drunk guard slurred at her as she stepped into the camp's torchlight.

Medea held up the berries. "I was on a forager detail. This is all I found."

The guard laughed. "We'll see how Ajax feels about that," he said, roughly grabbing her by the wrist and dragging her towards an ostentatious pavilion at the center of the tent.

Medea couldn't believe her luck, as she was being led straight for the Frouzean Prince of Gath, commander of the Imperial Army's backcountry division, but her excitement fought with her nervousness as she realized just how dangerous he really was.

The guard shoved her through the flaps. A tall, athletically built man, whom Medea supposed would be quite attractive if he weren't irredeemably evil, and a Mongol officer stood hunched over a map, clearly in the midst of an argument. The Frouzean, whom she could only assume was Ajax the Lesser of Gath, in the flesh, stood up from the map and looked over at her, annoyance crossing his riveting features.

"What is *this?*" he sneered.

The guard grunted. "One of the forager girls. Looks like she only found a few berries." Medea dutifully held up her hand, even as her eyes darted over to the tactical map. She suddenly, horribly, made eye contact with the Mongol, whom she assumed was General Nasir-al-Din; his eyebrows narrowed suspiciously at her apparent curiosity. Medea quickly turned her gaze back to Ajax.

Ajax stepped forward to examine the seeds. Then, he contemptuously turned her hand over, the tiny morsels of food clattering to the floor.

"Still the Wil'iahn cowards avoid a fight!" he thundered at Nasir-al-Din. "And here we traipse through blackened fields, with only birdseed to feed us! And where are the supply caravans we were promised? Already three should have arrived, and we haven't received so much as a loaf of bread!"

The plan is working. A thrill of hope surged through Medea, even as she fearfully looked on at the generals.

"We've run into this before," Nasir-al-Din said. "Dai Viet used similar scorched-earth tactics. We would be wise to turn back to territory with a more stable food supply."

"Retreat!? Retreat now, with Wil'iah on her knees!? Never! We must simply bring the Wil'iahns to battle."

"They know exactly what they're doing. They won't agree to a pitched battle until we're well and truly weakened."

Ajax pounded his fist on the map. "I just don't understand, where did they all go? We should have encountered at least a few terrified civilians to torment by now."

"That's a mystery to me as well. Clearly there is a larger plan at work. We would be foolish to walk straight into a trap."

Ajax bristled and rose to his full height, several inches above Nasir-al-Din. The Frouzean general looked down his finely-formed nose at the Mongol.

"Just who is in charge here?"

"This is an army composed of equals."

"Not here, it isn't! An army cannot have two bickering commanders. I, as the Prince of Gath, was invested in this position by Her Worship herself. You are merely an advisor."

"An advisor whose advice you would be wise to heed," said Nasir-al-Din fiercely, a dark look in his eye.

"And whose advice I am free to disregard."

Medea suddenly spoke, her voice purposefully tremulous.

"Might I suggest you turn to the east, rather than proceeding further north? There might be more food at the base of the mountains?"

"Did someone ask you to talk? Slaves have no voice in my tent, unless they are to whisper pleasing things to me," Ajax rudely responded, raising his hand as if to strike. Medea flinched. Ajax's hand hovered in the air for a moment, then dropped down, as if he decided he had better things to do. "We will proceed north. Tomorrow we will march twenty miles."

Thus dismissed, Medea was dragged back out by the guard, who forced-marched her over to the slave quarters tent and threw her inside. Medea found herself amongst a mass of women, who barely seemed to notice her.

"I'm hungry," one of them said.

"We're all hungry. None of us want to be here, but it's our lot in life. Just accept it already," another snapped.

Turning to Medea, one asked, "Did you see Ajax? I heard that he's Delilah's favorite, and if we win this campaign, he will finally get to marry her. After all, he got passed over for his brother last time. If he becomes the consort to the Frouzee, maybe our miserable lives will improve."

Medea disgustedly shook her head. One of the women finally noticed the new addition to the tent and flounced over. She looked Medea up and down, scoffing disapprovingly.

"Who are *you?*"

"My name is Medea," Medea responded. Her name was common enough in Frouzea that she saw no need for a disguise.

"I'm Cassandra. Why haven't we seen you here before?"

"I was in a different forager unit, but was transferred here."

Cassandra flippantly shrugged. "Whatever. I hope you found something when you were foraging. We don't have any extra food here. You can sleep in the corner."

The next morning, Medea rose and prepared to leave the camp with the forager detail. The group of women filed out of the camp and began to pick their way through the burned ground, looking for any potential morsels of food for the increasingly-starved army before it moved out on the day's march. Medea looked around. When she was satisfied that her unwitting compatriots were thoroughly engrossed in their tasks, she withdrew a small mirror from her pouch, looked toward a conspicuous mountain in the distance – as her memory served, this one was Mt. Bundella, home to a beacon-post – and began to flash the mirror in a coordinated pattern that relayed the information she had heard the night before. She waited on bated breath for a response.

Finally, two flashes answered from the mountain.

CHAPTER THIRTY-TWO

THE BALTHCUTTA BARRAGE

Balthcutta

Standing atop the ramparts of the Citadel of Balthcutta that jutted above a tall sea cliff at the entrance to the bay, Avora'tru'ivi's breath caught in her throat as she surveyed a veritable forest of masts clustered on the horizon. Heretofore, the enemy fleet had stayed out of range, blockading the city, but now they appeared to be closing in for an attack.

There must be at least a thousand of them, she thought as the great bells of the White Cathedral sounded the alarm. Thousands of troops, most of them Home Army personnel or reservists who had previously escaped service on the walls, streamed out of the waterfront portions of the city to their predetermined posts on the seawall. They busied themselves untying the great canvas bags that lined its battlements, revealing yet another battery of guns. A different crew of specialists, wearing hauberks emblazoned with the symbol of the sun, busied themselves unwrapping a series of curious objects spaced at regular intervals along the walls and at various strategic points on the citadel above.

Casting a doubtful glance at the sun that blazed overhead, Avora'tru'ivi questioned the sanity of the plan General Alinta, commander of Balthcutta's sea defenses, had devised.

Archimedes had better have been right.

The strangely shaped objects were revealed to be a series of parabolic mirrors that glinted in the sun. Avora'tru'ivi stole a glance at the tallest tower of the citadel, which normally functioned as a lighthouse. Today, it was crowned with the largest of the mirrors.

As the enemy fleet inexorably advanced, Avora'tru'ivi made out an odd assortment of technologically backward Frouzean trireme galleys and advanced Chinese junks, the latter most likely cannon-armed. Her eyes darted over to the circular-shaped quay nestled in the shelter of the citadel's guns where the Wil'iahn fleet normally docked. Fewer than fifty ships now rode at anchor there. They were outnumbered twenty to one.

A frontal assault would be useless.

However, the harbor of Balthcutta was not entirely without defenses. Across the bay stretched a great chain, the Balthcutta Barrage, in front of which floated, at regular intervals, barrels filled with explosives. Toward these barrels the enemy fleet advanced, led by the Frouzean galleys. As the first one neared the floating barrels, Alinta hissed,

"Now!"

A thin fuse rope attached to a steel cable ran from the ramparts of the Citadel down to the floating barrel in question, one of many such lines. A soldier touched a sputtering torch to the rope, which flared into life. The flame raced down the fuse and entered a hole in the barrel, which detonated an instant later in an earsplitting explosion. As the smoke cleared, the shattered galley was down by the bows, sinking fast. A cheer rang up from the ramparts of the citadel. The other Frouzean galleys retreated in confusion.

Avora'tru'ivi squinted as a group of Mongol junks broke off from the main firing line opposing the citadel and began to sail toward the Barrage. At a safe distance, they commenced opening fire on the barrels floating in front of it. One by one, they harmlessly exploded with a thunderous sound. Each time, Avora'tru'ivi winced.

There goes the first line of defense.

After they finished their tasks, the junks hauled around and returned to the main battle against the citadel. In their place a group of curious ships began to advance. These vessels seemed to float over the water, without any visible means of propulsion. While this type of vessel had often struck terror into the hearts of the Mongols' enemies, Zhang Shijie had informed the Wil'iahn Navy of their secret- manually-driven paddle wheels down the centerline, invisible to the outside -- and highly vulnerable to fouling. Unbeknownst to the Mongols, the Barrage was additionally fronted with a great net, held up by floats, which hung just below the surface of the water, virtually invisible. As the enemy paddle-ships grew close to the Barrage, the paddle-wheels churned into the nets, and the boats became caught like so many flies in a spider's web, struggling to free themselves.

Now the Wil'iahn fleet seized its chance. The remaining fifty warships, led by the veteran catamaran *Lion of Judah,* advanced on the Barrage, their forward batteries spitting flame. One by one the paddle-boats were smashed, their shattered remains sinking beneath the waves- and dragging the net down with it.

Undaunted, the Mongols sent forward their next wave. Two hundred ships of yet another curious design approached the barrage, flying the hated banners of the Yuan Dynasty. Primarily oar-powered, the ships featured a bow module that appeared to be detachable, piled high with barrels and pots. But once again, Zhang Shijie's intelligence reports included warnings about this type- the detachable module contained massive explosives. They were attempting to blow up the Barrage.

The Wil'iahn fleet formed into a line-ahead formation to attempt to combat this new menace, but there were simply too many Mongol ships. It seemed that, inevitably, one would get through. However, the Mongols had counted without the ancient wisdom of Archimedes.

"Now!" yelled Alinta as she waved her saber to the Citadel's tower above her. One of the great parabolic mirrors swung down, suddenly focusing an intense beam of light on the bow module of the nearest Mongol ship. Behind Alinta, up a signal mast ran a series of signal flags, and the castles across the bay answered with signal guns. The mirrors on their towers also swung into position, as did the ones positioned on the guard towers of the seawall. Their crews expertly tracked the slow movement of the explosive boats.

A wisp of smoke began to caress the sky from the bow of the lead Mongol ship. Her crew noticed the hazard too late, and her deck exploded into panicked milling about as the men abandoned their oars and raced for the rails. Suddenly, the mirror's beam cut through one of the dry barrels, and the ship disappeared in a blinding flash.

One by one, more than a dozen other ships similarly exploded down the Mongol line, joining several others that had been exploded by the Wil'iahn ships. A huge Mongol junk with five masts, by far the largest vessel in the enemy fleet and the presumed flagship, hauled herself into position behind the line of advancing explosive boats and ran up a series of signal flags. The remaining boats turned and ran.

A cheer rose into the sky from the seawall, but the battle was far from over. Several Hundred Mongol warships broke off from their assault on the resolute castles and formed a battle line near the barrage, seeking to destroy the Wil'iahn ships, but the Wil'iahns had a crucial advantage. Their naval guns, designed with painstaking meticulousness and thoroughly tested in anticipation of the inevitable conflict, outranged their Mongol counterparts. The *Lion of Judah* wore around and retreated into the bay, the other forty-nine ships following her, before they formed up into another line just outside of the range of the enemy weapons. The Wil'iahn guns dealt hammer blow after hammer blow on the enemy fleet, which ineffectually fired back in a fruitless response.

Finally, the Mongols had had enough, and determined to force the Barrage. The enemy flagship charged forward, intending to ram the chain and hopefully break it, or at least get close enough to deal damage to the Wil'iahn fleet. But the Wil'iahn ships retreated yet farther into the bay, and the Mongol missiles raised great enraged geysers of frothy, futile water. Still the Mongol battleship surged forward, until finally, with a crash, it slammed into the chain.

Avora'tru'ivi bit her fist with nervousness, wincing.

There's no way the chain could hold against a ship of that size.

But hold it did, and more than that. Unbeknownst to the Mongols, the Barrage was fitted at regular intervals with enormous spikes that jutted out into the ocean. One of these drove directly into the Mongol ship's hull. As the battleship reversed course and heaved itself off of the chain, the spike withdrew, and water surged in the gaping hole left behind. Down at the bows, the Mongol flagship was soon out of control- and well within the range of the Wil'iahn guns. The *Lion of Judah* now leapt forward to engage, her forward batteries spitting flame. One by one her expertly-aimed projectiles slammed into the junk, until one hit its mark- the powder magazine.

A great sheet of flame shot into the air as the Mongol flagship's entire store of gunpowder violently exploded, breaking the ship's back. Her panicked crew jumped into the water in droves, trying to escape the vortex of water that threatened to drag them down as the shattered junk sank beneath the waves.

Suddenly leaderless, the Mongol fleet began to mill about aimlessly. Finally, another large Mongol ship seemed to take charge of the operation. A four-masted junk, the ship ran up a series of signal flags. The remaining enemy ships wore around and headed back out to sea, bombarded not just by projectiles, but by cheers and jeers from the Wil'iahn ramparts.

Avora'tru'ivi and Alinta jubilantly hugged each other.

"I knew that chain would hold!" Alinta yelled.

Avora'tru'ivi looked at the remaining wreckage of the Mongol fleet, gurgling and burning as it slipped beneath the waves.

"Strike another junk!" she yelled, thinking back to her first sea battle at Bach Dang six years before.

CHAPTER THIRTY-THREE

GENERAL LUANA

Trukanamoa

𝒜 top the walls of Trukanamoa, terror reigned. In the aftermath of the disastrous Battle of Uluru, an inexorable sense of dread had settled over the city. A group of soldiers hung a giant black banner over the ramparts in mourning for those who had lost their lives, while a few dozen terrified reservists milled about on the walls in confusion. There was no sign of the enemy just yet, but everyone knew that it was only a matter of time.

"Just what is going on here?" A resonant voice cut through the din of confusion. A hundred pairs of eyes whirled around to see a woman confidently striding down the battlement. Clad in meticulously-polished scale armor emblazoned with an enormous Star of Wil'iah and with a pure-white cape billowing behind her in the gathering breeze, the silver-haired woman appeared aged but vital, the deep smile lines written on her caring face framing sparkling, fierce eyes. As she spoke, her very words crackled with an ancient power mixed with an incongruous hint of mirth.

"Come on, up, up!" she yelled, clapping her many-ringed hands together, the sound echoing across the walls far more than appeared possible given the woman's seemingly-unimpressive stature. "Back to your posts! This isn't the Trukanamoa I know!"

"And just who are you?" the gunnery captain responded.

"Who am I? WHO am I? Well, if you need that explained to you, I am General Luana, of course!"

"General…who?" whispered an artillery specialist to the man who crouched beside him. His compatriot shrugged, then turned back to gawk at the presence that effortlessly commanded the wall.

"Well, someone has to replace Eleazar, God rest his soul," she responded, briefly casting her eyes skyward. "The Powers that Be have invested me with that responsibility. Now, enough about me!" She looked briefly to her left and caught a glimpse of the giant black banner that slothfully flapped from the battlements.

"What on this Earth is this!? Get that thing down immediately. Is this a battle or a funeral!?" She snapped her fingers at the two soldiers nearest the flag, who instantly snapped to attention and began hauling down the black banner.

"Tell me we have a proper battle-standard around here! Honestly!" Two more soldiers scurried over to a locker and withdrew an enormous, multi-rayed flag.

"Well, *good!* I was starting to get worried!" The woman crisply but rapidly waved her hand over towards the now-bare pole, and the two soldiers sprang into action, running up the battle-standard, which instantly caught the breeze and billowed into life behind the general.

"Alright, now that we've got the basic housekeeping done, please tell me that these guns are all in working order."

"Yes Ma'am."

"And the oil vats are prepared?"

"Ummm…"

"Well, we'd better check, now shouldn't we?"

"Y-yes Ma'am!"

"Okay. Now, what about the rubble?" She surveyed piles of boulders and loose gravel that lined the tops of the walls behind the battlements, ready to be hurled downward through the machicolations.

"Alright, that seems adequate for now," she responded to her own question. "Well, everything seems in order. Where is the prince?"

"Locked up in his tower, Ma'am."

"EXCUSE me? Who does he think he is!?"

Two of the soldiers nervously looked at each other.

"Never mind, don't answer that. Leave him to me." Just as quickly as she had appeared, Luana power-walked over to the staircase that led to the ward below and descended, forcefully making her way towards the castle. One soldier noticed out of the corner of her eye that the General cast another brief glance skyward, then seemed to mumble something to herself. And then, she was gone.

🔆 🔆 🔆

Jeremiah sat in his chamber atop one of the twelve inner towers of the Castle of Trukanamoa, silently berating himself.

This is all your fault. If only you had listened and hadn't been so headstrong, he thought. *For years, we have been training for this moment, and what do you do? The instant the Frouzeans arrive, you forget everything and lose the plot.*

Images of dying soldiers and wailing mothers flashed before Jeremiah's mental eye, their haunting visages piercing straight to his heart. The images soon gave way to an even more disturbing visage- the City of Trukanamoa in flames, the Castle thrown down, and the Grand Cathedral desecrated by the Frouzeans. Suddenly, Jeremiah's eyes focused on something very real- his own reflection in a mirror that stood on a desk in front of him. With a guttural yell, he punched the face that greeted his vision, heedless of the pain that shot through his hand as the glass shattered into a thousand pieces.

"Oh, come on!" a voice echoed through the chamber.

Jeremiah whirled around, his bloodshot eyes searching for the source of the voice. They fell on a woman clad in full armor who stood in the center of the room, clucking with disapproval.

"How did you get in here!?" Jeremiah growled.

"Never mind that," the woman responded. "I am General Luana Va'a'kau'teva Kala'pa'i Zrai'vra'e, and I have taken command of the Army of Tjoritja. You are Jeremiah, Sovereign Protector of the Faithful Kingdom of Wil'iah, and don't you forget it!"

Jeremiah ruefully scoffed. "Some 'protector' I am. Maybe if 'protection' constitutes losing half of your army and dooming your people to destruction. I am worthy of no title save 'incompetent fool.' I am no longer worthy to even scrub the battlements of Trukanamoa, much less command them." With a dramatic flourish, Jeremiah ripped the badge of the Sovereign Protector from his breastplate and flung it at the ground.

To his surprise, with equal speed, the woman shot her hand out and slapped him.

"You are the son of Hezekiah Vrenga'ava'zora'vaua! It's time you acted like it! Besides, do you really think that you're so important that Wil'iah lives or dies by your decisions? We are under a much higher protection than the rash decisions of an inexperienced commander."

"Through my own stupidity, I have forfeited that protection."

"Nonsense. Do you think your father never made mistakes?" Luana involuntarily chortled with laughter. "There's a reason it took him thirteen years to beat the Frouzeans! He made error after error after error, but each and every time, he picked himself up and tried again. Do you think we would be standing here right now if he had just locked himself in a tower and wailed with despair the first time he lost a battle?"

"Well, I guess not…But I was so foolish…"

"I'm not going to argue with that. But the question of the hour is what lesson you learned."

"I thought I could be like David. I thought I could take out Goliath with one smooth stone."

"David had more than one stone in his pouch. He was prepared to try again and again until Goliath was slain. He ultimately didn't need them...because he listened."

Jeremiah hung his head in shame. "I have never been very good at listening."

"Well, here's your chance. Listen to me now! Here's what's going to happen. You are going to quit this lachrymose nonsense, you're going to put that armor back on, and you are going to meet me on the battlements in ten minutes. Do I make myself clear?"

"Yes ma'am," Jeremiah said, gathering his strength. He cast his eyes over to the armor that hung limply on a rack. He rose and walked over to it, then turned back to address Luana, but she was gone.

Curious. I never heard her leave.

Jeremiah paused for a moment, then shook his head, and began to buckle on the armor.

We have a city to defend.

CHAPTER THIRTY-FOUR

DELILAH'S LETTER

Balthcutta

*T*amino, Avora'tru'ivi, and Abigail, the gunnery captain, stood at their command post atop the St. Thomas Gate, once again directing the city's artillery batteries against the enemy.

Tamino turned in surprise as a courier ran up the stairs and snapped into a military salute.

"The north river wall reports a slightly lower level to the river than normal. It might be nothing, but they're keeping an eye on it."

"Curious. Tell them to report back to me if there are any changes," the king responded before returning his attention to his cannon batteries.

Suddenly, though, the enemy bombardment ceased its raging, and the projectiles that arced through the sky stopped coming. Tamino held out an arm to pause the Wil'iahn batteries.

A single horse streaked across the blackened plane, its rider holding aloft a shockingly white standard that seared the eyes against its dark surroundings.

"What is this?" Tamino said under his breath.

"Undoubtedly some sort of trick," Avora'tru'ivi hissed through gritted teeth.

The horse and rider thundered under the smoking ruin of the first barbican and came to a halt before the second, raising a loud voice trumpet.

"I come bearing an important message from the Frouzee Delilah! I ask that thou bid me enter!"

Tamino threw a rueful glance at Abigail, then called back.

"No Frouzean shall pass these gates until this war is over. Whatever you have to say, you can say it now, before all the walls." With a nod, he quietly ordered guns 321 and 323 to be trained on the herald.

"It is a letter, and I cannot read!" came the response.

After several more rounds of negotiation, Tamino arranged for the herald to leave the letter at the base of the gate and ride back to enemy lines. Then, the gate was opened just enough to retrieve the letter. Tamino was disturbed by its contents.

Your sister Jessica is in my custody. I am told she fought bravely against our naval forces, but nobody resists a goddess. To prove the veracity of my claims, I have attached a lock of her hair and her signet ring. If you want her to live for the next twenty-four hours, you will meet me in the tent that has been set just out of range of your Chinese playthings to discuss terms. You will come alone. Ignore this offer, and your nation's beloved princess will be killed in front of the walls of Balthcutta for all to see- and it will not be pleasant.

Tamino's shaking hands clutched the paper in shock. Forcing himself to regain his composure, Tamino narrowed his eyes as he noticed some odd capitalization in the letter. Stringing together the incongruous letters, he realized they spelled the word "invisible."

"Bring me a torch," he said grimly to Abigail. The gunnery captain gravely nodded and fulfilled the request.

Passing the torch under the paper, Tamino watched as a second message gradually darkened and became visible.

I don't want this war any more than you do. The inexorable might of Kublai Khan has forced my hand, but there is still a chance for us to defeat him if we are willing to work together. The only way for me to avoid the destruction of Frouzea was to pretend to go along with the Mongols' plan. Drawing them into Wil'iah was in fact an elaborately laid trap. Now we can strike. This is the real reason why I want you to meet. Frouzea chafes under the Mongol yoke as much as you do. We are prepared to turn our banners against theirs. But Khan's eyes and ears are everywhere, and a ransom negotiation is the only legitimate excuse I could come up with to meet with you in secret. Come, meet me in the tent. You will not be harmed.

P.S. I really do have Jessica, and if you value her life you will accept this invitation.

Tamino grimly looked up from the letter.

"Looks like I don't have much of a choice."

"Galbi, this is almost certainly a trap," Avora'tru'ivi pleaded. "Don't go. We can't afford to lose you."

"And I can't afford to lose my sister. If there's even a chance to save her, I'm willing to take it. Wil'iah will survive without me, if it comes to that."

"Galbi, I don't want you to go."

"Jessica is your friend, too. We must at least try to save her. If I go this way, only I am at risk. No other lives will be sacrificed, and the city's defenses will not be compromised."

"Do you realize how important to the morale of this city you are?" Abigail interjected.

"I am not the hope of this city," Tamino said, casting his eyes skyward.

"Very well," Avora'tru'ivi sighed. "But if she tries something, expect a rescue attempt. I don't want any lectures from you about 'the good of the many.'"

Tamino allowed himself a smile. "I always can count on you."

CHAPTER THIRTY-FIVE

THEY THAT BE WITH US

Trukanamoa

The sun's faint dawning rays broke over the Tjoritja Mountains, crowning their ancient ridges with golden light. A blanket of anticipatory silence lay over the city of Trukanamoa as the early light began to shine off of the burnished dome of the Grand Cathedral and the still waters of the Palaces of the Council of Uluru.

Suddenly, the silence was shattered by the lone wail of a conch shell. In answer, the deafening alarm bells of the cathedral blared their shouted warning, and the city instantly sprang into action, thousands of soldiers swarming onto the ramparts like so many ants.

Jeremiah, blinking sleep from his eyes, emerged in full armor from his ready-room atop the gatehouse. He wasn't surprised to find General Luana already on the ramparts, surveying the alarming scene below.

Stretching out as far as the eye could see stood the hordes of the enemy, their number seemingly as high as the grains of sand of the desert. A hundred siege towers, each one as high as the outer wall of Trukanamoa, ponderously lurched forward, pulled by mass teams of groaning slaves, who flinched at the incessant cracks of whips. A large covered structure stood at the center of the enemy army, which Jeremiah could only assume contained a battering ram. Most worryingly, hundreds of siege engines peppered the enemy lines, most of them currently out of reach of the guns atop the walls.

Jeremiah's eyes narrowed as four horses charged forward, their riders holding aloft billowing white parley banners. From his vantage point, Jeremiah could tell that they represented both the Mongol and Frouzean armies. One of the heralds lifted a voice trumpet.

"We bring the greetings and felicitations of Her Worship Frouzee Delilah and Kublai, Great Khan of All the World!"

Deafening silence greeted them from the walls. Jeremiah noticed the archers on either side of him grip their bows a bit tighter.

"These two monarchs admonish this highly-honored city to surrender now, before our mercy expires. As is widely known, the Great Khan prefers to be merciful, provided his future subjects show the proper respect. But defy us, and all shall die. It is the way of things. What is your answer?"

Without a moment's hesitation, Jeremiah grabbed the voice trumpet next to him and yelled his response.

"Let it be known that the City of Trukanamoa, and, more broadly, the Kingdom of Wil'iah will NEVER surrender to you or any of your hordes of darkness! Let it be known that we are not now, nor will we ever be, afraid by reason of your threats, no matter how severe they may be. You will never take Trukanamoa!"

The herald gave Jeremiah a wry smile.

"Very well. Enjoy your trip to hell!"

With that, the riders turned back, and the massive army began to lurch forward.

Luana smiled at Jeremiah. "I think these people need some more tangible encouragement. Something to rally around. You wouldn't happen to know of anything like that around here, would you?"

Jeremiah suddenly looked like he'd seen a ghost. "You don't mean…"

Luana threw up her hands. "What do you think I mean!? Jeremiah, you're the sovereign protector. That means you are one of the twelve people who know where it is kept. Go on, hop to it!" The general clapped her hands.

As if in answer, a roll of thunder clapped across the sky.

As Jeremiah disappeared to his mysterious destination, Luana surveyed the ranks on the wall, noting that their brown faces were a lighter shade than usual, and their knuckles stood out white as they gripped their weapons. Most of these people had never seen combat before, as the professional core of the Army of Tjoritja had perished at Uluru.

"Take heart," Luana said. "This battle is not yours."

These final words were almost drowned out as a deadly whine filled the air, and black clouds of arrows filled the sky. In response, the defenders atop the walls propped up folding shields designed to protect them from plunging fire. Dozens of boulders slammed into the walls, but the staunch structures barely shook from the blows. In response, just as at Balthcutta, the guns roared their defiance, and Trukanamoa's own missiles leapt forth from the trebuchets that lined the inner wall. Unlike Balthcutta, however, parched Trukanamoa lacked water defenses, and the siege towers inexorably marched forward, even as some of them collapsed from direct hits by Wil'iahn projectiles. Some siege ladders even managed to make their way to the walls despite the rain of artillery fire and arrows from the battlements. Noticing more than a dozen of the precarious ladders raise themselves against the slightly inclined wall, Luana barked out orders.

"Scythes!"

About ten feet below the battlements on the wall was a series of barely perceptible slits. From these sliced great, long scythes that effortlessly cut down the ladders, sending them toppling back over, the frightened yells of their occupants piercing the din of battle. Thus the thunderous battle continued, the waves of the enemy relentless, the walls staunch and unyielding. Fear and determination mixed in the eyes of Trukanamoa's rag-tag mix of defenders, as prime, fighting-age men and women hurled missiles against the enemy alongside the young and the elderly. Young children scurried behind the front lines, relaying orders, restocking ammunition, and carrying water to strengthen the defenders against the relentless desert sun. Even the youngest children refused to flinch at each blast of the enemy, their small, bright eyes filled with the ancient fire that had marked their ancestors for generations. Behind the two great, thousand-bannered walls of Trukanamoa and the three great concentric, multi-towered rings of the castle, the great dome of the Church of the Eternal Victory rose in open defiance of the Frouzean banners, the gold leaf that adorned it blazing like a beacon, reflecting the light of the sun and strengthening the hearts of those who rallied to its defense. Though the great structure, the very symbol of Wil'iah's determination, was a prime target for the Frouzee's siege engineers, not one missile of the enemy hit it, all of them falling short into the wards below.

Suddenly, a strange silence gripped the battlements as, one by one, the defenders came to rapt attention. Noticing the abrupt change, Luana whirled from her position between two merlons, and a wide smile spread across her careworn face.

Jeremiah and another knight slowly marched down the battlements, hefting two poles which supported a box veiled by a magnificently-embroidered, bright blue cloth. With each deferential step, they passed another defender, on whose face was uniformly written an expression of reverent, trembling awe, followed by an immediate dip of the head in a show of respect. Ever so gradually, the pair of bearers came to a stop at the exact center of the gatehouse, their faces breaking out with a sweat that had nothing to do with the heat of the sun.

General Luana, heedless of the missiles that whizzed over her head, addressed the defenders.

"From Egypt, to Canaan, and from there to this Far Garden on the long Maka'ivi, our people have been continually protected and guided. Even in the darkest valleys, in the deepest places of fear, in the deserts of doubt, the Almighty has stood over us, the great shield of our people. That power will not abandon us now. In all of the places we have traveled in search of a permanent home, this symbol has stood for this promise." With a flourish, she yanked the veil off of the object that stood before her, and a reverent gasp rippled out through the defenders.

A large box, meticulously gilded on all sides and crowned with two figures of angels, their wings outstretched to meet each other, stood atop the battlements. Though the gold that covered it reflected the sun, it appeared to add its own glowing brilliance, and the defenders could have sworn they felt the very walls shake with the power that seemed to effortlessly emanate from the box.

Before turning to face the massed enemy, Luana calmly addressed her enthralled audience.

"They that be with us are more than they that be with them."

※ ※ ※

On the plain that stretched before the staunch walls of Trukanamoa, Temur Khan, son of Kublai Khan, heir apparent to the throne, and commander of the Mongol armies in the central theater of operations, suddenly noticed a look of awed horror cross Menelaus' face. The once-smug Frouzean prince's mouth slackly hung open as his beady eyes filled with a pure terror and his short sword clattered to the ground.

"What's gotten into you?"

"I...I thought this was just a story..."

"What!?"

Without answering his Mongol compatriot, Menelaus urgently turned to the herald beside him. "Get your trumpet, now!"

"What? Why?"

"Fool! There is not time for your stupidity!" Menelaus gutturally yelled, shaking the herald by his collar.

"I just don't unders—"

"LOOK!" Menelaus jabbed his finger at the gatehouse.

The herald hazarded a glance at the imposing structure, and his face suddenly went as white as a sheet, his mouth trembling.

"Delilah said it was only a story..."

"Delilah says a lot of things, and you and I both know that over half of them aren't true! We need to retreat, NOW!"

With trembling hands, the herald grabbed a trumpet and pressed the mouthpiece to his shaking lips, but Temur Khan grabbed his arm.

"Just what do you think you are doing? This siege is proceeding according to plan. We have the Wil'iahns bottled up in their city like frightened animals. Our soldiers are now climbing the hills and will soon force the walls that crown them. Once that is successfully accomplished, the city will be ours. So far was we can tell, it is defended only by a rabble of old women."

"It was proceeding according to plan, until now!" Menelaus said, panic written plainly in his voice. "Can't you see it!? Look at the gatehouse!"

Temur squinted up at the structure. "All I see is a golden box. I don't understand all of this consternation. I am hardly afraid of a glorified gift container."

"You should be. That is not ordinary box. That—" Menelaus' eyes darted around like a deer being hunted by a pack of dogs, as if looking for somebody listening, "is the Ark of the Covenant. THE Ark of the Covenant. I thought it only existed as a legend designed to terrify the enemies of the mudfaces into submission, a sort of Biblical fairy tale that they used to justify their miserable existence. But there it is. We need to retreat to a safe distance, NOW!"

"What can a box do?"

As if in answer to Temur's query, another unlooked-for thunderclap shook both sky and earth.

"Stay here if you want. We're retreating, now. We'll starve them out. You couldn't pay me any amount, in gold or slaves, to launch a frontal assault on that gatehouse now. When the mysterious power of that so-called 'box' brings your mighty army to its knees, don't come to me for succor."

※ ※ ※

The awed silence on the walls turned to a deafening cheer as the inexorable tide of the enemy came to an abrupt halt, the blasts of trumpets ringing over the clamor of war. As swiftly as they had advanced, the massed hordes now turned tail in what began as an orderly retreat, but quickly degenerated into a panicked stampede. Everywhere Jeremiah looked, wide-eyed Frouzean soldiers darted like a herd of frightened sheep, leaving behind valuable siege equipment in their haste to escape the baleful glow of the Ark. Their bemused Mongol companions, unsure of the source of their terror but convinced of its efficacy, quickly added to the receding tidal wave of humanity.

"Consider the fall of Trukanamoa cancelled, indefinitely!" Jeremiah yelled triumphantly, pumping a fist into the air as the Ark glowed beside him. All along the walls, defenders shook swords and spears at the retreating enemy.

Luana patted the prince on the back. "Darkness always flees before the light. THAT is the natural way of things." She cast a glance at the Ark. "I think we've made our point. It may not be wise to leave this on the walls. Take it back, but put it in the center of the sanctuary of the Church of the Eternal Victory. The people must be able to see it, day and night, as a constant reminder of the Promise."

Jeremiah's brow furrowed. "Weren't we supposed to leave the veil on at all times?"

"I think this particular case required a more…dramatic demonstration. Don't worry, I have the necessary permissions," Luana said, more flippantly than Jeremiah thought appropriate, given the stature of the artifact.

Luana now turned to the rest of the defenders.

"They've retreated for now, but this battle is far from over. Now comes the hard part. The waiting. They will try to starve us out, since they don't dare launch a frontal assault now. I suggest we all become accustomed to smaller meals." She pointedly looked at the Ark, now passing back down the battlements toward the staircase that would send it on its journey to the cathedral.

"Nevertheless, we will be provided for."

CHAPTER THIRTY-SIX

DELILAH SPRINGS HER TRAP

Balthcutta

*T*amino nervously arrived at the seemingly isolated tent, following the instructions of Delilah's letter.

Spreading open the tent flaps, he lowered his head and stepped through the door. He instantly coughed as his lungs were assaulted by overpowering perfumes and incense emanating from hundreds of candles inside the tent, which was draped with pearls, corals, and jewels. It was also filled with large barrels overflowing with exotic fruits. Recovering, he looked up to see the Frouzee Delilah, splayed luxuriantly on a tufted couch beside a large gong. She wore a bizarre dress of scales made from inlaid mother-of-pearl, which iridescently shimmered in the candlelight.

The Frouzee, who had seemed momentarily lost in thought, started at his arrival, and rose with uncharacteristic haste from the recliner. She rushed over to the king and pulled him into an embrace. The king's eyes bulged as he tensed, ready for trouble.

"Tamino, thank God you have come!" she said, in an unusually breathy voice, a contrast to her normal contralto. She reached her hands up to caress the king's face and threw her head back, trying to lock eyes with him.

Extricating himself from her arms and stepping back, Tamino responded, "To what do I owe this greeting?"

The Frouzee advanced on him once more, this time with a completely devastated look on her face. To his surprise, she sunk onto her knees and grabbed his hand with both of hers, her eyes filled with pleading.

"O brave and valiant King, forgive me, for I have greatly wronged you! I desperately wished it would not be this way. But I am under duress! They made me do it! That wicked, evil Circle…they made me do it. The Khan made me do it." She shook his hand with hers, tears streaming out of her eyes. "You have no idea how strong the Mongol Empire is! They said they would pillage and destroy Frouzea if we did not go along with their plan. We were powerless to stop them, so we had no choice but to join them. And…the Circle…"

Tamino once again rescued his hand. "What Circle?"

Delilah sobbed. "Surely I told you of the Circle? The secret cult that actually controls Frouzea? I am but a figurehead. I am powerless to determine the destiny of my country. When I was a young girl, just a baby, I was kidnapped from my parents in the dead of night and taken to their evil convent, far out in the desolate and windswept

Nullarbor Plain. And there they twisted me to their will. I was broken, brainwashed, reprogrammed into what you see today. I was fed lies about what the old empire truly stood for. I was indoctrinated with the evil religion of Baal, Dagon, and Astarte, made to conduct sacrifices…of my classmates who were less pliable. And why? Because of their twisted plan to call into being a reincarnation of the Frouzee. I forgot how to love. They took my hate and turned it against me. Gradually I lost my humanity. I became an utter tool to them, the instrument that they would use to restore their twisted empire and launch their bid to rule the world. So, when the time came, I, their killing machine, got to work."

Tears now streamed down her face as a virtual torrent, her over-done makeup running down her cheeks. For the first time, Tamino could truly say that the Frouzee was a pitiful sight.

"And thus it was that I re-established the empire for them by systematically seducing and killing anyone who stood in my way. And then they took it all and threw it away by casting our lot with the Mongol Empire." She moved her hands onto his forearm and squeezed desperately. "And now we are slaves. We are all slaves. We might as well surrender to the Mongols now." Her nails now dug into his arm like the claws of a wild animal. "It is too late for my country – but it might not be too late for yours."

Tamino's brow furrowed in a mixture of confusion and concern. "I don't understand…"

"I had forgotten what love was before my first visit to Wil'iah. My whole life, I had been manipulated into believing that yours was a depraved and evil nation bent on our destruction, fueled by your fanatical belief in an unreal and evil god. I was told that our only recourse was to defend ourselves by effecting your destruction. But when I came to Wil'iah as a spy to begin to implement this plan, I could not believe my eyes. For before me was the great, honorable, and valiant nation that I had always dreamed of. There was the shining kingdom that was the true beacon to the world. It was everything that Frouzea wasn't. And then, of course, there was you."

"I don't recall any meeting other than our last one, which… did not go as you had hoped."

"During our dinner together, you said I was familiar. You weren't wrong," she said.

"I don't understand."

"Do you remember a certain moonless night, long ago, on the desolate wastes of Kati-Thanda? Do you remember seven escaping slaves, running for their lives? You saved them. You saved *me*."

Something vaguely stirred in the back of Tamino's mind, but he was confused.

"Why would you take advantage of the Exodus Road?"

"To spy out its secrets, of course. I was never really a slave. I was merely a convenient mole, going about the wicked business of the Circle. But then, you helped me up from the dirt, I looked into your eyes, and everything changed."

Tamino was beginning to feel thoroughly uncomfortable. Clearing his throat, he asked, "What are you proposing?"

She now stood up and placed her hands on his shoulders. She dropped her voice to a sultry whisper and cast her frightened eyes about, as if trying to ascertain if they were being watched. "I have valuable information about the arrangements of our armies and our plans. I have some generals who are personally loyal to me and not the

Circle. I am willing to switch allegiances and fight the Mongols, even at risk to my own destruction."

Tamino removed her hands from his shoulders. "Surely you demand a price."

With desperation in her eyes, she clutched at his armor. "A small one, a tiny one. Inconsequential next to the salvation of The Faithful Kingdom. When I saw you all those years ago, all the love that had been beaten out of me rose up again and set my heart aflame. I resolved to love you for the rest of my days. I demand nothing from Wil'iah. Only you."

Tamino recoiled. "As I have previously told you, I am married. I am not interested in anyone's advances."

Delilah's mouth quivered. "And that is why I love you. You are a strong and decent man. But think, Tamino, think. What a small price to pay to save your country. To keep your father's dream alive. To not be the one to finally end the story of the house of Israel. I offer you everything you could want. In fact, you can fulfill your end of the bargain right now!" She launched herself at him, clearly attempting to kiss him. Tamino grabbed her shoulders and forcefully set her down on the ground.

"My answer has not changed. I will not betray my nation to you. I will not betray my wife to you. If these are your conditions, Wil'iah will stand alone, and God will see us through to victory. If your story is true, I am sincerely sorry for how you have been treated. And although I cannot give you what you ask, if things are truly as you say they are, why not escape the Circle? We can offer you asylum and help you throw off Mongol control. But I will not assent to your demand."

Delilah recoiled like a cobra about to strike. Her eyes, which had been soft and doe-like a moment before, narrowed to slits, and her mouth curved into a wicked, closed grin. With a sinking feeling, Tamino realized he had been duped.

"So this is how it is going to be. Well! If you are a student of history, you will learn that what the Frouzee cannot get by asking…she takes!" With that, she struck the gong beside her recliner. Instantly, the room erupted in a shower of fruit as fully-armed guards sprang out of the barrels.

"I see you complied with our condition not to bring any weapons," she said as she looked the king over. "How honorable…and how stupid." A quick count told the king that he was facing twenty Mongol guards, all of them armed to the teeth. Grimly, he balled his fists and entered a fighting stance.

"Oh, this will be fun to watch," she cackled, her eyes flashing dangerously.

"It doesn't have to be this way, Delilah!" called out Tamino as the Mongols advanced. "I know who you really are! I know you know it, too! You are more than the culture that raised you! There is a higher way!"

Tamino noticed what looked like a flicker of doubt cross the empress's eyes, but she seemed to steel herself as she coldly spoke to her guards.

"Get him. I want him alive."

CHAPTER THIRTY-SEVEN

THE SPITFIRE AT SEA

Somewhere in the Coral Sea

*J*essica awoke, noting that the room she was in was oddly swaying. Wondering if it was just the whack she had received on the back of the head, she tried to reach for the throbbing lump that it had left behind- only to discover that her hands were tied. When she tried to cry out, she discovered that she was also gagged, but, at least she wasn't hallucinating. A quick glance at the swinging lantern above confirmed that she was indeed on a ship.

The door creaked open, and a Mongol sea-captain, resplendent in his multi-colored armor, stepped through the opening. Jessica redoubled her struggle at her bonds, to no avail. The captain greeted her efforts with a sneer.

"Ah yes, the spitfire Wil'iahn princess. I heard you put up quite a fight!"

"MMMPH!" came the response.

"Oh, come now, Princess, there will be plenty of time for conversation later. Our voyage to Xanadu will take some time. But don't worry, Princess, no harm will come to you. You are considered a valuable political prisoner-potential leverage for your brother. In the meantime, enjoy your trip!" The captain guffawed with laughter, then retreated from the cabin, shutting the door behind him.

So she was going to Xanadu. Jessica tried to think of a positive element of her situation, perhaps an advantage to be gained from her presence there.

She couldn't think of any.

CHAPTER THIRTY-EIGHT

DELILAH'S PRIZE

Balthcutta

f ear gnawed at Avora'tru'ivi as the dawn's faint rays fell on the bravely-polished dome of the White Cathedral.

He should have been back by now.

Suddenly, the air was pierced by five trumpets braying out a crass fanfare. Avora'tru'ivi started as she ran to the ramparts of the St. Thomas' Gate – and her heart nearly stopped.

Frouzee Delilah floated over the pockmarked ground in her sedan chair, flanked on either side by Homeric Guards carrying two white flags of truce. Behind them, yanked along by a chain, his arms and head immobilized by a stockade, was Tamino.

"Look who I found!" Delilah exulted. "You Wil'iahns are so gullible, with this stupid sense of justice and honor. Don't you understand that the world just doesn't *work* that way?" She turned back to Tamino, who was rough-housed into position next to her.

"At least it doesn't for you. The Universe clearly has some sense of justice, because I finally got what I deserve!" she cooed as she squeezed Tamino's cheeks with her hands. He rolled his eyes in response.

Avora'tru'ivi's knuckles turned white as she gripped the battlements in a cold fury. Teva'ivani grabbed her arm and squeezed it, trying to impart a modicum of strength.

"Let him go, Delilah!" Avora'tru'ivi called down from the battlements. She winced as the shocked murmur of the defenders on the battlements, who were beginning to realize what was happening, assaulted her ears.

"Or you'll *what?*" Delilah asked. "I hold all the cards now. Your fleet is destroyed and your resupply is cut off. Your city is surrounded by an army infinitely larger and better equipped than your own. Your entire agricultural region has been turned into a field of cinders. And, *now,* I have all that I wanted all along!" The empress began to laugh maniacally. "But," she said, raising a finger in a staying motion, "even now, in your moment of humiliation, I am willing to offer you a deal. I'll give him back, *alive,* if you surrender now. Otherwise, tomorrow, I will feed him to my beloved pet, Goliath, in front of you all!"

A wail rose from the battlements as several defenders caught Delilah's ultimatum.

But this time, it was Tamino who spoke.

"You know what to do!" he yelled, giving his best attempt at encouragement. "*Ivrae'ia Va'a'kau'lua!*"

The wailing on the battlements turned to a tentative cheer. A single tear rolled down Avora'tru'ivi's face. He was right. She couldn't give up the city for one person, no matter how dear. Even from her great height, she managed to make eye contact with her husband, who gave her a reassuring smile. She did her best to smile back.

"Shut up!" Delilah yelled, backhanding Tamino across the face.

Avora'tru'ivi yelled down, "Touch him again, and your little white rags won't mean much to me!" Avora'tru'ivi pointedly ordered two guns run out from atop the gatehouse. A sudden alarm filled Delilah's eyes as she realized who she was really dealing with.

"You wouldn't fire, not while he's here!" Delilah yelled.

"He's right, I know what to do!" the queen said as she reached for a flint.

"Get us out of here!" Delilah hissed to the slaves, who instantly lifted the sedan chair and began to run, dragging the battered King of Wil'iah behind them.

"Don't give up, Galbi! I'll find a way!" Avora'tru'ivi called after him.

Tamino called back to the ramparts.

"Take heart. I'm not really alone. One with God is a majority!"

Unbeknownst to Avora'tru'ivi, Zhao Bing listened to the whole exchange from a gunport in the outer wall, to which he had sneaked in the disguise of a regular wall soldier. He whispered quietly to himself.

"Well, you are the king's squire, after all. What do squires do but protect their knights? He'll thank you someday. Now is your chance."

CHAPTER THIRTY-NINE

THE WHIFF OF BAGHDAD

Balthcutta

"I don't understand! Why isn't it working?!" The Frouzee paced around her tent in a rage. "The Perfume of Jezebel *always* works! The Whiff of Baghdad never fails! And yet there he stands, eyes closed, a peaceful expression on his face. I don't believe it! She ripped aside a curtain to reveal racks filled with bottles of vile liquids from all corners of the known world.

"Now, it is time for me to prepare my most powerful concoction ever! I must have him, but he must come to me willingly! He *must!*" She whirled around to the two rather scared-looking slaves that stood awaiting her orders.

"Get over here, quickly!" She snapped. "I want Fire of Nineveh! I want Revenge of Lilith! I want the Spirit of Gomorrah! All of it! Now!"

One of the slaves stumbled over to the rack and pulled out a wicked-looking black bottle.

"You Fool!" The Frouzee hissed. That is only Bathsheba's Breath. That's used on easy men! That is not strong enough for this application! I would dock your salary- if you had one!" Delilah cackled, then rushed forward and shoved the slaves aside. One stumbled and fell, and she aimed a sharp kick at his backside.

"Idiots! Out of my way!" She pulled three bejeweled bottles off the highest shelf and rushed over to a steaming cauldron.

"I paid good money for these, and kissed more toads than I would have liked! That Chinese merchant better not have stiffed me!" Her eyes alight with a deranged fire, she stroked the first bottle. "Fire of Nineveh! From far Syria you have come to me across the ocean. Do not fail me now!" With that, she unstopped the floridly red bottle and poured its entire fuming contents into the spitting cauldron.

"That adorable dolt won't even know what hit him!" the Frouzee giggled maniacally as she uncorked the next bottle. "Revenge of Lilith! You snared Adam, and now you will snare his many-times great grandson! Forget that stupid apple! This will get him in far more trouble!"

The two slaves looked at each other, both wide eyed in a mixture of awe and terror. One of the Mongol guards, however, found the entire scene so outlandish that he was unable to stifle a snort of laughter.

Delilah instantly froze and looked up from the cauldron, her vulpine face framed in a wreath of putrid steam emerging from her concoction. Her eyes narrowed, and focused on the purple glass bottle, now empty, that had held the dreaded "Revenge of Lilith." Hefting it over her head, she hurled it at the guard and nailed him right between his eyes, which crossed as he fell to the floor. Both slaves winced and recoiled in terror.

"Nobody laughs at a goddess!" she said, her eyes even more unhinged than they had been moments before. Now, she picked up the last bottle, this one jet black.

"Last time....last time you worked your magic, the Hebrew so-called God was so afraid that he destroyed an entire city! Now you shall destroy the king's defenses!" She drew in a sharp, audible intake of breath as she poured the hissing black liquid into the cauldron, which responded with a volcanic jet of red steam. Grabbing a long iron spoon that hung from a meat hook, she began to stir the potion, humming an unnamed tune that would make a priest shudder.

After a few minutes of this, she ladled some of the dreadful mixture into a large goblet, then flounced over to the slaves.

"This should work instantly. In just a few moments, Wil'iah is ours!" With a mad flip of her hair, she cackled and ran out of the tent.

One of the slaves looked to the other and said, "She's crazy."

"Do you think it will work?"

"Probably. But I really hope not. I was beginning to like that Tamino character."

The second slave got a conspiratorial gleam in his eye and grabbed the forearm of the first. "I hope Wil'iah wins."

"Hush! Not now! We can pray for that victory later. She has eyes and ears everywhere. We will be strangled with a single thread if anyone so much as sees us looking in the wrong direction."

*   *   *

Frouzee Delilah paced toward the still-tied up King Tamino and proffered the goblet. Briseis looked on in fascinated horror, thinking back to the previous time Delilah had encountered Tamino.

All men are the same, Delilah had said. Briseis had believed her then, but Tamino had proved there was at least one exception to the rule. What would happen now?

"Water for the king!" she said, to no response from Tamino, who continued to keep his eyes resolutely shut and whispered something under his breath that she could not quite make out.

The king's eyes opened long enough to lock with Delilah. "I am not thirsty."

"You *will* drink!" She yelled, then snapped her fingers, her wickedly long nails clacking together. The two nearest guards sprang up and forced the king's mouth open. He struggled as Delilah poured in the liquid, now cooled to an acceptable temperature.

"There, that's better!" she said as she paced back and forth.

This potion is fast acting, Briseis thought. *It will only be a matter of moments.*

After a few seconds, the king opened his eyes again and stared directly at the Frouzee with narrowed eyebrows.

The king slowly shook his head. "Did you really think that was going to work?" With a look of complete peace and contentment, he closed his eyes again and began quietly humming a melody. Delilah recognized it from her intelligence training as the old Zebulite hymn "The Pillar of Fire."

"WHAT!!!" Delilah palpably felt rage boil up inside her. She reached up and backhanded the king hard across the face. "Hum all you want, Tamino. But remember this. What the Frouzee wants, she *takes.* You will eventually succumb to my wiles, just like all the others!"

For her part, Briseis regarded the peaceful expression on the king's face, completely unaffected by Delilah's rant.

I don't think he will. Maybe Delilah's wrong. They're not all the same.

CHAPTER FORTY

ZHAO'S CHOICE

Citadel of Balthcutta

Zhao Bing sleeplessly lay in his bed in his chambers in the Citadel. Beneath his night clothes, he wore a close-fitting black leather jerkin, and secreted beneath the bed lay a Ranger's cloak that he had purloined from Tamino's closet. He listened carefully for signs that activity in the Citadel was dying down. There was only one issue- a guard was stationed outside his door at all times.

Zhao noiselessly rose, pulling a wooden ship's belaying pin from beneath his pillow. He crept over to the door and gently pushed it open. The guard stood resolutely outside, his back to the door.

Sorry, Zhao thought to himself, then whacked the guard over the head with the pin. The guard crumpled to the floor.

"You'll thank me later," Zhao hissed as he closed the door behind him and stole out of the hall. He knew a way to get out of the castle – and the city -- without being spotted by any further guards. Coming to a bookcase against a wall, he strained to read the titles in the moonlight. Finally, he found the one he was looking for – a copy of Sun Tzu's *The Art of War.* He pushed the book back into the shelf, and was satisfied to hear a mechanism click. The entire bookcase swung out into the hall, revealing an unlit staircase that proceeded into uncertain gloom. Zhao closed the case behind him, lit a torch that he carried in his pack, and proceeded down the staircase, and the miles of tunnels that followed it. Finally, he reached his destination- a dead end in the tunnel with a slate roof. He tentatively pushed on one of the slate tiles above him; it gradually gave way and opened to reveal a square of stars. Zhao hauled himself out of the opening and found himself just outside the outer walls, hidden from view by a crook in the wall.

"Here I come, Your Faithfulness," he whispered to himself.

CHAPTER FORTY-ONE

MILCAH

Citadel of Balthcutta

"Where are we going?" asked little Princess Judith plaintively as she rubbed sleep from her eyes. The flickering torches that dimly lit the way down the hall delineated leaping, monstrous shadows on the cold stones. Judith gasped slightly as one shadow seemed almost to be a clawed hand reaching for her.

"Hush, child," hissed Milcah. "Your momma asked me to take you somewhere safe."

"But isn't this castle safe?"

Milcah rolled her eyes. "Not any more, sweetie. Your daddy has been captured."

Tears welled in Judith's eyes. "But…but Momma—"

"Shhhhh!" Milcah raised a finger to her thin lips. "Your momma has a whole army to deal with. She doesn't need to worry about you as well."

"But—"

"That's enough! If you are going to be safe, you need to be quiet!"

Just then, Milcah snapped straight with a start as footsteps and the creak of armor rang down the hall. Judith recognized the tall, thickset man approaching them as Vreva'zaua, a good friend of her daddy's. She felt Milcah's grip tighten on her hand- so much so that it almost hurt.

As he neared the pair, the knight dipped his head in a show of respect. "Madam Milcah," he said friendlily, his eyes twinkling in the leaping torchlight. "What brings you out at such a late hour?"

Milcah's face contorted in a smile that didn't quite reach her eyes. "Her highness couldn't sleep. She's missing her Daddy. *Aren't* you, sweetie?"

Judith nodded, a tear leaking out of one eye.

Milcah continued, "So I thought I would take her for a walk."

Judith opened her mouth. "I thought you sai"— her train of thought cut short as Milcah doubled the pressure on her hand, bringing more tears to her eyes.

"But we were just headed back to bed. Are you planning a rescue operation?" Milcah asked, her eyes briefly flashing out the nearby window towards the walls, flinching as a cannon boomed in the distance.

The knight nodded, a determined cast to his face. "It's not going to be easy, but we're not going to let Tamino stay in that vixen's clutches for long."

"See sweetie? Your Daddy will be home very soon. No need to fret!" Milcah cooed, then ruffled Judith's curly hair with her other hand. "Well, I won't keep you from your duty," she said, then began to walk down the hallway, Judith reluctantly following her.

Vreva'zaua dipped his head again. "Evening, madam," he said, then continued on his way down the hall.

"If Daddy's going to be home soon, then why are we leaving?" Judith asked.

Milcah whirled around, her flickering shadow on the wall looming over the princess. "Not another word from you, child!"

※ ※ ※

Avora'tru'ivi fought back a yawn as she forced herself to examine a battered map yet again. She hadn't slept in almost 24 hours, but she knew she wouldn't be able to rest while Tamino languished in captivity. Combating the horrific visions of Delilah's designs that danced in her head, the queen focused her attention on a tent hastily drawn on the map and circled in red ink.

"There's that witch's tent," growled Teva'ivani, the shadow of her sharp features splayed across the map. Her heart sinking, Avora'tru'ivi noted that the tent was surrounded on all sides by Mongol yurts, which inevitably housed vast numbers of heavily-armed guards. The entire tent complex was more than a mile from the walls, separated from the city's fortifications by forest of other defenses and suspected booby traps.

"A frontal assault would never work. It would only serve to weaken the city's defenses," the queen sighed.

"What if we tried to attack from the rear?" asked the general as she tapped a bony finger on a blank portion of the map.

"That would require that we sneak a significant force out of the city. I can't see how that would work. We're surrounded...*unless...*"

The queen's epiphany was interrupted by Vreva'zaua, who tromped into the room and slammed his sword down on the table. Noticing the queen at the table, he immediately snapped to attention and rendered the military salute.

"I see that none of the royal family can sleep tonight."

"What do you mean?" the queen asked, her brows furrowing.

"I just ran into Her Majesty and her handmaid Milcah. They were out for a walk. Apparently the princess can't sleep either."

"That's odd," said the queen. "Judy doesn't know about her dad yet. I'm hoping we can resolve this situation quickly without alarming her."

Avora'tru'ivi noticed a hint of concern cloud the normally-jovial knight's eyes. "I...I guess Milcah told her anyway. She said it was the reason they were out walking. I told them we were going to attempt a rescue...then again..."

"What?" asked the queen, butterflies beginning to flutter in her stomach.

"The princess seemed to think they were going somewhere else, but Milcah quickly corrected her."

Her nervousness exploding into full-blown panic, Avora'tru'ivi jumped up from the table. "Where were they?"

"In the tapestry hall two stories below. They seemed to be heading in the opposite direction to me."

"We need to get there, *now*. You're coming with me." The queen said, her heart hammering against her ribs. She hastily grabbed her saber and ran out the door, the somewhat bemused knight following her.

※　※　※

Milcah's clogs, wrapped in sound-deadening cloth, barely made a sound as the handmaid and the little princess hurried down yet another stone hallway. Judith, increasingly confused, had to run to keep as the bird-like woman's iron grip dragged her along.

"I'm tired," complained Judith.

"What did I say about you speaking?" hissed Milcah.

"I'm sorry," the little princess said, dipping her head in shame.

The two continued on in stony silence, descending a spiral staircase before approaching a heavy, arrow-looped door that led to the walls outside.

"When is Daddy coming home?"

Milcah lightly slapped Judith's hand. "Hush, child! We need to leave!"

"But you sai---"

Milcah whirled around and stooped to the princess' level, the moonlight filtering in through a nearby window throwing her pointed features into sharp relief. Her teeth bared, she opened her mouth to say something, but before she could, her eyes opened wide at the sound of grinding steel.

"Yes, just what *did* you say, Milcah?" a voice rang out.

Judith whirled around, wrenching herself out of the handmaid's grip.

"Momma!" she said, breaking into a wide smile as she ran toward the queen, wrapping her arms into a tight embrace around her armored knees.

Milcah recoiled and drew herself to her full height, her gaunt features appearing nearly skeletal in the harsh moonlight. She raised her head slightly, almost defiantly, before saying, "Yes, your majesty?"

"Where were you taking her, Milcah?"

Avora'tru'ivi noticed the handmaid's eyes briefly dart over to the window that flanked her to her right. Tightening her grip on the saber's hilt, the queen repeated her inquiry.

"Answer the question, Milcah."

The handmaid's eyes narrowed to slits, and her jaw clenched as her severe mouth resolved itself into a thin iron line.

Vreva'zaua stepped out from behind the queen, his hand pointedly on the hilt of his sword. "Why did you tell her that His Faithfulness has been captured? We were trying not to worry her."

"*One small mistake.*" The serpentine hiss of Milcah's voice was barely audible even in the quiet hallway.

"*Excuse me?*" Avora'tru'ivi advanced toward Milcah, raising herself to her full commanding height. Milcah began edging toward the window, then turned to face the queen.

Throwing back her shoulders and raising her head to an imperious angle, the handmaid spoke in a haughty, remorseless, steely tone.

"All hail Baal."

With that, she turned and hurled herself through the window, the queen flinching at the auditory assault of shattering glass. In a moment, she was gone.

CHAPTER FORTY-TWO

AVORA'TRU'IVI TO THE RESCUE

Citadel of Balthcutta

*A*fter tucking Judith back in and entrusting her care to Vreva'zaua, Avora'tru'ivi returned to her chambers to prepare for her next mission. She was buckling on her armor when she heard a knock at the door.

"Enter," she said urgently.

The door opened to reveal General Teva'ivani, whose features looked no less severe than they had in the planning room.

"What is it?"

"Zhao Bing is missing."

"What!?" Avora'tru'ivi, still recovering from the shock of Milcah's betrayal, found herself slipping into panic once again.

"The guard was found unconscious outside his chambers. He wasn't inside."

"Did Milcah get to him, too?" Avora'tru'ivi threw up her arms in frustration.

"No, I don't think so. He left this behind."

Teva'ivani produced a note. Avora'tru'ivi urgently snatched it out of her hand.

Tell the queen not to be upset. I'm doing this for His Faithfulness.

"Tell the queen not to be upset! That's rich!" Avora'tru'ivi flung the note on the ground. "I know it's our job to take care of him, but sometimes, he tasks me. Of course I'm upset. Now *two* important monarchs are at risk!"

"I'd tell you not to put a third at risk with this mission, but I know better," the general replied.

Avora'tru'ivi's eyes flashed dangerously to Teva'ivani.

"Don't even try to stop me."

A few minutes later, Avora'tru'ivi exited the Citadel and city, ironically by the same passages that Zhao Bing had used earlier that evening, though she was not aware of the coincidence. Finding herself in the crook of the wall outside the city, she drew a black cloak around herself and began to steal forward, using the Wil'iahn ranger camouflage techniques that Tamino had once taught her. Gradually, she approached the perimeter of the Frouzean camp, taking extra care not to make noise. Confident she hadn't been noticed by Delilah's listless, drunken sentries, she moved from shadow to shadow within the camp, painstakingly picking her way towards the tent where Tamino was suspected to be held. Suddenly, though, she tripped over a tent peg, and stifled a curse.

The noise was enough to attract the attention of a Frouzean guard, who staggered over, his bloodshot eyes widening as he realized that an intruder was present. Avora'tru'ivi fumbled at her cloak, trying to withdraw her saber as the soldier inexorably approached.

Suddenly, however, a whistling sound filled the air, and the man fell face-forward, a wickedly-sharp throwing star buried in the back of his head.

Starting in surprise, Avora'tru'ivi flashed her eyes to the black figure that blended in with the shadow of another nearby tent. The figure beckoned to her.

Looking to either side to make sure they weren't being watched, Avora'tru'ivi darted across the distance between the tents, drawing her dagger. The figure pulled her into the shadow, then removed the mask that had obscured his face.

Avora'tru'ivi nearly dropped the dagger.

"Zhao! You have no idea how upset I am with you right now!"

"Well, I did just save your life!"

"Yes, but I could have done it myself!"

"You can't do this all by yourself."

"Listen, you need to leave and get back to the city right now. That's an order."

"I've already broken one order tonight, what's another? I'm finally getting a chance to serve my country."

"China is your country, and as Galbi told you, your highest duty is to stay alive to give them hope."

"Wil'iah is my country now. Your people rescued me when I was just a child. Now I have the chance to return the favor. You and I both know it isn't right for me to stand on the sidelines while your people fight and die to keep me alive. That's no life worth living. You and Tamino are in this mess in the first place because China wasn't able to hold off the Mongols. I must do something to repay that debt. If I die in this war, China will go on without me. But if Wil'iah falls while I hide in a bedroom, I will never forgive myself. Please allow me just this once chance to set things right."

Avora'tru'ivi looked at the ground. "Zhao, I realize that if I were in your position, I would feel the same way. I cannot in good conscience stop you."

"Well, that's a good thing, because, if you did, you and Tamino would never escape this camp without a diversion."

"What do you propose?"

"I've been snooping around here for a while- after all, I'm Chinese, so I easily pass for one of the Yuan soldiers. I couldn't believe my luck when I discovered that their entire ammunition supply is stored in one big supply dump."

"That seems impossibly dumb."

"Remember that this is Frouzea we're dealing with," Zhao grinned.

"Are you thinking what I'm thinking?" Avora'tru'ivi responded.

Zhao withdrew a length of fuse and a match from his pack.

"I believe so," he grinned.

Avora'tru'ivi pulled the young man in for a hug.

"Take care of yourself," she hissed, then kissed him on the cheek.

CHAPTER FORTY-THREE

DARK PLACES OF FEAR

Imperia Army Camp, Nowra, outside Balthcutta

Jamino silently strained at the chains, but they only dug further into his wrists. Surveying the tent, he counted at least four guards inside the tent- and those were just the ones within his field of vision. With some relief, he noticed that these men were looking somewhat drowsy, but outside, there were undoubtedly more. With a sinking feeling, he realized that he was well and truly trapped. A shudder ran down his spine as he wondered what the wicked woman had planned for him. Surely nothing good.

All his efforts had come to this, and he had failed. The Frouzee's armies had overwhelmed the backcountry, and now Balthcutta was on the ropes. Her armies had probably taken other parts of the country as well. Suddenly overwhelmed by the specter of his failure, Tamino sank to his knees.

*If only my father were here...*he thought.

Through a small hole in the roof of the tent, Tamino could espy a single star.

I'm so sorry, Father. I tried. I tried so hard. And yet it was not enough. A single tear ran down his face, shaking as he trembled.

The star above seemed to pulse, almost imperceptibly, with a stronger light, and, somewhere behind him, Tamino could have sworn he heard a voice. In the gloom, its timbre was almost imperceptibly soft, but, at the same time, it pulsed with incredible power. Tamino shuddered involuntarily as its words washed over him.

Who says your Father *isn't here?*

Tamino whipped his head around, his eyes straining in the darkness to see whoever spoke. But he could make out no form behind the pole to which he was chained.

I must be going crazy, thought the king.

Suddenly, with a jolt, a memory flashed before his thought, almost as though it had come from an external source. Even Vrenga'ava'zora'vaua had had dark moments such as this, when he too had faced the chains of Gath. And in those moments he had not been alone. The king's mouth quivered as an unexplainable warmth began to fill his heart, and the inside of the tent seemed to grow inexplicably brighter.

Again, he seemed to hear a voice- quiet and tender, but full of strength.

Who was with the three boys in the furnace of fire? Who was with Daniel in the den of lions? Who was with Elijah in the cave? Who led Peter out of the prison? Who was with your father Vrenga'ava'zora'vaua in the square of Gath?

Tamino worked his mouth, trying to find words to answer the voice. In the end, only two came out.

"My God," he said under his breath, trying not to draw the attention of the guards.

Regaining his composure, Tamino silently tried to open his thought, as he had been taught to do as a child.

God, I am so sorry. I have failed thee. It was not for lack of effort, but ultimately, I simply wasn't strong enough, wasn't brave enough, to defend your kingdom.

A third time, the voice spoke.

Little one. Did you really think the defense of Wil'iah was solely your responsibility? Did you really think that by your will or your animal courage you could hold back the forces of darkness? Did you think that the kingdom was yours to lose?

His eyes welling again, Tamino trembled. Though he still could see nothing, he palpably felt surrounded by an incredible force, and his heart leapt with light.

I was with your people at the Red Sea, and on the long Maka'ivi, and I am with you now. Dear one, start always with the Truth, not the lie. What is the truth about my children?

Tamino's voice was a quivering whisper.

"The truth is that God's children are free, always."

And is it the sword and lance that guarantees that freedom?

"They are your instruments on Earth, when necessary."

Does the Almighty really need a piece of metal or a staff of wood to uphold his power?

His mouth agape, Tamino could not answer.

Dear one, the truth is that all of my children are free right now, because there is no power opposed to me. Do you understand this?

Finding his voice again, Tamino meekly answered, "Yes, Lord."

Then can these chains, forged from a lie, truly hold you? Do they mean anything next to the might of the omnipotent God?

It was then that the realization hit Tamino. The chains were material. God and his children were spiritual.

Get up.

A sharp cracking sound filled the tent, and Tamino started with alarm, breaking his reverie as he rose to his feet. Sharply casting his eyes about, he looked for the source of the sound. But there was no movement in the room. He noticed with surprise that the guards had crumpled to the ground, deep in slumber. But something about the chains felt different. Tamino felt the wrist restraints with his fingers. A long, jagged crack ran through both of them.

Once again the voice sounded, but this time, it thundered with all the glorious strength of the mighty Pacific. As its dulcet tones whirled around Tamino, he suddenly felt very small.

Remember, my son, that you are always free, and that it is not your responsibility to save your country. I have called thee by thy name. Thou art mine. You are compassed about with angels of deliverance. I am with you, always.

As suddenly as the light had seemed to fill the room, it was gone. Snapping out of his reverie, Tamino realized with a start that he was falling. As the wrist and ankle restraints broke away, Tamino tumbled into a heap on the ground, struggling to regain his footing after being restrained to the pole for so long. Panic momentarily gripped his heart, which still burned with the unexplained warmth, as he realized that the clanking of his armor would likely wake the guards. Yet, a quick glance indicated that they still slumbered on, oblivious to the miracle that had just occurred under their snoring noses.

Grateful for their unexplained stupor, Tamino gathered himself and prepared to walk out of the tent. His instincts told him to be careful of the guards outside, but something seemed to tell him simply to trust.

Yet, just as his hand reached forward to pull the tent flaps open, they were wrenched apart, and an altogether different light assaulted his eyes.

"Going somewhere?" his least-favorite voice sounded, dripping with an odd mixture of derision and triumph. Standing before him, flanked on either side by two of the fearsome Homeric Guards, stood Delilah, her smirking face and deranged eyes framed in the lurid cobra headdress crowned with two ivory horns and a gold disk.

A hissing sound escaped her lips that made Tamino's skin crawl. His eyes cast about for a means of escape, but as he backed back into the tent, they only found the once-slumbering guards stirring around him. At least the chains were broken. But that didn't help him much, unarmed in this manner.

Suddenly, a ripping sound filled the room as a blade slashed the fabric of the tent. Starting in surprise, the Frouzee turned to the gash, and grimaced as Avora'tru'ivi, bedecked in full armor and wearing two sword scabbards, charged through the opening.

"STAY. AWAY. FROM. MY. GALBI!"

Avora'tru'ivi's fist swung like lighting and slammed directly into the Frouzee's face with an audible crack. The empress's eyes crossed, and she toppled to the floor. Yet it seemed the queen was too late, for one of the guards held a spear securely to Tamino's throat.

"Drop your weapons, or your precious king dies," he growled.

Stay away from my Galbi!

"Not today!" yelled Tamino, grabbing the guard's thickset arm that restrained him and, with rapid precision, twisting the man around and hurling him to the ground. Grabbing the spear as it clattered to the floor, Tamino ran towards the queen and declared, "I am married to the greatest woman in the world."

The queen cast him a brief radiant smile, then hefted her saber to meet the onslaught of three guards. Sensing movement behind him, Tamino whirled around in time to parry the thrust of a Frouzean short sword with the spear staff. Soon, the two monarchs stood back to back, facing a steadily advancing ring of some ten Frouzean guards.

"You forgot this!" hissed the queen as she reached down with her free arm to her second scabbard. With the rasp of steel filling the tent, she unsheathed the Zrain'de'zhang and tossed it to her husband, who deftly caught it as he cast the Frouzean spear aside. The sword of

Vrenga'ava'zora'vaua gleamed in the flickering torchlight, seeming to reflect their feeble rays back with its own renewed strength. The guards recognized the weapon, their eyes growing large.

"Yes, the Zrain'de'zhang, sword of light, the divine weapon that fell from Heaven to forge the Faithful Kingdom of Wil'iah! Look on it, and despair!" yelled the queen. Her words were punctuated by a sudden sound like thunder that shook the tent. The guards, seemingly forgetting themselves, dropped their spears and ran.

The queen grabbed Tamino's arm and yanked him toward her.

"We must make haste. I managed to sneak in here unnoticed, but surely our friends here will raise the alarm. If we are to make it out alive, we must fly as we have never flown before," she hissed.

His heart still filled with warmth, Tamino nodded, but with an easy smile, replied, "It will all be alright, dear heart. For we are already free."

Sensing movement in her peripheral vision, Avora'tru'ivi whirled around to see the Frouzee Delilah stirring on the ground. She hefted her saber and raised it over her head, ready to strike a killing blow, when she felt a gentle hand on her arm.

"This is not who we are, Avora." Said Tamino.

"I have had more than my fill of her!"

"Remember the Sixth Commandment."

Avora'tru'ivi rolled her eyes.

"What happens to her is between her and God. She will get her justice without us losing ours."

With a heavy sigh, the queen lowered the saber. "Fine. But if she pulls something else, I am not responsible for my actions."

For his part, Tamino turned to squarely face the squirming empress, who had only just now fully woken up. Her eyes focused on the king of Wil'iah and widened, the flickering torchlight illuminating the desperation that filled them.

"Don't go, Tamino! I love you!" she cried.

"That's it!" Avora'tru'ivi growled under her breath as she hefted her saber. Tamino gently placed a staying hand on her shoulder, then turned back to face the "eternal empress."

The king pushed his shoulders back, and with a determined set to his face, opened his mouth.

"You know, for such a famous temptress, you're *really* bad at it."

With that, Tamino spun on his heel and strode purposefully out the tear in the tent, leaving the Frouzee sputtering on the floor.

"I HATE YOU!!!"

"For such a famous temptress, you're really bad at it."

CHAPTER FORTY-FOUR

FOR CHINA

Imperial Army Camp, Nowra, outside Balthcutta

Zhao stole towards the ammunition dump in the center of the Frouzean camp. Great piles of cannon balls, naphtha bombs, and kegs of gunpowder lay strewn about in a disorderly fashion, but the whole assemblage was brightly lit with an array of torches.

Casting the black cloak aside, Zhao donned a Mongol uniform he had stolen from a supply tent. Then, relying on sheer audacity, he walked over towards a pyramid of gunpowder barrels, doing his best to discreetly unroll the fuse into the long grass as he went. He confidently swaggered up to a gunpowder barrel, as if he owned the entire camp, and, at first, the other guards in the area didn't seem to pay any attention to him. However, when Zhao knelt to tie the end of the fuse to a barrel, a Mongol captain began to approach him.

"Hey, you, just what do you think you are doing!?"

"Oh, well, I was, inspecting the barrel to make sure it wasn't leaking."

The captain's eyes narrowed. "I haven't seen you before. What's your rank?"

"I am a Jagutu-iin-Darga."

"A Jagutu-iin-Darga would have no business inspecting barrels," the Captain retorted. Zhao's stomach fell.

I should have studied Mongol ranks more closely.

Suddenly, the Captain's eyes fell on the fuse that snaked from the barrel through the grass. His eyes narrowed.

"What is this!?"

Zhao was running out of options, and he knew it. In a quick, blinding motion, he drew his dagger and lunged forward, burying the weapon in the captain's stomach. The captain toppled forward with a gurgling sound, instantly capturing the attention of the other guards. Zhao leapt over the corpse of the captain and raced to the end of the fuse, producing the flint and striking it. He let out a breath he didn't realize he'd been holding as the end of the fuse ignited into life, but, when looked up, he was surrounded by a ring of spears.

"Just what is this all about?" sneered one of the guards.

A smile crept up Zhao's face as his eyes caught the glint of the flame as it raced up the fuse toward the barrel of gunpowder. He turned to squarely face the guards, stood up straight, and thrust out his chin proudly.

"For China."

CHAPTER FORTY-FIVE

TAMINO'S ESCAPE

Imperial Army camp, Nowra, outside Balthcutta

Once they were both outside the tent, the queen took a second to focus on her husband's face. Something seemed…different. His eyes were not those of someone who had been held prisoner and publicly humiliated. Instead, they were full of an indescribable light.

"What happened?" she asked.

Tamino smiled again. "We do not have time to speak of it here. But our escape is assured. Let us go before more guards arrive."

"I think they will have…other matters to attend to," the queen grinned.

"What do you mean?"

"We have made…certain arrangements."

As if on cue, an ear-splitting explosion shook the earth, and the surrounding camp was, for a moment, lit as though it were noonday.

"That should keep them occupied for a while!" The queen turned around and shook a fist at the now-blazing ammunition depot in the center of the Frouzean camp. All around them, panicked Frouzean soldiers ran in every direction, heedless of the two outsiders in their midst.

The two monarchs ran to a wild-eyed, stolen Mongol horse, which Avora'tru'ivi had hitched in the shadow of another tent. They quickly mounted, and Avora'tru'ivi dug in her heels. The horse reared, then tore off at a full gallop.

As their horse thundered through the camp at a full gallop, Tamino whispered in Avora'tru'ivi's ear.

"Does this remind you of anything?"

The queen smiled, remembering the first time they had ridden a horse together as they rescued the Scroll of St. Thomas from the clutches of Hosania.

"I care a lot more about you than that scroll, you know."

The walls of Balthcutta loomed ever larger in the darkness as the horse seemed to fly across the blackened plain, flecks of foam splatting onto the monarch's faces. For a moment, it seemed like they might make a clean break, when Tamino suddenly forced Avora'tru'ivi's head down, just in time to miss an arrow that whizzed overhead into the azure sky beyond.

"Some friends decided to tag along!" he hissed, hazarding a glance at five Mongol riders that had appeared behind them, each of them expert marksmen with the dreaded bows.

Avora'tru'ivi swerved left and right to avoid the barrage, but it was getting too close for comfort. One arrow managed to fly through her voluminous hair, its feathers getting tangled, leaving the arrow hanging from the queen's midnight locks.

"I like it. You look fierce." Tamino said as he ducked to avoid another arrow.

"It's certainly better than that stupid snake hat," came the reply.

Suddenly, one of the riders gave a gurgled cry as an arrow, coming from the opposite direction, embedded itself in his chest.

"We're in range of the walls," Avora'tru'ivi hissed. In front of them, Tamino could now clearly make out the St. Thomas Gate, as well as the drawbridge that lowered with painful deliberateness to give them passage over the moat. Despite the danger, the riders behind them continued their relentless pursuit, steadily gaining on their quarry.

Avora'tru'ivi realized that, at the rate they were going, the bridge wouldn't be fully lowered by the time they reached it, and they couldn't afford to wait, a fact punctuated by yet another arrow.

Time to remember your dressage tricks, she thought. As they reached the edge of the moat, she coaxed the horse into a flying leap that just barely cleared the edge of the still-lowering drawbridge. The horse and its two riders plunged down the sloping side of the bridge, which suddenly stopped its descent and began to raise again, barring entry to their pursuers, who came under a barrage of fire from the battlements. Avora'tru'ivi and Tamino roared through the gatehouse, passing beneath the deadly portcullises and murder holes, before emerging in the inner ward, where they were greeted by a huge crowd of cheering soldiers.

After dismounting, Tamino pulled Avora'tru'ivi into a tight embrace.

"What would I do without you to keep rescuing me?" he said.

"Let's try not to find out," the queen replied.

"I love you," Tamino said, then leaned down for a kiss.

CHAPTER FORTY-SIX

REUNITED

Citadel of Balthcutta

"Daddy!" Judith scrambled out of bed and hurled herself across the room at her father, who scooped her up and pulled the little princess into a tight embrace.

"How's my brave, sweet girl?" asked Tamino as he gently bounced Judith.

"How did you get away from that mean lady?" she asked.

"Well, God helped me, and, with some more help from your momma, we got away."

"Where is Momma?"

"Right here, sweetie!" another voice rang out as the queen strode into the room. Taking Judith from Tamino's arms, she gently laid her back down in the bed and kissed the princess on the forehead. "It's past your bedtime, sweetheart." The queen arranged the princess' stuffed animals around her. "Now, look at this! You've got your kangaroo, and your wombat, and your koala, all watching over you! Good night, sweetie!" The queen bent down and gave the princess one more hug.

"Good night, Momma. Thank you for saving Daddy." Judith said drowsily, her eyelids growing heavy.

Tamino pulled Avora'tru'ivi in for another hug. "Yes, thank you, if I haven't mentioned that already."

Vreva'zaua grinned at the queen. "I'd bet that Delilah didn't know what hit her!"

"You have no idea!" chuckled Tamino. "I always said I'd never hit a lady –"

"But I have no such compunctions," finished Avora'tru'ivi. "And, as far as I am concerned, that *pagh* is no lady." With that, she walked back out of the room, blowing one more kiss to the now-slumbering princess.

Tamino followed her out the door. As soon as it had closed, Avora'tru'ivi placed a staying hand on his shoulder and began to speak.

"Galbi, there's something you need to know."

"What?"

"While you were gone, she tried to take Judy."

"Delilah?" Tamino's eyebrows narrowed as he clenched his fist.

"Yes, I believe so, but she had help. She has had an agent in our midst this entire time."

"I can't say I'm surprised. Frouzea's intelligence network is apparently much more extensive than we thought. Who was it?"

Avora'tru'ivi winced. "Milcah."

Tamino's staggered back, looking like he'd been struck. His eyes, normally calm and reflective, filled with a cold fury as his jaw worked helplessly. Finally gaining his composure, he clenched his teeth and growled,

"Where is she?"

"She is dead."

"She'd better be grateful I wasn't here," Tamino said, an uncharacteristic note of hatred creeping into his voice.

"Galbi, don't let her win from beyond the grave. I was just as mad as you are, but, in the end, Judy's safe, and that's all that matters."

Tamino closed his eyes, clenched his fists, and took a deep breath, the inner battle written plainly on his face.

"Galbi, remember who we are."

Tamino slowly nodded, then opened his eyes again. Avora'tru'ivi was relieved to see the old twinkle tentatively flare back into life.

"Now, I think you needed to know that, but, putting that behind us, you have some explaining to do, Galbi. I came prepared to bust you out of your chains, but it appears you beat me to it."

Avora'tru'ivi was surprised to see the last vestiges of darkness in her husband's eyes instantly vanish, replaced with a wistful, faraway, awed expression.

"Somebody beat you to it, but it wasn't me."

"Who? Did that little maid Briseis finally come to her senses?"

Tamino laughed. "No, but I haven't given up on her yet." The mirth disappeared almost as soon as it had arrived, replaced once again by the serious wonderment. "Do you remember what happened to Peter in the prison?"

"Of course. Everyone knows that story."

"Peter wasn't making it up."

Avora'tru'ivi took a step back, stunned.

"What do you mean, Galbi?"

"Take heart, valiant Queen of the Faithful Kingdom. For we are compassed about with songs of deliverance. This fight was never ours to begin with. And there's only one possible outcome. Darkness and chains, as always, are no match for the Truth."

A look of wonder crossed Avora'tru'ivi's face.

"Then I am confident he will be protected, too."

"Who?"

Avora'tru'ivi looked at the floor. "Galbi, Zhao Bing snuck out to try to save you while I was dealing with Milcah."

"What!?"

"He was responsible for the explosion that gave us the diversion we needed. He said he could handle it, but I fear the worst. That said, just as God delivered you from Delilah's chains, he can protect Zhao."

Tamino cast a glance back in the direction of the Frouzean camp, a faraway look filling his eyes.

"We can know that for him. I'm infuriated that he would leave the safety of the castle, but at the same time, I'm proud of him."

Avora'tru'ivi followed his gaze into the distance.

"God save him."

CHAPTER FORTY-SEVEN

WHISPERED HOPE

Imperial Army camp, Nowra, outside Balthcutta

Seracles' snores cut through the predawn gloom as he slumbered away, heedless of the irregular cannon fire that periodically erupted around him. He did wake with a start, however, when a long-nailed hand passed a jar of cloying salts under his wide nostrils.

"What!?" he grunted, reaching for the short sword he kept under his pillow at all times. As his befuddled eyes came into focus, they saw Delilah looming over him.

"We're leaving."

"Leaving? For where?"

"We've done all we can do here. Our presence is needed elsewhere. I have informed Minos and his lieutenant, Achish. They agree that the situation here is under control. Pack your bags for a long trip."

"Is the whole retinue coming?"

"No. The illusion must be maintained that I am still here."

"But, will you be able to travel…comfortably?"

"As *comfortably* as you will be able to orchestrate," Delilah sniffed as she imperiously raised her chin. "Sometimes, even goddesses have to make sacrifices."

※ ※ ※

Meanwhile, on the other side of the camp, a group of Chinese soldiers excitedly whispered in the shadow of a tent.

"This campaign is getting worse and worse. Now, the Wil'iahns have destroyed our ammunition supply. I'm beginning to think we're not going to win," one of them said.

"Isn't that what we're hoping for?" another said.

"Yes. The emperor lives, and Wil'iah holds out hope for a free China. If they prevail, we might be saved!" a third soldier interjected.

"Hush! We can't speak of that here. Who knows who might hear?"

Suddenly, another figure loomed out of the darkness. The Chinese soldiers jumped back, startled and prepared to make excuses for their treasonous speech. However, as the figure stepped out of the shadows into the light of the moon, they relaxed slightly as they recognized a fellow Han Chinese soldier, probably no older than twenty-one.

He leaned forward and whispered, "Yes, the emperor indeed lives. I've seen him myself."

CHAPTER FORTY-EIGHT

THE HOME ARMY

Barranbinya Nation, Maranoa, eastern Wil'iah

"*W*e're almost there," Jiemba hissed at the tired group of men and women as they trudged through low-lying prairie grasses. Ahead of them lay the rolling hills that Vreva'iava, a soldier in Jiemba's detachment, vaguely remembered hearing about in a geography lesson as a boy. Apart from guessing they were somewhere near the border with the Judgate of Maranoa, Vreva'iava had no idea where they were. Jiemba squinted at two of the hills to their left and sang his song once again beneath his breath. After visibly thinking for a minute, he stood straight up and pointed. "That way, next." He flatly stated.

"Can someone please tell me what's going on?" Vreva'iava recognized the voice as coming from Tirzah Va'i'teva, a woman from the neighboring village. "We've been traveling now for two weeks. We haven't had a square meal in that long. I don't know about you, but I'm sick of running. When are we going to turn and fight? This isn't how Wil'iahns respond to invasions."

Jiemba turned back to her. The Wiradjuri tracker's eyes narrowed conspiratorially. "We're almost there. You just have to trust me. Nobody is running away from anything. I cannot yet reveal what the plan is, but rest assured that there is one."

"How can you expect us to follow a plan we don't know? I don't think there really is a plan. This defense was doomed to failure from the very beginning," said another disgruntled woman in the group as she wiped perspiration from her brow.

Suddenly, the oppressive heat of the downs was punctuated by the blast of a conch shell. The heads of the bedraggled travel group immediately snapped to attention. Jiemba regarded them with a triumphant smirk.

"Just over the rise now."

Vreva'iava scrambled over the rise, took a deep breath, and looked down.

His heart soared as his eyes focused on a great fluttering battle-flag. Beside it flapped another banner displaying a Star of Wil'iah emblazoned on a green background.

The Home Army.

Surrounding the central battle flag, stretching out nearly as far as the eye could see, was a vast blanket of tents, with a forest of pikes holding aloft dozens of standards emblazoned with the coats of arms of various units of

Wil'iah's national militia. The air was filled with the whinnies of horses, the groans of camels, and the clinks and clangs of blacksmith's hammers hitting home on half-forged weapons. He felt a hand slap his back as Jiemba joined him on the rise.

"What did I tell you?" Jiemba's eyes flashed as he recognized someone in the crowd. Vreva'iava struggled to keep up as Jiemba bounded down the hill toward an enormous, imposing woman who stood like a statue next to the giant battle-flag. Her hair was pulled into a severe bun crowned with a wicked, burnished spike that, like her armor, almost blindingly reflected the light of the noonday sun. Strapped across her back was a gigantic two-handed sword, while her fist held an eight-foot-tall spear in an iron grip. The woman's steely eyes seemed to bore right through him but relaxed as she recognized Jiemba.

"Good, you're here! I think that's everybody." When the woman spoke, her voice reverberated through the camp like distant thunder. Vreva'iava squinted, trying to make out a badge pinned to the woman's breastplate. He sharply drew an intake of breath as he recognized the symbol.

Jiemba snapped into a military salute, then turned to his ragged group. "May I present Lady Deborah of Dhirari, Captain of Zebulon."

The leader of all of Wil'iah's armed forces.

Two knights holding conch shells stepped up to flank the captain. Bringing the shells to their lips, they let off three long blasts, which were punctuated by a thunderous roll on a giant drum behind them. The camp sprang into action as the scattered standards around the site began to coalesce around the central clearing with the flag. Soldiers streamed out of the tents to take anticipatory stances around the clearing. Deborah cleared her throat, and their excited chatter instantly fell silent.

"Citizens of the Kingdom of Wil'iah!" she bellowed. "You have answered your country's call to duty and come many miles to this place, not knowing where your guides led. Undoubtedly, you wondered what was happening, if there was a plan, and why your forces were running from the enemy rather than charging directly into battle. Let me now reassure you that a secret plan for the defense of our nation, prepared long before that vixen in Gath ever appeared in a puff of red smoke, has put itself into action. Our forces were not running. They were gathering. This is the Barranbinya Muster Point of the Home Army of Wil'iah. There are six other such points flanking us to north and south."

A surprised murmur ran through the crowd.

"It is true that the Imperial Army of Frouzea and their Mongol allies have roared through our beloved backcountry, seemingly sowing destruction and fire wherever they went. Village after village has fallen, and farm after farm has been burnt to a crisp. But in their flush of apparent victory, Ajax the Lesser's Army has run headlong into a well-laid trap."

A gasp rose from the assembled armies.

"By putting our villages and farmlands to the torch, we have denied the enemy the supplies he needs to sustain his conquest. He has advanced so far into our territory that he is now too distant to be immediately resupplied from the empire. And, unbeknownst to him, we have arrayed forces in secret that now will emerge to destroy his supply caravans before they can reach him. The great city of Wagga Wagga has held fast, and the highly-trained forces of the Order of the Flame of Zebulon are even now emerging from their hidden fortress in the Snowy

Mountains to choke off the enemy's lifeline. Ajax's forces are exhausted, hungry, and thirsty. And now, our great game shall come to an end. We have arranged our forces into two great jaws that now surround the Imperial Army on all sides- and outnumber it. Now, these jaws shall snap shut and smite the enemy!"

A great cheer rose from the surrounding forces, followed by a guttural rendition of the war grunt, "Hiu!"

"Now we must take a muster-call of our forces," Deborah continued. She placed an open palm beside her, which was immediately filled by a scroll held at the ready by an aide. Deborah snapped the scroll open and began to call out the names of the nations assigned to this muster point.

"Barundji!"

"Gunu!"

"Barranbinya!"

"Wongaibon!"

"Wailwan!"

"Kullilla!"

"Budjari!"

"Kunja!"

"Upper Wiradjuri!"

"Yuwaalaraay!"

"Yuwaalayaay!"

"Muruwari!"

Each time she yelled out a name, a great cheer erupted from a section of the camp as the corresponding battle-standard was hefted aloft.

"Today stands one-seventh of the strength of the Home Army of the Faithful Kingdom of Wil'iah in the East! Many times I have heard our dear nation referred to as a dream impossible, perhaps a flame that burns bravely against the darkness but will inevitably be snuffed out. Today, I know differently. I know that our dream will never die as long as it burns on in our hearts. And, as our brave king has told us many times, the wind that lifts our banners is more powerful than even we could ever imagine. Today, let the assembled armies of the Kingdom of Truth rise as one to defend this dream!"

Her final words were almost deafened by the thunderous applause from the assembled army. As its final breaths were carried off by the winds of the downs, the Captain of Zebulon began to sing the "Yah'Hele'vanu," the rallying song of Wil'iah. At the conclusion of its last strains, the army cried out in unison.

"'Ivrae'ia Va'a'kau'lua!"

CHAPTER FORTY-NINE

MANNA FROM HEAVEN

Balthcutta

Tamino squinted his eyes as columns of blackened dust rose in the distance.

"I think they're coming back for another frontal assault," he whispered to Avora'tru'ivi, who nodded grimly.

"Well, when the faithfulness of my Galbi's heart undermines their dastardly schemes, they have to resort to their previous unsuccessful methods. We'll repel this one as well," she responded as she drew her sword.

✳ ✳ ✳

"She left strict orders. The rest of the men aren't to know," Minos said to Achish, who shook his head in amazement.

"And just where does she think she's going?"

"She said that her mission was vital for the war effort, but it was equally vital that the Wil'iahns continue to believe that she's here. I have no idea what she's up to. If you ask me, she's off to sulk because that mudface didn't succumb to her wiles."

"I have to hand it to him, that's better than any of us could do," Achish responded with grudging respect. "I've said it before, and I'll say it again, Wil'iah was never that bad to Ashkelon."

"Watch your tongue, if you wish to keep it," Minos said conspiratorially, his eyes suspiciously flicking from side to side. Attempting to steer the conversation away from the jagged rocks of potential whispered treason and back to the real subject at hand, he continued. "At least she left us detailed instructions. The river diversion project is to continue as planned. And, now we get to carry out 'Operation Manna from Heaven.' She certainly has a way with cruel words."

Achish grimly nodded. "The furnaces are ready."

✳ ✳ ✳

Tamino held a telescope to his eye, surveying the advancing enemy forces. He could make out a mobile battery of siege engines surrounded by blocks of archers, but his pupil dilated in surprise as he saw a pink sedan chair carried along behind the trebuchets.

"She doesn't usually participate in the full-on attacks like this. She must be really angry," he said.

"Well, you know what they say about women scorned," Avora'tru'ivi laughed in response. "At least this time she has no gunpowder artillery to back her up."

"What would I do without you?"

For what seemed like the hundredth time, Tamino called Balthcutta's artillery batteries and archers into action. Flights of arrows whizzed through the sky as thunderous blasts from the guns shook the walls. But, this time, the enemy siege engines didn't stop to fire, their inexorable advance continuing until they were well within the accurate targeting range of the cannons, as well as the trebuchets on the inner wall. One by one, the enemy engines fell to ruin as the stone cannonballs and projectiles found their marks. Yet, still they advanced.

"What are they doing?" Tamino asked, his eyes filling with a mixture of triumph and alarm as he realized this attack didn't correspond to previous patterns.

"I don't know, Galbi. This seems like a waste of equipment. What do they hope to accomplish with this?"

Suddenly, the remaining enemy siege engines ground to a halt, barely three hundred feet in front of the outer wall. One by one, their counterweights plunged, and the great trebuchets swung into action, their baskets lobbing glowing red shells in great arcs. Tamino's head passed over his shoulder as his eyes followed one of the projectiles over all three sets of walls.

"*What?*" he whispered under his breath.

Suddenly, cries of alarm emanated from behind the inner wall, followed by an angry glow. This process was repeated all along the inner wall as more and more shells soared over the defenses.

The color drained out of Avora'tru'ivi's face.

"The crops. They're going after the crops."

Tamino turned to Abigail, the artillery officer, who stood beside them, her face contorted in alarm.

"Destroy all of those siege engines, *now.*" He and the queen began to stride over to the staircase that would lead them to the bridge to the inner defenses. "We need to handle this situation. We'll hopefully be back shortly."

Shaking herself from her dismay, Abigail snapped into a salute, then turned to her gunners.

"OK, let's blow these things to bits!"

A short time later, Tamino and Avora'tru'ivi emerged onto the battlements, and looked out in horror at the scene that unfolded before their eyes in the outer city. Before them, the neatly-arranged crop rows that fed the five hundred thousand hungry mouths of Balthcutta lay in flames as the Mongol naphtha bombs finished their deadly arcs.

After allowing a moment to compose herself, Avora'tru'ivi sprang into action. "Well, we still have the dry food storage facilities in the inner city. Many of the crops had already been harvested. And we still have the fish ponds and Lake Wollombulla."

Just as she said that, an alarmed, exhausted messenger ran up to them.

"Your Faithfulnesses! The fishponds…"

"What about them?" A dark look crossed Avora'tru'ivi's face.

"Enemy warships attacked the Wollombulla Seawall this morning, but instead of attempting to batter the walls down like they have in the past, they threw…something over it into the lake. Now all the fish are dead."

Tamino's shoulders slumped as Avora'tru'ivi involuntarily put a hand to her mouth in shock.

"We should have known they would try something like this. Is there any other bad news?" Tamino asked hesitantly.

"The River Wall reports that the water level has been steadily decreasing over the past several days."

"Just as I suspected, they may be trying to divert the river. I've heard of the Mongols doing that in other campaigns," Tamino sighed. "Are the cisterns full?"

"Last I checked," said Avora'tru'ivi.

"Good. We'd had better make them last."

Avora'tru'ivi nodded grimly.

"Galbi, do you know any good rice recipes?"

CHAPTER FIFTY

THE TURN OF THE TIDE

Zrain'novahi, Vrenga'nui, eastern Wil'iah

*N*ervously casting her eyes about, Medea once again crept to the edge of the Frouzean camp, anxious to relay the latest set of tactical information that she had gleaned from listening around the camp. While she had now done this at least a dozen times, she didn't feel any less nervous as she took out her concealed mirror and began flashing it toward the mountains, her movements practiced and precise. Her tongue crept out from between her lips as she concentrated, her ears listening for any sign that she was being noticed. She thought she heard a rustling in the distance, and began to increase the speed of her signals in response.

Just one more message to convey.

Suddenly, a brusque voice pierced the morning air.

"YOU! What are you doing?"

Her heart exploding with alarm, Medea whirled around to see a huge Frouzean guard approaching her, a grimace cut across his bearded face.

She decided on one last desperate attempt at deception. Coquettishly flipping her hair, she held up the mirror.

"I was just admiring my own reflection, of course!"

"Likely story. With the reflective part of the mirror pointed *away* from you?"

Medea's heart sank as she realized she was caught.

"Well...I...."

Suddenly, the guard's eyes narrowed as two answering flashes came from the mountain. Medea winced.

"You're coming with me," growled the guard.

Medea kicked and scuffed to no avail as he dragged her along. He tore open the flaps to a command pavilion and flung her through the opening.

Ajax the Lesser of Gath luxuriantly sprawled across a recliner, his arms languidly folded behind his head as a cohort of bondwomen fanned him with great plumes of emu feathers in a fruitless attempt to combat the oppressive heat of the backcountry. The air inside the pavilion was stifling and still, but that apparently didn't hinder Ajax's enjoyment as juice dribbled down his chin from the grapes that he expertly caught in his mouth from the flinging hands of yet more women. His eye caught by the disturbance at the entrance to the pavilion, he hoisted himself up on his elbows.

"And who is this?" he sneered.

"A bondwoman from your retinue, my lord," replied one of the guards. He spat in Medea's direction. "A *traitor.*" Ajax studied Medea's face with half-interest. "Ah yes, what was your name? Mina?"

"Medea," she replied through gritted teeth.

"A shame, that such beauty could mask deceit. What did she do?"

The second guard replied. "We caught her at the edge of the camp with a mirror. She was waving it back and forth, with the reflective part facing out, as if to send some signal. I think she's working for the Wil'iahns."

Ajax flicked his finger, motioning for Medea to come closer. When she didn't immediately comply, the guard shoved her over to him. Ajax now studied her more closely, an eerie leer crossing his face.

"Now, why would a pretty girl like you be working for the enemy?"

Medea decided to try one last desperate gamble. "I did have a mirror, but it was only to ensure that my makeup was perfect. I live only to please you."

Ajax scoffed. "Don't insult my intelligence. If you were admiring yourself, why was the reflective part of the mirror pointed away from you? I think there's only one way to find out if you are true to me." He suddenly lunged up from the recliner and forcibly kissed Medea, who squirmed in protest. Instinctively, she recoiled and slapped him hard across the face, satisfaction and regret instantly mixing in her heart as she realized she had truly given up the ruse.

Ajax leaned back on the recliner, a triumphant, wolfish look on his face. "So it's true. More's the pity. Well, it's no matter. After they have fed you to the snakes, there will be plenty of women eager to take your place. Serving me as your lord is a great privilege, you know."

Medea bared her teeth in answer. "The only privilege I know is to serve the *real* Lord!"

The guards stepped forward and grabbed Medea's arms, preparing to drag her away. Medea frantically cast her eyes around the tent, searching for a means of escape. She briefly locked eyes with one of the women fanning Ajax. She gave Medea a brief, sympathetic gaze before looking away.

"No, wait, not yet," said Ajax. "I want her to witness the next village assault from here. I want her to see just how powerless her Wil'iahn friends are." Ajax alit from the recliner and snapped his fingers at two of the women, who brought forward his armor and began to clip it on. He leered at Medea.

"You know, I was raised with stories about how fierce the Wil'iahn Army was. I think they were all lies. We have now penetrated hundreds of miles into Wil'iahn territory and have yet to see serious resistance. Every village we reach has already been abandoned. The much-vaunted Wil'iahn Army has yet to appear in any serious numbers. The triumph of my Imperial Army will be remembered for a thousand generations!" His armor now fully assembled, he grabbed Medea's arm in a steely grip and dragged her out of the tent, where he was met by General Nasir-al-Din.

"Who's this?" sneered the Mongol general as he beheld Medea.

"She's nothing. Just an unwilling witness to our latest triumph!" Before them stood a Yuwaalaraay Village that the Wil'iahns called "Zrain'nui'novahi," if the map was to be believed. Behind them stood the vast Imperial Army, although, Medea noticed with no small amount of satisfaction, its soldiers all looked rather worse for wear as they wilted in the sun and burned with hunger. A group of heralds splendidly dressed in the regalia of Gath stepped forward and let off five blasts from brass trumpets, the sound reverberating through the still air.

The village remained silent.

"Just as I thought. Those cowards turned and ran rather than face our majesty!" Ajax smirked at Medea. "Nobody will save you today, beautiful. Isn't that what you were hoping fo"--

Ajax's last word was interrupted by a thunderous report as a cloud of white smoke rose from the village. A whine filled the air as a cannon ball screamed over their heads and plunged into Ajax's pavilion behind them, collapsing the gaudy structure.

Hope leapt in Medea's heart. *Today is the day!*

"Ah, good! Somebody finally wants to challenge me!" Ajax drew his short sword and thrust it up into the air, the blade gleaming in the mid-day sun.

Over the modest castle that stood sentinel for the village, a flapping banner began to raise. Medea's eyes strained to make it out- it was a yellow star on a green background. The hope that had begun to kindle in her heart now leapt into a roaring flame. *The Home Army.*

Ajax, still dragging her along, marched out ahead of the assembled Imperial Army, beat his chest with his free arm, and yelled a guttural war cry at the village. It was joined by a deafening rendition of the same growl by the rest of the Frouzean Army, the overwhelming sound seeming to punch right through Medea's slight, trembling frame.

The low, determined wail of a conch shell floated over from the village in answer. Medea's heart leapt again at the sound of her adopted home. Ajax snorted, then laughed – an ugly, screechy sound.

"Is that all you have in answer? I will smash this village like a gnat!"

Suddenly, another conch shell rang out. This time, it was to their left.

Then another. This one to the right.

Ajax whipped his head from left to right, squinting into the distance. He laughed again. "Nice try. Send conch-blowers to either side to make it look like they have more forces than they really can deploy."

Then, a roaring blast of sound hit them from both sides. This time, it sounded more like a thousand conches. Medea triumphantly noticed a hint of alarm cross Ajax's piercing eyes. Then, the still air was split once again by a deafening blast of shells, magnified yet more- but this time, from behind them.

Forgetting his grip on Medea, Ajax whirled around, brandishing the sword, confusion mixing with awakening terror in his eyes.

"*What?*"

Suddenly, the ground shook as an even more thunderous roar of sound hit them from all sides. As it died down, it was replaced with a low hum that gradually resolved itself into a menacing, yet rousing, song. Medea instantly recognized it.

Tear Down the Gates of Hell.

A thin black line, seeming almost like a distant forest, appeared on the ridge to their left, punctuated by occasional glints of light. Her peripheral vision catching a hint of motion to her right, Medea turned to see an identical pattern on the hills in that direction. As the final strains of the song roared through the air, they were succeeded by a final, deafening war cry that assaulted the Imperial Army from all directions. On cue, a forest of battle-standards hoisted themselves above the mass of troops crowning the hills. On a second, larger flagpole crowning the keep of the village castle, an enormous battle-standard of the Kingdom of Wil'iah unfurled, flapping defiantly in a sudden breeze that blew from the north.

Abruptly, the sunlight grew visibly darker as thousands of arrows filled the sky.

Medea hazarded a glance at Ajax. He stood completely still, his mouth agape as his eyes registered total shock. Similar expressions played themselves out on the faces of the other Frouzean leaders around her.

Deciding this was probably as good a time as any to make her escape, Medea broke and ran- headlong into a hulking Homeric guard, who leered down at her, his lips pulled back into a cruel growl.

"Going to join your friends, sweetie?"

Medea didn't dignify that with a response. Instead, she shot out two outstretched fingers in a lightning strike at the pressure point on the guard's neck. He crumpled to the floor, and Medea began to run again, throwing off the impractical high heels that she had been forced to wear as a "bondwoman." Casting a glance back at Ajax's crumpled pavilion, Medea winced as a pang of guilt gripped her heart – and an arrow buried itself in the ground an inch from her foot.

She reversed course and raced back to the crumpled Homeric Guard, who now resembled a pincushion as several arrows protruded from his back. She yanked his sword from its sheath and brandished it, giving herself half a second to admire the gleaming blade before running back to the pavilion. Cutting a hole in its side, she pushed through and was confronted with the sight of the bondwomen whimpering at the thunderous sounds of battle outside. They instantly looked up at her entrance, and ran toward her.

"Is it true?" Cassandra entreated.

"Are you really working for the Wil'iahns?" another woman whom Medea did not recognize asked excitedly.

"If you want freedom, now's your chance," Medea said, motioning to the tear in the tent with her sword.

"But what if the Wil'iahns capture us? They will roast us on a spit and eat us!"

Medea rolled her eyes. "I don't know who told you that; it's not true. If we can escape to their lines, you will not be harmed."

The other woman, her face betraying surprising determination, grabbed one of the tall fans and ripped the emu feathers off, transforming it into a long stave. She turned to face the other hesitant women and pointed to the gash in the tent fabric with her makeshift weapon.

"Let's go!"

However, before the women could exit, another person staggered into the tent. To Medea's shock, it was Ajax. His face smeared with blood and his eyes wild like a horse caught in a burning barn, he yanked the battered tent clothes back together behind him and exhaled deeply, grateful for a place to hide. Then, his eyes focused on the women, all his former slaves.

"Well, hello, ladies," he said, weakly attempting to be seductive.

"Coward," Medea derisively scoffed. After a moment of hesitation, the women surged forward and dogpiled Ajax, whacking him with the staves. Ajax was quickly unconscious.

"Let's go. He's no longer a threat," Medea entreated.

"We're not finished with him yet," came a cold reply.

"I can't in good conscience kill a defenseless man. I'm a Christian," Medea responded.

The gleeful ex-slaves responded in unison.

"WE'RE NOT!"

CHAPTER FIFTY-ONE

THE IMPERIAL ARMY

Imperial Army camp, Nowra, outside Balthcutta

Minos stared angrily at the whitewashed walls of Balthcutta, now streaked with the char-marks of gunpowder and cracked in a thousand places from his repeated, fruitless assaults. The Prince of Ashdod waved an angry fist at the tallest tower of the main gate, atop which still defiantly flapped the hated, thirty-two rayed flag of the enemy. Minos flinched as a thunderous sound shook the earth and an ominous whine filled the air, resolving itself into an explosive roar somewhere behind him.

Those blasted guns. If only we still had ammunition to fire back. Minos rued the day he had allowed all of the siege ammunition to be placed in one location. It was out of range of the Wil'iahn guns, his advisers had said. It wasn't out of range of Wil'iah's queen.

The warning sound of a horn caught his ear, and Minos whirled around, heading toward the entrance to the camp where the horn had sounded.

Something's wrong. Minos couldn't shake the feeling as he accelerated his pace into first a jog, then a full-on run. He wasn't prepared for the sight that greeted his eyes at the gate.

A bedraggled horse foamed at the mouth, while its exhausted rider tottered unsteadily on its back. His wild-eyed face was streaked with dirt, his helmetless hair rebelled in wild clumps, and his eyebrows had apparently been singed off. His once-gleaming uniform was in tatters, the Imperial emblem ripped clean in two. At the sight of Minos, the man lost his grip on the reins of the horse and toppled into an unruly heap on the ground, before a trembling, grimy hand shot up for assistance. Minos reached down and brusquely yanked the man to his feet.

"You are a soldier of the empire! Act like one!" he yelled, backhanding the messenger across the face.

The soldier's eyes manically flicked back and forth. He looked as frantic as his horse, who looked like it was facing an unescapable barn fire.

"Ruin....disaster...they're everywhere..." he breathlessly gasped.

"Who is everywhere?"

"It was going so well…we had penetrated even into Murrinui…we were as an almighty tempest that scattered all before us…we were so foolish."

"What happened!?" Minos bellowed, alarm starting to gather itself in his stomach.

"Surrounded…no escape…destroyed…"

"Where is the Imperial Army!?"

The soldier seemed to gather himself and stared directly into Minos' eye.

"What Army?"

Minos stepped forward and grabbed the man by his frayed shoulder straps, shaking him.

"Don't test me!" He bellowed.

"They were all around us. Their horns and their cries filled the sky. Their arrows blocked the sun. Their cannon shook the earth. It was all a trap. It was all a giant trap."

"Where did these forces come from? Our intelligence indicated there were less than forty thousand troops in the east of Wil'iah."

"I don't know…they came from all sides…they outnumbered the sands…"

"How much of the Imperial Army survived?"

The man gave a half-crazed, wry grin. "I am the Imperial Army. I am all that's left."

In shock, Minos dropped the man, who crumpled to the floor, broken and defeated. Minos instantly began doing the math. If the mighty Imperial Army had been destroyed by this massive Wil'iahn force that had arrived seemingly out of nowhere, his forces stood no chance. Unless….Minos cast a quick glance at the walls of Balthcutta.

The messenger, hauling himself up once more to a standing position, entreated, "I must speak with Her Worship. She must be told."

Minos shook his head. "Her Worship isn't here. She left eleven days ago. She said the situation in the east was under control, so she was going to assess the assault on Trukanamoa."

Achish, who had rushed over to join the questioning of the master, shook his head in disgust. "She knew! She *knew!* She has left us all to our deaths!"

The messenger spat out, "You will not blaspheme our empress in such a manner! It was our privilege to die for her. I am only ashamed that I survived! But now…"

With an unhinged look, the messenger lunged forward and seized Achish' short sword, then raised his eyes skyward.

"All hail Baal! All hail Dagon! All hail Astarte, our eternal empress!" With that, he plunged the short sword deep into his midsection and fell forward onto the ground, his face lit with a deranged smile.

Achish regarded the soldier with a contempt-filled sneer, then turned to Minos, the disgust in his eyes unsuccessfully attempting to mask the cold fear that burned beneath.

"Now what? In next to no time, we will have a massive army at our backs."

Minos stroked his beard, letting his hand sink deep into the luxuriant fibers. "As I see it, we have three options. We can move into the mountains and make our stand there, attempting to delay the Wil'iahns as long as possible, we can assault the city with one last mighty push, take it, and then fortify ourselves inside it against the enemy, or we can retreat to our own lands and prepare a defense there."

Achish spat on the ground. "To retreat would be humiliating!"

"I am not yet ready for that. In order for the enemy to reach us, they will have to negotiate the mountain passes to our rear. If we can occupy those passes, we could hold them off indefinitely. Our great ancestor Leonidas did much the same at Thermopylae."

Achish shook his head. "Leonidas died."

Minos gave a humorless smile. "Yet we still talk about him. Would you rather die forgotten in a bed?"

"That doesn't change the fact that the Wil'iahns know those mountains much better than we do. We could never hold them. There may be other passes and passages that we don't know about. Besides, there are many Wil'iahn forces already in the mountains to begin with."

A sudden realization dawned on Achish as he grabbed Minos' forearm and whispered in his ear. "Why are we here, Minos? Our Principality was forced to surrender to Delilah or face certain death. Ekron's prince was dropped in a pit of spiders. Now that the Frouzee is gone and has abandoned us to our fate, why keep fighting this pointless war? We shouldn't stay here. We should return home and fight for the independence of Ekron and Ashdod. That would not be a retreat; it would be a victory for our people!"

Minos recoiled and gave Achish a harsh sneer. "I will not tolerate treasonous speech in this camp. You'd best be careful. If Delilah were here, she would have you strangled with a single thread. Just because she's gone doesn't mean she still doesn't have ears everywhere. Sleep with a sword under your pillow tonight."

Achish snorted. "Well, if you won't heed my advice, I suppose our only option is to take the city. We have been trying to do so for three weeks and have exhausted every weapon in our arsenal, up to and including Delilah's ridiculous love potions. Do you have any other ideas?"

Minos furrowed his brows in thought. "Clearly the Wil'iahns planned their trap in the north for some time. It is the lynchpin of their defense strategy. If their battle against the Imperial Army had failed, all would have been lost for them, and they know it. It is impossible for news to travel so quickly, our messenger of course being an exception," Minos said, briefly casting his eyes on the soldier's corpse that lay strewn at their feet. "We have the city surrounded. There's no way the enemy could get a message through. If we can convince them that their plan has failed, they might be demoralized enough to let their guard down. They would never surrender, but they might slip. It might give us the chance we need to use trickery where brute force has failed."

Achish' mouth twisted into a sickly grin. "I see. It sounds like it's time for us to start spreading the Good News."

CHAPTER FIFTY-TWO

THE GAROTTE OF GATH

Imperial Army camp, Nowra, outside Balthcutta

The next morning, Minos spread open the tent flaps, disgusted at Achish's lack of punctuality.

"Fool! Last night was not the time for drunkenness! That time will come when Balthcutta has fallen."

The form in the bed gave no response.

He must have really had the night.

Minos marched over to the bed and shook the general. Still there was no response. Then he noticed it. A thin purple line across Achish's throat. His stomach sinking,

Minos tore off the blankets, suppressing a retch at what he discovered. Carved into Achish's chest was the symbol of the Goddess Astarte, and pinned to his navel was a note, on which a message was scrawled in suspiciously-red ink.

Thus befalls all traitors.

CHAPTER FIFTY-THREE

A DAMSEL IN THE DESERT

Trukanamoa

*J*eremiah stirred as the predawn light filtered through the arrow loop that provided the only illumination in his ready chamber. As usual, it took him a few moments to fully wake up, but his eyes suddenly shot wide open as he realized something unusual was occurring. Complete silence.

Usually some racket indicated the presence of the enemy army just outside the range of Trukanamoa's defensive artillery. But this morning, all Jeremiah could hear was the grumble of his own stomach. He ruefully looked at his complaining gut.

Enough. This is how we get through sieges. I don't want any more complaints from you.

After hastily putting on his armor, Jeremiah emerged from the ready chamber onto the walls. To his shock, the enemy army was gone, leaving only heaps of garbage and abandoned equipment.

"What on earth?" he said out loud, almost involuntarily.

"Curious," a voice said behind him. Jeremiah whirled around to see Prime Minister Allira walking toward him.

"This seems like a trick. We all know that the Frouzeans are, at the end of the day, ultimately spineless, but it's not like the Mongols to just give up like this," Jeremiah said. "In fact, as I know all too well," he said ruefully, "they love to pretend to retreat, then strike when you let your guard down."

Allira nodded. "I don't for an instant think they're really gone."

Jeremiah shook his head. "I wish General Luana were here. She would know what to do. Where is she?"

Allira looked surprised. "I thought she told you. She said she's been reassigned, and that the situation here is now under control."

"What? Reassigned by who?"

"She simply said that the ultimate authority reassigned her, and she needed to go somewhere else."

Ultimate authority? She must have meant Tamino. If we get out of this alive, I'll have to ask him, thought Jeremiah.

"Well," he responded, "in that case, I think it's best if we try to ascertain their whereabouts. It would also be helpful to see if we can reconnect with the guerilla forces.

I can only hope they've succeeded in cutting their supply chain back to Frouzea, or at least constricting it," Jeremiah responded.

"Such a mission would be highly dangerous. This desert is probably crawling with the enemy."

"Which is why I, and a few handpicked rangers, are going to go," Jeremiah said.

"I won't stop you, but I need you to be careful," Allira said.

Two hours later, a scraping sound filled the still desert air as a panel in the formerly-smooth face of the outer wall slid back to reveal a dark opening. Jeremiah and seven mounted riders, clad in the rust-red camouflage robes that characterized the King's Rangers of the Order of the Flame of Zebulon, emerged from the gaping doorway. As soon as the last rider cleared the wall, the panel began to slide back into place. Soon, the only hint that the opening had ever been there was a hairline crack that outlined the postern gate.

The riders made their way towards the remains of the besieging army's camp. They paid special attention to the kitchen rubbish spaced periodically throughout the site.

Jeremiah's nostrils flared with disgust.

"They're eating their own horses."

"The Mongols have been known to do that when their other food supplies run out. They even drink the horses' blood," one of the knights responded.

"Well, it appears the Army of Anangu is doing its job, then," Jeremiah said gravely.

The search party continued forward, following the myriad of tracks that marched south, away from the city. They grimly noted the burned-out shells of the outer castles that defended the southern approaches to the city atop the lower ridges that preceded the Tjoritja Mountains. Jeremiah sadly dipped his head at each one.

The search continued for hours, and, although there were plenty of indications that the enemy army had passed this way, including the grisly sight of the abandoned corpses of Mongol horses, there was no sign of the army's current whereabouts. At length, Jeremiah called for a rest, and the riders dismounted, letting the horses graze on the scraggly tufts of grass that intermittently forced their way out of the parched dust. Jeremiah had just sat down to eat some dried meat when a loud scream reverberated through the desert. Jeremiah motioned for the other riders to drop to the ground, then listened carefully. The scream sounded again. It didn't sound more than a few hundred meters away, most likely emanating from a small gorge that opened up to the west.

Putting the skills honed from five years on ranger duty to use, Jeremiah crept forward, his cloak making him nearly indistinguishable from his surroundings. His knights did the same, the group moving forward in a broad arrowhead formation. A third scream, this time accompanied by cruel laughter, confirmed they were heading in the right direction.

Finally, they rounded a corner in the gorge and came face to face with their quarry. A woman in a simple white shift, with a gold band on her arm, screamed in terror as she was tossed between four burly men in Frouzean military uniforms. The men laughed and leered, occasionally planting kisses on the hapless slave. Jeremiah instantly felt his stomach boil with anger, and withdrew a deadly throwing star from his bandolier. Suddenly, though, he felt a hand grab his.

"The soldiers could be valuable sources of tactical information. We'll take them, but we should take them alive," one of the knights hissed.

The wisdom of the man's word's managed to cut through Jeremiah's seething rage. He replaced the throwing star and instead withdrew a boomerang, flinging the weapon with expert precision and just enough force to stun.

The next soldier who was supposed to catch the woman instead toppled to the ground with a sickening crack as the boomerang found its mark. The woman, rather than falling into his arms, plummeted into a discombobulated heap as the other three soldiers drew their swords, looking wildly about for the source of the marauding missile. But, just as quickly, they were all rendered unconscious as the strange thumping sound of the other knights' boomerangs reverberated through the gorge.

The soldiers dispatched, Jeremiah emerged from hiding and rushed forward to the woman, who struggled to get up from the desert ground. He grabbed her arm and gently lifted her to her feet. The woman had striking features and raven black hair, not uncommon for her people.

"How can I ever thank you for saving me?" she breathlessly asked.

"Never mind that," Jeremiah responded. "Are you attached to the main Frouzean Army?"

"I was, until now," she nodded enthusiastically.

"Then, if you don't mind, you're coming with us," Jeremiah responded.

"Trust me, I have no love for them," she said contemptuously as she surveyed the unconscious forms of her tormenters as they were unceremoniously flung across the backs of the horses by the knights and tied to the rear of the saddles.

The party gradually made their way back to Trukanamoa, stopping several times to allow the slave girl to rest. Jeremiah found his heart filled with pity for the woman as he imagined the horrors she must have faced as a slave to the Frouzean army. At length, they found themselves once again facing the staunch walls of Trukanamoa, now lit in the nighttime darkness by a thousand flaring torches. A pair of conch shells announced Jeremiah's return, and the postern gate once again slid open, revealing the hidden passage through the outer wall. The slave woman's eyes widened.

"Ah, yes, we have a few tricks up our sleeve," Jeremiah said proudly.

Once inside, they were greeted by Prime Minister Allira.

"Well, Your Faithfulness, I see you were successful in your endeavor...and you have an unexpected guest," she said, looking the slave woman up and down.

"Faithfulness? You're...you're..." the slave said, her eyes widening to the point where they reminded Jeremiah of a cow. He rendered a flourishing civilian salute in response.

"Yes, I am Jeremiah, Prince and Sovereign Protector of the Faithful Kingdom of Wil'iah." Color rose in his cheeks as he realized he had forgotten an important courtesy. "Pardon me, I realized I forgot to ask your name."

"Oh, Your Faithfulness, you never have to apologize to me! You saved my life!" Batting her eyes, she dropped into a deep bow.

"I am Iphigenia."

CHAPTER FIFTY-FOUR

THE GOOD NEWS

Balthcutta

*T*amino hunched over a map of the city of Balthcutta, noting the parts of the outer walls that were nearing collapse. He winced as another trebuchet projectile slammed into the wall, but the noise was drowned out by a blast of trumpets as a group of heralds announced the arrival of Minos of Ashkelon, bearing a message.

"Give up, Tamino! Spare yourself before this last bastion of Wil'iah is reduced to rubble! Your army in the interior has been met in pitched battle and defeated! Your nation's lands are in flames, your armies are scattered and destroyed, and the flags of our empire fly all over your backcountry. You and I both know that this was inevitable. Your kingdom stood for a time, but its high-minded ideals were never going to last in this world. The tide of our empire, and our allies in Asia, is inexorable. There is no reason for you to be ashamed. It is perfectly normal for small countries like yours to fall in submission before great empires. It is the natural way of things. We will be generous. If you submit now, we will be merciful. You may even find your new way of life pleasurable. Look around. This is pointless! Surrender now while you still have a chance!"

Tamino laughed in response. "If you for a moment thought that I, or any of my countrymen, would surrender to such bald-faced lies, you were sorely mistaken. I do not believe that Wil'iah is lost or that her armies are destroyed. Even if they were, and even if, as you state so speciously, that over our walls flutters the last battle-flag of the Faithful Kingdom, then Balthcutta would steadfastly resist you. For we insist that the wind which lifts our banners, the eternal truth that set alight the ancient Flame of Zebulon that has sustained us down the centuries, is an almighty force beyond your comprehension. We do not for a moment quake in fear, for we know what is at our backs, and we understand that, if Balthcutta be the last city to resist your advance, she does not stand alone."

Despite the boldness of his words, Tamino felt his stomach clench. *What if he isn't lying? Our plan hinged on the success of the Home Army.*

"Brave words from a king that has presided over defeat after defeat and was even foolish enough to deliver himself, unarmed, into the hands of our empress! If I were a mudface like you, your leadership would not inspire confidence!"

"Then you would be placing your hope in the wrong vessel. I do not lead the defense of Wil'iah. God does. And before that, our ultimate defense, your army, vast though it is, quails into insignificance. Begone, herald of despair! You are not welcome here! Your retinue has two minutes to retire to your lines before we open fire!"

Minos sputtered in response, but he waved his men back and began to retreat toward the Frouzean lines.

Avora'tru'ivi whispered in Tamino's ear.

"Galbi, this situation is serious. I know that a miracle delivered you from the Frouzee's chains, but we need another one now. I'm not sure how much longer we can hold out."

"Avora, I don't believe his statement that the Home Army has been destroyed. You and I both know that there is a plan, and it has, so far, been carried out."

"We have been cut off from information from the outside for some time now. We have no way of knowing if they are telling the truth or not."

"In my experience, if the person saying something is a Frouzean, nine times out of ten, they are not telling the truth."

Avora'tru'ivi gently laughed. "I trust the word of Captain Deborah much more than I trust Minos of Ashkelon, that's for certain."

Suddenly, Tamino's peripheral vision caught a flash of light. He turned from his wife and stared out into the west. Avora'tru'ivi saw a wide smile break over her husband's face. Curious, she followed his gaze.

A brave green flame burned atop Mount Cambewarra.

CHAPTER FIFTY-FIVE

VICTORY IN THE EAST

Balthcutta

*A*ll along the River wall of Balthcutta, the fog of war reigned supreme. Since this wall was ostensibly protected by the fast-flowing river, it was much less stout than the three main land walls that defended the primary western approaches to the city. But, now that the river had run dry, redirected by Delilah's dam, the wall faced the full brunt of a land-borne assault by the entire remaining strength of Minos' forces. Trebuchets flung great stone projectiles at the wall, which responded with its own spitting cannon fire, while a tidal surge of humanity rushed the wall, hefting thousands of siege ladders.

There's no way we'll be able to stop all of them, Tamino thought as he surveyed the scene from atop a wall tower. Avora'tru'ivi stood beside him, directing the cannon batteries on either side.

"Gun 624! Get that trebuchet!"

Even as the words left her mouth, seven ladders poked their malevolent heads over the battlements beside her. The supply of oil and rubble for the machicolations long since exhausted, the defenders were forced to resort to long poles to push back the ladders, but they just kept coming.

"The enemy positions in front of the St. Thomas Gate are all but abandoned in favor of this assault," Tamino yelled to his wife. "Maybe if I lead a force out of there, we can attack this group from behind and do something to break the siege."

"Galbi, that would be suicide. We can't muster any force large enough to make a difference. You would all be slaughtered. Our best chance is to defend this wall, and, failing that, to retreat to the Middle City."

Suddenly, an urgent conch shell blew up from the ward below. Tamino rushed down the stairs toward a man who lay with his ear pressed to the ground.

"I think they're tunneling under the wall here," he said.

Images of the explosion of the "Goliath Bomb" at the outer wall flashed before Tamino's eyes, and panic filled his heart as he realized that Avora'tru'ivi was directly over where the wall would likely collapse.

"Get down from there!" he yelled in alarm, motioning to the likely position of the tunnel. Avora'tru'ivi quizzically looked at him for a moment, before horrified comprehension dawned in her eyes, and she scrambled to the ward below, the rest of the troops following her.

"If the wall is breached here, we won't be able to hold them back. We'll have to retreat to the Middle City!"

Avora'tru'ivi grimly nodded. She reached to a ram's horn that was buckled to her bandolier and blew on it seven times. The command was relayed by tower commanders up and down the wall. The section of wall in question was flanked on either side by two towers connected to the wall by wooden drawbridges, which were rapidly withdrawn to reveal deep pits lined with iron spikes. "Hopefully, that will delay the enemy long enough to secure the defenses of the Middle City," she said.

Tamino gravely nodded. "I'll sound the retreat. This is my responsibility." He withdrew his own ram's horn and gave off nine blasts. The defenders on the walls quickly began to carry out the plan, shoving off as many siege ladders as they could before doing what they could to disable the remaining cannons. Then, they abandoned the wall en masse and began to run across the ward toward the middle wall complex, whose drawbridge ponderously lowered to admit the retreating masses. Tamino blew on the ram's horn again three times, and a cadre of knights formed up behind him and the queen, grimly leveling their lances at the portion of the wall that was expected to collapse, preparing to cover the retreat of the wall defenders. All along the wall, the towers remained manned, cut off from the rest of the defenses by the spiked pits, with ziplines to the middle wall as a last escape path.

Suddenly, a hideous cracking sound filled the air as the wall in front of them collapsed, sending up a cloud of dust and rubble. Through this curtain of debris rushed a tide of enemy soldiers, brandishing weapons and yelling guttural war cries.

Tamino hefted his shield and drew the Zrain'de'zhang, the blade gleaming in the sun.

"When the enemy shall come in like a flood, the spirit of the Lord shall raise a standard against him," he said, his voice oddly calm.

To the east, General Alinta and General Teva'ivani stood atop the Wollumboola Seawall, looking at the advancing enemy fleet with consternation. A veritable forest of masts confronted them, with a fogbank beyond. The seawall's guns continued to spit flame, their projectiles smashing into the Frouzean and Mongol ships with deadly accuracy, sending fragments of wood pinwheeling through the sky. But there were simply too many of them.

"We're running out of ammunition," Alinta growled. "And the barrage across the river mouth has failed."

"I don't understand. If they continue on this course, they're going to run aground," Teva'ivani responded.

Alinta squinted at the lead Frouzean galley, her eyes widening in alarm.

"They've built ladders, siege towers, and drawbridges on the ships. They mean to rush the wall." She looked doubtfully at the exhausted, ragged defenders of the seawall.

"Then we'll repel them," Teva'ivani said, hefting a wickedly-sharp halberd.

Suddenly, a cannonball screamed out of the sky and struck one of the Frouzean ships in the rear of the advancing line of malevolent vessels.

"What?" asked Alinta under her breath. The cannonball had not come from the walls. As she squinted more into the distance, she realized that what she had identified as a fog bank was in fact a mass of sails, and the wisps of mist that had seemed to emanate from it was gun smoke. She reached out to grab Teva'ivani's arm.

"Look!"

"What?"

"There are more ships coming!"

"Wonderful. Just what we need."

"No, they're ours!"

As the new fleet grew closer and closer, Alinta whipped out a spyglass and began to make out details. The fleet appeared to be composed of a wide variety of ships, from double-hulled Wil'iahn war canoes to giant Indonesian Jongs. Her heart leapt as she beheld the ensigns of Wil'iah flapping at many mastheads – but not all of them. The majority of the ships flew other flags – the flags of Ephraim-Manasseh, Singhasari, Champa, and Dai Viet. But, most surprisingly of all, the lead ship flew an entirely different flag – the flag of Song China.

As this new flank of the enemy thundered down on them like a tsunami, Delilah's ships halted their advance on the wall and sounded the alarm, trying to execute a mass turn to meet this new threat. But the Frouzean-Mongol fleet was not well practiced in joint maneuvers, and many ships crashed into each other with sickening crunches. Soon, the entire fleet became one interconnected morass of men, wood, and canvas, virtually immobilized. And still the allied fleet bore down on them, their forecastle guns belching flame in concert with the guns atop the wall. Gradually, the enemy fleet was pounded into junk, the ocean littered with severed masts and fragments of brightly-painted ships. Fire belched from dozens of enemy ships as the cannonballs and catapult projectiles found their mark. As ships sank, they often dragged down nearby entangled vessels with them, even as their crews frantically tried to sever the connections. Alinta, in between directing cannon volleys, noticed the one ship flying the Chinese flag veer off from the rest of the allied fleet and head toward the mouth of the river.

Tamino and Avora'tru'ivi frantically swung and hacked with their swords as their force was driven steadily back toward the gate. Tamino's shield resisted uncounted blows from the enemy as they fought to keep themselves from being surrounded. Nearer and nearer to the gate they backed. Through his peripheral vision, Tamino could see that most of the outer wall's defenders had made it through, and he silently blessed the archers atop the walls who provided precious covering fire. All the same, the gate was a long way away, and more and more Frouzeans and Mongols were streaming through the breach in the wall.

We're not going to make it, the thought crossed his mind. He instantly batted it way, attempting instead to focus on what he had to do.

Just then, his eye caught a flicker of movement in the sky above the battered river wall, in the eastern section where some water still flowed from the sea into the bed of the now-redirected river. A blue flag fluttered in the breeze atop a masthead. The Flag of Song China.

He wasn't the only one to notice. Many of the Chinese soldiers in the Mongol force stopped their advance and turned to gawk at the ship as it stopped at the beginning of the River Wall. Avora'tru'ivi followed his gaze, a wide smile breaking over her face even as she parried a jab from an enemy pike.

"I knew it! I knew he wasn't really dead!" she yelled.

"It'll take a lot more than a lousy Frouzean battlefleet to get the Fox of China," Tamino smiled back, the Zrain'de'zhang cleaving a Frouzean short sword in two.

Suddenly, a figure appeared atop the tower that formed the junction between the Seawall, the Middle City Wall, and the River Wall. Clad from head to toe in Song Dynasty naval armor, he was unmistakable.

His appearance was greeted by a rippling murmur as the Chinese troops under Mongol command began to coalesce into a mob in front of the Middle Wall.

Admiral Zhang thrust a gleaming sword in the air, unfurled a Song Dynasty banner behind him, and simply yelled,

"FOR CHINA!"

The Chinese troops needed no second bidding. En masse, they instantly turned away from the Middle Wall and faced their Mongol overlords.

"FOR CHINA!" they yelled, and charged, casting aside their Mongol Yuan Dynasty banners.

The sudden strength of thousands of disaffected Chinese soldiers added to his own meager force, Tamino stopped retreating and began to push forward again. Gradually, the remaining loyal Mongols and Frouzeans were pushed back through the breach in the wall. Tamino came face to face with a Chinese soldier, who looked at the Zrain'de'zhang with a mixture of awe and fear.

"It's good to be on the same side again," Tamino smiled, then charged out the breach in the wall.

Outside, the scene was much the same. All along the dry riverbed, the Chinese soldiers had thrown down their Mongol emblems and joined the allies, reinforced by a steady stream of League troops that disembarked from ships that pulled ashore where the river mouth had been. Behind them, the drawbridge lowered again, and yet more Wil'iahn troops, mostly levied from the former outer wall defenders, streamed out, yelling war cries. Though they were still outnumbered, the allied forces surged into the enemy with such vehemence that the Frouzean formations were broken and thrown back, and the enemy was soon in open retreat along the river bed, seeking to reach their more fortified positions in the broad plain that fronted the main Outer City Walls.

They never got there.

As the Frouzean army broke out onto the open plains in a panicked flight, they were greeted by a wall of sound as thousands of conch shells sounded.

Standing squarely in their way were several hundred thousand troops of the Home Army, an enormous battle-standard of Wil'iah flanked by the individual pennants of hundreds of local Home Army units. Standing at the fore was Lady Deborah, resplendent in her full burnished battle armor. She hefted an enormous two-handed broadsword.

The Frouzean stampede ground to a halt as it found itself stuck between a hammer and an anvil.

Tamino lifted a hand to stop his forces, which formed up into more ordered ranks as both sides awaited the next move.

※ ※ ※

Minos hyperventilated in unabashed panic, his eyes frantically darting back and forth. Toghon managed to shove his way through the milling morass of terrified soldiers and came face to face with his ally.

"Just what do you plan to do about *this*, Frouzean?" he spat.

"I don't suppose the Wil'iahns will allow us to surrender?"

"Mongols never surrender."

"Speak for yourself," Minos said as he ran toward Tamino's force, his eyes casting about for an authority figure, as well as some way to indicate his non-combatant status. Finding no white flags around, he instead unbuckled and threw off first his sword belt, then his armor. His eye finally caught who he thought he recognized as Tamino, and he, now clad only in his white tunic, ran toward him and fell prostrate on the ground.

"Yes?" Tamino said quizzically, keeping the Zrain'de'zhang pointed at the Frouzean prince.

"Mercy!"

"Would you have shown us mercy if the tables had been reversed?"

"No," Minos sobbed.

"Well, you'd better be grateful that we will," Tamino responded flatly.

Tamino confronts Minos

"You're not going to eat us?" Minos moaned.

Tamino laughed, an incredulous look on his face. "You people keep bringing that up. They only do that in Fiji."

"What are your terms?" Minos entreated.

"The Kingdom of Wil'iah demands the unconditional surrender of all Frouzean and Mongol forces. Once that has been extended, all of your weapons will be confiscated, and your troops will be held prisoner until this conflict is concluded. They will then be free to go home. They will be cared for with the best humanity we can muster given our limited resources. Your people must each individually promise never to attack Wil'iah again. In addition, all principalities and territories of the Frouzean Empire must release all Aboriginal people who are currently enslaved and allow them to resettle in Wil'iah."

"You...you're going to let us go home?"

"Eventually, yes. At least you have a home to go back to. Thanks to you, many of my people don't. If I were you, I'd spend the next few months thinking about that."

Minos nodded pitifully.

"Alright, do I have an answer from you?" Tamino asked sternly.

"I, Minos of Ashkelon, on behalf of Her Worship—"

"Cut the 'Her Worship' business."

"Fine, I, Minos of Ashkelon, on behalf of the fraud known as 'Frouzee Delilah,' offer the unconditional surrender of all Frouzean forces in the east."

"That's better."

Behind Minos, an audible sigh of relief emanated from the cornered Frouzean army, followed by a cacophonous clatter as thousands of weapons and armored breastplates dropped to the ground.

Tamino cleared his throat and yelled.

"Where is General Toghon!?"

The Mongol leader sheepishly emerged from a mass of Mongol troops, who now numbered about twenty thousand- outnumbered three to one by the Chinese defectors alone.

"General Toghon, as you are so fond of telling us, you have two choices: surrender or death. I ask you to choose wisely. After all, isn't this the 'natural way of things'?"

Toghon visibly bristled and puffed out his chest, placing a hand on his sword hilt. In response, Tamino hefted the Zrain'de'zhang more pointedly. Toghon cast his eyes about, taking in the blanched faces of his own troops, then looking with disgust at Minos. Then, he slowly, deliberately drew his sword, the sound of grinding metal filling the tense air. Tamino fluidly but quickly entered a fighting stance.

Toghon raised the sword … then dropped it.

A cheer erupted from both the Mongol forces and the Wil'iahn Army. Tamino let out the breath that he didn't realize he had been holding. Avora'tru'ivi rushed forward and pulled him into a tight hug.

"We did it," she whispered.

Tamino strode over to Admiral Zhang and snapped into a military salute.

"It's good to see you, Admiral."

"Likewise."

"I knew they hadn't really gotten you."

"It was a near one, but we managed to get way with much of the fleet intact. I'm sure they told you the whole thing got destroyed."

"Naturally."

A dark look crossed Zhang's face. "I'm sure you heard about the princess…"

Tamino hung his head. "I did. Delilah said she was captured, but given that she is a singularly unreliable source of information, and that particular 'fact' was part of a gambit to capture me, I'm sure she's already organizing the defenses up in heaven," he said, his voice breaking.

"That may be premature. Her ship was indeed captured, not sunk. There's a chance she's alive. It's not time to give up hope," Zhang responded.

Tamino felt hope rekindle. "I suppose not."

The two leaders turned to the assembled mass of Chinese soldiers. Tamino began to speak to them in

Mandarin, doing his best to imbue the multi-tonal language with a level of warmth.

"You came here as enemies, but you don't have to leave that way. In fact, you don't need to leave at all. We always knew that your service to the so-called 'Great Khan' was under duress. Your choice today to cast your weight in the side of light will not be forgotten. As I'm sure you may have heard by now, Wil'iah is prepared to grant clemency to you. I know that many of you likely have families back in China. But, given your choices today, I imagine it will be difficult for you to return. You are safe here, should you choose to remain. There is always a place in Wil'iah for hearts brave enough to defy the will of a tyrant."

In response, many of the Chinese soldiers began to bow in gratitude. Tamino raised a staying hand.

"Not here. In Wil'iah, we bow to no temporal person. Take your time. Think about it. If you choose to go back to China, we will grant you the safest passage we can arrange, but we cannot guarantee your safety once you return."

Tamino turned back to Admiral Zhang, who seemed to be peering into the grouped Chinese soldiers, squinting. Suddenly, the Admiral seemed to recognize someone, and stepped back in surprise. Tamino had to tap him on the shoulder to get his attention.

"Admiral, I have some bad news."

"What is it?"

"Emperor Zhao is missing in action. He blew up an ammunition dump to cover my escape from Delilah. He hasn't been seen since, and we fear the worst. I'm so sorry. I did everything I could to protect him, but he snuck out against orders to try to rescue me."

To Tamino's surprise, Zhang gave a knowing smile. "Tell me, Tamino, how old was your father when he made the decision to leave everything he knew to fight for his lost country and claim his rightful throne?"

"Twenty. Everyone knows that."

Zhang turned back to the Chinese soldiers, looking at the same place where he was before, but he continued to speak to Tamino. "And how old is Emperor Zhao?"

"Well, he *was* twenty-one…"

Tamino followed Zhang's gaze. Suddenly, he knew exactly what the aged Admiral meant.

"Perhaps there's hope for China yet," Tamino said, his face masking his sudden comprehension.

Leaving the Chinese forces behind, Tamino caught a glimpse of Lady Deborah, and ran forward to wrap her in a tight embrace.

"I knew you could do it," he said.

"Was there ever any doubt?" Deborah chuckled, but then her face grew serious. "I knew *you* could do it," she said significantly as she jabbed a finger at the Star of Wil'iah emblazoned on Tamino's breastplate.

Tamino nodded in gratitude. "I expect a full campaign report."

"Oh, you'll get nothing less than a proper opera," Deborah smiled as she led him over to the home army units. "Victory would not have been possible without our woman on the inside. She did valuable work for us, reporting the locations of the Imperial Army." Deborah motioned to the assembled crowd of knights and soldiers to her left. Medea, heeding the call, squeezed her way between two mounted knights and stepped forward, rendering the military salute.

Deborah continued. "This is Medea. We all owe her a great debt."

Tamino kindly regarded her. "At ease, Medea." As she raised her face from the salute, he suddenly smiled with recognition. "I know you from somewhere…"

Medea involuntarily blushed. "Yes, your faithfulness, you saved me from some slave-catchers long ago."

Tamino laughed. "Ah, yes, that moonless night in Kati-Thanda. Of course I remember! How could I forget? That was the same night that "Iphigenia" first arrived in Wil'iah to cause problems!"

"Yes, your faithfulness. I only regret that I did not become aware of her treachery then. I could have saved all of us a lot of trouble."

"Nonetheless, you have demonstrated great courage and heroism. Sneaking into a Frouzean camp is not for the faint of heart. We all owe you a debt of gratitude."

The color in Medea's cheeks deepened as she involuntarily batted her eyelashes. Avora'tru'ivi's eyes narrowed.

"I felt I had to repay my debt to you for rescuing me, and to this great nation for granting me freedom!"

Tamino smiled. "Well, I think you have more than proven yourself worthy." Drawing the Zrain'de'zhang from its scabbard, he tapped her on both shoulders, then on the head. "I name thee Dame Medea, Knight of the Order of the Flame of Zebulon!"

The crowd erupted into cheers as Medea smiled.

"Thank you, Your Faithfulness!"

Tamino gave a military salute, then turned to congratulate some of the other soldiers.

Medea noticed the queen approach her. Avora'tru'ivi smiled radiantly at the newly-christened knight.

"Congratulations on your knighthood, and thank you for your brave and selfless service." Avora'tru'ivi pulled her in for a hug.

As Tamino strode back toward the battlements of the relieved city, he suddenly stopped dead in his tracks.

"What is it?" asked Avora'tru'ivi, her eyebrows narrowing in concern.

Tamino's eyes were filled with a suddenly-remembered worry.

"Where's Delilah?"

CHAPTER FIFTY-SIX

ON TO THE WEST

Citadel of Balthcutta

"Sweetie, It's all going to be okay now. The bad guys lost," Avora'tru'ivi said as she hugged Judith tightly.

"Oh, I know."

"What do you mean?"

"It's all okay. Daddy told me."

Avora'tru'ivi's eyes snapped to Tamino, who responded with a quizzical look and a shrug.

"Are you holding out on me, Tamino? When were you back here sneaking hugs?"

"No, Momma, DADDY told me." This time, the emphasis was audible.

Avora'tru'ivi and Tamino both involuntarily flicked their eyes skyward, sudden comprehension dawning in them. Just then, a gentle gust of wind blew through the room.

"…Oh," Avora'tru'ivi responded.

"If 'Daddy' tells you anything else, please let us know," Tamino smiled.

After tucking in their daughter, Tamino and Avora'tru'ivi proceeded to the War Room in the depths of Balthcutta Castle. Lady Deborah and Admiral Zhang were waiting for them, hunched over a map of Wil'iah's east.

"Alright, now that the celebrations are over, what is the current situation?" Tamino asked.

"Following our initial defeat at the hands of the Frouzean-Mongol fleet, the Eastern Fleet regrouped north of Djubuguli, where it was eventually joined by reinforcements from our League allies," Admiral Zhang replied. "Even before the fleet fully assembled, we sent our fastest ships to interdict Frouzean convoys resupplying the besieging forces. The current fleet is somewhat eclectic, but is an effective fighting force. So far as we can tell, the Frouzean Navy is almost totally destroyed, at least in the east."

"Very good," said Tamino.

"Predictably, Ajax's lust for conquest drove him deeper and deeper into Vrenga'nui, and eventually even South Murrinui and Maranoa," Deborah said. "But, all units reported to the muster points as expected, and our forces smashed the Imperial Army on the downs. All went according to plan. The knights at the Hidden Fortress were able to cut the enemy supply lines, and even launched a few military raids into Gath. Wagga Wagga held firm and tied down the enemy's rearguard, rendering them unable to defend their own supply caravans. By the time the Home Army assembled on the downs, the Imperial Army was ragged and starving, and most of them were only too happy to surrender. The battle was an almost immediate rout, and most of the Imperial Army is currently held prisoner by Home Army units in east Maranoa."

Tamino nodded. "Excellent work. What of the civilians in Vrenga'nui?"

Deborah continued, "Civilians in Vrenga'nui evacuated as planned to the National Redoubt. The Imperial Army never discovered their location, despite committing over 50,000 troops to the effort. Once we closed our trap on the downs, the Home Army proceeded south and mopped them up. The civilians, defended by the Home Army and Army of Vrenga'nui units initially assigned to the Redoubt, will remain there for the duration of hostilities, resupplied from the North."

"Does the Hidden Fortress or Balawan indicate any sign of a second wave from Gath?"

"According to our intelligence reports, the Frouzeans mustered nearly every able-bodied, fighting-age man in the Empire to create this invasion force. Seeing as their culture prohibits women from serving," she said ruefully, "they barely have anything left to defend their own cities, much less assemble another army. In fact, we've heard that there are food shortages and riots in the streets. I'd say now was the time to strike, but we still have other things to worry about."

❋ ❋ ❋

Minos languished in a holding cell in the dungeon of Balthcutta, though even the dank surroundings chiseled into the rock outcropping on which the castle was built were better than the best prisons he'd seen in Frouzea. He started as he heard the jangle of keys, and the door to the cell slid open with a screech, the flaring torch illuminating two faces he hadn't expected to see: Tamino and Avora'tru'ivi.

"Your Faithfulnesses!" he glibly entreated, throwing himself prostrate on the floor in a pitiful display of submission.

"Never mind that," Tamino said gruffly. "We need you to answer some questions…unless you want Deborah to do the asking?"

A look of fear crossed Minos' grimy face. "No… of course not…what do you want to know? I swear, this whole invasion was never my idea anyway. I knew this plan was flawed from the start. If only people hadn't listened to that *woman*…"

"Watch it," Avora'tru'ivi sharply retorted.

"Oh, not to say that all women"—

"Whatever. We need to stay on topic," said the queen, rolling her eyes.

"Where is Delilah?" asked Tamino pointedly.

"Who knows? She simply told me that she had 'other business to attend to.' If you ask me, she knew we were going to lose and got out of here before the jaws closed on her too. That was probably her plan all along, although I can't imagine why."

"Did she give any indication of her destination?"

"No. In fact, she left most of her retinue here to give the illusion of her continued presence, but her lapdogs Briseis, Salome, and Heracles went with her."

"Hmmm," said Tamino.

"What do you know of the plans for the invasion of central Wil'iah?" Avora'tru'ivi asked forcefully.

"That I can tell you, if I'm thanked properly."

The queen looked contemptuously down her nose. "You are not in any position to bargain. As far as I'm concerned," she gave her husband a slightly peeved look, "you have already been thanked with your life. When this is all over, I suggest that you familiarize yourself with the Sixth Commandment. It's the only thing that saved you from oblivion."

Minos looked at the ground. "Point taken."

"I should hope so."

Minos cleared his throat, then divulged what he knew. "The Center Force, like the Eastern Force, is composed of Mongol and Frouzean units. The Frouzean forces are under the command of Menelaus of Gaza, while the Mongol forces are under the command of Temur Khan, Kublai Khan's grandson. Their mission was to take the capital, then proceed east and meet up with us once we had conquered Yaringa, Vrenga'nui, and South Murrinui. Some of the force was also to proceed north to complete the destruction of Manasseh," he said, wincing at the withering look he received from the queen.

"And how large was this force?" Tamino continued.

"Of equal size to our own, but primarily Mongol. They committed thirty tumens."

Three hundred thousand Mongols, in Tjoritja. Tamino felt a chill run down his spine.

"And in the west?" Avora'tru'ivi asked.

"Tanitania's large battlefleet was intended to engage Wil'iah's western fleet and destroy it. The Tanitanian army was to march north, ravage Pilbara, then proceed to besiege Trujustakanoa. Once Jason took Manasseh, he was to pivot west and complete a pincer maneuver with the Tanitanians to capture Issachar."

"Do you have any updates on the status of these initiatives?" Tamino asked.

"Communication from the west and center has been almost non-existent. I'm no better-informed than you."

"And do you know of the whereabouts of my sister Jessica, who went missing when our fleet was defeated at the cape?"

"Delilah had some special plan for her, but she didn't divulge it to me. She isn't the best with communication."

"I see. Do you have anything else to say for yourself?"

"Only this. The vast majority of Frouzea's leadership thought that this war was a fool's errand from the beginning. And none of us believes that Delilah is really a goddess"— Avora'tru'ivi snorted – "But she won such fanatical popular support from the people that we had no choice. We simply were swept up in the tide of her own megalomania. Any of us who didn't go along with her plan were killed, up to and including Diomedes."

"I was wondering what happened to him," Tamino said.

"Yes, he had a lunch date with her pet crocodile, Goliath."

Tamino suppressed a shudder.

"Oh, *that's* what that crocodile was for in that tank we captured," Avora'tru'ivi replied. "He's been released back into the river system. Hopefully he can live his days out in peace."

Tamino regarded Minos. "Alright, thank you for your cooperation. I'm sure that you understand that I can't thank you for anything else."

Minos stared ashamedly at the ground.

"I suppose I'll have to research that Sixth Commandment."

After departing the dungeon, Tamino and Avora'tru'ivi conferred.

"We need more information about the situation in the center before we send an army over there," Tamino said.

"Yes," Avora'tru'ivi responded, "but we might be able to get a message through to them via the beacon system and the signal corps. As I recall we have a standard "victory in the east" signal. We won't be able to get much detail back from them, but they may be able to at least tell us if Trukanamoa has fallen or not. We can try a similar tactic with Ephraim-Manasseh. It will take hours to get a response, but it's much better than going uninformed."

※ ※ ※

That night, the beacons once again erupted in flame, spreading the news of victory in the east across the nation. Where the mountains ended and the flatlands began, as dawn spread its friendly light, white smoke rings from the highly-trained signal corps rose into the sky, sending the news ever westward. Where the Tjoritja Mountains began their march across the center of the continent, the beacon-fires once again took up the message. Finally, a brave orange flame burned atop the highest keep of the East Guard.

Prime Minister Allira, from the command post atop the gate of Ntaripe, watched the fire in triumph, her mouth trembling with emotion.

"There's hope," she excitedly exclaimed to the fellow troops on the wall. "Victory is ours in the East. Send a message back to Balthcutta – tell them Trukanamoa is still under siege, but we hold firm. Yellow fire."

※ ※ ※

Hours later, a bright yellow flame roared to life atop Mount Cambewarra, and Tamino pumped his fist in triumph. "I knew that Trukanamoa would hold out!"

When a similar flame flare up on the mountain four hours later, an identical answer came from the north. Reconvening in the War Room in the Citadel of Balthcutta, Tamino explained the plan to the assembled generals.

"I will take twelve divisions west to Trukanamoa. It's not as much as I would like, but I think it's all that we can support logistically. Avora'tru'ivi will take eight divisions to the assistance of Manasseh. That should be enough to help defeat Prince Jason's forces that we presume, based on the beacon response, to be besieging Shechem."

Avora'tru'ivi winced as she thought back to the revolting prince's advances ten years before. Forcing the unpleasant memory out of her thought, she addressed the generals.

"I am loath to leave Wil'iah in this hour of need, but we cannot allow our allies to fall."

Lady Deborah gravely nodded. "Your place is at the side of the people who raised you. We can handle the home front."

"Alright, that settles it," Tamino said. "Begin mustering the troops, equipment, and logistical trains. We will depart in two days." His eyes catching a painting of the city of Trukanamoa lovingly framed on the wall, he thought of his brother, bravely commanding the defense of the city.

Don't lose hope, Jeremiah. We're coming!

Rallying the troops to march west

CHAPTER FIFTY-SEVEN

THE WRONG PRINCESS

Palace of Xanadu, northern China

"**M**ore wine!' slurred the Great Khan as he struggled to shift position on his throne. Bao, his latest Chinese minister, flinched at the harshness of the command as he gingerly picked up the platter and prepared to return the kitchen. His eyes watering at the acrid fumes from the three pots of wine already lying mostly empty on the platter, he wondered how much was going to be too much for the Emperor.

How this man managed to conquer China escapes me, he thought as he began to hurry out of the room. The obese drunkard currently splayed across the throne was not the living nightmare he had been brought up to fear.

His thoughts were abruptly interrupted as the doors to the throne room flew open. Kublai Khan grunted in surprise, and Bao froze at the sight that greeted his eyes. Four burly Mongol guards dragged an enormous woman through the door, expending significant effort as she quite literally dragged her feet. The statuesque lady was like nobody Bao had ever seen, her voluminous, frizzy hair framing a head that towered over the already-large guards beside her. Bao estimated that she must be over six feet tall. Her bared teeth formed a harsh juxtaposition with the bronze color of her angular face, and in her angry eyes blazed a fire that made Bao's blood run cold.

Is this what we're up against?

Suddenly, with a growl and a great surge of effort, she wrenched her arm out of one of the guards' grip and backhanded him across the face, the force of the blow sending him flying against a column, which creaked ominously. Balling her hand into a fist, she slugged the other guard to her right, whose eyes crossed as he crumpled to the floor. Seeing the commotion, the additional guards flanking the Khan's throne rushed forward to restrain her, one of them cursing under his breath as he barely missed another wild swing of her fist. Finally, one of the guards managed to wrap a thick arm around her neck in what he thought would be an effective restraint, until the woman dipped her head and bit the exposed arm. The guard howled in pain and released her, but, by this point, she was up against no fewer than twelve guards.

The scuffle continued for another minute before the woman was eventually restrained again and dragged before the Great Khan, her teeth once again bared in a perpetual growl.

"Well, the famous Princess Jessica, in the flesh. I've been told you were a firecracker." the Khan said, his words dripping with contempt.

The Princess of Wil'iah spat on the ground. "If there is a hell, you'll burn in it!"

"Strong words from a prisoner of the world's greatest empire!"

Jessica's nostrils flared as the stench of alcohol hit her nostrils.

The Khan continued. "Now, Princess, I am willing to be lenient. Let's be civilized here. I will provide you comfortable accommodations with my wives. You won't be harmed. Trust me, you are more valuable to me alive. Perhaps your brother will be willing to make certain…concessions in exchange for your release."

The princess snorted in disgust. "You're one to speak of civilization. All that you and your grandfather have done is destroy civilization. I can promise you that your dastardly attempt at exacting ransom will fail. My brother knows what he must do to defend his country. My presence here is irrelevant, and he knows that. So, you might as well kill me now," she pointedly looked the Khan up and down, "if you think you can."

Kublai laughed, his chins bobbing up and down. "I won't be baited into giving up my leverage. I'd love to kill you, but I won't give you the satisfaction. We'll see if your attitude changes after a few days here. I'm surprised that you are so rude. I at least had the impression that the Wil'iahns were a dignified and respectable people. I guess your father's parenting left a bit to be desired." Turning to the guards, he yelled "Take her away!" with a dramatic gesture.

As the guards dragged her away to Kublai Khan's harem, she looked over her shoulder and yelled in response.

"Whatever you think of him, I am the daughter of Hezekiah Vrenga'ava'zora'vaua. You just kidnapped the wrong princess!"

As her words echoed in the chamber, Bao resumed his course towards the kitchens, shaken by what he had witnessed.

She may be right.

As Jessica was dragged away, she began to get a better look at her surroundings. The splendid, gilded room was intricately painted with images of flowers and animals.

Such beautiful art, for such a barbarous ruler, she thought.

However, as she thought back to her unwelcome trip to Xanadu, she couldn't help but be impressed. Clearly, Khan had gone to great lengths to appear civilized. The enormous palace had a diameter of sixteen miles and numerous gardens overflowing with exotic plants, pleasant pavilions, and picturesque lakes. The splendid Marble Palace where she now found herself imprisoned was joined by a second complex, the equally-intricate Cane Palace, elsewhere on the grounds.

The guards dragged Jessica, kicking and screaming all the way, to a doorway with two proud columns with carved dragons wrapped around them, their gilded heads supporting the lintel of the doorway. Two stern-faced eunuchs guarded the doorway, but they swept open the double doors to admit Jessica entry. She was unceremoniously tossed into the room, and then the doors slammed shut.

As Jessica shook her head to clear it, she focused on the scene before her. Dozens of dainty women froze, stunned at the appearance of the newcomer. A few iron-featured, elderly women attended to them, but even they looked shocked.

Great. I must be in the harem.

Recalling her training in Mandarin Chinese, Jessica said "Don't be alarmed" as she rose to her feet. However, this seemed to have the opposite effect, as the women recoiled in fear. With a wry smile, Jessica realized that she was almost a foot taller than most of them – and she was sure none of them had seen a Wil'iahn before.

"I am a prisoner of the Great Khan," Jessica said. "I don't know why I have been taken here, instead of a regular cell."

"Perhaps the Khan fancies you," one of them said, recovering slightly from her shock.

The thought turned Jessica's stomach, but the gears of her mind were already working on a solution.

Jessica got as settled as she could in her new surroundings, fighting off an attempt by two of the older women to "evaluate her." At first, the two bat-like women had insisted on attempting to give her a "carat rating," whatever that meant, but when Jessica finally bared her teeth and audibly growled, they skittered away. Her mind still racing, Jessica decided that all she could do in the circumstances was try to get some sleep. She was just about to nod off when she felt something gently poke her back.

Jessica rolled over in a flash, fists balled and eyes wide open – only to see the woman who had addressed her earlier, who gasped and recoiled. Jessica let her features soften.

"What is it?" she asked.

"Is it true? Are you from Wil'iah?" the concubine asked.

"Yes," Jessica responded.

"And are women really free there?"

"Yes. I take it you aren't here willingly?"

"We are all from the distant province of Kungarat," the concubine responded. "Kublai Khan has four main wives, and thousands of us concubines. Every year, his men come to our province and take four or five hundred of us. Then, we are evaluated, and if we are over twenty-one carats in beauty, we are accepted into his service." Suddenly she clapped a hand over her mouth, her eyes widening in terror. Jessica soon understood the reason why. One of the elderly handlers was swooping in.

"I take it these are here to watch and control you?" Jessica whispered. The concubine silently nodded. Jessica decided to take matters into her own hands. As the old woman approached, a chastising expression on her face, Jessica rose to her full height, grabbed the old woman by the collar, and lifted her off the floor with one arm, bringing her to eye-level. The old woman's face immediately turned from triumphant glee to naked fear.

"You will leave us alone," Jessica growled. The old woman nodded, and, when Jessica put her back on the floor, scurried away.

The concubine watched her retreat with an awed expression. Jessica turned back to her and continued her questioning.

"I take it you won't ever get out of here?"

"Not alive. Khan regularly changes out his concubines. About two hundred are culled each year. I've already been here too long."

Jessica felt like she was going to be sick, but quickly fought for control.

You are a princess of Wil'iah and an admiral of the Royal Wil'iahn Navy. Act like it!

"Have any of you ever tried to escape?" she asked.

"Escape?" the concubine responded in wide-eyed confusion, as if it were a foreign word.

"That's right. We're going to get out of here. *All* of us."

CHAPTER FIFTY-EIGHT

IPHIGENIA'S TOUR

Trukanamoa

Jeremiah and Iphigenia walked through the outer ward of the Castle of Trukanamoa, the damsel's wondering eyes taking in the massive defenses as they approached the gatehouse that led to the city beyond.

"I must thank you, Iphigenia. The tactical information you have given us is invaluable."

"Anything for the valiant nation that rescued me," she said, batting her eyelashes.

Jeremiah turned slightly red and cleared his throat. "I'm not surprised that the cowards turned and ran after the scare we gave them. But, as you indicated, I'm sure they'll be back."

"I still don't understand why they're so afraid," Iphigenia said. "After all, they are way more powerful than your defenses."

Jeremiah allowed himself a smirk as the portcullis raised to allow them to exit the castle. Standing foursquare before them was the Church of the Eternal Victory, every bit as proud and defiant as the fortress that shielded it from the darts of the enemy.

"Allow me to show you," he said with a note of pride.

"By all means," Iphigenia said, motioning him forward.

The enormous gilded doors of the church, inlaid with the patterns of the twelve tribes, slowly swung open. The interior of the Grand Cathedral, which soared above them into the heavens, was bathed in the golden light of a thousand braziers that flickered mysteriously. But the attention of all in the church was instantly drawn to the plinth in its center. There, aloof, proud, and untouchable, in all its ancient wonder, stood the glittering Ark of the Covenant, the golden wings of the seraphim that crowned it seeming to glow with their own unearthly power.

"What is *that?*" Iphigenia asked breathlessly, her eyes filled with wonder.

"That," Jeremiah said, notes of pride and a certain awed terror mixing in his low voice, "is the Ark of the Covenant, the ancient symbol of God's promise to save our people."

"Can I touch it?" Iphigenia asked innocently.

Jeremiah laughed. "I wouldn't recommend it. No living Wil'iahn has touched it."

"Oh," Iphigenia said, her eyes widening in surprise.

"Well, I think that concludes our tour," Jeremiah said. "We'd best get you to your new living quarters. The castle's just about maxed out, so we're going to have to put you up in one of the guest rooms in the palace."

"My goodness, I've never been in a palace before," Iphigenia said, open wonder filling her voice.

"Don't get too excited. Our palace is only as large as it needs to be. My father had no desire for extravagant expenditures."

As they exited the cathedral and began to walk toward the palace, Iphigenia spoke again.

"It must be difficult, being so close to the throne and yet so far."

"I don't know what you mean. My brother is an able and capable ruler."

"Is he? He allowed the Frouzee inside the gates of Trukanamoa two years ago. Isn't it a classic rule of war that you do not allow your enemy to inspect your defenses? I think your country would be better off with you at the helm."

"I did not agree with that decision. That woman is not to be trusted."

"Indeed, she is not."

"However, I trust the ultimate judgement of my brother. He is a good and caring man who loves his people very much, and would do anything to defend this nation."

"Indeed, from what I hear, he could -and did- ...anything."

"What do you mean?"

"I overheard some of the soldiers speaking. Apparently your brother…entertained the Frouzee more than he led you to believe."

"What!? I don't know what you are talking about."

"From what I heard, she snuck into his chambers after the official state dinner and offered him a military alliance in exchange for certain …shall we say, favors?"

"My brother would never do that. He loves his wife more than I think anybody has loved another in recent memory."

"Yes, but does he love her enough to pass up an opportunity to secure an alliance against the inexorable Mongol Hordes?"

"Clearly such an alliance was never concluded, else you would not be here."

"Ah, your highness, you think like a Wil'iahn. You and I both know the depth of the Frouzee's duplicity. Tamino is naïve to a fault. Surely she took advantage of him and then reneged on the deal." Her voice dropped to a whisper. "It is widely known within the empire that the Frouzee fancies your brother. Yes, she has had many husbands and even more "gifts" from outlying provinces, but she finds them all dull and unsophisticated. As we both know, her reputation as a temptress has reached even the shores of Persia. No man in Frouzea can resist her- do you think your brother could, especially when assurance of his country's safety was offered on a silver platter?"

"Ma'am, I do think like a Wil'iahn, which is why I know Tamino would never even consider such an action. She may be able to instantly snare a man in Frouzea, where the men are widely known to run about after anything that moves, but such tactics do not work in Wil'iah. Tamino is a brave, honest, loyal, and faithful man. He is my best friend, and I know him well enough to know that he would rather die than betray his wife and his country, especially to a viper so vile as the Frouzee."

"And would he rather see the nation his parents sacrificed so much to build go down in flames?"

"I know I speak for all of Wil'iah when I say we would all rather die a thousand times by fire than enter into such an unholy alliance, as I am sure you are finding out now."

"Such fire, such strength. This is why Wil'iah needs you to lead. This is why oppressed people like me everywhere need someone like you. Someone who would slam the gates at evil, not invite it in to the bedchamber."

"Wil'iah has such a man, my brother. I refuse to believe you. Tamino would under no circumstances entertain such a motion. So far as I am concerned, the matter is closed."

"Well, I am glad you trust him. I hope your admirable faith is well-placed, especially in the coming weeks. I only hope he did not reveal too much about Trukanamoa's defenses." Suddenly, her eyes lit up with delight. "Ah, is this the palace?" she said motioning to the small building that stood before them.

"Yes, Ma'am!"

"How *cute!*" Iphigenia squealed.

"You will be well-taken care of while you are here. I pray that hostilities will not last too much longer. I'll have to speak to Tamino, but I'm sure he will grant you clemency to stay here afterward." Jeremiah motioned to the portly man approaching them. "This is Enaua'ivanu, the head of the staff here at the palace. Enaua'ivanu, this is Iphigenia, a former slave of the Frouzeans who we rescued on our scout mission. She has provided us some valuable information. Since the castle is filled to the bursting, I thought it was a good idea to put her up in the guest room."

Enaua'ivanu nodded curtly, then turned to Iphigenia. When his eyes met her face, he paused for a moment, his brow briefly wrinkling as he seemed to study her doe-like features. Then, he quickly shook his head from side to side and snapped into a civilian salute.

"Forgive me," he said. "I will show you to your quarters." He turned around and began walking into the palace, but not before looking once more over his shoulder at the woman who followed him.

CHAPTER FIFTY-NINE

THE FISH FIGHT

Imperial Army Camp, Tjoritja, Central Wil'iah

*B*riseis stepped outside of her tent in the Frouzean Army's camp and deeply inhaled the cool desert air as she marveled at the blanket of stars draped over her head. She didn't understand it, but she felt some sort of strange power in the breeze that gently ruffled her hair. Suddenly, her eyes narrowed as she noticed light spilling out of the enormous red pavilion that belonged to Delilah.

How odd. She isn't here, Briseis thought. A suspicious glimmer in her eye, she snuck toward the tent and gingerly spread open its flaps.

Inside, the tent was brightly lit by candles, which illuminated a platter piled high with decaying fish that Delilah had brought from the coast for the "calling ceremony" whereby she would be "coaxed into appearing" for the main army, the majority of which was not yet aware that she was here. But it wasn't the fish, however foul their stench, that alarmed her. Sitting at the vanity on the far end of the pavilion was Salome.

Next to her, splayed out over a cushion, was Delilah's presentation costume, and, with it, the famous snake headdress. Salome gently, almost reverently, bent down to pick up the headdress. Then, slowly, with a gravitas Briseis didn't know the officious damsel possessed, she lowered it onto her head. Her stone-serious face was suddenly lit by a wicked smile that Briseis could see all too clearly.

Salome trying the hat on for size

"Just *what* do you think you are doing?" Briseis challenged.

Starting in shock, Salome whirled around to face her rival, her smile instantly turning into an ugly grimace.

"How dare you walk in on me like this!?" she shrieked in response.

Briseis advanced forward, balling her fists in fury.

"Never mind that, you officious, scheming, bootlicking—"

Salome shot up from her pouf. "Watch your tongue!"

"Forget my tongue, you'd better watch yourself! Who do you think you are? How dare you place the headdress of the eternal empress on your pitiful, unworthy head?"

Briseis marched forward, until she was mere inches from Salome's indignant face.

"This was your plan all along, wasn't it? Ingratiate yourself, insert yourself into Her Worship's life, and then, when the moment comes, seize it all for yourself? I knew that you were actually conspiring with Diomedes, and it wasn't just a trick to flush him out! How could you, after everything she's done for you? I knew you were rotten to the core right from the start!"

Salome didn't respond. Instead, her eyes darted over to the platter of fish. Then, in a sudden, blinding motion, she grabbed a large snapper and slapped Briseis across the face with it. The rotting flesh squelched on impact and sprayed all over Briseis's face and clothes, leaving a shocked visage behind.

"How *dare* you?" Briseis seethed with anger. She felt rage boil in her stomach, rapidly overcoming whatever sense of decorum remained. Her eyes now shot over to the plate and eyed a flounder, whose dead eyes blankly stared back at her. Briseis grabbed the fish and, swinging it with all her might, smacked Salome across the face, knocking her back into the vanity. The snake headdress toppled off her head.

There was no going back now. Salome picked up a slimy sea cucumber and hurled it at Briseis, who responded with a fusillade of shrimp and slugs. As the aquatic bombardment continued, the unrefrigerated bounty of the sea soon became an indistinguishable, frothy morass of scales, organs, and entrails. Briseis slipped on some residue left over from a squid and landed directly in a pile of sea worms, gagging at the stench that filled her nostrils. Seizing the advantage, Salome dove down and wrapped a limp, dead moray eel around Briseis' neck, tightening the organic noose while Briseis kicked and scratched, fighting to draw breath.

"This is the last time you insult me!" Salome screamed as she viciously tugged on the eel.

"You---insult---yourself---every---time---you---look----in----the---mirror!" Briseis forced out her reply.

Salome shrieked in disgust, and then in pain, as Briseis' free hand clobbered her over the head with a lobster. But still she tightened her grip on the eel, and Briseis' flutterings grew more feeble even as her vision began to go dark.

Suddenly, a deep voice cut through the violence.

"Just what is going on here?"

A hulking form stood at the entrance to the tent. Heracles.

The giant bodyguard strode over to the two women, forcibly separated them, then lifted them both up, kicking in protest, by the scruffs of their necks.

"She started it!" Salome gasped.

"She is trying to usurp Delilah!" Briseis countered.

"That's enough. I want both of you to be quiet. You should be ashamed of yourselves. Wasting Her Worship's sacrificial bounty for a childish food fight. You can be certain Her Worship will hear of this when she returns." He marched over to the opening of the tent and threw both women out, leaving them crumpled heaps on the desert ground.

"I always love being carried by a big strong man," Salome giggled as she batted her eyelashes.

"Whatever," Heracles rolled his eyes as he walked away.

Salome turned back to Briseis.

"This isn't over," she simply said, before slinking away into the darkness.

CHAPTER SIXTY

DELILAH'S DECEPTION

Trukanamoa

The four soldiers that had fallen victim to Jeremiah's raiding party languished in a holding cell deep in the bowels of one of Trukanamoa's wall fortifications, rubbing their ankles at the shackles that bound them. Their dirt-streaked faces were only lit by a single sputtering torch that looked like it was going to go out at any minute. One looked doubtfully at another, and was about to open his mouth, when a scraping sound announced the presence of a key in a lock. The men started at the ugly rasp, and blinked in a mixture of wonder and adoration as the door swung open to reveal a woman in a simple white shift.

"I think it's time to put the Imperial Frouzean Moving Service to Work," Iphigenia said as a serpentine smile played across her face, a ring of keys jangling in her hand.

"How did you get in here?" one of the guards asked.

"The Wil'iahns always talk about speaking to their God. I guess I helped a few of them do so a bit more *directly*," she said as she unlocked the shackles. "Alright, on your feet!"

The men, led by the woman, slowly crept their way through the darkened corridors of the dungeon, pausing to hide behind the corners any time they heard a guard pace through. The woman deftly navigated the twists and turns of the subterranean maze, finally emerging in a wide field that backed the walls. Sticking to the shadows, hoping to avoid spying eyes from the walls above, the party continued to move. Standing directly in front of them was the Castle of Trukanamoa, and, beyond that, the Church of the Eternal Victory.

"What now?" one of the soldiers said.

"Now we wait," the woman hissed as she crouched in the lee of one of the massive towers.

They didn't have to wait long. Seemingly out of nowhere, an angry orange glow lit the sky as a fireball arced down toward the wall. The battlements instantly became a flurry of activity as alarms sounded all along their lengths. The bells of the church suddenly boomed in panic, and the ward before them exploded into a frenzy as sleepy soldiers rushed to their posts.

Two men rushed right past where the party hid.

"I don't understand. I thought they were gone. I thought they were afraid of the Ark," one said to the other.

"Apparently they've gotten over it," came the response.

Once they had passed, the party darted through the crowded ward, passing under the guns of the great castle. The harried defenders didn't notice them. Within minutes, they stood directly before the Church of the Eternal Victory, moving into the shadow of its many towers and spires.

"Now for the fun part," the woman said as she untied a cloth that had been fastened it to her waist and put it over her head, instantly transforming her appearance into that of a pious pilgrim.

"Wait for me here," she said, then slipped into the door. After what seemed like an eternity, the soldiers heard a muffled cry, followed by silence. A few moments later, the woman emerged, a self-satisfied smile on her face.

"Well, that should put them to sleep for a while," she said as she quietly suppressed a cough. "The Mist of Hypnos has yet to fail me." She hurriedly motioned toward the doors. "Hurry, you fools! Our window of opportunity will close soon!"

The men charged into the church.

Standing before them was the Ark of the Covenant.

CHAPTER SIXTY-ONE

APHEK RELIVED

Trukanamoa

*J*eremiah awoke the next morning to the sound of bereaved wailing.

As soon as the import of what he was hearing registered, he sat bolt upright in bed, and, not even having time to buckle on his outer armor, rushed down from his command post atop the wall, rubbing sleep from his eyes. He hadn't gotten nearly enough last night.

I hate 3 AM raids, he thought. This one had been strange, too. A sudden, furious attack with a handful of siege engines on a specific section of the wall, after which, the enemy army had simply melted back into the desert. Something was wrong.

As Jeremiah descended the stairs to the flat ward below, his eyes strained to make out the source of the commotion. All around him, people milled about, excitedly talking. Some of them threw up their hands in gestures of despair, while some of them wept and moaned. Increasing dread filling his stomach, Jeremiah finally grabbed hold of a frantic adolescent who was running away from the church.

"What is it?"

"It's—It's gone!"

"What's gone!"

The child wordlessly pointed at the church, then burst into tears and kept on running.

Jeremiah now ran in the opposite direction, his thundering strides soon bringing him to the doors of the church, where a mob of people frantically groped at the doors. The crowd parted as they recognized the prince, and Jeremiah forced himself through the doors into the Church.

As soon as he entered, his mouth ran dry, and he stopped in his tracks.

The great stone plinth in the center of the church was empty. The Ark was gone.

"*What?*" Jeremiah hissed under his breath.

The Patriarch of the church, noticing him, swiftly walked over, his face ghostly pale.

"It's gone," he said, his voice trembling.

"I can see that, but I don't believe it," Jeremiah said. "I don't understand."

"Neither do I," the Patriarch said. He motioned for another clergyman, who ran over, his eyes filled with tears.

"I was in the church last night, along with the guards," he said, his voice choking with despair. "It was a quiet night just like any other. Suddenly, the room filled with a strange smoke, and that's the last thing I remember. The next I knew, we were on the floor, and the Ark was gone."

"How is this possible?" Jeremiah shook his head in bewilderment.

Suddenly, steps rang out as a soldier breathlessly ran into the church.

"They're gone!"

"What now? Who's gone?"

"Those soldiers you captured yesterday!"

Jeremiah's stomach dropped to the ornately-tiled floor.

"*No,*" he said under his breath, sudden comprehension dawning.

"I need to go to the palace, now," he said. "I'll be back soon, and we'll continue the investigation." With that, Jeremiah spun on his heel and ran.

Fortunately, the palace wasn't far. The two guards who stood at the front door noticed his approach and instantly swung the doors open. Jeremiah had barely entered the palace when his ears were assaulted by an ear-splitting scream.

Racing towards the source of the noise, Jeremiah arrived in a hallway – and barely suppressed a retch.

A maid from the custodial staff stood over the lifeless body of Enaua'ivanu, his glassy eyes staring at the ceiling above.

Forgetting himself, Jeremiah brusquely shook the maid's shoulders.

"Where is she!?"

"Who?"

"The slave girl!"

"I---I don't know—"

Without giving the woman more time to respond, Jeremiah ran down the hallway, emerging into the courtyard at the back of the palace. Before him was the guest house, its doors hanging limply open.

Jeremiah charged into the guest room, which looked immaculate- except for a bunch of flower petals oddly strewn on the table. Jeremiah stood a little taller, recognizing a pattern. The seemingly random petals resolved themselves into a gut-turning shape.

The symbol of the Frouzean Empire.

Just then, the bells of the church rang out with a new alarm.

CHAPTER SIXTY-TWO

I AM THE ENEMY

Trukanamoa

*T*earing his eyes away from the ghastly flower arrangement, Jeremiah ran back out of the palace and on to the walls, his chest heaving with effort. He was already winded when he reached the battlements, but he suddenly felt like the wind had been knocked out of him.

Standing in full battle array before him was the vast Frouzean-Mongol Army.

A sedan chair approached the walls of Trukanamoa, flying a flag of truce. Jeremiah rushed to the crenellations, noting with no small amount of satisfaction the rows of cannons staring grimly out at the massing enemy, just out of range.

The slaves carrying the sedan chair stopped about eighty feet from the wall. The silk curtains parted to reveal...Iphigenia, luxuriating on a couch, still dressed in her innocent white shift.

"Iphigenia!?! You are working for the enemy that enslaved you?" He called from the walls, his mouth working in shock.

A wicked smile, plainly visible even from atop the walls, splayed across the woman's face. She raised a hand to daintily pull on the silk cord that hung next to her, causing a tinkling bell to chime. Two women ran forward, carrying something on a soft pillow. Iphigenia reached forward and picked it up. With a lurch of his gut, Jeremiah realized it was a snake hood-shaped headdress crowned with two horns and a hissing cobra. Iphigenia slowly, dramatically placed it on her head, then locked eyes with Jeremiah.

"I don't work for the enemy. *I am the enemy!!*"

Jeremiah's stomach plummeted as he realized he had never actually seen the Frouzee Delilah in the flesh, for he had been away during her infamous state visit two years before. Had he really been so gullible?

"Well, well, well. Brave Prince Jeremiah. Courteous, yes. Honorable, perhaps. But intelligent? Hardly. Not even as much as your brother, who, cute as he is, does not set a standard for smarts. It was a pleasure getting to know you-- and your city's defenses."

Apoplectic, Jeremiah raised his fist and worked his jaw, trying to prepare a retort. But, before the words could leave his mouth, the gauzy curtain abruptly yanked itself up again. Delilah smiled at him.

"Oh, and, my prince, have you been…missing anything lately?"

With a contemptuous flick, she yanked on a second silk cord. The silk curtain behind her, which Jeremiah had surmised was the back of the sedan chair, yanked open to reveal the Ark of the Covenant, chained to a velvet pillow.

Jeremiah felt his face turn red as the kingdom's soil as his fingernails dug far enough into his palms to draw blood. The soldiers flanking him gasped almost in unison, and a murmur began to rise from the inner wards of the city as the news of the devastating capture spread.

"Yes, yes, the famous Ark of the Covenant! Who knew that all the power of a nation, all the hope of a people, could be contained in such a small box? Well, it is lost to you now. What even Babylon could not accomplish, I have. Now your city has lost its light. It is become small, weak, and ready for the taking. What strength you once had is gone. I suggest you surrender now…" she briefly looked at the Ark and smirked, "For I am not bound by its commandment not to kill!" With that, she raised her arm above her head. The giant army behind her began to ponderously advance, the groan of the wheels of the siege towers filling the air.

"Why don't you open it!" yelled a soldier from further down the wall. Despite the bravery of the declaration, Jeremiah could see naked fear writ large on his eyes. Glancing down the battlements at the exhausted assortment of old men, older teenagers, and elderly women that mostly manned them, Jeremiah realized that Trukanamoa's defenses weren't going to last long against the forces arrayed before them. Not without the Ark.

This is all your fault. If only you hadn't been so stupid.

Jeremiah suddenly stood bolt upright as he realized there was a chance. A small one, but a chance at that. Grabbing a voice trumpet that stood on a stool next to him, Jeremiah yelled at the retreating sedan chair.

"It is well-known that the Philistines have a proud tradition of trial by combat!" he yelled.

The sedan chair stopped, and Delilah looked contemptuously over her shoulder.

"And it's well-known that you mudfaces don't."

"All the more reason for you to prove yourselves," Jeremiah said. "In the name of the Faithful Kingdom of Wil'iah, I personally challenge you or a champion of your choosing to personal combat, to the death. To the victor will go the Ark."

"And why on my green Earth would I acquiesce to such a ridiculous request?" Delilah said, her lips curling into a sneer.

"If I am truly of an inferior race, as you aver, then you have nothing to worry about. Nonetheless, your culture's sense of honor, what little of it exists, demands it."

Menelaus of Gaza, who now stood next to the sedan chair, gave a Delilah a nervous look.

"He's not wrong," he hissed. Delilah rolled her eyes.

"What are you afraid of, Delilah? I would think an *eternal empress* would have an endless array of formidable warriors eagerly awaiting the change to crush a 'mudface' like me!"

"We would look like cowards if we refused," Menelaus said through gritted teeth.

A sudden look of piqued curiosity crossing her face, Delilah raised her chin imperiously.

"I always appreciate a little…entertainment. I do have such a champion." She extended her little finger in the air with a beckoning motion.

"Heracles, come here."

Jeremiah swallowed hard as the Frouzee's enormous bodyguard emerged from the shadows behind her sedan chair.

Delilah whispered into Heracles' ear.

"Achilles is dead. Ajax is defeated. I know how you feel about me. Now is your chance. Defeat this mudface, and…"

A look of longing wonder crossed Heracles' face.

"Now be a good boy and get your weapons."

Heracles, Champion of Frouzea

CHAPTER SIXTY-THREE

CLASH OF CHAMPIONS

Trukanamoa

eremiah grimly strode down the broad avenue that led from the Elysium gardens to the castle, and beyond that, the gates of Trukanamoa. Clad from head to toe in the finest armor Wil'iah had to offer and hefting an enormous, two-handed broadsword, he seemed a picture out of an ancient heroic legend, an impression reinforced by the intense scowl that lay across his face. Both sides of the avenue were lined with exhausted and frightened-looking citizens- young children and elders. But the fear had not completely won. Behind the terror that clouded their eyes lay a last desperate hope. Jeremiah swallowed hard as he realized he was that hope. The citizens flung flowers and leis at him. Some of the older women even blew him affectionate, motherly kisses. As he approached the gates, Jeremiah's eyes focused on the Wil'iahn battle-flag that still snapped defiantly atop them, and his heart simultaneously leapt and sank.

It's all up to me now.

Delilah rubbed her hands together in anticipation as she stared at the gates.

"This will be so much fun!" she crooned as she squeezed Heracles' bulging bicep, the bodyguard taking in a sharp intake of breath in response as his nostrils dilated and a slightly red tinge crossed his face.

Temur Khan approached the empress, a doubtful look crossing his face.

"This is a foolhardy plan. You hold all of the advantage. You have no reason to give him this chance to take back the ark."

"This is merely a formality, son," Delilah said, Temur bristling at the last word. "Our proud warrior tradition requires it," she continued.

"And if he wins?"

"No matter."

"Then you don't mean to uphold your end of the bargain and return the Ark?"

Delilah looked insulted. "Of course not!"

Suddenly, their conversation was interrupted as the gates creaked open and the drawbridge dropped to cross the ditch.

A lone figure strode out of the gate, the massive structure seeming to vicariously lend him strength. The morning sun shone on his burnished armor, illuminating the Star of Wil'iah emblazoned across his breastplate and the giant shield he carried bearing the Cross of St. Thomas.

"Well, well, the prince of the mudfaces," Delilah sneered, "come to die."

Jeremiah didn't respond. Instead, he hefted his spear at Heracles, who stepped forward, accompanied by five long blasts of trumpets. The hulking bodyguard looked like a vision of Goliath, his golden armor and feathered helmet joining with a fearsome javelin, spear, and sword to complete the picture.

"Well, get on with it, we don't have all day," Delilah waved her hand impatiently.

The two warriors needed no further bidding. Heracles, in a single fluid motion, hurled his javelin, which traveled with lightning speed toward the Prince of Wil'iah. But Jeremiah's eyes were faster, and, using his woomera, an Aboriginal weapon intended to increase the range and accuracy of a spear-thrower, flung his own spear with expert precision. As Heracles' javelin arced down on its deadly course, it was met in mid-air by Jeremiah's spear, which split the inferior Frouzean weapon in two. The harmless halves clattered to the ground, accompanied by a hearty cheer from the ramparts above.

In response, Heracles bellowed with rage and charged forward, his steps shaking the earth. The javelin discarded, he now leveled an enormous lance at Jeremiah, who had no such equivalent. Jeremiah simply danced to the side, holding up his shield with both hands for protection. Around and around they danced, Heracles grunting and bellowing with each thrust of the lance as Jeremiah's eyebrows narrowed in concentration. But finally, inevitably, the lance struck home, smack in the center of Jeremiah's shield. Heracles struck the blow with such force that Jeremiah, despite throwing his full weight into resistance, was pushed back several feet, his heels scraping sand off the desert ground. But, miraculously, the shield held, and the Frouzean lance shattered against it, leaving the spearpoint buried in the center of the Cross of St. Thomas.

Roaring with rage, Heracles withdrew the enormous sword that was slung across his back. Jeremiah, realizing that his own, equally-formidable weapon could only be effectively yielded by two hands, and that the shield had served its purpose, cast the shield aside. With a practiced, elegant motion, he withdrew his own enormous broadsword from its scabbard that was slung across his back. His eyebrows arching over widened eyes in an expression of animal ferocity, Jeremiah bellowed out his own battle-cry and charged forward.

The air was filled with thunderous crashes as the swords struck and struck and struck. Sparks rained onto the desert ground like a rare rainstorm as the blinding blades whirled about and met with bone-shaking, brain-rattling blows. With each strike, both men gutturally yelled. On and on they fought, jabbing and parrying with the two huge weapons, each of which weighed five pounds. The ragged defenders on the ramparts winced and gasped with each blow, but neither man seemed to gain the upper hand.

But suddenly, incredibly, everything changed in an instant. The quality of the Pilbara steel and the workmanship used to make swords in Wil'iah had already become legendary, while Frouzean blade smithing was much less so. And it was this quality of engineering and craftsmanship that carried the day. It was blow like any of the other thousand that the two swords had dealt that day. There was nothing remarkable about the way that Jeremiah swung the longsword, hollering in fury. But, this time, the Wil'iahn blade struck a weak point in Heracles' sword, and the massive weapon sheared in half. The top half of the blade spun out of control, whirling through the air like a boomerang, finally crashing into the watching contingent of the enemy and severing the obsidian cobra from the top of Delilah's snake headdress. Even as she shrieked in shock and fury, the defenders on the ramparts erupted into a jubilant cheer.

Heracles, not expecting his sword to suddenly give way and lose resistance, lurched forward and tumbled to the ground. By the time he regained his faculties and rolled over, the point of Jeremiah's sword hung like the Sword of Damocles over his throat.

Jeremiah's chest heaved with a mixture of exhaustion and triumph. The fire of rage that roared in his stomach urged him to push forward, to finish the job, to spill the man's blood into the ground, where it would imperceptibly mingle with the red soil. The thought of Delilah's duplicity, of Enaua'ivanu's unjust death, and of the deadly threat facing the innocent children inside Trukanamoa egged him on.

Your hated enemy is two inches from death. Bridge the gap.

But, all at once, another voice spoke to him. It was a voice he didn't often like to heed, but a grudging acquiescence at once began to bloom in his thought.

Sixth Commandment.

Jeremiah took a close look at the man who pitifully sprawled in front of him. Behind the hulking frame, behind the formidable visage, were a pair of eyes filled with terror – and something else. Was it remorse? Was it guilt? Was it shame? Jeremiah couldn't tell. But somewhere inside the seemingly hateful heap of flesh was a spark of innocence.

Internally rolling his eyes, and gritting his teeth, Jeremiah addressed the "eternal empress," not moving his sword from its attack posture.

"Alright, I've played by your rules, and I've won. You will return the Ark, and I will let this man live."

"How *predictable,*" Delilah sneered. Suddenly, she snapped her fingers at the cadre of Homeric Guards who anxiously watched the scene. "Seize him!"

Jeremiah whirled around, his face filled with indignant shock.

"This wasn't the deal!" he cried as he leveled the broadsword at the fifty warriors who now encircled him, heedless of the fact that Heracles scuttled away behind him.

"Goddesses don't have to keep promises!" Delilah said. "Get him-- but don't kill him, yet! I want him alive!"

Jeremiah grimly assumed a fighting stance, but it was hopeless. The defenders watched in anguish from the ramparts as he gave a valiant effort, felling over a dozen of the fearsome guards, before he was overwhelmed and dragged away.

CHAPTER SIXTY-FOUR

JEREMIAH'S DARKEST HOUR

Imperial Army Camp, outside Trukanamoa

Briseis watched in fascination as Jeremiah, trussed up like a turkey, was kicked and prodded into a miserable tent in the middle of the Frouzean camp, where he was unceremoniously tied to a pole. Focusing on his intense features, presently contorted with rage, Briseis thought back to the first time she had met the hostile prince of Wil'iah, during her first visit to the country several years before. He hadn't been friendly then, and nothing seemed to have changed. Suddenly, the prince made eye contact, and the disgusted expression that greeted Briseis made her feel as though she were about the shrivel up.

"Well, look who's back," he hissed.

Briseis quickly tore her eyes away as Jeremiah was dragged into the tent.

Suddenly, she felt a presence to her left, and turned to see Delilah, a triumphant smile livening her face.

"Come, darling, we have a special visitor."

Briseis reluctantly followed the empress into the tent.

"*Well,*" Delilah purred. "The *other,* less interesting, prince of Wil'iah, finally in my power." She seemed to scrutinize him for a moment, then moved close in, leering at him with her serpentine eyes.

"Not quite a scrumptious as your brother, but I suppose you will do in a pinch." She turned to Briseis. "Get the Whiff, darling."

"But that didn't work—"

"The Whiff. Now."

Jeremiah glared at Delilah. "I don't know what you're plotting, but it isn't going to work."

Delilah reached out to stroke his chin, which he promptly tore away. "This doesn't have to be so bad for you, Jeremiah. We could have *fun* together."

"Not even if hell freezes over."

Briseis heard the exchange as she left the tent, and, to her surprise, she felt pride leap in her heart at the prince's resistance. A few short minutes later, she returned holding the vial, looking at it rather sadly before handing it to Delilah.

"Now," the empress said as she uncorked the vial, "You may think you're some virtuous knight, but all men are the same."

"Excuse me, Your Worship, but not all"—Briseis' attempted interjection was promptly silenced by a murderous glare from Delilah. The empress then passed the vial under the nose of the squirming prince.

"Soon you, and all of Wil'iah's secrets, will be mine!" she gleefully cackled.

Briseis waited in anguished anticipation as the seconds ticked by, unsure of what outcome she desired. It would help their cause if he was ensnared by Delilah's wiles, but something in her hoped that Tamino wasn't an anomaly.

Delilah leaned in, puckering her luridly-painted lips, but Briseis noted that Jeremiah appeared neither flushed nor hyperventilating like so many of the eternal empress' victims.

"I'd rather kiss a bird-eating spider," he said calmly.

Briseis suppressed a triumphant smile as Delilah's face contorted with rage. She slapped Jeremiah hard across the face, her razor-sharp nails leaving three red scratches on his cheek. All this got her was a sarcastic grin from the prince.

Rounding on him, Delilah decided to try a different tack. "I can't figure you out, Jeremiah. I don't know if you are smarter or more stupid than your brother."

"Leave Tamino out of this!"

"Oh, don't worry, Tamino hasn't been left out of *anything.*"

"What are you talking about?"

"Honesty is not one of my faults," Delilah sneered, "But during my delightful little foray into your wretched city, I didn't lie about everything." She reached into her bodice pocket and withdrew something, then flung it at Jeremiah. All he saw was a flash of red before something hit his face and fell to the floor. When his eyes focused on it, his blood ran cold.

Crumpled on the dirt was a red waratah flower.

"No…" he whispered.

"The ability of the men of Wil'iah to resist temptation is renowned throughout the world. Yet it didn't take much…I suggest that the next time you see your brother, you ask him why he abandoned Trukanamoa to my armies and went instead to Balthcutta."

Bile filled Jeremiah's mouth. "NO!" he bellowed.

"Yes, yes. Oh, yes, your brother is *fun*. Not like you. You are such a dullard. More's the pity. Look upon me and despair, Jeremiah, ye who were born too late to save your country! For soon, very soon, you will kneel before me as your goddess, just as all of your provinces in the east have, just as the smoldering ruins of the slum you once called Balthcutta have! You are all fools to think you could defy the divine power of my eternal empire!"

Suddenly, though, the prince seemed to remember something, and a fire of hope ignited to replace the anguish and sorrow filling his intense eyes. "I don't believe you, for three reasons. One, my brother would never do that, no matter what you say. Two, you could get a crumpled waratah flower anywhere. Three, contrary to your claims of the destruction of Wil'iah's provinces in the east, we have been informed that have in fact achieved victory there, a fact which your presence here confirms. We're not desperate, you are. Y*ou* are the fool if you think you can conquer Wil'iah! We defeated your degenerate empire before, and we'll do it again. Our freedom is forever! If you think that by stealing a box you have done anything to touch the power that defends us, you are even more of an idiot than I thought! We will never surrender this city, and help is on the way!"

Delilah smiled.

"We'll see. Now my armies, unheeded by your silly box, even now march upon your city. They will burn it to the ground, and everyone in it. And *you* will get to watch!"

As Delilah flounced out of the tent, she motioned for Briseis to follow. She stole one last glance at Jeremiah standing tied to the pole with a triumphant smile on his face. She couldn't help but feel a bit proud of him.

Tamino isn't the only one.

CHAPTER SIXTY-FIVE

THE LIONESS OF ZEBULON

Trukanamoa

 eremiah's words, brave as they were, weren't heard by the defenders on the walls, who now watched in cold horror as the enormous enemy army, in its full terrifying array, marched inexorably forward. Elderly men and adolescent women looked nervously at each other, tears streaming down their faces, as the full horror of the morning's developments struck home. Jeremiah was gone. The Ark was gone. And, so it seemed, their strength was gone.

Nevertheless, elderly women passed down the walls, bringing precious, life-giving water from the Springs of Mparntwe to quench the thirst of the defenders as they prepared for the final fight to save Trukanamoa. One soldier gratefully accepted the water and took a deep swig. Suddenly, he croaked and clutched his throat, then, his eyes crossing, toppled over. The water bearers looked on in disbelief, their eyes filling with alarmed terror.

"Stop what you're doing! Don't drink the water! Someone's poisoned the springs!" the frantic cry echoed down the walls.

And still the enemy army advanced, its steps shaking the earth.

Suddenly, the clamors on the wall fell silent, as all eyes turned to a figure slowly ascending the stairs. She climbed with a restrained grace, the magnificent mane of her iron grey hair blowing in the wind uninhibited by any sort of head covering. She was bedecked from head to foot in burnished gold and silver armor; on her breastplate was emblazoned a burnished Star of Wil'iah, with rays of red, white, and blue emanating from it in all directions. Draped from her shoulders, an enormous cape of red and royal blue fluttered, upon which was emblazoned the emblem of the Tribes, with the one central star and four smaller stars blazing around it. Below them on the cape was an enormous Ship of Zebulon. The woman was armed to the teeth, with a magnificent saber strapped to her waist and seven bejeweled daggers hanging from her bandolier. In one hand she carried a shield upon which was emblazoned a giant Cross of St. Thomas; in the other she hefted an enormous Wil'iahn battle-flag, its pole topped with a wicked-looking barb. Her face was set into a fearful glare that, had it been a weapon itself, would have given even Genghis Khan pause, her eyebrows narrowed dangerously and her hard eyes set resolutely against the marauding army. Then, all at once, she mounted the top of the wall; it seemed to the massed defenders as though she had stepped from the mists of legend, a mythic figure rousing herself from an age long past. Adirah of Mangala, Lioness of Zebulon, the woman whose fierce name was the central signet of every bedtime story told to children across the kingdom, had returned from the slumber of mourning to gird herself for battle.

Adirah, Lioness of Zebulon

She wordlessly strode to the battlements, attended on all sides by gasps. The Defenders before her parted like the Red Sea, silently dipping their heads and placing a fist over their hearts, all of them wide-eyed in wonder at the sight before them. Even in her golden years, she towered over the battlements, her head held high, her hair whipping behind her in the gathering wind even as her battle-flag defiantly flapped, the slapping sounds it made ringing across the ward below. With a start, one of the defenders realized that her flag was in fact the self-same banner that she and Vrenga'ava'zora'vaua had sewn together to rally the disparate members of the Council of Uluru on that fateful night in 1243. Warmth gripping his heart, he hazarded a whisper to his neighbor: *"Mother is here. We are delivered!"*

After regarding the invading armies for a moment, she turned to the defenders and passed the battle-flag to the nearest soldier, who looked as though he were holding the True Cross itself. Adirah then opened her mouth and began to sing, the power and timbre of her voice undiminished by her advanced years. The voice of the Great Mother of Wil'iah echoed off the ramparts of the city of the faithful and was gradually joined by the voices of thousands of defenders, their voices defiantly raising the Song of Deborah.

As Adirah sang, the hearts of the men and women defending the capital of Wil'iah were filled with a new fire. A great cloudbank that stood over the city parted, and rays of sunlight suddenly illuminated the burnished dome of the Church of the Eternal Victory, which shone like the greatest and brightest beacon in all of the world. With each stanza of the Song of Deborah, terror and confusion spread amongst the Frouzean ranks.

"Who is that, up on the walls?" asked one Frouzean soldier to another. "I don't know," came the answer. Then, however, the man stiffened, a look of horror crossing his face. "Oh gods, it's Adirah! I recognize her only from the nightmare stories told to me as a child!" The ranks of the Frouzeans began to break their formations, their men milling about in confusion.

Temur Khan viewed the scene from his command post. "What is the problem?" he asked, turning to his Frouzean Attaché, who for his part looked like he had seen a ghost.

"That-that is Adirah of Mangala, sir."

"I don't understand why your much-vaunted armies should be so afraid of a solitary old woman singing a song in a language we do not understand."

"If you knew her, you would be scared, too. You will be soon enough."

As Adirah finished her song, the walls fell silent once again. Then, she turned to face the assembled ranks of her soldiers. She reached down and withdrew a saber from its scabbard and, brandishing it over her head, once again opened her mouth to speak.

"Men and Women of Wil'iah! Most of you do not remember a time when we lived in shackles, enslaved by the likes of the men at the base of these walls! It is because of the courage and determination of men and women like you that this is the case. Our freedom is forever, and the Flame of Zebulon burns as an eternal fire in our hearts!" Turning her attention to the battery of enormous cannons beside her, she hoisted the saber, point skyward, before bellowing out a single word.

"Shekinah!"

With that, the battery of cannons roared as one, their thunder shaking the very earth beneath the feet of the Frouzean armies. Everywhere, the ground erupted into great geysers of dirt and fire as the cannons' deadly gifts struck home. As the roll of thunder reverberated through the skies and the smoke cleared, it revealed the Great Mother of Wil'iah still standing defiantly beside the smoking hulk of one of the great guns, embers of its fire glowing in her hair. Now she directly addressed the assembled enemy horde, seeming not to heed the thousands of arrows that whizzed about her in all directions, but never seemed to hit home.

"Look, and despair, O Forces of Evil! For thou hast cast your lot against our Ultimate Defense! We are not afraid of you, and we never will be. And to the hordes of the Great Khan, know this! Your wave of conquest has stunned the world, but it shall break upon the rock that is Wil'iah! You have no idea what you have wrought, and your armies will pay the price for your arrogance!" With that, she leveled her saber at the invaders and turned her head to her forces.

"Ivrae'ia Va'a'kau'lua!" she screamed, her voice piercing the din of battle.

Temur Khan turned to his Frouzean adviser as a Wil'iahn projectile screamed over their heads. "I see what you mean."

CHAPTER SIXTY-SIX

THE PRISONER

Imperial Army Camp, outside Trukanamoa

eremiah grunted, straining at the manacles that bound him to a post in the middle of the tent. His eyes tearing up at the overpowering incense with which Delilah had filled the tent, Jeremiah gathered his strength. Growling a guttural war cry, he surged against the chain. Jeremiah thought he felt an almost imperceptible movement of the post, and, for a brief moment, a spark of hope lit itself in his heart. Preparing for another assault on his fetters, Jeremiah was interrupted as the flaps of the tent opened to admit a woman that he recognized as the Frouzee's handmaid, Briseis.

"I bring you water, Prince of Wil'iah."

"I don't want your water," he growled. *It's probably poisoned or drugged,* he thought.

"Well, I guess that's your decision. I have some bread for you as well."

"I'm not hungry."

"Surely your exertions have drained your energy?" Briseis regarded the sweat running down the sovereign protector's face.

"Nonsense. I'll do this until Armageddon if I have to."

Briseis advanced towards Jeremiah, who bared his teeth in what was almost a snarl. After gingerly setting the bread and the goblet of water down on the sand, she sat down next to him.

"What are you doing?" asked the prince, his face registering surprise.

"I have a few questions for you."

"If you are looking for tactical information, you won't get it."

Briseis managed a weak smile.

"Tell me, Prince of Wil'iah, why are your people so fiercely committed to the Hebrew God? Your holy books were written hundreds of years ago. How can anyone be sure they are true? It seems it would be much easier for you to simply sail with the tide."

"Even tides break on sufficiently steadfast rocks."

"Perhaps." Jeremiah noticed that Briseis had in her eyes an unusually distant look. His curiosity piqued, he responded.

"Why do you ask?"

Briseis, seemingly startled from some sort of reverie, sharply drew her breath. "I—I was just wondering. There are many things I don't understand about your people."

"I'm surprised you even bother to try. It is well known that the Frouzee's only goal in this war is our extermination."

Briseis didn't challenge his assertion, but instead asked, "Why is the Ark of the Covenant so important to your people? If it is truly the source of Wil'iah's power, and it is lost to you, why don't you simply give up?"

Jeremiah laughed, a sound Briseis found surprisingly jovial given the prince's general severity. "Give up? There is no word in the Wil'iahn language for…what do you call it…*surrender.*" His last word dripped with disgust. The prince continued, "Even if the Ark were the sole source of our might, we would fight on to the very end. Every last man, woman, and child is prepared to resist your invasion to the utmost. When our swords are broken and our spears dashed to pieces, we will switch to rocks. When we have exhausted our rocks we will use our hands, and, when we have lost those, we will bite and spit to our last breath. Your armies will pay the ultimate price for every square inch of this kingdom."

"Brave words for a man in chains."

Jeremiah clenched his jaw, then responded, "Our people know what to do."

"It doesn't have to be this way. If you simply agree to our terms" —

"There are no terms that you could write that we would assent to. And the scenario I have outlined won't come to pass. For our power is not in the Ark, and never was."

"I don't understand."

"You and your people place their hope in physical gods and idols. Our trust is in something much greater."

"But the Ark is what defends your nation – everyone knows that."

"The Ark is merely a symbol of our covenant with the eternal God. But his power is not confined by material limitations. Your strategic plan is sorely flawed if you thought that capturing the Ark would really change anything."

Briseis frowned. "Your God is hated and feared in my country. He is a deity of wrath and ruin. He is our ancient enemy."

The prince responded, "I'm sure that's exactly what you have been taught. But you are mistaken. Our heavenly father-mother is a God of love." He almost seemed as though he were reminding himself of this idea. Briseis could palpably see some of the fire and venom draining from his face.

"How is that possible? He loves even his enemies?"

Jeremiah smiled, a wistful, faraway look in his eyes. The prince looked more peaceful than Briseis imagined possible. "*Especially* his enemies."

CHAPTER SIXTY-SEVEN

THE ARK AND THE ANGELS

Imperial Army Camp, outside Trukanamoa

ater that night, Briseis slinked between the rows of
Mongol tents, her hands cradling a single piece of bread
intended for the prisoner. The camp was quiet as the
Mongols slumbered before the walls; only a few guards
languidly strolled about, haltingly illuminated by leaping
torch flames. Above, the stars defiantly blazed against the
darkness, while watchfires flickered in the distance atop the
stern walls of Trukanamoa. A gentle desert breeze breathed
through the encampment, tenderly fluttering the flaps of

some of the tents and carrying on its wings faint strains of music from the city.

How can they celebrate at a time like this? the handmaiden wondered. *They have lost their ark and their prince is in chains. Yet it is almost like they aren't even afraid.*

Briseis stole between two Mongol yurts, and suddenly found herself standing in front of a much taller, scarlet Frouzean tent bedecked in embroidered symbols of the Philistine Gods. Flanking its entrance on either side were two towering members of the Homeric Guard, their burnished armor reflecting the torchlight. A shiver passed through Briseis' slight frame as she realized the tent contained the captive Ark of the Covenant. She knew she needed to continue on her mission, but something about that tent called to her.

Sidling up to the nearest of the guards, she dropped her voice to the husky contralto that she knew usually got her what she wanted.

"So, it's in there, isn't it?"

The guard stoically looked ahead, but, as Briseis gently touched his shoulder, she realized he was incredibly tense and almost imperceptibly shaking. The flickering torchlight illuminated tiny beads of sweat on his brow, which shouldn't have been present in the cool air of the desert night.

The Wil'iahns aren't scared, but he sure is.

Batting her eyelashes, Briseis entreated, "Do you mind if I take a look? Just a tiny peek? My goddess shall reward you handsomely."

Only momentarily breaking his concentration to dismissively view the handmaiden, the guard grunted his assent.

Briseis slipped inside the tent, and instantly lost her breath. Before her stood the legendary Ark of the

Covenant, which had managed to evade all the efforts of the Frouzeans to capture it- until now. She noticed with a wry smile that Delilah had placed her idols all around it. In particular, a statue of Astarte stood just slightly taller than the famed box. Yet, somehow, even thus encompassed, the Ark dominated the interior of the tent.

As she stared at the Ark, an imperceptible warmth began to spread in Briseis' chest. She gingerly reached out a hand to caress one of the gold cherubim that crowned the top of the Ark, then thought better of it, remembering the whispered tale that the Ark delivered instant death to all who touched it.

As she withdrew her hand, a low sound like thunder seemed to surround her. Briseis jumped, the warmth near her heart instantly running cold as the ground began to shake beneath her. Suddenly, the statue of Astarte that had seemed so sturdy moments before began to ominously waver. As the shaking continued, it creaked for a few moments, then toppled over, its face planting itself in the red soil. Yet the Ark remained completely motionless.

Covering her mouth in horror, Briseis turned and ran out of the tent. As she exited, she noticed that there were now five guards standing watch over the tent. She rushed over to the nearest one.

"Something is happening inside! I think the Ark destroyed one of the idols!" She breathlessly intoned, realizing that this must be the new guard who had joined the other four.

This time, the guard turned to look her directly in the eyes. Briseis stepped back, for the man seemed to be looking right into the deepest parts of her soul.

"Thus befalls all false gods." he said calmly, all appearance of the alarm she had sensed in the other guard no longer evident. Then, in a movement highly uncharacteristic of the brusque Homeric guards, the man gently took her hand. Unlike anything she had ever heard, his deep voice washed over her. "You are loved, Briseis. He knows who you are. And He will lead you safely home." All at once, Briseis' eyes filled with tears, as an indescribable longing filled her being. The man spoke once more. "Be not afraid, for the Ark of the Covenant is indeed guarded tonight. Take heart, little one. For now you know the way. Now you must walk in it."

"I-I don't understand," she choked out. She whirled around as another voice, this one decidedly less soothing, rang out behind her.

"I don't either, sweetheart." Briseis's gaze was greeted with the jarring, wolfish face of one of the other guards. "Who are you talking to?"

"What do you mean?" She asked. "I was talking"— she turned again to point out his compatriot, but, where the strange man had stood just a moment before, only desert sand swirled now.

"Maybe next time, lay off the wine a bit, darling," the guard said, rolling his eyes. He then returned to his station and didn't deign to look at Briseis any further.

Struck with a strange mixture of awe and terror, Briseis realized she knew what she had to do.

What she didn't notice in her moment of wonder was the shadowy shape slinking in the darkness, or the vulpine eyes that followed her every move.

Briseis' moment of awe

CHAPTER SIXTY-EIGHT

TREACHERY

Imperial Army Camp, outside Trukanamoa

Jeremiah awoke with a start as he heard someone rummaging around the prison tent. A spark briefly blazed out in the darkness, followed by a warm glow from a torch, whose leaping flames illuminated the face of Delilah's handmaid, Briseis.

"What do you want?" growled the prince.

"Hush!" she said as she withdrew a short sword from her robes.

So this is how it ends. Murdered by the Frouzee's maid.

"Wow. She can't even kill me herself. I thought I at least warranted a public execution. I'm almost insulted."

"Fool!" hissed Briseis. "Delilah does not know I'm here!"

Her lack of an honorific piqued Jeremiah's interest. "Well, whatever you're doing, do it quickly. But know that, though I die here, Wil'iah doesn't die with me. Our flame will burn on long after your empire is reduced to a cautionary tale for those who follow false prophets."

Briseis drew close to Jeremiah's face, her eyes betraying a surprising earnestness. "Tell me, Prince Jeremiah. What is it like to live free?" she whispered.

Jeremiah's eyes widened in surprise. "What do you mean?"

Briseis put her mouth to his ear. "I have heard the good news."

Jeremiah's eyebrows narrowed. "I am not as gullible as my brother. I admire your attempt at deception, but you picked the wrong brother to try it on."

Briseis managed to look hurt. "No, you don't understand, your highness. I was once Delilah's most loyal servant, but for a long time I have questioned what I was taught in the empire. I was told that Wil'iahns were fanatical savages bent on our extermination. But, now that I'm here, the picture is completely different. You are decent, kind, and honorable people. I cannot continue to assist with your destruction. And"— her eyes narrowed conspiratorially --"It has come to my attention that something *much greater* is defending your nation than we could ever muster."

Jeremiah cocked his head quizzically.

Briseis reached into her cloak and withdrew a small brass key.

"I know the way. Now I must walk in it. Or so He told me?"

"Who told you?" asked Jeremiah.

Briseis knowingly glanced upward. Stepping forward, she unlocked the hand and leg cuffs with the key. Jeremiah stepped out of his restraints, rubbing his wrists. Briseis proffered the sword.

"Make haste, Prince of Wil'iah! And take this sword, that you might defend yourself in this evil day!" she entreated.

"I cannot abandon you to your fate. If you are discovered, I would not conscience the blood of a lady such as yourself -- a thousand deaths would be preferable."

"I will not be discovered. I am the Frouzee's closest confidante. She will never suspect me. Now GO!"

Just then, both started as the curtains of the tent were ripped open, to reveal Frouzee Delilah – and Salome, who flashed a triumphant smile. Jeremiah's stomach fell to the floor.

"TREACHERY!!!!" screamed the empress as she withdrew a stiletto from its sheath and hefted it over her shoulder. Her eyes, full of cold fury, narrowed to slits as she beheld Briseis.

"*You. YOU*...how could you...GUARDS!" yelled the empress as she hurled the stiletto directly at her handmaiden.

"NO!" Jeremiah threw himself in the flight path of the blade, which buried itself in his midsection. He groaned and staggered backwards, clutching at the handle as his short sword clattered to the floor and skittered over toward the Frouzee, who picked it up with a wolfish look.

Briseis rushed forward to confront her. "This is not what it looks like! Your worship, he was menacing me, forcing me to help him with dire threats."

Salome rolled her eyes.

Delilah's mouth contorted into a twisted smile. "You are *forgiven*," she purred, then yanked a squirming Briseis into a tight embrace. "Allow me to reward you for your loyalty!" Delilah forcefully kissed the terrified damsel on the lips.

Jeremiah recovered from the initial shock of the blow, forcing his thoughts through the pain. Realizing that Delilah must be wearing her infamous lethal lipstick, he gathered his remaining strength. *I swore I'd never do this...*

Briseis's squirms and muffled protestations grew weaker as Delilah continued her attack. Suddenly, Delilah's eyes crossed as a fist connected with the back of her head.

The last thing Briseis saw before she blacked out was Jeremiah standing over the collapsed empress.

"That's for Avora'tru'ivi!"

For her part, Salome, suddenly realizing the danger she was in as Jeremiah's murderous eyes moved to her, turned and ran.

Jeremiah realized he didn't have much time before he lost consciousness too. Abandoning his plan to attempt a rescue of the Ark, he realized he needed to get back to the gates. Looking at the unconscious forms of the two women, he pondered what to do next. Ordinarily, he would have taken Delilah prisoner; even in his current state of agitation, he would not abide the thought of stooping to cold-blooded murder. But if he left Briseis here, she was sure to die. He was confident that the efforts of the priests would be enough to revive her from the Frouzee's black arts. Hearing stirrings in the camp, he realized he only had seconds until guards arrived. Stooping to pick up the short sword, he winced as his gut screamed in pain. With his other arm, and no small amount of effort, he slung the damsel over his shoulder and ducked out of the tent.

CHAPTER SIXTY-NINE

A CURSE AGAINST HEAVEN

Imperial Army camp, outside Trukanamoa

Heracles snored soundly in the tent, oblivious to the chaos outside.

"Your Excellency!" hissed a voice as two timid hands attempted to shake Heracles' muscle-bound arm. The hulking Homeric Guard grunted, a drop of drool wicking into his beard, but he didn't otherwise respond.

"Your Excellency! You must awake! We are under attack!"

Still there was no response as the Frouzee's mousy servant vainly shook the soldier.

"Your"— the servant's squeaky voice was cut short as a massive hand shot out and hefted him up by the neck as Heracles rocketed out of bed.

"WHAT!??" he bellowed, shaking his head in an attempt to clear his bloodshot eyes.

"We are under some sort of attack, sir!" wheezed the guard as he fruitlessly kicked at the air, struggling to free himself from Heracles' iron grip.

"Attack? Where!" Heracles opened his fist, and the servant fell to the floor in a heap, clutching at his throat. Heracles hastily buckled on a hauberk and grabbed his short sword before lumbering out of the tent.

As he spread the flaps open, he instinctively covered his eyes with his free hand as the angry light of a blazing fire invaded his vision. The tent in which the Ark of the Covenant was held prisoner burned with otherworldly fury as an incredibly loud, low-frequency buzzing sound shook the earth and assaulted his ears, drowning out the alarmed cries of men trying to put out the blaze.

Maybe this fire will finally rid us of that stupid box, he thought as he struggled to regain his faculties. But, as his vision cleared, his brief hope was crushed. For, though the idols that had surrounded the ark were all consumed, the Ark stood completely untouched in the center of the fire. The cacophony of the strange throbbing emanating from the Ark was reinforced by a sudden ringing clap of thunder directly overhead, which shook even the mighty Heracles to his core. Rain suddenly poured down in thick sheets, a rare occurrence in this part of the desert. Yet, inexplicably, the flames only grew brighter as they licked at the blackened idols. Another crack sounded across the camp, but this one didn't emanate from the heavens. The great stone statue of Baal-Hammon split in two and crashed to the ground as the frenzied flames thrashed at it.

"I knew this was a bad idea," Heracles overheard one soldier confide in another. Whirling around, he espied the man who had made the traitorous comment and marched toward him, rearing up to his full towering height.

"How dare you question the commands of the goddess Astarte!?"

The man quailed before the huge Homeric Guard, but his friend was more bold.

"If she is truly the goddess Astarte, surely she can put an end to this madness? We have angered greater powers than her tonight."

Heracles sneered. "There is no greater power. There is no other power. What you witness here is sabotage, and the weather is a coincidence. And," he said, whipping out the short sword and pointing it directly at the smaller soldier's Adam's apple, "You would be wise not to speak such treason, if you ever wish to speak again," With that, he lunged forward and lightly pricked the man's neck just enough to draw blood. The soldier howled in pain and ran away, clutching his neck.

Suddenly, another light filled the sky, this one red, as a plume of smoke rose next to the Ark. As the artificial fog cleared, the Frouzee Delilah emerged, dressed as the goddess Astarte and wielding her scepter. The excited cries of the crowd instantly died as all attention focused on the empress.

"You fools!" she crowed. "To think that this was some sort of divine display! You give our enemies too much credit. All they have accomplished here is to sabotage us. I even know who it was! It was my trusted handmaiden, Briseis!" The crowd gasped.

"Yes, my erstwhile most faithful friend. Well, not anymore!" Delilah pointedly smacked her lips. "She has been properly *rewarded* for her treachery, and has embarked on her swift journey to hell! Such befalls all who betray me!" The empress now turned to directly face the fire surrounding the Ark of the Covenant.

"And to fear a box is preposterous! As I have proven conclusively many times, the so-called Hebrew God does not exist! And this glorified shipping container certainly didn't come from him. There is only one deity here, and you are looking at her!" she cried, throwing her arms wide and shaking the scepter for emphasis. Flinging her head backward, she screamed at the sky. "Oh so-called Hebrew God, I defy thee! Do your worst, for you are unreal and have no power! You are nothing next to my infinite power!"

Her challenge was met with silence as the rain continued to pour down from the heavens. A murmur began to rise again from the crowd.

"That's what I thought!" yelled the empress. "You are so powerless"— Her boast was summarily cut off by an enormous clap of thunder as a sizzling bolt of lightning hurled itself into the ground not six inches from the empress's feet. Hurled back by the force of the discharge, the empress collapsed to the ground, her headdress flying off to reveal a wild mass of hair rendered frizzy by static electricity.

The devastating strike was instantly followed by a massive gust of bitterly cold wind that blasted through the camp, knocking over tents and instantly extinguishing every torch or source of light in the camp-- save one. The preternatural fire continued to burn around the Ark as everything else was plunged into darkness.

Delilah scrambled to her feet and shook a fist at the sky. "CURSE YOU!!!"

CHAPTER SEVENTY

IN THE CLOISTERS

Church of the Eternal Victory, Trukanamoa

*B*riseis' eyes fluttered open, registering the warm glow from a series of yellow candles that surrounded her. A vaulted ceiling arched overhead, shadows flickering across it as the candle flames licked at the air. Briseis heard a low murmur outside the room, which was sealed with a heavy wooden door.

Suddenly, the crack of a releasing deadbolt filled the air, and the door began to laboriously swing open. A tall figure stooped below the opening and stole into the room. As it drew closer, the flickering flames revealed a familiar face: Jeremiah.

Briseis smiled in greeting, but then her brows furrowed in confusion.

"Where am I?"

"You are in the lower cloisters of the Church of the Everlasting Victory."

Briseis' eyes widened as she realized she was inside the city that her masters' armies had been trying to breach for weeks. "How long have I been here?"

"You were out for five days."

"What happened?"

"Well, it appears that Delilah had a kiss for you – but certainly not the kind of kiss anyone would want."

Briseis suddenly went completely white as she weakly held a hand in front of her face.

"H-how am I still here? That kiss…people don't come back."

"There are powers in this world that overrule the venoms of a delusional woman. In fact, if what you told me in the tent was to be believed, you have encountered them yourself."

Briseis narrowed her eyes as she focused on Jeremiah's midsection, which showed no signs of a mortal stab wound.

Maybe he's right.

"You saved me. Why? I am the enemy."

Jeremiah smiled. "I did what anyone would do in that situation. And anyone who displayed the courage that you did, helping to free me and defying your supposed mistress, no more deserves to be called 'enemy' than my own mother."

"What shall become of me?"

"The priests have done their duty, and the poisons of your mistress are nullified. Rest a while. You will be back on your feet soon. In the meantime, though, I need to know everything you do about the enemy's plans."

Briseis struggled to sit up, then opened her mouth to answer.

"We are getting desperate. The supply caravans that were supposed to come from the south never made it."

Jeremiah pumped his fist in triumph.

"I knew that the Army of Anangu wasn't completely destroyed!"

Briseis continued. "Anyway, we are running out of food. The Mongols drink their own horses' blood to sustain themselves, then eat them when the blood is exhausted. Tensions are high between the Mongol command and Delilah. That's why Temur left."

Jeremiah's eyebrows arched in surprise. "Temur left? Where did he go?"

"My understanding was that it was supposed to be some sort of flanking maneuver. Something about the north wall of Trukanamoa being weaker…they said that the fortresses guarding the ends of the mountains had fallen, allowing this maneuver."

The color drained out of Jeremiah's severe features at the news.

"In that case, we'd best prepare to defend ourselves on our north flank. Thank you for the information." He turned to leave.

Briseis called after him.

"Jeremiah, thank you."

Jeremiah stopped and knelt gently on the floor, an unexpected tenderness in his eyes.

"No. Wil'iah thanks *you*."

CHAPTER SEVENTY-ONE

THE ARK COMES TO XANADU

Palace of Xanadu, Northern China

"**H**ush!" Jessica said to the excited women around her, annoyed that their excited tittering might give away her plan. She knew that a guard would arrive with food at any minute. It had turned out that the rest of Kublai Khan's concubines were just as disgusted with him as she was, and they had readily assented to her plan. She had been individually, clandestinely training them over the past few days, dodging the inquiring eyes of the chaperones. Jessica had finally begun to set the plan in motion by knocking out the old handlers who watched the concubines' every move – and even smelled them at night to make sure they remained sweet for the Khan. Jessica hadn't relished clobbering the elderly ladies over the head, but she hadn't seen much of an alternative. Now, she thought ahead to how she would ensnare the guard who was bringing the food.

I can't believe I'm about to do this. Well, I guess if it worked for Judith and Holofernes, it will work for me.

Mustering her best attempt at a flirtatious smile, a concept utterly foreign to her, she awaited the fateful knock at the door.

About two minutes later, a sharp rap indicated that the moment to set her plan in action had arrived. Jessica, attempting a sweet voice, said, "come in!"

A burly guard entered, his well-muscled arms carrying a platter loaded with dumplings and steamed buns. His beady eyes narrowed at the princess, and with a wolfish smirk, he said, "'Evening, Sweetheart."

"Oh, I'm famished! I'm so glad you came!" Jessica said, forcing her voice into a breathy higher register as she flounced over to the guard. "How can I ever *thank* you?" Jessica placed her hands on the guard's shoulder as he set the platter down.

The guard flushed, his eyes opening in surprise at the unexpectedly warm reception from the notoriously fiery princess. "Well...I...."

Jessica placed a single finger on his lips, doing her best to channel the Frouzee Delilah. Her stomach churned at the mere thought of the woman, but she knew the "eternal empress's" methods had been effective at courting the favor of Kublai Khan and his henchmen.

"Hush. Let me do the thanking," she purred at the soldier. Jessica saw the man relax, and knew his guard was down. Seizing the opportunity, she sprang into action, throwing the guard into a headlock, hefting him over her shoulder, and body-slamming him onto the ground. The man's eyes crossed, and his tongue lolled out, as he lost consciousness.

"Now, that's all the thanks you are going to get!" Jessica hissed as she confiscated the ring of keys and the man's sword. She knew that the additional guards right outside the doors would come running at any moment to address the commotion.

Sure enough, two armored men came clattering in through the door, their eyes widening in surprise at the sight of their compatriot splayed out on the floor with a wild-eyed woman standing over him. Instantly drawing their swords, the men moved into an attack position.

"Are you boys ready for some training?" called Jessica, tightening her grip on her saber.

The leftmost of the two guards noticed some movement, his eyes flashing to his left just in time to see a Shang Dynasty bronze urn come flying at his face. He crumpled to the ground, his sword clattering on the tile as it dropped out of his hand.

"Tell your master that I want a divorce!" cried a concubine, noting her handiwork with satisfaction from her vantage point above the doorway.

The other guard whirled to face her and sneered, preparing to attack, but his head snapped back to Jessica as she opened her mouth and uttered her mother's famous battle-cry.

"Shekinah!"

The clash of swords was brief but furious, the ringing of the blades accentuated by the sparks that flew around the room. But Jessica's superior training manifested itself, and in less than a minute, the guard found himself with an empty hand as his sword flew across the room and buried itself in a column, batted out of his grip by an expert swing from the princess. Facing her disarmed opponent, Jessica prepared to strike the final blow, when a gentle voice seemed to speak into her ear from her right shoulder.

"Sixth Commandment."

Oh Brother, she thought, her eyes rolling as she lowered the saber. The guard's eyes registered surprise at the action, but then they widened in fear as a bronze-colored fist flew in at lightning speed. The guard toppled over, joining his two companions on the floor.

Shaking her fist as it rang from the blow, Jessica turned to the other wives and concubines, who somewhat nervously surveyed the scene. Drawing herself to her full, intimidating height, she raised the sword over her head and called to them.

"Let's get out of here!"

Even Jessica was surprised by the fervor which filled the responding cheer. The women facing her hefted torches, brooms, candelabras, and a myriad of other household wares.

This is not the army I expected to command in this war, thought Jessica. *But it will do.*

With that, she charged out of the door, the excited women streaming out behind her.

For her part, Jessica tried to make for the entrance of the Marble Palace, hoping to sneak out through the main gate, but she soon found herself hopelessly lost as the sounds of distant commotion echoed through the hallway. Jessica realized she had made a wrong turn when she found herself face to face with a cinnabar screen, with the throne room beyond.

The enormous emperor lay sprawled on the throne, folds of fat rippling down to the floor. The entire room was filled with the acrid smell of alcohol. Jessica reached up to hold her nose, and held out a hand to urge her compatriots to silence. Her eyebrows narrowed as a Frouzean herald entered the room. He slammed his staff on the ground and bowed to the Khan.

"Yes?" Kublai's grizzled voice weakly rose from the throne.

"Delilah, Empress of China and all the lands of the Mongol Empire, has a gift for you."

"Bring it in," said the Emperor.

Jessica's jaw dropped to the floor as four slaves walked in bearing...The Ark of the Covenant. Her heart seemed to plummet through her stomach into the tiles of the floor itself as she realized what this meant. Trukanamoa was lost.

"No," she hissed in anguish, but she managed to restrain herself enough that none of the Khan's sycophants in the throne room heard her exclamation. Some of the Khan's wives crowded over the screen. Jessica silenced them with a single finger to her lips.

"As you can see, the war is going well, your Highness," said the Frouzean herald, "For this box, the fabled Ark of the Covenant, contains special gifts seized by Her Worship from the great treasure-houses of Wil'iah. They are a weak and broken people, and it is only a matter of time before the flags of our alliance fly all over the continent."

Jessica's nostrils flared with rage. *Not on my watch,* she thought. While the implications of the Ark's presence in Xanadu were terrifying, somehow, she felt a strange warmth spreading through her- for the Ark reminded her that God was there too. And with this warmth came an inexplicable strength as the despair seemed to drain out of her. Suddenly, a thought occurred to her. *'This box contains?' Did she put something in it?*

Kublai Khan laughed. "Good, good!"

The herald continued. "Her Worship includes a message with this gift." Jessica leaned forward behind the screen with interest.

'Dearest Kubi. Allow me to express the depths of my devotion to you with the baubles in the box. Go ahead and open it. I can assure you it's quite safe."

Khan laughed, the folds of fat that cascaded to the floor jiggling in rhythm. "Finally, I have a worthy successor to my dear Chabi. Bring the Ark to me."

Jessica raised an eyebrow as she watched the proceedings, the words of Delilah's curious note ringing in

What is she up to?

The slaves brought the Ark to a position about three feet in front of the throne.

"Open it. I want to see what's inside."

The four Frouzean slaves looked at each other nervously, their eyes betraying their fear at what they were carrying.

"OPEN IT!" Khan bellowed. "WHAT ARE YOU WAITING FOR? THIS IS A GIFT BOX, ISN'T IT?"

Bao gingerly raised a finger. "Don't the legends say that to open the Ark would deliver instant death? Chabi"—

"*Chabi* may have been a follower of this misguided religion, but I've never paid much heed to the rantings of the Christians or their Jewish allies. Do you really believe this superstitious balderdash? It's a gift box, nothing more. *Open it.*"

It's too bad the Ark isn't actually deadly, Jessica thought. Though she always treated the object with reverence, Jessica had never believed the legends about the Ark's lethal powers. It was only a symbol.

Wincing, the slaves gingerly lifted the top of the box, their chains jangling as they perceptibly trembled. They placed it on the ground with a quiet thud. A strange hissing sound began to fill the throne room.

What? Jessica thought.

Khan leaned in over the Ark, a greedy leer crossing his corpulent features.

The hissing sound continued.

Suddenly, Khan convulsed and began to frantically cough. Staggering back toward the throne, he wildly gestured at his sycophants for help. Transfixed by the scene, none of them moved.

Khan collapsed back onto the throne, gurgling incoherently as foam began to bubble at the corners of his mouth. His weight overbalanced the throne, which crashed onto its back, leaving the ruler of the world's largest empire in a heap. He gave one last great spasm, and then all was still.

Khan's retinue stared at the Ark in silent, slack-jawed horror.

Even Jessica was impressed. *Delilah must have put some sort of poison in the Ark.* Anger that the holy relic had been thus desecrated fought with begrudging admiration for the devious empress, and gratitude that her machinations had just eliminated one of Wil'iah's most dangerous enemies.

Of course, maybe the legends are true…

Khan's entourage slowly recovered and began to wordlessly file out of the throne room. The Ark stood undisturbed at the center, as if nothing had ever happened. Once the chamber emptied, Jessica emerged from behind the screen and walked over to the toppled throne of the Great Khan. One look at the glassy, vacant stare in his eyes told Jessica that he was no longer there.

She turned around to face the Ark, only for her eyes to catch unexpected movement. The four slaves that had carried in the Ark were stirring, their faces tableaux of terror.

Jessica rushed over to the nearest one, who was hyperventilating, trembling, and drenched with sweat.

"Come now, dear one. Stand and be strong. For today is the day of your freedom!"

The slave, his eyes filled with astonished horror, looked down at his ankles and wrists. His fear suddenly melted into wonder. Jessica followed his eyes. The shackles were gone without a trace.

Jessica's eyes darted back to the Ark as her stomach clenched with awe.

Maybe that box has more tricks under its lid than I give it credit for.

"Yes, yes, God loves you," she said, "And now it is time for us to take this Ark, this symbol of His promise to us, away from this place. Now, we have to figure out how to pass the guards."

"Take it," a voice rang out behind her. Jessica nearly jumped out of her skin, whirling around with bared teeth.

Bao stood staring at Khan's corpse, his face an emotionless mask.

"We have no need for that box here," he said. "As far as I'm concerned, Khan's misadventures across the ocean died with him. Take it and leave."

Jessica regarded the minister with a nod.

"Thank you," she said.

As she and the freed slaves left with the Ark, Bao said one more thing, his voice a trembling whisper.

"Long live free China."

Jessica, Princess of Wil'iah

It is related in stories in China that the princess and the four freedmen together carried the Ark from the Palace of Xanadu all the way down the mountain to the river, accompanied by the liberated concubines and additional slaves who escaped from the palace. Not once were they questioned or stopped, for the legend of the Ark moved before them, and all could palpably feel the power of the protection under which they walked. When they reached the river, the princess asked a boatman to convey them to the sea, and he wordlessly nodded. And thus it was that the Ark of the Covenant passed unscathed out of the very den of the Great Khan.

At length, the group reached the port of Tianjin. As they stole into the harbor area, the Ark shielded by a commandeered veil, a smile spread across Jessica's face as she beheld a familiar catamaran tied captive at the quayside. Her eyes lit up as she read the gilded letters that announced the vessel's name: *Ava'ivi.*

"Hello, old girl," Jessica whispered triumphantly.

CHAPTER SEVENTY-TWO

THE WRONG SIBLING

Shechem, Kingdom of Manasseh

*A*vora'tru'ivi put a telescope to her eye and examined the scene in the distance. What she saw made her blood run cold.

The Citadel of Shechem stood, blackened in a thousand places by the blasts of the enemy, before the massed armies of Prince Jason. But, oddly, no fighting seemed to be in progress. The enemy army simply stood there. Avora'tru'ivi panned the telescope over to the citadel's highest tower, and her breath caught in her throat.

A white flag hung from the keep.

"*No…*" the queen whispered.

"What is it?" the scout next to her asked.

"It appears my brother has decided to surrender," Avora'tru'ivi replied grimly. "I think it's time somebody talked some sense into him."

A plan was already beginning to coalesce in her mind. She snapped a series of instructions to the scout, then wrapped her heavy ranger cloak about her, hoping that it would conceal her well-enough to carry out the crucial first step of her plan.

Alone, she picked her way through the shrubs toward the citadel. She noticed a gap in the Pelesetanian lines, the army having grown lax in its vigilance during the apparent truce. Barely making a sound thanks to the stealth techniques that Tamino had taught her, Avora'tru'ivi ghosted through the enemy lines and came to a stone in the wall that she knew very well. Hidden in the corner between a watchtower and the main wall, it was concealed from nearly every possible enemy vantage point. She pushed in just the right place, and the stone noiselessly swung into a gaping maw of darkness. The queen slipped inside, and the stone returned to its position, leaving nary a trace.

Now engulfed in blackness, Avora'tru'ivi picked her way forward, remembering the passage by heart. Finally, she emerged at her destination- a hallway in the citadel wall that was covered by an expensive foreign carpet. The wall panel swung open as she actuated a latch, revealing the back of the carpet. Drawing her dagger, Avora'tru'ivi gingerly pushed the carpet aside and stepped into the hall.

She stifled an exclamation of dismay as she realized she was not alone. Two tall guards stood in the hallway, clad in the armor of the Royal House of Manasseh. Avora'tru'ivi tried to duck back behind the carpet, but it was too late. The guards whirled, around, drawing their swords. But, as soon as they saw who stood in the hallway, the swords clattered to the ground.

Both guards broke into wide smiles.

"Your Highness!"

"Hush! Now is the time for discretion. Where is Gideon?"

Melancholy clouded on of the guards' faces.

"He is in the throne room, preparing to sign the surrender papers."

Avora'tru'ivi grimaced.

"Whatever possessed him to do such a thing?"

"He thought it was the best way to ensure everyone's safety. He was convinced that this is a lost cause, and that surrender is the best way to protect the people of Manasseh. Prince Jason promised to be lenient."

Avora'tru'ivi wanted to spit on the floor, but she restrained herself.

"This war is anything but lost. I have forty thousand troops outside the walls waiting for my signal."

The guards' face lit with unlooked-for hope.

Avora'tru'ivi sprang into action. "Go prepare the wall defenses for the resumption of hostilities. I have a surrender ceremony to cancel." With that, she snapped into a military salute and bounded down the hall.

The two guards looked at each other in triumph.

"The wrong sibling ascended to the throne," one said.

CHAPTER SEVENTY-THREE

A COURSE IN COURAGE

Citadel of Shechem

"**W**hat are you waiting for, sign it!" Prince Jason of Pelesetania leered at Gideon, who sat in humiliation at a long table in the throne room of Manasseh. The king's hand trembled as he tried to maintain his composure, spraying the surrender document with dots of ink. Gideon looked sadly around the room, his eyes suddenly focusing on a portrait of Gamaliel that hung on the wall. His father's determined visage stared into the distance, a faraway look in his eyes, as a great battle-flag flapped behind him, symbolizing Manasseh's lone resistance to the original Frouzean Empire.

Forgive me, Gideon thought as he fought back tears. He lowered the pen to the paper.

"Just *what* do you think you're doing!?" A voice suddenly rang through the still chamber. All of the heads in the room snapped to the far corner, where Avora'tru'ivi stood in full battle armor, seemingly having appeared out of nowhere like a wraith of a Frouzean nightmare.

The queen drew her saber and leveled it at Prince Jason, who looked absolutely gobsmacked.

"What...what are *you* doing here?" he sneered.

"Not marrying you, that's for certain," Avora'tru'ivi retorted as she marched forward. Even now, the very thought of Jason's threat-filled proposal nearly ten years before filled her with loathing. With an expert flick of the saber, sent the feather pen flying out of Gideon's hand. She then reached forward and picked up the surrender document.

"Hmphf," she snorted, then tore the sheet in two, flinging the pieces to the floor before pointedly stepping on them. She then pointed the saber directly at Jason's heart. The prince's eyes filled with panic as his two guards rushed forward to protect him, levelling spears at the queen.

"There will be no surrender today," Avora'tru'ivi said proudly. "While I am sorely tempted to gut you like a fish right as you stand, the laws of truce that you have invoked give you permission to return to your lines before we reopen fire. You have five minutes to get out of this castle before I start to forget that rule."

Prince Jason stood completely still, as if paralyzed, a petulant expression crossing his face, not unlike a toddler who had been denied a new plaything.

Avora'tru'ivi lunged forward, the saber catching the light of the chandelier above.

Startled into action, Jason turned and ran out of the room.

Avora'tru'ivi turned to her brother.

"We'll have a lesson in something called a 'backbone' later. For now, we have a city to defend." With that, she bounded out of the throne room.

Gideon collapsed onto the table, burying his face in his hands.

※　※　※

Atop the citadel, two guards sadly looked at the white flag that flapped in the breeze.

"I really think we could have fought it out," one of them said.

"Yes, but it would only be a matter of time. Gideon really only had one choice."

"I would rather die than surrender. It's what Gamaliel and Sheerah would have wanted."

The debate was suddenly cut short as a burnished figure emerged from the spiral staircase that led to the parapet. Both guards were stunned as they recognized their princess.

"Consider the surrender of Manasseh permanently cancelled," Avora'tru'ivi said as she walked up to the flag and, with a look of extreme satisfaction on her face, tore it down from the pole. She turned to the guards.

"I assume that you have the proper adornment for this pole lying around somewhere?"

The guards looked at each other, and, needing no second bidding, sprang into action, running over to a trunk on the far side of the parapet and pulling out a massive battle-flag of the United Kingdom of Ephraim and Manasseh.

"Now *that's* better!" Avora'tru'ivi said delightedly.

Together, the three hoisted the flag up the pole. As it reached the top, it almost instantly unfurled in the gathering breeze, snapping its defiance to the Pelesetanian lines. An excited murmur, followed by a hearty cheer, rose from the battlements below.

Avora'tru'ivi now looked to the south, where, from a small knoll, a light flashed three times. The signal she had been waiting for.

From the gate below, Prince Jason and his retinue thundered out, fleeing openly for his lines, a flag of truce flapping overhead. As soon as he reached the Pelesetanian vanguard, Avora'tru'ivi called down to the battery of trebuchets on the wall below.

"Fire!"

"Our pleasure, Your Majesty!" the crews called back. The trebuchets groaned, sending enormous missiles vaulting through the air into the enemy lines. The Pelesetanians scrambled to respond, their own siege engines hurling projectiles in response as clouds of arrows filled the air. Avora'tru'ivi surveyed the scene and grimly realized that the Pelesetanian forces still greatly outnumbered the army she had brought from Wil'iah. But it would simply have to be enough. She briefly closed her eyes in a wordless prayer.

As if in answer, the sound of conch shells and trumpets filled the air as the Wil'iahn Expeditionary force made its presence known, another hearty cheer rising from the walls of Shechem in response. The Wil'iahn forces, in a headlong cavalry charge, emerged from hiding and smashed into the right flank of Jason's army, driving deep into the

Pelesetanian lines. But, after a few minutes, the charge got bogged down, and the battle degenerated into a vicious, hand-to-hand brawl. Nobody noticed Prince Jason, his purple toga in tatters, slink away from the battle. Avora'tru'ivi turned to the guards atop the tower.

"I think it's time we stopped hiding behind our walls and faced these cowards in the open."

The guards nodded triumphantly, immediately raising ram's horns to their lips and letting out a series of blasts. Reserve forces, held in case the walls had been breached, began streaming out of barracks in the citadel and forming into ranks in the courtyard before the main gate. Avora'tru'ivi raced down the steps, suddenly finding herself face-to-face with two very familiar figures.

Gideon stood holding the reins of her father's horse, the magnificent war-charger's mane billowing in the wind.

"Father would have wanted you to ride him into battle," he said simply. Avora'tru'ivi, handed a lance by a guard, mounted the charger and began to walk to the head of the forming line of cavalry, where Gideon joined her on his own horse, his face a mixture of sheepishness and determination. He looked to his sister.

"Maybe it's time for lesson one in your course in courage," he said as he drew his sword and hefted a shield emblazoned with three arrows.

Avora'tru'ivi smiled. "Better late than never."

With that, the gates opened, and the queen screamed, at the top of her lungs, the great battle-cry of the women of Wil'iah.

"Shekinah!"

CHAPTER SEVENTY-FOUR

THE END OF JASON

Shechem

𝒜vora'tru'ivi hacked and swung with her saber, periodically screaming war cries as she fought for her birth country's life. But, all around her, the picture wasn't encouraging. Jason's forces had recovered from their initial shock of the combined assault of the Manassite garrison and the Wil'iahn Expeditionary Force, and their greater numbers were beginning to turn the tide. On all sides, the allied forces were being pushed back, and a quick glance over her shoulder told Avora'tru'ivi that she was only a few hundred meters from the gate, which loomed closer and closer with each passing moment.

She narrowed her eyebrows, gritted her teeth, and renewed her determination. But in her heart, she knew it wouldn't be enough. She thought of Tamino, and the similar thoughts he must be feeling as his forces fought their way to an uncertain fate at Trukanamoa.

Godspeed, Galbi.

Suddenly, a cry of alarm from the Pelesetanian forces rose above the din of battle. Avora'tru'ivi's head snapped to the north, where the Gulf's sparkling waters stretched into the distance. But the waters were far from empty. A great fleet of ships spread in glorious array across the sea. All at once, hope ignited once again in her heart.

The lead ship flew the battle-standard of Dai Viet.

An attack on one is an attack on all, Avora'tru'ivi thought as the spark of hope leapt into roaring flame. *I knew they'd come through.*

A thunderous report accompanied a puff of white smoke that issued from the lead Vietnamese ship's forecastle.

Thus heartened, Avora'tru'ivi drove once again into the mass of Pelesetanian troops, the garrison force behind her buoyed by the unexpected development.

One by one the Vietnamese ships, as well as an equal number flying the flag of Champa, reached the shore, sending boards crashing down to allow the troops they carried to charge onto the beach. This renewed strength swelled the determination of the allied forces and added to the terror and confusion of Jason's troops, whose once-inexorable advance was almost instantly reversed. But nobody was prepared for what happened next.

A particularly large Vietnamese ship, flying a standard which Avora'tru'ivi recognized as the personal standard of General Hung Dao, reached the shoreline and lowered its drawbridge.

Suddenly, to Avora'tru'ivi's surprise, another ship hauled into view – a very familiar one. The *Ava'ivi,* flagship of the Wil'iahn Eastern Fleet and presumed lost at the Battle of Cape Nadgee, reached the beach and lowered its own drawbridge. A figure whom Avora'tru'ivi never thought she would again see charged down the bridge in full Wil'iahn battle-armor, her sword flashing in the sun. Princess Jessica was followed by four bearers carrying a great burnished box: the Ark of the Covenant.

Joy mixing with bewilderment at the development, Avora'tru'ivi let out a triumphant shout as all eyes on the field turned to the curious sight.

The ancient legends about the Ark of the Covenant had not been lost on the Pelesetanians. This last blow to their morale was simply too much, and Jason's command structure collapsed. Soon, Pelesetanian soldiers deserted en masse, running off the field in all directions. The allied forces surged forward, until soon enough they had complete command of the field. The remaining Pelesetanian soldiers dropped their weapons, and the hated flag of the principality came crashing down, replaced with a white banner.

Avora'tru'ivi turned to Gideon.

"Return to the castle and tell the staff that it's time to draft up an entirely different set of surrender documents."

For his part, Prince Jason crashed through the underbrush in a headlong dash away from the battlefield, his eyes wide with panic. He had been so close to victory—so close to the humiliation of Avora'tru'ivi and her wretched country that he could almost taste it. Now, the sudden reversal of fortune had cost him his army – and likely his kingdom. The full import of Avora'tru'ivi's presence in Manasseh registered with him – it must mean that the Wil'iahns had won in the east, and Delilah was defeated.

He was doomed.

A panicked moan involuntarily left Jason's mouth as he hurtled along as fast as his corpulent legs would carry him, completely heedless of the direction in which he traveled. He just had to get away, as far from the avenging forces of justice as he could. He was so absorbed in his thoughts that he didn't notice the hard-packed ground beneath him gradually grow spongier, nor the pounding of his heavy footfalls turn into audible squelches.

He was completely unprepared when the ground below him gave way completely and he found himself neck-deep in a billabong. Now in utter terror, Jason began to flail around like a dying fish, fully aware that he couldn't swim—and, for once, there were no slaves or sycophants to help him.

A horrible thought crossed his mind. Even if there were, they probably wouldn't. Suddenly, in this moment of clarity, Jason focused on a pair of beady eyes watching him, just above the surface of the water.

Jason froze, petrified in fear.

The eyes, and the scales that surrounded them, began to move toward him with ever-increasing speed.

Willing himself to try to escape, Jason began to flail once more, vainly trying to propel himself toward the billabong's edge.

He was too late.

CHAPTER SEVENTY-FIVE

THAT'S OUR QUEEN

Citadel of Shechem

The throne room of the Citadel of Shechem was filled with excited voices as Jason's remaining lieutenant grimly approached the twin thrones where Gideon and Avora'tru'ivi sat. Before them was the same table where Gideon had almost signed the surrender papers only a few hours before. Behind the thrones hung the flags of Ephraim-Manasseh and Wil'iah.

Avora'tru'ivi was the first to speak.

"The long Frouzean occupation of the Peninsula has reached its end. In exchange for sparing your miserable life," she gave Jason's lieutenant a pointed stare, "the so-called Principality of Pelesetania is hereby dissolved. The territories which formerly comprised the western provinces of the Kingdom of Manasseh are to be returned at once. The remainder of Pelesetania's territories are to be turned over to the Yonlgu Confederacy and be given over to Aboriginal rule. Any Pelesetanian citizen who is willing to peacefully abide by these terms and follow the rules and statutes of the government in whose jurisdiction they find themselves is welcome to stay as a private citizen. Any who does not will be deported and granted passage back to Frouzea, or whatever is left of it by the time this war is over. Any remaining Pelesetanian troops in Manasseh, must, regrettably, be held prisoner here for the duration of hostilities. These are the terms we generously offer you."

Jason's lieutenant looked nervously around the room at the eyes which radiated hostility from all directions. He then reluctantly picked up a feather pen and, wincing, signed the document. The throne room erupted in cheers. He then hauled himself out of the chair, walked forward, and threw himself prostrate on the floor before Avora'tru'ivi, kissing the tiles.

The queen looked exasperated.

"Oh, please. Get up, and then get out."

The lieutenant scurried out of the room, watched ruefully by the queen's guards. After he slid through the large double doors, they slammed shut with a monumental finality.

Avora'tru'ivi involuntarily let out a breath she didn't realize she'd been holding, then looked over at Gideon, a wide smile spreading across her relieved face. For his part, though, her brother simply looked sheepish.

"I failed you, Avora," he said softly.

"We all have times of weakness, Gideon. At least I arrived before it was too late."

"What if you'd hadn't?"

"Let's not think about that."

"No, Avora, we need to think about that. I may be older, but I think we both know the wrong sibling ended up with the crown."

Suddenly embarrassed, Avora'tru'ivi quickly averted her gaze and looked at the floor.

"Gideon, I never"—

"No, you didn't. You don't have to say it, because I'm saying it for you."

"I have a life of my own now, in Wil'iah. I have responsibilities there."

"Personal unions exist. True leaders like you make it work. There is no reason why you couldn't rule Manasseh and Ephraim from a seat at Trukanamoa with your husband."

"Maybe, but what happens when I step down? Ephraim-Manasseh must retain its independence."

"What happens then can be decided at a later date. What I know is that, right now, in these challenging times, our country needs the leadership it deserves, and, as I so ably demonstrated during this siege, that isn't me."

Avora'tru'ivi took a deep breath. "We don't have time for a lengthy, drawn-out coronation right now. We have to get our armies to Trukanamoa, immediately, or this is all for nothing."

A half-smile played at Gideon's face, even as his eyes betrayed regret for his previous weakness. To Avora'tru'ivi's surprise, he began barking out orders with a crisp precision.

"Call Parliament, and tell them to assemble in the Mother Church immediately – skip the finery! Tirzah – get some oil! Meshach – get the orb!"

Before Avora'tru'ivi knew what was happening, she was squired out of the throne room into the main auditorium of the church, whose clanging bells announced to the populace that something important was happening. Scores of people plunged through the doors, curious looks on their faces as they craned their necks to see what was going on.

Gideon nervously cleared his throat.

"Citizens of the United Kingdom of Ephraim-Manasseh, I thank you for your courage and fortitude during our recent struggle with the forces of the reconstituted Frouzean Empire. I only regret that I did not share them in the appropriate quantities. Thanks to the enterprise and initiative of my sister, however, I was saved from making the worst decision of my life."

A confused murmur spread through the crowd.

Gideon continued. "I have thought on this, and I have reached a decision. I am not the best choice to be the leader of this kingdom. She is."

A shocked gasp rang through the auditorium as the full import of his words registered with the citizens. Avora'tru'ivi blushed with no small amount of embarrassment, but she kept her steely gaze fixed ahead.

Gideon wordlessly walked over to Avora'tru'ivi, then, with great deliberateness, took the crown off his head and placed it on hers. He snapped to the Patriarch of the Cathedral, who scurried over and offered the Orb of Ephraim and the Scepter of Manasseh to Avora'tru'ivi on velvet pillows.

"Do you, Avora'tru'ivi, daughter of Gamaliel IV the Defiant of Manasseh and Sheerah, War Queen of Ephraim, solemnly vow to defend their United Kingdom with all thy might, and to rule in justice and peace with all thy wisdom? Do you swear to uphold the ancient laws and standards of the kingdom, and to treat its citizens with equanimity and mercy? Do you swear to ever hold our banners aloft with thy courage?"

"I do," Avora'tru'ivi said confidently.

"In the haste of these times we have been forced to abbreviate this ceremony. A more complete coronation must follow, but some things must still be done." The Patriarch produced a cruse of oil and anointed Avora'tru'ivi.

"By the authority invested in me by the Church of Manasseh and by the laws and statutes of this kingdom, I declare the Avora'tru'ivi I, first Queen Regnant of the United Kingdom of Ephraim and Manasseh!"

Avora'tru'ivi's eyes darted over to Gideon, who smiled as he rendered her a full military salute. The crowd erupted into a chorus of cheers.

"Long live the queen!"

Avora'tru'ivi, Queen of Ephraim, Manasseh, and Wil'iah

CHAPTER SEVENTY-SIX

DAWN

Trukanamoa

*J*eremiah winced as a giant Frouzean siege projectile smashed into the cannon four crenellations down the battlement from him, destroying the gun's mount and sending the heavy barrel crashing down from the wall, attended by panicked shrieks. Casting his eyes with a mixture of sorrow and pride at the ragged defenders, clad in an irregular assortment of rags and bits and pieces of armor, Jeremiah swallowed hard and refocused on the seemingly endless sea of torches that spread out before him.

You will not win, he silently defied the enemy.

Suddenly, he looked over and saw a soldier sprawled on the battlement, collapsed from thirst. Jeremiah snapped into action.

"Get him down to the ward!" he snapped at two other nearby soldiers, themselves looking like they had been wandering the Sinai for forty years. They snapped into shaky salutes and then tottered down the stairs, unsteadily carrying the exhausted fighter between them.

All at once, a familiar, deadly whistle filled the air. Yet another trebuchet projectile.

"Get down!" Jeremiah yelled as he hunkered behind a merlon.

But this time, the giant ball sailed harmlessly over the defenders' heads, slamming into the ward below.

Jeremiah never expected what happened next.

Rather than the terrified cries that usually accompanied an artillery strike, jubilant shouts floated up from the ward. In bewilderment, Jeremiah whirled his head around.

From the crater left behind by the ball jetted an enormous geyser, its sweet waters sparkling in the moonlight like so many jewels. Heedless of potential danger, soldiers rushed toward it like madmen and danced in the spray, letting their open mouths catch the droplets as they arced back to earth. Jeremiah held his breath, uncertain of what to make of the surprising development and silently praying that the water hadn't been reached by Delilah's poisons.

But the triumphant dance didn't end in death. Instead, more and more people rushed to the geyser and drank their fill. And, to Jeremiah's unending disbelief, the geyser refused to abate. It simply continued to fill the night sky with its splendor, drenching the parched earth all around in life-giving rain.

Jeremiah's eye was suddenly caught by something in the east -- an indescribable glimmer.

Dawn had come.

CHAPTER SEVENTY-SEVEN

THE WEST GUARD

Trukanamoa

amino and a handpicked group of scouts inched their way forward across the desert ground, putting their well-practiced ranger techniques of camouflage and evasion to the test. A couple of miles behind them, the Wil'iahn Army waited in silent anticipation, sharpening its weapons for the inevitable charge against the enemy. But it needed to know what the headlong attack would run up against. The team carefully made its way over a rise, and all let out a nearly inaudible gasp as a terrible sight greeted them.

Before them, the walls of Trukanamoa burned, both with uncontrollable fires and with the still-defiant blasts of its guns. Before the staunch but weakening fortifications, the enemy stretched into the indiscernible distance like a flood. Tamino grimly clenched his jaw and withdrew a Chinese-made telescope from his bandolier, surveying the vast army before them.

"That's odd, I don't see any Mongol flags," he whispered to one of his fellow scouts.

"They must have gone around to the rear of the city."

A dark look crossed Tamino's features. "The northern defenses are the weakest, except for Tjoritja Cast"— suddenly, the dark look turned to pure horror as Tamino's telescope focused on something else.

The flag of the Frouzean Empire flapped from the tallest keep of the Castle of the West Guard.

"Never mind the Mongols, we have no time to waste," Tamino said, his voice shaking with terror. With that, he wordlessly motioned for the scouts to follow him and headed back toward the Grand Army with the best speed he could muster.

CHAPTER SEVENTY-EIGHT

TRUKANAMOA'S LAST STAND

Trukanamoa

*J*eremiah was right. Dawn had indeed broken over Trukanamoa, but its ostensibly friendly rays were anything but. Tamino was not the only son of Vrenga'ava'zora'vaua to notice the developments on the West Guard.

"*No....*" a whisper escaped Jeremiah's exhausted lips. The hated red banner of Delilah gloatingly waved in the gathering morning breeze as a burning Wil'iah flag was draped from the battlements. One by one, the soldiers that joyously drank from the still-flowing geyser looked up in alarm. Jeremiah's stomach churned as he realized the implications of the capture of the West Guard. Squinting in the early-morning gloom to make out details, Jeremiah felt his spirits sink even further as he noticed black cylinders poke out from the city-facing battlements of the castle.

Suddenly, an angry belch of fire issued from the castle, and a projectile screamed into the defenseless city below, setting a house in the inner city on fire. Panicked civilians began pouring out of their homes, milling about in terror. But they simply had nowhere to go, no stronghold to escape from the perfectly-positioned guns on their vantage point atop the mountain. Volley after volley from what was once the West Guard tore into the vulnerable mud brick buildings. Most of the civilians seemed to decide on a common course of action, a final safe haven from the blasts and darts of the enemy – the Grand Cathedral. The great church's doors ponderously swung open to admit the horde of refugees, who streamed in like citizens fleeing the city of Pompeii as cannonballs fell all around them like so much volcanic ash.

Snapping himself from the awful tableaux, Jeremiah sprang into action.

"Turn guns 24 and 28 on the West Guard! Do it! Now!"

As exhausted gun crews manhandled the bombards into position and piled rubble below their wheels to gain the proper elevation, Jeremiah ran a series of flag signals up the mast beside him to Trukanamoa Castle, whose ninety-six resolute towers still stood behind the weakening main wall. A flash of light from one of the twelve highest inner towers confirmed receipt of the message, and the largest castle in the world opened up on its former compatriot.

As Trukanamoa's own castles hurled missiles at each other, the resulting distraction had presented the Frouzean army with a rare opportunity. They now surged in like a tsunami, a wild, hungry, desperate look in their eyes. For as ragged and exhausted as Trukanamoa's defenders were, its attackers were more so, denied any of the supplies that had been promised from Frouzea by the Armies of Anangu and Kati-Thanda. On towards their prize, their glittering jewel, their salvation, they rabidly drove, many of them beginning to scale the walls without even the aid of ladders.

Heedless of the fusillade from Trukanamoa Castle and the walls, the West Guard inexorably turned its guns on the Grand Cathedral, setting its burnished dome directly in the cannons' sights. Jeremiah's heart leapt into his throat as a horrifying image of the great dome crashing down on the terrified civilians within flashed across his mind.

"No!!!" he gutturally yelled as he lunged forward and yanked the pull-cord on the nearest bombard, a thunderous report announcing the projectile that he hurled at the West Guard.

But it was to no avail. The cannonball fell short. The wall's guns simply couldn't elevate high enough. The cannons of the West Guard let out a hideous, brutal volley, and a dozen missiles sped through their deadly arcs, heading directly for the church, accompanied by an equally offensive bombardment of obscenities and jeers from the captured castle.

Jeremiah helplessly closed his eyes, unwilling to watch the beloved structure come crashing down. In the resulting darkness, he braced himself for the inevitable.

But it never came.

The screaming whistle of the projectiles ended, followed by thunderous reports as the cannonballs found their marks. But no groaning thunder of a crashing dome followed. The silent seconds ticked by, and Jeremiah finally wrenched his eyes open.

The dome looked like nothing had ever happened. In the eastern skies, two angry clouds parted to admit a blazing ray of the rising sun. The shaft of light gently lit the polished dome, which gleamed in response with a golden, resolute light that outshone even the brightest beacon. In response, fuming red flame belched out from the West Guard's ramparts once again, sending a second deadly hail onto the defiant dome. But, to Jeremiah's wondering eyes, the balls bounced off the structure and fell harmlessly into the Cathedral gardens below.

The West Guard's third volley was drowned out by a thunderous cheer as the defenders realized that somehow, against the odds, the Church of the Eternal Victory refused to fall. The joyous shout redoubled as an answering missile from the Castle of Trukanamoa slammed into the flagpole atop the West Guard and sent the Frouzean banner tumbling down.

But the celebrations were premature. Jeremiah whirled around in horror as a grappling hook clattered onto the battlement beside him, even as the gatehouse shook from an enormous battering ram that the Frouzeans carried above them as they gleefully slammed it repeatedly into the gates.

"Oil!" yelled Jeremiah to the machicolations below, even as he rallied the wall defenders to repulse the crawling sea of enemy soldiers that scaled the walls.

"We're out!" came the reply. "No more boulders, either!"

Jeremiah sharply took in his breath as he realized what he had to do. He signaled to the seven heavily-armored knights that stood with him atop the tower and began to descend the spiral staircase to the ward below, wincing as dust fell from the stairs with each crash of the ram.

After the first gate were many others in the three outer walls of the city, with portcullises in between. It would take some time for the enemy to penetrate the gates. But with nothing to pour through the machicolations and murder holes, time was all Trukanamoa had – and not much of it. Only a desperate last stand by the knights would forestall a flood of ravenous enemy troops upon the exhausted and defenseless city.

Again and again the ram came, like a mallet beating on a drum. But, to Jeremiah's surprise, once again, the attack of the enemy was greeted not with anguished cries from the ramparts, but with jubilant shouts, and, from somewhere in the far distance, beyond the resolutely thick walls of the gatehouse, the blare of a thousand conch shells and an equal number of trumpets. Wordlessly, Jeremiah turned around and ran back up the stairs, the other knights needing no second bidding to follow.

CHAPTER SEVENTY-NINE

A LION ROARETH

Trukanamoa

*T*amino sat tall and proud atop his charger, the magnificent horse snorting in anticipation as the burnished spike that sprouted from its forehead armor gleamed in the sun. On either side of the king, two standard-bearers rode. One held aloft an enormous battle-flag of the Kingdom of Wil'iah, its thirty-two rays seeming to outshine the sun itself. The other proudly waved the royal standard, its four quarters displaying the Star of Bethlehem, the Stripes of Uluru, the Ship of Zebulon, and the Lion of Judah. All along the front of the line of cavalry, thousands of brightly-colored banners waved in the bright morning sun, emblazoned with personal coats of arms and the divisional emblems of individual army units. Conspicuous were the great guidons of the Armies of Yaringa, Vrenga'nui, Maranoa, Kati-Thanda, and Anangu.

This is probably the moment for some great speech, but we don't have time for that, Tamino thought to himself.

Instead, he simply drew the Zrain'de'zhang, hefted it over his spiked helmet, and yelled with all his might,

"Ivrae'ia Va'a'kau'lua!"

A hundred thousand voices yelled in return, their strength swelled by the blasting of trumpets and conch shells. Tamino briefly looked with his own mixture of sadness and pride at the gleaming line of thirty thousand mounted knights that surrounded him on either side. His eyes then flicked to the battle-flag fluttering above his head, focusing on the boldly-embroidered star.

Not mine, but Thine, is this field, he thought silently, then looked straight ahead at the massed enemy, his large brown eyes narrowing with a fierce determination as he fought down the butterflies that attempted to take flight in his stomach. Gripping the lance just a bit more tightly, he quietly nickered to his horse and dug in his heels. Needing no further bidding, the magnificent charger surged forward, neighing in challenge.

On either side of him, the line of knights lurched forward, haltingly at first, but then with increasing speed. Soon, the red earth shook with the thunder of their hooves as they seemed to fly over the ground like an inexorable storm.

The jeering of the teeming hordes that crawled up the walls instantly stopped as every Frouzean head snapped to the East, met with the blinding, blazing sun and a surging tide of gleaming armor and deadly lances. It was as though a whirlwind from the heavens had descended to forge its avenging, dreadful path through a harvest-field of wickedness.

Louder and louder the thunder grew, until attacker and defender alike could plainly make out the battle-flags. Gasps and cheers rose from the walls as the defenders recognized the banners of the Armies of Yaringa and Vrenga'nui, and a wide smile played across Jeremiah's face as his eyes alit upon the royal standard.

So you were true to us after all. I knew Delilah was wrong.
He turned to the other knights atop the gate, who only moments before were preparing for their last stand.

"Well, are we going to make my brother do all of the work?"

CHAPTER EIGHTY

THE EMPIRE COLLAPSES

Trukanamoa

*D*elilah, atop her once-secure command post on a siege tower outside the range of Trukanamoa's guns, looked on in horror as the charge bore down on her once seemingly invincible army. Her face, which only moments before had been filled with wicked, gloating glee, now was as white as a sheet. Menelaus, a shocked, gormless look on his chiseled face, wasn't much better.

"D-Do something!" Delilah screamed as she frantically brandished her scepter. Heracles rushed forward to steady her, concern filling his face as the full impact of the sudden turn of events registered.

Some of Delilah's better-disciplined units heeded her hysteric orders and formed a shaky, tottering line to face the charge. At its center, squarely between Tamino's knights and Delilah's command post, stood the Homeric Guard, it alone having the composure to form a nearly-perfect phalanx, its deadly lances pointed directly at the armored hearts of the horses that thundered down on them.

However, Tamino was prepared for that eventuality. The tide of horses and knights split like the Red Sea around the potentially deadly phalanx and instead smashed squarely into the disorganized conscripts on either side. The phalanx's row upon row of sharpened pikes pointed harmlessly into a void in the Wil'iahn line, but the infantry forces that flanked it crumpled like tissue paper before the enormous force of the Wil'iahn charge. Soon, the phalanx was an island in a sea of horses that surged ever forward, driving back the terrified Frouzean infantry lest it be trampled underfoot. As the last of the Wil'iahn horses cleared the phalanx and the cyclone of red dust began to clear, it revealed instead a row of polished field guns and mangonels that had been dragged into place by the Grand Army's infantry forces as the charge proceeded. The receding thunder of the cavalry was succeeded by a new blast as the guns roared, sending their missiles crashing into the phalanx's shields. And thus, in an instant, the proud discipline of the Homeric Guard disintegrated.

Just then, to everyone's surprise, the gates creaked open. The soldiers manning the battering ram let out a brief triumphant cheer which was almost instantly choked as another group of knights, with the standard of the sovereign protector flapping above them, came charging out of the opening, sweeping away the battering ram crews. This new sortie from the city slammed squarely into what was left of the Homeric guard, and the air was filled with the clanging of clashing swords.

The mass of Frouzean infantry was pushed ever westward, but, gradually, the marvelous strength of the Wil'iahn charge began to fade. The advantage of the cavalry beginning to disappear, the Wil'iahn infantry, the majority of the Grand Army, now surged forward to support the knights as they jabbed with their remaining unbroken lances and hacked with great broadswords. Most sense of coordination was gradually lost as the battle descended into a chaotic melee.

But for Tamino, the goal was quite clear. A lurid, red siege tower stood, haughty and aloof, in the distance, and his squinting eyes could just make out an equally garish figure above.

It's time to put an end to this. She must be captured.

Tamino and six other knights formed an arrowhead formation that gradually, but relentlessly, pushed forward toward the command tower. The Zrain'de'zhang flashed in the morning sun, the legendary weapon dealing much more psychological damage than physical; legends of the sword's invincibility had already spread through the Frouzean ranks, and at the mere sight of the weapon, and the royal standard that announced its presence, the sea of enemies parted before the king and his compatriots.

His progress did not go unnoticed atop the command tower.

"Heracles, you may have another chance to redeem yourself," Delilah said nervously. To her right, Salome audibly gulped as her frightened eyes surveyed the changing fortunes of the Frouzean Army. A desperate, hungry light filled Heracles eyes as he hefted his giant broadsword.

"I will dispatch him for you, Your Worship. A son of Hezekiah Vrenga'ava'zora'vaua will not defeat me this time."

"Good boy."

Heracles turned to head below, and Salome whispered to Delilah.

"All is lost!"

"Oh hush, child. All is not lost. After all, do you forget that fully half of our force, our Mongol allies, even now beats against the northern defenses of the city? It surely shall fall, and then our strength against this rabble shall be redoubled. This is but a temporary setback."

Heracles dashed down the stairs to the base of the siege tower, where a few dozen of the remaining Homeric Guards, who had been held in reserve as Delilah's personal guard, stood in a stern, resolute, fanatical circle.

Heracles brushed them aside as he advanced towards Tamino.

"He's mine."

CHAPTER EIGHTY-ONE

SALVATION IN THE NORTH

Trukanamoa, northern approaches

On the other side of the city, the situation was substantially less triumphant. The great Irlpme Castle, a concentric fortification with two mighty walls that stood atop a hill on the north end of the city, stood resolutely in the way of the Mongol hordes, but even the huge fortress looked small compared to the forces it faced. On either side stretched the North Wall, a fortification that was still powerful by any measure, but not so great as the walls facing south, toward the direction where an attack was expected by the city's architects. This lack of foresight had now become a problem. The wall was ablaze in three dozen places, and even the castle, elevated though it was, was partially consumed by fire as its main keep burned from incendiary Mongol shells. Somehow, the Wil'iahn Flag still flapped beyond the reach of the flames, but the sight seemed only to amplify the defenders' desperation.

Prime Minister Allira, herself a military veteran, had assumed command of the northern defenses when General Vrenga'ivi had fallen. She grimly surveyed the situation from a corner tower in the castle, wincing as a tide of Mongols broke over the battlements to the west and began to engage in hand-to-hand combat with the weary defenders, most of whom were elderly, as the northern defenses had been considered a secondary priority when the troop assignments were created. She also feared that sappers might be at work, but her forces lacked the manpower or resources to counter them.

Suddenly, her fears were confirmed as a thunderous explosion shook both sky and earth. As the smoke cleared, a gaping hole yawned in the wall to the east of her, through which streamed hundreds of Mongol Troops. Her heart leapt into her mouth as Allira realized that the siege of Trukanamoa would likely be over in a matter of minutes. A shaky line of old men and women formed up behind the rubble to counter the Mongols, but Allira knew they wouldn't last long.

Suddenly, Allira squinted into the distance as a thin, dark line, almost like a forest, appeared on the horizon, followed by a sound like distant thunder. Her heart sank as she realized that yet more Mongol reinforcements, or perhaps Pelesetanians fresh from the destruction of vanquished Manasseh, must be on the way. Gripping her sword hilt tightly, Allira resolved to go the gap herself and fight to the last for her beloved country. She cast a brief, grieving glance at the flag that still bravely waved above the flames.

It was a beautiful dream.

But just as she turned to descend the spiral staircase to the ward below, something caught her eye. A flash of unexpected color. The flag that she could barely make out in the distance was not the dark blue, triangular banner of the Yuan Dynasty, or the blood-maroon flag of Pelesetania. It was red, and white, and blue, and gold. And in its upper left corner was a very familiar sixteen-pointed star.

How?

As the sudden charge grew nearer and nearer, another standard became visible. It had four quarters, containing the emblems of Judah, Zebulon, Manasseh, and Ephraim.

Now that's *my queen,* Allira thought triumphantly.

CHAPTER EIGHTY-TWO

THE TRUE ENEMY

Trukanamoa, northern approaches

Temur Khan whirled around in his saddle as a thunderous sound filled the air behind him, drowning out the battle-cries of his own troops as they ravenously surged through the gap in the wall.

The sight that greeted him was not a welcome one. A forest of lances leveled themselves directly at him and his men, and at their fore was a terrifying woman with a massive mane of black hair that flared out behind her like wings of an avenging angel as she bore down on them, an enormous spike sprouting from her forehead.

So this must be the oft-mentioned Queen of Wil'iah, he thought as he noticed her standard flying alongside her.

If there's one thing the Mongols know how to do, it's a cavalry charge, he thought. He instantly began barking out orders, and his lieutenants began to issue commands through their intricate flag signaling system. Almost instantly, three tumens of soldiers formed up around Temur, ready to face the new menace. But one glance at the troops' glassy eyes and hollow cheeks told Temur Khan that his men were in no condition for a true cavalry charge against the enemy. He snapped out more commands, and instantly, massive flights of arrows blackened the sky, furrowing towards the approaching enemy. But they were not yet in range. As they drew closer, to Temur's surprise, he began to notice other banners. The flags of Dai Viet, Champa, and Ephraim-Manasseh also fluttered bravely alongside the flag of Wil'iah, as well as several others that he did not recognize. Temur found himself oddly proud of the strange alliance that refused to surrender to him, even as he rallied his forces to destroy it. If he could pick off enough of the enemy charge with arrows, they might be weakened enough that his remaining strength could dispatch it, even though they were currently outnumbered.

But then, his eyes focused on something else. Carried aloft atop a huge cart drawn by four chargers and driven by a fearsome woman was a gleaming gold box. A very familiar gold box.

Temur wasn't the only one to notice it. An audible gasp ran down the line of Mongol archers as they all recognized the fabled Ark of the Covenant- an Ark that was supposed to be safely in China. Temur squinted again as recognized the banner that flapped above the cart-- the personal standard of Princess Jessica.

How? Delilah told me that she had been taken to China.

Another voice spoke to him, a voice that had been speaking to him for months, that he had been doing his best to ignore.

Delilah told you a lot of things.

Suddenly, the cavalry charge stopped just out of range of the Mongol arrows. The woman on the cart, who Temur presumed to be Princess Jessica, lifted a voice trumpet to her mouth and began to cry out.

"Behold, the Ark of the Covenant, recovered from Xanadu!"

"You must lie, the Great Khan would never allow you to escape, much less take the box with you!" Temur responded.

"The Great Khan is dead!" she simply responded.

A sudden gasp rang out down the Mongol line. Temur ruefully noticed that the gasp sounded more hopeful than anguished from the Chinese soldiers.

"Delilah sent him the Ark of the Covenant with a note saying that there was a present for him inside. Khan opened it, and was killed," Jessica responded.

Temur's blood suddenly ran cold.

She knew. She planned the whole thing.

Clenching his fist, Temur said to Bayan of the Baarin, his mentor, "She's nothing if not consistent. We should have seen this coming."

"Are you thinking what I'm thinking?" asked Bayan.

"She knew! She sent the Ark to him knowing it was deadly – or, for all we know, she engineered it to achieve the desired effect. She never had any intentions of carrying through this alliance. She probably thinks she is the rightful ruler of China now."

Bayan disgustedly looked at the carnage around him, at the hundreds of Mongol corpses piled at the base of the wall.

"I'm tired of fighting that duplicitous woman's war for her."

"She's more than duplicitous. She is a murderer. She murdered my grandfather. These Wil'iahns may have defied us, but they have comported themselves honorably even in this, their most desperate hour. Have you ever felt like, just maybe, you were fighting on the wrong side?"

"I will do anything for my Great Khan," the old general replied. "But now that Kublai is dead, I consider *you* the rightful heir to the throne. I owe that woman no loyalty. The choice of how to go forward rests entirely on you, not on that scheming empress."

Temur grimly nodded, then turned back at the huge, assembled army facing him.

"It is my understanding that Wil'iah recognizes the right of parley!"

The queen wryly smiled. "I find it amusing how you only seem to recognize other countries' rights when you try to exercise them for yourself, but yes we do."

Temur hesitantly began to ride forward meeting the queen in the middle of the battlefield.

"Am I correct in my interpretation of events, that the Frouzee Delilah deliberately sent the Ark of the Covenant to my grandfather for the express purpose of killing him?"

The queen smirked. "You know her better than I do, thankfully. What do *you* think?"

Temur looked sheepishly at the ground.

"I think we have all been duped."

"I knew you were smart."

"Well, seeing as Delilah has killed Kublai Khan, which is unequivocally an attack upon the Yuan Dynasty and the Mongol Empire, she is officially an enemy of the Mongol State, and you know the saying, the enemy of my enemy"–

"I wouldn't go that far," said Avora'tru'ivi, "but it does seem our swords should be pointed in the same direction, doesn't it?"

Temur motioned to the Tjoritja mountains that stretched into the distance on either side.

"In order for my forces to reach her and assist you, we would have to either go all the way through the mountains, or go through the city. Only one of those ways would get us there fast enough to save your capital."

Avora'tru'ivi laughed. "I may recognize our mutual interests, but I don't trust you *that* much. Your army will remain here. One false move, and our truce is called off. You, General Bayan, Princess Jessica, and I will proceed through the city to announce your changed allegiance."

Temur gravely nodded.

Avora'tru'ivi whisked her horse back around and returned to the allied line.

"It seems that our Mongol friends have experienced a change of heart, courtesy of the treachery of everyone's favorite walking fraud." Her announcement was met with a deafening cheer from the allied soldiers. She turned to General Hung Dao.

"General, I have made it clear that the Mongol Army is to remain here. If they make any false moves, you know what to do. Can you stand guard over them?"

"With pleasure, Your Faithfulness."

Avora'tru'ivi, her guards, and Jessica, still driving the cart with the Ark, advanced forward as the signal corps informed the gatehouse of the new developments. They met Temur Khan and General Bayan at the Mongol line, which parted to let them pass. The North Gate ponderously swung open, to reveal a jubilant Prime Minister Allira, who ran forward to hug the queen.

"Don't thank me yet. This battle is far from over," Avora'tru'ivi said through gritted teeth.

The strange entourage passed wordlessly through the streets of Trukanamoa. The few remaining civilians not huddled inside the Grand Cathedral quietly lined the sides of the street, whispering excitedly to each other as their beloved queen, standing tall, proud, and fearsome as ever, passed before them, with the legendary Ark of the Covenant and the two curious Mongol leaders following behind.

One young girl whispered to another,

"That's my queen."

CHAPTER EIGHTY-THREE

I KNOW WHO YOU ARE

Trukanamoa, southern approaches

*T*amino, still atop his charger, suddenly found himself face-to-face, once again, with Heracles. He gripped his sword just a bit tighter and swallowed nervously as he took in Heracles' massive stature.

"Get off that pony and fight me like a man," Heracles growled.

Tamino obligingly dismounted.

"It doesn't have to be this way, Heracles," he said as he entered a fighting stance, hefting the Zrain'de'zhang in front of him.

"It's too late for that," Heracles snarled as he ran forward, bellowing and whirling his giant sword about like the blades of a windmill. But, beneath the bravado, Tamino could have sworn that he detected a note of wistful longing in the man's voice.

Tamino steeled himself to meet Heracles' assault. He didn't have to wait long.

Steel rang against steel as the Zrain'de'zhang rose to meet Heracles' broadsword, sparks flying in all directions as the blow reverberated through the air.

"Why did you have to do this to her?" Heracles howled as he swung the sword with such force that Tamino was nearly knocked over. But he dug in his heels and held firm, the legendary sword of Vrenga'ava'zora'vaua refusing to yield to Heracles' assault.

"It seems to me that Delilah is the one who has been the aggressor," Tamino calmly responded.

"All she ever wanted was to be loved. You could have given that to her."

"I do love her, the same way I love all of Go's children."

The response was sincere, but it only served to enrage Heracles further. Tamino was driven back by a furious fusillade of blows that the king was hard pressed to parry. But, another glimmer of understanding dawned as he looked into Heracles' enraged, inflamed eyes.

"You can do better, Heracles. She has only ever used you."

"No. She is my savior, my goddess!"

"Do you really believe that, Heracles?"

The hulking bodyguard's only response was an enraged, animalistic bellow and a redoubled swing of the sword, which impacted the Zrain'de'zhang with such force that Tamino skidded back five feet, his boots carving great gouges in the red soil. But this was Heracles' crucial mistake, for, as in ages past, the mysterious, otherworldly craftsmanship that had forged the Sword of Light carried the day. Heracles' sword was cleaved in two, and, before Tamino could stop it, the Zrain'de'zhang buried itself deeply in Heracles' midsection, cutting through his substandard leather armor like butter.

"*No,*" the word escaped Tamino's mouth as a whisper. The king lunged forward to catch Heracles as he lurched and fell, clutching his abdomen.

This isn't right. This is not how this ends, Tamino silently, frantically thought.

The spectacular duel had caught the attention of the surrounding combatants, and the battle had actually died down in the surrounding area as both sides paused to witness the great confrontation between the King of Wil'iah and the Frouzee's closest and most devoted servant. Now, they watched with even more curiosity as Tamino gently laid Heracles on the ground and knelt down next to him, his eyes shut as he seemed to furiously think.

After what seemed like an eternity, Heracles stirred. And still Tamino knelt on the ground, his eyes tightly shut against the testimony of the world.

Suddenly, a gasp rippled through the onlookers as Heracles sat up and Tamino opened his eyes, an expression of profound peace writ large on his kindly face.

Heracles, for his part, looked like he had seen a ghost.

"*What did you do?*" he quietly hissed.

Tamino smiled.
"I know who you are."

CHAPTER EIGHTY-FOUR

THE FLIGHT OF DELILAH

Trukanamoa, southern approaches

"WHAT!?" seethed Delilah from her distant vantage point atop the siege tower as Tamino lifted Heracles to his feet and gently led him off the battlefield, the nearby opposing forces too stunned to keep fighting each other and instead parting to let them pass.

Delilah's surprise was short-lived, for just then, a much bigger problem presented itself.

The attention of the armies was instantly captured by the blare of trumpets, which turned into a deafening cheer as the Wil'iahn forces beheld Queen Avora'tru'ivi standing triumphantly atop the Gate of Ntaripe, flanked by Princess Jessica with the Ark of the Covenant – and Temur Khan. None cheered louder than Tamino, whose face lit up brighter than the beacon of Mount Cambewarra when he saw his wife.

Delilah lurched forward in shock, forcing herself to hold onto the railing for support, her long nails digging into the poorly-cured wood.

Surprisingly, it was Temur who spoke first.

"My grandfather, Kublai Khan, is dead, by the indirect, treacherous hand of that woman!" He spitefully pointed in the direction of Delilah's distant siege tower. She gasped in shock, giving her best attempt at feigned insult.

"How dare you?" she yelled, although she was barely audible over the distance.

"And, as the ranking officer of the Mongol Empire in this theater of war, I consider this treacherous attack on the person of the Great Khan to be an act of war by the Empire of Frouzea upon the Yuan Dynasty and the Khanate of the Great Khan. Thus, from this moment forward, there exists a state of war between the Mongol Empire and the Empire of Frouzea! Hostilities between the Mongol Empire and the Kingdom of Wil'iah and its allies," he nodded at Avora'tru'ivi, "have been suspended for the duration of this conflict."

Delilah looked like she had been physically struck.

Her army was no better. As the news began to spread to the areas where the din of battle still reigned supreme, looks of anger and horror fell across the Frouzeans' faces as they realized that their cause was lost. Any remaining semblance of order broke down in a matter of minutes as the Frouzean army disintegrated into a panicked, milling morass.

Delilah, for her part, seemed to recover quickly, but panic was still plainly written in her eyes. She physically shoved General Menelaus. "Don't just stand there, *do* something!" She rapped him on the head with her scepter. The general sheepishly descended the stairs to the ground and ran forward, ostensibly to rally the troops. But, instead, he made a direct line to Tamino and hurled his sword to the ground. Delilah snorted in disgust, turning to Salome.

"It's time we made our exit."

"What do you hope to do at this point? All is lost!" Salome wailed.

"Nonsense. Whatever that weakling Temur might say, *I* am still the empress of China. They know nothing of Temur's treasonous decision today. We shall flee there, and in that great nation rebuild our strength to carry on our fight."

"Do you really think that will work?"

"Have I failed us before?"

Salome questioningly cast her eyes over to the disastrous battle before them.

"Don't answer that question," Delilah hastily added.

Delilah and Salome wrenched a couple of horses away from two dazed Frouzean soldiers who stumbled about as though they were sleepwalking, and began to ride south at flank speed. At this final sign of Frouzea's defeat, the Frouzean collapse was complete. A few Frouzean soldiers surrendered, but most of them, fed propaganda about supposed Wil'iahn cannibalism of defeated enemies from a young age, broke and ran south, hoping to follow their empress. The Wil'iahn cavalry, thus extricated from the chaotic melee, began to form into a pursuit force. Suddenly, Tamino stepped forward with a staying hand.

"Wait."

"Now, in our moment of victory? We must seize the moment and destroy them!" Temur responded incredulously.

"We are not in the business of wholesale slaughter," Tamino replied calmly. "Look out there. That army has no supplies and nowhere to go. There is no need for us to stain our hands with their blood. In fact," he said with the slightest hint of a smile, "I have another plan."

CHAPTER EIGHTY-FIVE

VICTORY IN THE CENTER

Trukanamoa

*A*s the smoke of battle cleared, day fully broke over the battered, but undefeated, city of Trukanamoa. As the final vestiges of the Frouzee's army fled into the wilds of the south, the bells of the Church of the Eternal Victory pealed in triumph, the sound surrounding the dome that gleamed in the rising sun.

Once again, the battered gates of Ntaripe opened, although this time they admitted no cavalry charge. This was a charge of a different kind: Avora'tru'ivi, Jessica, and

Queen Adirah ran out to meet Tamino, whose chest heaved with exhaustion even as his eyes filled with triumphant tears. Avora'tru'ivi was the first to wrap him in an enormous bear hug. He responded by picking her up, armor and all, and twirling her around.

"I knew you could do it," he softly said.

"I knew *you* could do it," she responded.

Now Jessica stepped forward. Tamino's face broke into a visible tableau of relief as he rushed forward to embrace his sister.

"I was so worried."

"It's not me you should be worried about. They kidnapped the wrong princess!"

"Is Khan really dead?"

"You and I both know better than to open the box," Jessica wryly responded. "Clearly, Khan never read the Scriptures. I think the Ark's legendary powers got a bit of help from our least favorite empress." Suddenly, she got a faraway look in her eyes. "That said, I don't think they're just stories. The slaves' chains vanished without a trace."

Tamino gave a triumphant smile. "That's not the only mysterious deliverance from chains that has occurred during this war."

Queen Adirah rushed forward and gave Tamino a kiss on the cheek.

"Your father would be so proud of you," she said, her voice choking with emotion. Tamino's only response was a single tear that leaked out of his right eye.

Jeremiah trotted over, still atop his giant war-horse. He dismounted and pulled Tamino into a hug, slapping his brother on the back.

"I knew she was lying!"

"About what?"

"Well, she implied that, well, you and her---"

"She can dream on!" interjected Avora'tru'ivi.

Tamino laughed. "Well, I was in her clutches for a time, but thanks to the greatest woman in the world, she didn't get anywhere with her schemes, whatever they were," he said with a shudder.

Jeremiah chortled as he turned to Avora'tru'ivi with a twinkle in his eye.

"What did you do?"

Avora'tru'ivi smiled. "I acquainted her face with my fist!"

Jeremiah looked sheepishly at the ground. "You're not the only one."

Avora'tru'ivi feigned shock. "You did *what?*"

Another voice cut across the clearing.

"It was only to rescue me," Briseis said as she walked out of the gate, clad in a simple white peasant dress.

Tamino's eyebrows arched in surprise, but his eyes twinkled as though he really wasn't. However, Avora'tru'ivi's eyes narrowed.

"What is *she* doing here? Don't you know who she is?"

"It's a long story," Jeremiah chuckled. "I led a scout party to determine the disposition of the Frouzean forces, and 'rescued' a 'damsel in distress' by the name of…Iphigenia."

Tamino's face fell. "*No…*"

Jeremiah looked at the ground. "Yes. We took her in, treated her with all the courtesy that is customary, and what does she do?"

Tamino looked to Jessica. "Is that how…"

Jeremiah indignantly shook his fist. "She *took* it! So of course I had to go try to get it back, but even that was a trick, and soon I found myself in the clutches of the Vixen of Gath, much like you apparently were. But this lady," he said admiringly as he gestured to Briseis, "apparently had a change of heart and risked her life to help me escape. We weren't quite fast enough, though. Delilah arrived, and, well…" he said as he conspicuously rubbed his clenched fist.

Avora'tru'ivi snorted. "It couldn't have happened to a nicer 'goddess.'"

Briseis cleared her throat. "I have a confession to make."

The entire Wil'iahn royal family turned to her.

"Delilah isn't really a goddess."

The Wil'iahns burst into laughter as they yelled in unison,

"WE KNOW!"

Jeremiah suddenly got a puzzled look on his face and turned to Tamino. "By the way, why did you have General Luana reassigned from Trukanamoa? We could have used her longer. Come to think of it, how did you even transmit the order? I didn't see any smoke signals or beacon fires."

Tamino gave him a blank stare. "General *who?*"

"You know, the force-of-nature woman who showed up in the hour of Trukanamoa's greatest need and whipped us into fighting shape in time to defend the city against the Mongols? You sent her, right?"

"I've never heard of any General Luana," Tamino shook his head. "She told you I sent her?"

"Well, no, she said she was there because of the 'powers that be' and the 'ultimate authority'" – Jeremiah suddenly looked like he'd seen a ghost.

With sudden comprehension dawning in his eyes, Tamino asked, "And she mysteriously appeared in the darkest hour and promptly disappeared when it was passed?"

"Yes…and she was surprisingly casual about the Ark."

A smile worked at the corners of Tamino's mouth. "I see."

Something suddenly caught Briseis' eye. She ran toward a figure that stood aloof in the shadow of the wall.

"Heracles!"

The bodyguard turned to Briseis, shocked to see her. His face broke into a rare smile, which died almost instantly as he saw Avora'tru'ivi walk up behind her. He hastily genuflected on one knee.

"I don't quite understand what happened to me today," he said, "but the time has come to transfer my servitude to your household."

Avora'tru'ivi's eyes focused on the brass bands around Heracles' forearms. She shook her head.

"No. Stand up. Your servitude, to anyone, has come to an end."

Heracles, for his part, looked like he had been struck.

"What should I do? Where should I go?"

"Whatever, and wherever, you want. You are welcome to stay here. I think you will find that you will not be mistreated, as you were in Frouzea. We put our differences with the Anakim aside long ago."

"Anakim?" Heracles looked puzzled.

"I'm sure you've noticed that you're a bit bigger than your countrymen?"

"I might have," Heracles said bashfully.

"If our legends are to be believed, you are not alone. Feel free to peruse the Library of Trukanamoa if you wish to learn anything more." Avora'tru'ivi snapped her fingers at a nearby soldier, who rushed over. "Find a blacksmith. Those slave bands are coming off today."

"Right away, Your Faithfulness."

Heracles collapsed to the ground, overwhelmed by the news. Briseis rushed forward to steady him. Heracles turned to his fellow former Frouzean.

"You were right."

Avora'tru'ivi returned to where Tamino, Jeremiah, and Jessica stood in council.

"What happens next?" she asked.

Tamino cleared his throat. "Well, for starters, we apparently have an entire Mongol Army standing awkwardly outside our northern gate. I suppose we should do something about that before we move onto the next problem, which is what to do with Delilah."

CHAPTER EIGHTY-SIX

NEGOTIATIONS

Trukanamoa

"You must understand, Your Highness, that I have at my command two hundred-fifty thousand very angry men with a lust for conquest." Temur Khan entreated. "The Empire of the Great Khan does not take kindly to being betrayed. There are those that we fight who fight with honor, like yourself and your country. Then, there are those that have no honor, like the Frouzeans. They deserve to be trampled underfoot. I think it is clear from the events of the past twenty-four hours that the Mongol Empire does not have a future in Wil'iah. However, our rage must be vented somewhere. Join me. We will crush Frouzea together. They will never bother you again."

Tamino and Avora'tru'ivi looked at each other. Temur Khan could tell that the look conveyed more than just affection- it was an instant, wordless communication. Tamino cleared his throat and leaned forward on the table, lacing his fingers together.

"Khan, when Wil'iah began planning the defense of our nation against the treacherous and duplicitous invasion orchestrated by Ms. Delilah, we immediately established that we would defend Wil'iah the right way. Our armies abide by a very important code. We never act in offense. While our standards are different than yours, we know that the Mongols too have a code. Surely you can understand us."

"What are you saying? You do not wish to exact your revenge for all the woes that the Frouzee has wrought on you and your people? You do not wish to finish the job that your father started and exterminate, once and for all, this treacherous scourge from your continent?"

"The only job that my father started was building this country- a nation that always acts in accordance with its principles." Now Tamino stood up from the table, his commanding frame towering over the Mongol prince.

"The stated purpose of the League of Trujustakanoa was to defend its members, and, in our case, to defend our continent, against any invasion or occupation by the Mongol Empire. We stand by our original commitments."

"But Frouzea was never part of this League."

"Frouzea's people are a misguided flock that followed the wrong shepherd. They were fooled by the Frouzee just as you were. Does this make them worthy candidates for extermination? Hardly."

"Then you will not assist us with the cleansing of Frouzea."

Tamino gave a wry smirk. "Not only will we not assist you with your putative 'cleansing' of Frouzea, we will not permit it. Your armies have been repeatedly defeated in pitched battle by our forces and the forces of the League of Trujustakanoa. It is time for you and your armies to go home."

Temur Khan recoiled and stood up to face Tamino, but, even standing, he couldn't reach up to look him in the eye.

"Do you really think you can force us to leave?"

Tamino smiled again. "Yes. But that is not my goal. I think something better can come from all of this. You and your forces came to Australia as enemies. But I think you can leave as friends."

Temur Khan took a step backward, clearly taken aback.

Avora'tru'ivi rose from her seat. "Listen, Temur. These repeated wars cannot have been good for the Yuan economy. You have lost army after army, and fleet after fleet. Even China's resources are not unlimited. And now, to boot, the Great Khan is dead. But now there is a new Great Khan. You. You get to decide what your legacy will be. Will it be failed conquest after failed conquest, leading to national ruin and a personal spiral into depression and madness, like your grandfather? Or will it be something else?"

Temur looked stung by her words, but Avora'tru'ivi could tell in his eyes that her words hadn't completely missed their target.

"Alright, what do you propose?"

Avora'tru'ivi cleared her throat. "You will have your chance to strike at the Frouzee, but not in the way you intended. Our western provinces, as far as we know, are still under siege by the Frouzean Army's Tanitanian legions. We plan to march there; you will accompany us and help us to defeat them. In exchange, we will permit you to embark on unarmed ships, with Wil'iahn naval escort, from our western ports and return to China. We will then normalize our diplomatic relations with the Yuan Dynasty and resume our trade partnership. In addition, you will promise never to attack Wil'iah, or any of the member states of the League of Trujustakanoa, including Singhasari, Champa, Dai Viet, and our northern continental allies, again. You will also withdraw your forces from the island of Ithaca and cede control to a Wil'iahn expeditionary force. Ithaca will then be allowed to decide its own fate. While we will allow your ships to visit our ports, for a customary period until trust is fully established, direct trade between Frouzea and the Mongol Empire will not be permitted."

"You drive a hard bargain."

Tamino interjected. "The choice we offer you is very simple. How do you want to be remembered, Temur? As the man who brought stability, peace, and prosperity to the Yuan Empire, or the man who drove his country to disaster pursuing the useless vendettas of his grandfather? Because, if you continue to pursue your campaigns of conquest, we will continue to resist you, and this war marks the sixth consecutive defeat for the Yuan Empire. Genghis Khan's aura of invincibility is long-dispelled. Your people are growing exhausted and dissatisfied."

"As much as we disliked you, your wisdom has become known even in our empire, Tamino," Temur conceded. "And my grandfather's spiral into madness has not gone unnoticed. As much as Delilah and her forces have proved themselves to be duplicitous and treacherous, Wil'iah has proved herself to be courageous and honorable. I will admit that there were many times in this conflict that I suspected we were fighting on the wrong side."

Temur fell silent for several moments as he clearly pondered the offer. Avora'tru'ivi found herself involuntarily scooting forward on her seat. Finally, Temur looked from side to side at his soldiers, noting their bedraggled appearance.

"Something has to change. I will accept your offer."

Avora'tru'ivi found herself breathing a sigh of relief. But, suddenly, she made eye contact with one of the Yuan soldiers, this one clearly a Han Chinese conscript. "Khan, I have one more thing to add to our proposal."

Temur winced. "And what would that be?"

"A significant portion of your forces is made of native Chinese conscripts. Within living memory, China was a fast friend of Wil'iah. As I'm sure you know, many of their hearts simply weren't in this war."

Temur grimaced. "I may have noticed."

"Your armies will still be granted safe, but escorted, passage back to China. But I will add to our demands that any Han Chinese soldier who wishes to remain here rather than return to their occupied homeland must be allowed to do so. Wil'iah will extend asylum to these individuals. In addition, you must promise that no retaliation will come to their families in China." She noticed a flash of gratitude cross the soldier's face.

"You ask for too much, Your Highness," Temur responded.

"Khan, if you wish to stabilize your grandfather's decaying Empire, you must win the loyalty of the local population. The Han are a powerful and numerous people. Without their cooperation, you can never hope to hold China for any significant period of time. What better way to improve relations with the Han than by releasing them from their unwilling service?"

Temur stroked his wispy beard. "It appears that the king has found for himself someone equally wise."

"Trust me, she's wiser," Tamino interjected.

"Very well. Any Han soldiers that wish to remain in Wil'iah will be allowed to do so. Now is that it, or are there any other 'requests' that you would like to add?"

"No, that's all," Avora'tru'ivi said. "This will be formalized tomorrow as an agreement between the member states of the League of Trujustakanoa and the Yuan Empire. We will sign the treaty at the Great Hall." She caught the eye of the Han soldier once again. While he attempted to maintain a suitably stoic expression, gratitude was writ large in his eyes.

"*Xie xie,*" he mouthed.

Temur Khan stood up and extended a hand to both the king and queen, who each shook it in turn.

"Here's a sentence I never thought I'd say," said Tamino. "To the friendship of the Yuan Dynasty and Wil'iah!"

CHAPTER EIGHTY-SEVEN

A HIGHER WAY

Trukanamoa

$\mathcal{D}$eep in the Castle of Trukanamoa, Tamino, Jeremiah, Avora'tru'ivi, Adirah, Jessica, and Briseis gathered around a conference table. A large wall map of the Judgate of Tjoritja hung behind them, with the expected path of the Frouzean Army, or whatever was left of it, marked in red. Tamino folded his hands and leaned forward on the table.

"Here's the situation. We have a large number of Frouzean soldiers staggering through the desert. While they were roundly defeated in the last battle, they still remain a threat."

"Best to crush them now, before they can cause any more problems!" hissed Jessica.

Tamino held up a staying hand. "It *may* come to that. But I don't think it will."

"What do you mean?" Jessica responded combatively, folding her arms and leaning back in her chair.

"There are two ways to destroy an enemy," Tamino said softly. "One way is to kill him. That is the lowest way. There is a higher way. To make him into a friend."

Jessica scoffed. "That will never happen."

Tamino pointedly looked at Briseis. "It already has."

To Tamino's surprise, Jeremiah spoke out in support.

"It can happen again."

"What are you proposing?" Avora'tru'ivi asked, folding her hands together and leaning forward on the table.

"Perhaps Briseis can confirm this," Tamino said, "But, based on what I heard from the Army of Anangu, the Frouzean Army is starving, exhausted, and terrified. They are now staggering through one of the most inhospitable deserts in the world with virtually no supplies and even less leadership. We could probably just sit here and let the desert solve our problem for us. But that would not be the higher way."

Briseis nodded. "Everything was falling apart even before I defected. None of the supply caravans that we expected made it through, and there was virtually nothing to eat in the surrounding areas."

Tamino smiled. "As our Aboriginal friends know, there is actually enough, if you know where to look. But that's beside the point. I propose that we take a large force south, powerful enough to meet the Frouzeans in combat if need be, but with a different primary mission. We will carry food and supplies with us to relieve the Frouzean troops."

Jeremiah's face fell. "It's a nice idea, but I don't think we even have enough food to feed ourselves, much less the enemy!"

Tamino gently shook his head. "We will have the supplies we need. Anangu and Kati-Thanda captured almost all of those supply caravans Briseis was talking about. There will be more than enough to share."

Jeremiah looked somewhat mollified, but still skeptical.

"Furthermore," Tamino continued, "I think you are the perfect person to command Wil'iah's first humanitarian mission in aid of Frouzea."

"What!?" the sovereign protector responded.

"I know you well, my brother, well enough to know that you could use this lesson in forgiveness. But this will only succeed if we have inside information to use to our advantage." He pointedly looked at Briseis, who looked surprised to be regarded at all.

"Briseis, consider yourself the recipient of a field promotion. You and Jeremiah will lead this resupply effort, although the queen and I will accompany you." Tamino suddenly stood up. "That settles it. Prepare eight divisions and enough food and water to relieve the Frouzean Army. We have a war to end."

CHAPTER EIGHTY-EIGHT

SACRIFICE

Lake Pantu, Sovereign Judgate of Anangu, south-central Wil'iah

The Frouzean Army staggered on, in the vague direction of Tanitania, which might still offer them a stronghold – and passage to China. Delilah had managed to muster up another sedan chair, on which she luxuriated while four sweating slaves stumbled across the desert, their ribs plainly showing. Delilah did her best to combat the oppressive heat with a plume of emu feathers, but the merciless, lidless sun beat down on them all, the parched earth radiating back most of the heat. Day after desperate day had passed like this, the army held together only by the will of their eternal empress as she drove them to their uncertain destination. No horses remained, all having either fled, been captured, or eaten by the remaining soldiers. The last few bags of water had run dry earlier that day.

Suddenly, the lead column halted in the distance. Delilah sat up with interest, noting also that, in the very remote distance, the rock of Uluru was just visible, as were the domes of Kata Tjuta. But, between the army and the famed rocks stretched a great mirage, as far as the eye could see in either direction. A cheer erupted from the army as they thought they saw a large lake.

But the cheers died quickly as the first group of men reached the "water's" edge. What stretched before them was no lake with living water, but a great expanse of salt. One man reached down and scooped up a handful, letting the salt crystals run through his fingers before throwing the last small bit down in disgust. The news that there was no water spread like wildfire through the exhausted army, and the sky was soon filled with moans and groans.

Little did they know that the problems of the Imperial Army were just beginning. A cry from the rear of the army turned Delilah's head, and in the distance she could see an ominous red cloud sweeping down on them. She stifled a curse as Salome ran to her, her eyes filled with alarm.

"What is it?"

"A dust storm, darling. We'd better draw the curtains closed on the sedan chair." Delilah languidly pulled the silk cord that closed the gossamer hangings, but, as soon as they drew shut, they were wrenched open by an infantry captain, his feathered helmet askew.

"Why don't you explain why the gods have abandoned us, O 'eternal empress!?' First, the water runs out, and we are cheated by an impassable salt flat. Then, the sky fills with dust!"

Delilah struggled to find the right words to answer him. In her moment of hesitation, the captain brusquely grabbed her arm and yanked her out of the sedan chair. She tumbled to the ground and shrieked as she skinned her elbow on the hard-packed earth.

"How dare you!?" she responded, her eyes filled with a livid fire and her nostrils flaring like a bull.

The captain didn't respond. Instead, he stood positively gobsmacked, his mouth open in shock as his wide eyes focused on the blood that dripped from her elbow.

Red blood.

Delilah's insides seemed to turn to terrified mush as she realized what had just happened.

The captain's shock turned to anger as he lunged forward and grabbed Delilah's arm once again, dragging her to her unsteady feet and lifting the elbow up for all the surrounding troops to see.

"Look at this!" the captain gutturally yelled. "This is no golden ichor! This is not the blood of a goddess!" He threw her back to the ground, where she crumpled in an undignified heap. "This is a fraud, an impostor, a *woman,*" he said, spitting on her. Delilah reached to wipe away the spittle and retorted.

"Don't listen to this imbecile! Am I not your eternal empress? Have I not led you to victory after victory? This is just a temporary setback! Once we return to Tanitania, we will renew our greatness!"

Suddenly, another soldier spoke.

"She has no intention of leading us to any more victories. She is only going to Tanitania so she can get on a ship to China. She is abandoning us! I overheard her say this to her lackey!" He pointed at Salome, who shrunk away in terror before she was roughly grabbed by two more soldiers, who shoved her into the center of the circle, where she fell to the ground next to Delilah.

The captain continued. "Her treachery has angered the true gods! Now we are punished for her sins! What is the only way to appease the anger of the gods?"

"*Sacrifice!*" yelled another man from the crowd.

"That's right, sacrifice!" yelled the captain.

"How dare you!" yelled Delilah, her bravado failing to mask the naked fear that filled her eyes.

"SACRIFICE!" came the deafening answer from the army.

"Prepare an altar! This must be done in the proper way if it is to work!" the captain barked.

With very little in the way of building materials, the men began piling spears, staves, and other weapons into a roughly altar-shaped pile. The screaming, protesting Delilah and Salome were tied up and placed on the altar, while the troops obscenely danced around it in a great, frenetic, fanatical circle, cursing at the top of their lungs and making vulgar gestures.

The captain mounted the altar and withdrew his dagger, which gleamed in the deadly, merciless sun. He held the dagger high over his head and began to chant.

"Oh great Dagon, great Baal, true Astarte, forgive us for our transgressions! Accept the blood of this woman and her foul, sniveling accomplice as recompense for our sins!"

Delilah cowered on the altar and closed her eyes, waiting for the inevitable as the jeers of the soldiers assaulted her ears from all sides.

Suddenly, the taunts died as an ear-splitting sound reverberated through the air.

Conch shells. Delilah had never thought she would be happy to hear them.

The Frouzean soldiers forgot their diabolical dance and looked to the east, where a long, dark line stretched across the horizon, kicking up a dust cloud of its own as it thundered over the earth. The troops scrambled to form some sort of defensive line, but most of their weapons had been given over to Delilah's sacrifice pyre. Some even picked up stones as they waited in quiet desperation. Delilah and Salome, tied as they were to the altar, craned their necks to see what was happening.

Just outside of bowshot, the Wil'iahn line stopped, and four figures trotted forward- Tamino, Avora'tru'ivi, Jeremiah, and Briseis. Delilah sharply drew her breath as she caught sight of her accomplice.

"What do you want?" jeered the captain at Tamino.

The king calmly responded, "We want this war to be over. We offer you that chance now." Tamino's eyes narrowed as he spotted Delilah atop the pyre.

"Sacrificing her isn't going to solve your problems."

The captain snorted. "The gods have been angered by her treachery. We must do something to appease them. I can't imagine you're sorry to see her go."

Tamino flicked his eyes to the approaching sandstorm, now just minutes away, then locked eyes with the captain.

"Your problem isn't the wrath of nonexistent gods. It is your own false beliefs coming to roost, your own lack of understanding. Take her down," he said coolly as he drew the Zrain'de'zhang. At the sight of the legendary weapon, the Frouzean line flinched.

"Galbi, it does seem an odd sort of justice for her"—

"—This is no justice. Nobody is beyond redemption." Tamino returned his gaze to the captain and said flatly, "Off the pyre. Now."

"Or you'll what?" leered the captain.

Tamino quietly nodded to the line of cavalry on either side. They locked their lances into attack position in perfect unison.

The disorganized rabble of Frouzean troops began to nervously murmur as they realized they would never be able to stand up to another cavalry charge. The captain cast his eyes about with increasing panic, realizing that his support was eroding. Finally, he stepped aside, the soldiers behind him parting as well to allow Tamino's charger to pass. He slowly walked over to the pyre, and, with an expert flick of the tip of the Zrain'de'zhang, cut the ropes tying Delilah and Salome to the pyre. For the briefest instant, he locked eyes with Delilah, and saw what he expected to see. Beneath the layers of venom, loathing, and frustration, he saw a spark of something- maybe it was gratitude. Delilah didn't say a word.

"I'll deal with you later," Tamino said flatly, then turned to look at the swirling maelstrom of sand that barreled down on them. He rode back out to join the other Wil'iahn leaders, then turned back to face the Frouzean captain.

"Your so-called gods had nothing to do with that sandstorm, and neither does the True God." He then whispered to his compatriots. "Remember-- God is not in the storm."

Avora'tru'ivi quietly nodded. The four riders turned to face the sandstorm and grasped hands. Tamino, Avora'tru'ivi, and Jeremiah all noiselessly closed their eyes in concentration. Briseis briefly looked confused, then did the same. Gradually, behind them, the rest of the Wil'iahn army followed suit in silent defiance of the angry storm whose menacing tendrils reached out to engulf them in a stinging darkness.

The whole Frouzean army stood transfixed at the apparent silent battle as eight divisions of Wil'iahn soldiers stood absolutely still. The gathering wind howled, tousling the hair of the Wil'iahn soldiers and setting their banners frantically flapping, but they refused to move, standing tall and resolute, fearless in the face of the fury of wind and sand.

Gradually, almost imperceptibly, the scene began to change. The howling grew ever so quieter, the advance of the storm just slightly slower. Minute after minute ticked by, and still the sandstorm didn't engulf the armies. Finally, it halted its progress, whirling about harmlessly and helplessly just beyond the armies.

Abruptly, the wind changed, and the storm began to be pushed back, receding, slowly at first, but with increasing speed, into the north, weakening with every foot it was pushed back. Finally, when it had almost retreated out of sight, its last malevolent puff of sand collapsed to the ground, leaving only a clear blue sky.

The Frouzean soldiers stood nervously transfixed by what they had just witnessed. None of them noticed Delilah slink off the pile of weapons and slither back to the sedan chair, where she secreted herself, Salome following behind.

Tamino slowly opened his eyes, greeted with the clear skies he had been expecting to see. He breathed in a deep gulp of fresh desert air, then turned back to the Frouzean Army.

"You are probably expecting us to now slaughter you wholesale," he said. The Frouzean soldiers snapped out of their awed trance and began to nervously murmur, fidgeting uncomfortably.

Tamino continued. "But, contrary to what you may have heard, that is not how Wil'iahns choose to live their lives. We understand that you have been led to this extremity by false prophets and fraudulent shepherds. Our enmity is with evil, not with you." He turned behind him and nodded to the line of cavalry, which parted to reveal carts piled high with food, water, and supplies. An audible gasp rose from the Frouzean ranks.

"So, if you promise now to throw down your weapons and never again attack the Kingdom of Wil'iah or its allies, we are prepared to offer you amnesty, and provide the food and drink that you so desperately need."

The captain worked his mouth in shock, searching for words. "Wh…wh…why would you do this…after everything we have done to you?"

Tamino smiled. "We are to love our neighbors as we do ourselves. Last time I looked at a map, Frouzea was Wil'iah's closest neighbor. We're just following orders."

The captain looked questioningly at the soldiers on either side, whose expressions wordlessly answered the unspoken query. He then looked back to Tamino, raised his short sword over his head, and let it clatter to the ground.

The surrounding desert rang as thousands of other weapons were similarly dropped, then reverberated with thunder as desperate feet ran towards the carts.

Tamino turned to the cavalry, which until that moment had stood tense, lances at the ready.

"At ease."

An audible sigh of relief rippled through the Wil'iahn Army.

Avora'tru'ivi reached across to wrap her husband in a tight hug, but then suddenly pulled away, a dark look on her face.

"What is it?" Tamino asked.

"Where's Delilah?"

CHAPTER EIGHTY-NINE

THE BEAUTY OF POLYTHEISM

Lake Pantu, Sovereign Judgate of Anangu, south-central Wil'iah

Delilah was hiding inside her sedan chair, when the flaps opened and a voice sounded.

"What do we do now, Your Worship?" Salome breathlessly intoned. "All is lost!"

Delilah hastily put down the snake headdress, which she had just been putting something in, and whirled around to face her assistant.

"Not all is lost," Delilah crooned. "And the question is not what I will do, but what *you* will do."

Salome looked shocked. "What *I* will do?"

"*Yes,*" Delilah said. She pointed over to the snake headdress, which sat undisturbed on the seat.

"Dear Salome, I know what you have always really wanted."

"I don't know what you mean."

"I must flee and rebuild. I, of course, shall return. However, someone needs to assume the mantle of the Frouzee here while I'm gone. You have proved the depths of your loyalty during your service to me. You have earned the right to wear the headdress."

Salome looked bashful. "I could never replace you, Your Worship."

"Of course you couldn't. Not in truth. But you would make a very convincing interim Frouzee indeed. Put it on."

Salome nervously walked over to the headdress and picked it up.

Delilah saccharinely nodded, an entirely fabricated smile plastered across her face.

Salome raised the headdress over her head, her self-conscious expression turning to triumph as she lowered the headdress onto her head.

Just as soon, however, her expression changed to naked fear as a serpentine hiss escaped the famous adornment.

A wicked smile spread across Delilah's face. "After all, the beauty of polytheism is that you can have *more than one* goddess."

Horror filled Salome's eyes. "You knew!? You heard me talking to Diomedes?"

"Goddesses hear *everything.*"

Delilah continued to smile as she produced a lit match.

"All hail the Frouzee."

CHAPTER NINETY

THE PYRE OF AN EMPIRE

Lake Pantu

Tamino's eyes darted to the west as a sudden angry light flared up. He wordlessly drew his sword, dismounted, and ran, the queen, Jeremiah, Briseis, and Heracles following as he raced over toward the enormous, billowing tent that could only have been Delilah's sedan chair. Teams of soldiers followed his lead and began to hack the chair's flaps apart, smothering the burning strips of fabric with heavy blankets. Finally, only the smoldering ruin of the chair's framework still stood, revealing the charred interior.

At the center, sprawled across the floor, was a blackened corpse, unidentifiable but for two unmistakable ivory horns that lay broken on the floor near the body's head. Tamino suppressed a retch as Briseis ran forward with an expression of dismay. A great sob shook the woman's slight frame. "Defiant to the end. She never saw the light."

Jeremiah rushed forward to comfort her.

A great sadness spread through Tamino's spirit as he realized Briseis was right. He hung his head in sorrow, not for the passing of Wil'iah's most formidable enemy, but for what might have been. He turned as he felt a gentle hand touch his armored shoulder.

"You did your best, Galbi. Some people just refuse to be led to the Higher Way."

"I really thought"—

"I know. But the peace she couldn't find here, she may find on the next stage of her learning experience. And," the queen smiled sheepishly, "I certainly won't miss her."

Tamino nodded sadly, then looked briefly skyward.

Lead her to the freedom that I was unable to give her.

CHAPTER NINETY-ONE

WELCOME TO WIL'IAH

Gardens of the Elysium, Trukanamoa

Briseis walked through the Gardens of the Elysium, surveying the splendor that had somehow remained mostly untouched during the siege, protected from the darts and projectiles of the enemy by the staunch walls of Trukanamoa. Standing tall and proud, its defiant, undamaged dome gleaming in the low afternoon sun, was the Grand Cathedral, its towers and semi-domes spread like a mothering, protective blanket over the grateful people that streamed in and out of its doors.

The Grand Cathedral, Trukanamoa

Briseis smiled to herself, happy that the building had withstood its bombardment from the West Guard, whose now-blackened walls still loomed above, the Frouzean flag that once flapped over it long-replaced with a Wil'iahn banner. All the same, Briseis' relief at the salvation of the city was tinged with sadness at the realization that she was a stranger in this place, and she could never go home.

She looked down at her hands, their fair skin contrasting with the darker tones of those around her. She didn't look like, speak like, or think like the whirlpool of strangers that flowed around her in the garden. However, somewhere in the recesses of her mind, a spring of hope flowed – hope that the gulf could be bridged, that these differences were not irreconcilable. She thought back to the first time she had seen these gardens, the night when Tamino had squired her around the city in a vain attempt to turn her in the direction of peace, to thwart Delilah's plans.

It wasn't in vain, she suddenly realized. *You knew then. You knew she was wrong.*

And then, of course, she thought back to those strangest of nights in the Frouzean tents, as the city lay in mortal danger, when the Prince of Wil'iah languished in the chains of Gath, and when the tiny seed of freedom that had been planted in her heart during the first visit began to sprout into a mighty crop, and she had finally dared to do the unthinkable…

"I never got a chance to properly thank you," a voice said behind her.

Briseis whirled around, and her eyes were greeted with the severe features of Jeremiah. Yet today they seemed just a bit softer- the eyes a bit less piercing, the eyebrows a bit less like the slashes left behind by a saber.

Briseis averted her eyes and began nervously handling a boronia flower. "It was nothing. A decision I should have made a long time ago."

"It was not nothing. To defy Delilah is not for squeamish, callow weaklings. You risked your life to save me, and you knew it. I only wonder why," Jeremiah said, a slightly sheepish edge creeping into his voice, to Briseis' surprise. "After all, I have been a poor example of Wil'iahn courtesy."

"Your nation was under attack. I was the enemy. What else would you be but hostile?"

"Wrong. I was wrong."

Briseis finally looked back at him, and was surprised to see a mixture of shame and earnestness, an expression of which she didn't think he was even capable.

"I let my own prejudices get the better of me," Jeremiah said. "I thought that Wil'iah had a sworn enemy, a perpetual nemesis, that could only be defeated through its destruction. I didn't realize that Wil'iah was at war with evil, not with the people evil had deceived. And I failed to discern that a spark of good was right before me, in the unlikeliest of places."

Jeremiah's eyebrows arched in surprise as a tear slipped out of Briseis' eye and dribbled down her cheek.

"What's wrong?" he said as he rushed forward, concern filling his voice.

"These gardens are beautiful," Briseis said.

"Well, yes, I suppose they are – I'm ashamed to admit I never paid much attention to them."

"And this beauty my people tried to destroy. I have no doubt that I made the right decision when I defied the Frouzee, but I'm afraid, Jeremiah. I am now a woman with no country. After what I've done, no good people would ever accept me. I certainly cannot return home. There, I am a traitor."

"Who says this cannot be your home? Jeremiah said as he reached to brush the tear away, but Briseis recoiled at his touch.

"Look around, Jeremiah. I am not one of you. I am different. That will never change. Your people will never be able to look on me as anything but an enemy. You are a Zebulite, I am a Philistine. Such is the way of things."

"It is there that you are mistaken, Briseis. Wil'iah is not a people. Wil'iah is an idea. An idea whose embrace stretches beyond border and sea, transcends color and creed. Once I was foolish, and did not realize this, but now I see that in difference there is beauty."

Briseis looked up in surprise to meet his eyes, noting that his voice seemed to tremble with emotion.

"I- I don't understand."

"Listen to your heart, Briseis. I think you do understand. I have learned to listen to mine. Before this war, I was a cold, maybe even heartless, individual. I was cynical, and I believed that this world was made of the good and the irreconcilably evil, and I had to stoop to their level to stop them. But, in the unlikeliest of places, in a Frouzean tent of torments, someone showed me that I was wrong. Somebody showed me that love was stronger than the darkness, and the only thing that would truly defeat it in the end, not swords, not catapults, not cannons. You may have entertained ethereal visitors, but the guardian of the Ark was not the only angel in the Frouzean camp that night."

"Y-you can't possibly mean…"

"Your spirit is strong and brave, and your soul is beautiful, Briseis."

"I hadn't dared hope…"

"You restored my hope," Jeremiah said, then stepped forward and kissed Briseis. They lingered for a few moments, then she stepped back.

"I grew up a slave, in more ways than one," she said. "In Frouzea, I thought that all men were a certain way, that to serve them was my lot in life, and that was simply the way the world worked. I was taught that Wil'iah was the enemy, a land of bloodthirsty savages who would stop at nothing to destroy us all. But there was another way -- a higher way – and a brave, noble knight in bright, burnished armor cut through the chains to show me the path to freedom, even in the darkest depths of his own despair. For, that, I will always be grateful. You saved me."

Jeremiah shook his head.

"No, you saved me." He offered his arm to Briseis, who hesitantly took it. He beamed down at her, smile lines crinkling around his eyes for the first time in as long as he could remember.

"I think it's time we gave you a proper introduction to your new home. Welcome to Wil'iah."

CHAPTER NINTETY TWO

THE TREATY OF TRUJUSTAKANOA

Trujustakanoa, Marduwarra, western Wil'iah

The Palace of Marduwarra, the center of administration for the Judgate, rose in a massive, bewildering pile of domes, columns, and towers, facing a broad, smoothly-paved plaza surrounded on all sides with a riot of brightly-colored consulates in dozens of unusual foreign architectural styles, while the enormous Church of the Eternal Resistance loomed in the distance across the square. Today, the square was packed to the bursting with the largest crowd it had ever seen as all of Trujustakanoa's citizenry, and virtually the whole population of the surrounding region that had barricaded itself within the city's staunch walls, excitedly focused its attention on a wide platform that crowned the Palace's portico, supported by massive columns crowned with geometric capitals. Atop the platform stood a row of flags: Dai Viet, Singhasari, Champa, Wil'iah, Pilbara, the Yolngu Confederacy, Murrinui, Ephraim-Manasseh, and Issachar, representing the sworn nations of the League of Trujustakanoa. To their right stood, alone, aloof, and somewhat awkward, the flag of the Mongol Empire.

One by one, the dignitaries arrived, heralded by a line of a dozen trumpeters. Tamino greeted the delegation from Dai Viet, consisting of Emperor Tran Nanh Tong and General Hung Dao. Next, Prince Harijit of Champa arrived and greeted Tamino with a firm handshake. Tamino turned to the figure to the prince's right and recoiled in surprise as she cast back her hood.

"Minh! What are you doing here? Tamino asked his former fellow operative from Champa."

"It seems our victory provided the occasion for me to finally see Wil'iah," she said. "I can't say I'm disappointed."

Tamino saluted her, then greeted the next group of dignitaries from Pilbara. Then the trumpets sounded for Singhasari, and, to Tamino's surprise, not King Kertanegara, but Raden Wijaya, the general, stepped through the door onto the parapet.

"General, it's good to see you," Tamino saluted.

"I see you have not been kept informed of events," Wijaya said somewhat severely.

"Forgive me, sieges tend to cut off information flows,"

"We had a siege of our own. The Mongols attacked Java, with the help of some of our own treacherous nobles. Kertanegara is dead. Singhasari is no more."

Tamino's face fell. "I'm sorry we couldn't be there to help."

"No matter. I pretended to cooperate, but led them into a trap. The Mongol fleet has been destroyed, and Singhasari has expanded to become a new empire, Majahapit. But, perhaps that is a story for another time."

Concern filled Tamino's face. "And the princesses?"

"They're fine. To protect them, I married them."

"All of them?"

"Well, you had your chance." Raden Wijaya continued on to the long table where the treaty documents were laid out, sat down, and picked up a quill pen, beginning to intently read the document. Gradually, the rest of the dignitaries arrived and took up their positions.

Tamino turned to the Mongol delegation, consisting of Temur Khan and Bayan of the Baarin.

"Gentlemen, there is one more delegation that we need to welcome to our proceedings today."

The crowd gasped in surprise as General Zhang Shijie walked out onto the parapet, hefting an enormous Song Dynasty battle flag.

Temur began to rise in protest, but a sharp look from Tamino put paid to the notion.

"Since Emperor Zhao apparently gave his life in service to our nation, General Zhang will represent the interests of Chinese citizens-in-exile here in Wil'iah during these proceedings. You will treat him with the same courtesy and respect as the other governmental representatives."

Temur exchanged a worried glance with Balin, but then slowly, gravely nodded.

A herald, expertly trained in projecting his voice, dramatically unfurled a gold-filigreed copy of the treaty and read its terms to the crowd below, who watched and waited with bated breath. Finally, he drew to a close.

"This concludes hostilities between the Mongol Empire, including all its vassals and the Yuan Empire of China, and the nations comprising the League of Trujustakanoa!"

At this last announcement, the plaza erupted into joyous applause, relief palpable in the air. Each delegation signed the treaty in turn. At last, it was Temur Khan's turn.

He seemed to steel himself for a moment, winced, then dipped the pen into the inkwell and signed his name in the curious vertical script employed by the Mongols. As soon as he lifted the pen, a battery of cannons began to blast out a salute, with one thunderous report for each allied nation. Temur Khan rose and curtly dipped his head to Tamino and Avora'tru'ivi, who saluted in return.

"May this newfound peace between our nations benefit us both," Temur said.

"Agreed. I'm glad our conflict ended this way."

The treaty-signing completed, the Wil'iahn and Mongol delegations wended their way through the city's narrow streets and emerged outside the wall, where the Mongol army waited. Temur climbed atop a platform and began to address the gathered troops.

"Many of you are, regrettably, here against your will, dragged from your homes and sent to fight in a war that was not your own. In a display of equanimity that I find surprising, the king of Wil'iah has something to say to you."

Tamino mounted the podium and cleared his throat. "Wil'iah and China have long been fast friends, and it greatly saddened us to find our countries on opposite sides of this titanic struggle. You may be surprised to learn that, in the east, a large number of Han Chinese conscripts in the Mongol Army defected to Wil'iah."

A shocked murmur rippled through the Chinese ranks.

"We made the decision," Tamino looked back at Avora'tru'ivi, who smiled sweetly, "to allow them to remain in Wil'iah, and extended that option to any Han Chinese conscript who wished to do so. Today, we make that same offer to you. As part of our signed treaty with Temur Khan," Tamino regarded the future emperor of the Yuan Dynasty, "full amnesty will be granted to anyone who makes this decision, and there will be no retaliation to their families in China. Wil'iah is also prepared to welcome these families if they choose to come here to join you. The choice is yours. Ships are waiting in the harbor to return you to your homeland if you wish. But, should you so choose, our red desert can become your new homeland."

Tamino noticed a rare tear leak out of one of the Chinese soldiers standing near the front of the group. Stunned silence from the army greeted his announcement, but, gradually, the full import of Tamino's words began to register. Chinese soldiers began to break out into wide smiles and slap each other on the back, and the army quickly began to split into two groups- the ones who would remain in Wil'iah, and a much smaller group that elected to return to China. Tamino stepped down from the platform and began to walk back toward the city with Avora'tru'ivi.

As they neared the gate, they turned back to watch as the Chinese soldiers joyously began to prepare for their new life.

A voice sounded behind them as a figure emerged from the shadows.

"Your father would have been proud of you, and Emperor Zhao would want this," Zhang Shijie said.

"I'm so sorry we were unable to keep him safe," Tamino hung his head. "But he clearly felt his right place was fighting for his people. I only hope his sacrifice isn't in vain."

Zhang reassuringly patted him on the shoulder. "Let's not talk of sacrifice just yet. He may be 'missing in action,'"-- Zhang winked – "but I have a feeling the world hasn't seen the last of Zhao Bing. Someday, China will control her own destiny again. We will continue to watch and work toward that day. In the meantime, we have secured more rights for the Chinese people. I have high hopes that Temur will be more reasonable than his predecessors."

"You're right," Tamino sighed.

"No more long faces," Zhang chided. "For China!"

CHAPTER NINETY-THREE

WE DID IT

Trujustakanoa, Marduwarra, western Wil'iah

*T*he great organ of the Church of the Eternal Resistance, the giant cathedral of Trujustakanoa, thundered out hymn after hymn, the very stones of the building shaking as a nation gave voice to its gratitude for its deliverance. But the joy was tinged with solemnity, for after an appropriate selection of readings, Tamino produced a scroll entitled "Heaven's New Recruits," and began to read off the names of those who had given their lives in defense of Wil'iah, his voice trembling with emotion. At the close of the ceremony, the assembled congregation rose and blasted out the undying classics: *Tear Down the Gates of Hell, The Flame of Zebulon,* and, last but not least, *The Vow of Wil'iah.*

As the grateful citizens of Trujustakanoa poured from the doors of the church and jubilantly danced along the glittering strand, with the diamond-flecked waters of King Sound sparkling in the distance, Tamino and Avora'tru'ivi walked to the parapet that guarded the city against the unknown reaches of the sea, the king holding Princess Judith in his arms. In the west, the last dying beams of the sun still lit the sky with brilliant red, while the first brave stars ignited against an azure celestial banner in the east. The air was filled with triumphal music as a nation feted its victory and gave gratitude for its deliverance, punctuated by brilliant, thunderous fireworks that filled the sky with a thousand colors. Avora'tru'ivi leaned over and tightly hugged her family.

Tamino leaned over and kissed the top of her head, then met her eyes, noting how the bright fireworks reflected in them. His kindly face broke into a wide smile.

"We did it."

EPILOGUE

Wiluna, southwestern Wil'iah

*F*ar away from the battlefields of the war, from the staunch ramparts of the castles of Trukanamoa and the Gates of Balthcutta, remote even from splendors of Tanitania and the squalors of Gath, the full moon bathed the still desert in its gentle, pale light. The scene of peaceful desolation was broken only by a few glimmers of sputtering torchlight coming from a low mud structure that seemed to grow out of the ground itself. On the dusty track, barely discernable against the desert ground, that wound its way from the building's crudely-rendered door, a lone figure scuttled. Her head tightly wrapped in a shawl and her body enveloped in a traveling cloak, only the woman's face was visible. As her staggering footsteps drew her close to the door, a glance at the symbol emblazoned above it confirmed she had, against the odds, reached her destination. Tentatively raising a trembling hand, she knocked three times, then waited.

After a few agonizing moments, a small panel in the door opened to reveal a kind, round face set in a homespun habit.

"What is it, child?" the kindly nun asked, her many-lined face crinkling in concern as they beheld the ragged figure on the other side of the door.

"I wish to join your order," came the whispered response.

Her tone told the nun everything she needed to know. She unbolted the latch and pulled the protesting door open, then quickly stepped forward to envelop the waif that stood in the threshold in a grandmotherly hug.

"What is your name, child?" she asked softly.

The woman looked up at the nun, her face lit with a sly smile.

"Iphigenia."

OUR CHARACTERS WILL RETURN

IN

THE RANGER OF

WILUNA

Book Three of the Annals of Zebulon

AND NOW, AN EXCITING GLIMPSE INTO THE NEXT CHAPTER OF WIL'IAH'S STORY...

*P*erhaps she was being superstitious. There was no sign of any signaling happening from the buttes -- not even a bird call. Yet there was something...

The hairs on the back of her neck stood on end. Judith whirled around in her saddle, the crisp desert air filling with the rasp of steel as she drew her saber almost involuntarily.

All she saw was emptiness, the majestic desolation of the desert stretching into the vast forever behind her.

Taking a deep breath, she refocused on the trail ahead and pressed forward. She passed another butte, when she thought she heard a snap behind her. Once again, Judith stopped and turned around. Again, nothing was behind her, just a small, grassy mound here and there interspersed between the majestic natural castles that marked the landscape.

Small, grassy mounds...

Were her own tactics being used against her? Judith gently turned Skydancer around and carefully approached the nearest of the mounds. She drew her sling from her bandolier and hurled a smooth stone at it. The stone impacted with a thud, but it left a clearly-visible crater in the sand. This was a true mound.

Judith dismounted to pick up the stone, not wishing to waste precious ammunition, then got back on her horse and continued to three other visible mounds, repeating the process. All were natural. Judith shrugged to herself, shook her head, sighed, then remounted, turned around – and froze.

The silhouette of a rider stood before her on the trail, black against the moonlight that illuminated him from behind.

Judith had not been wrong.

She had two options – she could run, and assuredly escape, as Skydancer, being a Tanamian, was undoubtedly the fastest horse in the judgate. Yet, if she ran, this scout would return to the Red Dingo, who would then know he was being followed. Judith knew what she had to do. She must dispatch this scout.

Her anxiety instantly dissipating in the thrill of the moment, Judith dug her heels in. Skydancer leapt forward, a blinding missile streaking across the desert. While her adversary might have been expected to challenge her, instead he turned and ran. Judith's eyes suddenly noticed a streak of color that, even in the moonlight, was unmistakably red.

It's him.

ACKNOWLEDGEMENTS

The Author would like to thank Ginger Clark, Clara Lowenberg, Susan Tsuji, and Beth Whittenbury for reading this book and providing enormously helpful feedback. Beth has been a constant source of support, ideas, and knowledge through the entire process of creating this series. He would also like to thank Wade Waterstreet for his continued support of this series and the world of Wil'iah. He would also like to thank all those who have stood up for what is right, even when the odds were against them. Wil'iah isn't a real country, but the idea it stands for lives all over the world.

'Ivrae'ia Va'a'kau'lua!

ABOUT THE AUTHOR

William Whittenbury drew inspiration for this story from an imaginative game he played with his friends as a child. He previously co-authored the novel *The Shapeshifter's War* (2014) with the Bohemia Chapter of the National English Honor Society and *The Seven Thunders* (2020), the first book in this series. In addition to writing, William is an aerospace engineer and holds a degree in Manufacturing and Design Engineering from Northwestern University. William is a heritage speaker for the US Naval Historical Foundation and the co-host of the maritime history podcast *In the Drydock*. He is also involved in efforts to save the critically-endangered vaquita porpoise.